Dave,

CW00551900

Happy Birthday.

Hope you enjoy

ASH

About the Author

Alan was born and raised on the outskirts of Glasgow. He has worked in the Oil & Gas Industry here in the UK and abroad. He lives in Stirling with his wife.

To Jennifer and QPGC (For Wee Eddie)

Alan Ash

CONVERSATIONS WITH A KILLER

AUSTIN MACAULEY
PUBLISHERS LTD.

A CIP catalogue record for this title is available from the British Library.

ISBN 9781786120328 (Paperback)
ISBN 9781786120335 (Hardback)
ISBN 9781786120342 (E-Book)

www.austinmacauley.com

First Published (2016)
Austin Macauley Publishers Ltd.
25 Canada Square
Canary Wharf
London
E14 5LQ

Foreword

This idea of writing a book came to me a long time ago. To be truthful it was while I was working in the British Steel pipe works at Tollcross in Glasgow's east end when I was doing nightshift. (The place was demolished years ago and is now a housing estate).

I was an experienced industrial radiographer and I had a radiographic assistant trainee to accompany me through the 7 p.m. to 6 a.m. shift. In between bouts of work we would retire to our office and develop the radiographs of the pipe welds and sit and read all the newspapers our dayshift colleagues had left. We used to take a sheet of A4 foolscap and challenge each other to write an alternative story, on a chosen headline from one of the national newspapers. Six weeks later we had it down to a tee and some of the stories we had both penned were indeed worth printing. It made the nightshift somewhat tolerable. My trainee confided to me one night around 3 a.m. that he was getting sick of this work and it wasn't really what he wanted to do in his life. I asked him what he really aspired to do.

He explained that in his spare time he wrote short stories and that he had written some 65 to date and that he was working on a book.

You can imagine my surprise at that. I told him if that's what he wanted to do then he should pursue his dream of

1

becoming a journalist or a novelist. We sat down and he got the teas in and he pondered long and hard. He had made the decision by knocking off time. He said "Thanks Alan. You're right. I'm off." He handed his notice in on the Friday.

The book he was writing was *The Wasp factory*.

Our paths took different directions and we never met again. I followed the oil and gas engineering route and he became a famous author.

A couple of years ago there was a question and answer symposium in Stirling University's Macrobert centre with Iain. I was working in the Middle East and I missed it by 2 weeks. I wanted to sit in the audience and ask him if he remembered cold nightshifts in Tollcross, but I never got the chance.

Alan. S. Haggarty.

Conversations with a Killer.

The Oxford Dictionary defines the word conversation as a noun and an informal exchange of ideas by spoken words.

Conversation is an everyday occurrence. One needs conversation in order to survive each day. How boring this world would be if not one soul conversed. Think about how much heartache you would cause if you did not converse with loved ones and family. Think about how much gossip would be saved, if not for exaggerated conversation. Tabloids would simply cease to exist for not having to write stories based on the snippets of overheard conversation. Truth or hearsay let them have a conversation about it.

Pause and think for a minute and imagine just how many conversations take place daily on our planet; unimaginable.

The following is of a conversation, which took place over several days in Glasgow's Barlinnie prison wing for extremely dangerous prisoners. The prisoners on this wing are in solitary confinement as they are either, a danger to, or require protection from, the rest of the inmates. Barlinnie is located in the East End of Glasgow.

I will let the story unfold a little bit before I explain my part in it.

The following conversation was secretly recorded.

The following conversation was obtained without written permission.

The following conversation cannot be used as evidence in a court of law.

Chapter 1

You know something; I really don't think you should say that.

Why not?

Because I don't think you should.

And I'm asking you why not?

Because by saying what you're saying, you could get us in trouble.

Ha ha ha.

Don't laugh, I'm telling you. We could get into real trouble.

You mean worse than we're already in?

No. Nothing could be worse than this.

But you're blaming me for our current situation.

If the truth has to be told

So it's my entire fault is it?

Wasn't it? Let's be honest. It was all down to you. You, my man, are the sole reason we find ourselves here today in this little predicament.

So you're putting all the blame on me. That's charming.

Truth hurts sometimes

Can you really be so sure it was my entire fault and it wasn't the fault of society?

Society had nothing at all to do with any of this.

Are you one hundred percent sure that it wasn't our upbringing that has caused this upheaval in our lives?

Of course it was.

Of course it was what? I can blame society or our upbringing?

You can blame whoever you want!

Then I want to blame society and our upbringing equally for me and I stress the word me for getting us into this mess.

Well that's awful noble of you accepting the blame, but if it wasn't for your actions where would we be? I mean where would you want us to be at this moment in time, somewhere else?

Well you tell me, smart arse, where do you think we would be?

Anywhere but here, that's for sure,

And where would you want to be?

Ah changing the course of the conversation. That's very clever of you. Making us converse about a different subject rather than face the truth about our predicament. As I say, very clever.

I am not changing subjects, I …

Well tell me. I asked you where you wanted to be at this moment in time. Then you asked me. I was first so can you think about it. Of all the places in the world where would you pick as your first choice?

Do you mean at this exact moment in time?

Yes.

Man, that's a good one. I'd really have to stop what I'm doing and have a real good think about that. Let me … No I don't think I could come up with one specific place I mean …

Oh come on. Stop what you're doing and think. You make me laugh that's a good one. It's a simple question. I asked you where you would like to be just now. There are a million places to choose from.

I said I don't think …

You don't think. That's your problem you don't think! We wouldn't be in this rat hole if you had thought just once.

Calm down. Don't get tetchy with me. I'm thinking.

Tetchy, is that a new word you've added to your vocabulary? Tetchy, I like that word. Do you know the average person has less than 1200 words in their vocabulary?

Yeah I read that somewhere. That's how you know, I told you that.

You did not!

I told you that ages ago and you're just remembering that fact. So what was your question again?

I asked you…

Oh that's right I'm thinking about it

As I said that's a laugh, come on answer me. Where would you want to be?

For goodness sake give me a minute. I think I'd like …

Go on

I think, I'd like to be sitting on a beach, in the warm sunshine, sunning myself, watching tanned girls in bikinis play beach volleyball

Which beach? Somewhere exotic or do you mean Blackpool beach?

Somewhere exotic like Bondi beach and I would be drinking free cocktails

Ooo listen to him. I would be drinking free cocktails. You would be actually drinking alcoholic cocktails that you don't have to pay for?

That's what free means dummy.

I know damn well what free means. Free means we wouldn't be cooped up in here.

Then I would pick out one of the girls and we would go out to dinner and order lobster and a big juicy steak and a bottle of red wine.

You'd pick surf and turf?

That's what I said.

You're insane.

What do you mean? You asked, it's my choice and I choose to dine on Surf and turf?

Not that. You said you'd pick up a girl.

I said pick out a girl not pick one up.

Pick out or pick up it's the same thing.

No it's not!

You'd never pick up a girl because you haven't the balls to ask. You never have and you never will.

I have so!

No you haven't! You seem to forget I know you. And have for some time.

I have so picked up girls.

No you haven't. So don't lie.

I'm not lying.

Yes you are.

No I'm not. You were away when I picked up that girl.

7

Which girl?

The one with the red hair, you remember? She was my girlfriend, you know, the little redhead?

Oh yes her the imaginary little redhead?

She wasn't someone I imagined. She was real.

No she wasn't. She was a figment of your imagination.

I'm telling you she was lovely.

You imagined her. You forget I know you.

No you don't. So piss off.

We know why she had a red head don't we? You gave her the red head when you clubbed her and split her head open.

No I didn't and now who has the imagination running away with himself eh? And I did pick up that girl!

No you didn't.

I did so!

You said girlfriend. She wasn't your girlfriend was she? Because I know you've never had someone of the female gender that wanted to be that close to you before.

I have so. You're boring me now.

So you'd have a Lobster and steak dinner with wine eh?

What?

I said

I heard you.

Well then you'd have ...

Yep I reckon that's what I would have.

Gone all American on me now have you?

What because I mentioned surf and turf and that sounds American to you does it?

No because you said yep.

Surf and turf isn't an American thing.

Yes it is. Now tell me what kind of wine you would pick. No let me guess. I think you would go for a cheeky wee Californian red to accompany your American style dinner, or would it be?

It would have to be a French one.

But you're eating Lobster remember. Wouldn't you pick a delightful, light, white, crisp Chablis?

Mmmm ice cold Chablis, well maybe now you mention it.

Well would you or wouldn't you?

I said maybe.

That's just like you, always non-committal. I mean it's a straight choice between Chablis and Beaujolais.

I never mentioned Beaujolais.

You never mentioned a young Beaujolais Nouveau? Ah! I can almost taste it.

It'll be a long time before we taste that again.

In fact we'll never get that chance to sample the fine wines again because of you.

I told you it wasn't my entire fault.

It was you know.

No it wasn't.

It was so.

Oh my fucking head. You do my nut in do you know that? You're always blaming me.

I'm always blaming you because it was you that put us in here. Why can't you accept that fact?

Shut up and go away.

Go away that's a laugh .Where do you suggest I go? Disappear off to Paris, London or to the beach? Ha, or to the other side of the room? I mean I would and could and I'd still be able to talk to you. You couldn't shut me up altogether. I mean have you seen the size of this place?

Of course I have. I exist here! Just go away and leave me alone for a little while.

You'd like that wouldn't you?

Like what?

Admit it; you would like me to go away. You'd really like that. Wouldn't you?

More than ever.

But then where would you be eh? You'd be all alone in here surrounded with these four grey walls to stare at. But you'd like that would you?

Piss off.

But that's where you're wrong, my friend. I can't just piss off now can I? I'm stuck here with you. So pissing off is not an option now is it?

I suppose not.

You suppose not. Who the hell are you to suppose eh?

I can suppose anything I want to suppose.

Oh heaven help us. You don't even know the meaning of the word suppose.

I do so.

No you don't. You were thick at school and English was not one of your stronger subjects my friend.

No I wasn't thick I was just …

Own up to it, you were not the brightest bulb in the class. If it wasn't for me helping you you'd have been a complete dummy. The rest of the kids bullied you and made fun of you, until I showed up. Then they stopped their daily teasing of you.

That's because they were scared of me.

Scared of you? It was because of me, you fool. Not you. You were a wimp.

I was not.

Yes you were. Wimp! Wimp! Wimp!

Stop it!

Wimp!

I wasn't a wimp when I got a hold of that bully on that Friday afternoon after school.

Was I there?

No. It was just me.

Are you sure?

Yes, it was just me on my own.

What happened?

He was always threatening me. So I spat at him.

You did not.

I did so.

You big brave thing. Good for you.

I spat at him and it landed on his trousers. He was very angry and said he was going to get me after school.

Were you afraid?

No.

Are you sure?

Well maybe a bit.

So what happened?

Well he never saw me after school.

I thought you just said he did.

I mean he didn't see me right after school, but it was later when I was playing on the rope swing down at the river. He must have sneaked up on me.

Go on this is the best part.

Well he must have watched me climb the tree and catch the big boy's rope. They used to hide it and tie it up the tree so the wee ones like me would never get a shot. But I could climb. I loved climbing.

I know that. You seem to forget I know you.

Well I got up that big beech tree and I sat on the knot in the rope and jumped out from the big branch and it was a brilliant feeling. I was a big boy swinging. My stomach was in my mouth. I shut my eyes as I first jumped out and I wouldn't let the rope go. But it was great swinging there.

So what did he do?

He waited till I was nearly at a halt and then he swore at me called me, you know.

You don't like people swearing at you now do you?

No!

So did he get a hold of you or what?

I'll tell you in a minute. Schhhhh. There might be people listening.

There's nobody listening but me.

You don't know that, the guards sometime stop and listen.

So what? Let them listen to you prattle on, what are they going to hear?

I don't want them to hear anything I say, all right? They want to know everything about everyone in this place. Knowing things about us and they feel like it gives them some sort of a power over us.

Aye OK. But there's no one listening but me. So go on.

Anyway I couldn't take my eyes off him. He was shouting at me saying he'd get me now.

He started spitting at me as I swung past him. Then he went to find a big stick to beat me with.

Did he find one?

Yes.

And did he hit you with it?

Yes.

Was it sore?

Yes.

So what did you do then after he started hitting you with the stick? Did you cry?

Well he hit me as I passed him and I fell off the swing.

But did you cry.

No I was too scared to cry.

So did you run away?

I tried to.

Did he chase you?

No he didn't have to. He hit me with the stick on my leg as I tried to run.

Did you fall down?

Yes.

And then what did he do?

He stood over me gloating and laughing. He was holding the big stick over me threatening to hit me with it, waving it at my face.

Was there anybody else there to see all this?

No.

So there was no one there to help you.

Not a soul.

So he was gloating over you with a big stupid grin all over his face.

Yes. And then he unzipped his trousers and took his penis out and was going to pee all over me.

Did he?

No.

Why not?

Cause I managed to get up somehow and I bit his penis.

Was it not the fact that he took out his penis and asked you to kiss it?

I don't remember.

But I do. That's what happened.

Was it?

Yes it was and then when he put his cock in front of your mouth that's when you bit it and tore at it like a dog with a rabbit.

Aye and the end came right off! There was blood everywhere.

That's hilarious. I bet you he was yelling and screaming then.

Not really. He was too stunned to scream I think.

Stunned? You think he was too stunned to scream? I'd say he was a bit more than stunned. He just had a chunk of his cock bitten off and he didn't know what to do. I'd say he was a wee bit more than stunned. The end of his cock lying on the ground and I can only imagine the pain he was in. I think intense pain, don't you?

So what if he was in intense pain. I spat the thing out at his feet and he just stared at it. And then he started whimpering like a wee dog. He was trying to stop the blood flowing down his legs by holding his hands in front of his cock. I started laughing at him. There was blood all over his hands and his legs. He started to shake and tremble. There were tears in his eyes and he fell to his knees.

What did you do then?

He had dropped his stick and I picked it up and started to hit him with it.

Well he did hit you with it. How ironic was that then? You were hitting him with his own stick. Now I find that funny. That would have shown him who was boss.

It certainly did. He was crying as I hit him with it again and again. I hit him really hard, right over his head.

Did he bleed?

You could say that. His head opened up like a cracked walnut. He fell down and I hit him a couple of times again.

You hit him 65 times.

I couldn't have, I didn't hit him that many times.

Yes you did.

Was it really that many times?

Yes it really was.

You counted?

I did my friend 65 times.

His head looked like mince when I was finished with him.

He died you know.

I know. Cause I buried him in the woods under that big chestnut tree.

It wasn't a chestnut tree now was it? It was a Rhododendron bush you buried him under.

Are you sure?

You know it was.

Oh yeah, It's all coming back to me, I remember now.

That's a laugh you remember now.

Are you mocking me?

"I would never mock you! You're my source of inspiration. You're my only hope of getting out this shit hole.

Chapter 2

I feel obliged to give you the reader a brief quick snapshot of the history of Barlinnie prison. I'll attempt not to overload you with too much information because that sometimes puts off reading further.

Barlinnie Prison or the Bar-L as it is often referred to, was built from rock carved and shaped by Scottish masons in 1880. Yes it has been around that long. The site location on the Eastern outskirts of Glasgow was chosen at that time because it was well away from the centre of Glasgow. The site was picked for the geological reason that the whinstone bedrock foundation was supposedly not liable to suffer dampness or flood. It was envisaged that the prison would be surrounded by green fields and nothing more.

It would stand alone out in the countryside.

In those days transport was by horse and cart and to service the new prison decisions to utilize the nearby Monklands canal were taken. This was the bonus that they could sail barges with all the supplies the prison required along the canal to the dropping off point. From there the supplies would be taken by more traditional Shire horse and cart.

It was initially planned that the prison would never be overlooked by any other buildings.

They could never have imagined that Glasgow would have turned into a large sprawling metropolis.

Barlinnie's first hall, "A" Hall, was completed and opened to take prisoners in August 1882; halls B, C and D were completed by 1892 some ten years later. This time the construction was solely by prison labour. The prisoners under the watchful eye of the stone masons, cut and quarried the granite and transported it to site, where it was used to build the accommodation for the rising prison population. By 1892 there were 900 prisoners all housed at Queen Victoria's pleasure!

The prison was hailed at the time as a modern necessity for the unlawful and harsh times occurring during the Queen's reign.

Scotland's criminals had a new establishment to languish in. nights. This was somewhere different for their atonement for their abhorrent crimes. The cells were cold and with the cold came the inevitable damp.

The whinstone bedrock failed to do its job of keeping the damp at bay. The prison walls could not keep out Scotland's harsh cold wet climate. However the cells proved one thing and that was that they were escape proof. Not one prisoner managed to escape from the vice like grip Barlinnie held them in.

Barlinnie was just the place that all the scum of Scottish society deserved. This was the place for real punishment.

The previous choices of where to incarcerate Scotland's convicted were the two main prisons at Peterhead in the north of the country and Greenock in the west. They were the two largest prisons in Scotland by far and by no means, any easier places to do your time. Far from it as both were extreme and brutal places and hundreds of prisoners died from the inhospitable conditions.

Now this new magnificent Victorian two storey prison located in the East end of Glasgow was a hotel in comparison to the other two.

The Riddrie district of Glasgow would eventually grow up and surround the prison and the hustle and bustle of the area would now include a new building for common people to talk about. The surrounding high walls and barbed wire fencing would keep the scum inside and keep the normal riff raff out.

As you can imagine, the described conditions in the prison were being compared to the early 20th century gulags in Russia, cold, extreme and harsh.

The prison has always been synonymous with a hardened criminal fraternity, the murderers, armed robbers and the criminally insane. Societies fuck ups and all those mad bastards that you couldn't control. You'd just lock them up in Barlinnie and throw away the key and forget all about them.

Decisions were made easy for the Judiciary way back then. They had a new deterrent and that was the several big stone buildings on the outskirts of Glasgow.

It was hoped that this prison would beat the notoriety out of you.

You would go in as a so called hard man and come out as a pussy cat.

That was the theory put down.

Sentences of up to twenty five plus years in a hell hole like the "Bar-L" would hopefully have a sort of mellowing effect on your character.

Whether it worked or not is still up for debate.

The 1950s and '60s saw the shift in the type of prisoner locked up in Barlinnie. The new crimes of Sex offences meant that prisoners required protection from the other prisoners. Those were now housed there. Short term transfer prisoners who were classified as extremely dangerous were also locked up tight.

A couple of the more notorious and recent inmates from the 70s and 80s have been, Jimmy Boyle and the Lockerbie bomber, Abdel Baset Ali Mohammed Al Megrahi. He was the person convicted of and was serving out his 20-year sentence for masterminding the bombing of the Pan Am flight 103 on the 21st December 1988 over the Scottish village of Lockerbie.

Boyle on the other hand was a notorious Glasgow gangster from the 60s and a real Glasgow hardman and one of the first prisoners, to be housed in the pioneering, infamous "Special Wing" solely for reformers.

Today's prison has been modernized somewhat with funds that were made available from the Scottish office, but today's prisoners are now categorized into two factions.

First – the sex offenders who cannot be helped and are an extreme danger to our society. These are the paedophiles and sexual predators that prey on the weak and the young.

Second – the mad, murderous bastards that the Liberals among us and the so-called goody goodies think will reform and one day will be welcomed back into general society.

As they say the jury is still out on that one.

Then there is the Special Security Wing or the SSW as it is fondly called. An annex stuck on the back of "C" hall. This houses Scotland's worst offenders. There are 8 cells, 8 doors and 8 prisoners currently housed at her Majesty's pleasure.

Since Capital punishment was abolished and we no longer have the Death penalty here in the United Kingdom, there are still many today, that would welcome its return.

There are others that you talk to, that appreciate the Chinese approach, death by firing squad and the murderer's family, being charged for the bullet.

Those inmates which the authorities genuinely think can be helped and are of no danger to themselves still have the degradation of cleaning their own filth and slopping their individual cell out. They are fully supervised while cleaning and are allowed disinfectant to use on their very own toilet; after all you wouldn't want them to catch anything now, would you?

The ones who cannot be helped have cells with the European squat holes in the floor. These shit holes have a wall mounted electronic button flush.

The European Commission for Prisoner reform and rehabilitation has never been invited to survey the conditions of the SSW.

The bureaucrats in Brussels have, to be honest, never approached the British government for a site visit to see and check on the prisoners civil and human rights.

The Scottish Prison Office is well aware of the wing but they have never visited it either. To visit it, is to publically acknowledge it and that my friend, is as big as a political banana skin you could ever want to step on.

The monetary funding for the Special Security wing (Where the conversation was alleged to have taken place) was earmarked by the Scottish office in the early 90s and the refurbishment work was completed and paid for in the third quarter of 1996.

The special security wing is only for solitary confinement.

The special security wing has the sole purpose of punishing Scotland's real criminals.

The special security wing is never mentioned at cabinet or at any other ministerial level.

The special security wing sends shivers down your spine when you step through the door.

The special security wing exists.

Chapter 3

Footsteps could be heard squeaking along recently polished tiles. Rubber soles meeting the newly tiled surface. Irritating, soul destroying squeaks, walking up to a numberless cell door. The prisoners never knew if the squeaks were destined to stop outside their cell. Each individual on the corridor lay and waited. Their imaginations could run wild. Every high pitched squeak was a stark reminder that there was another side to the locked door.

This time however the prisoners could make out that there were two sets of squeaking footsteps in their corridor.

There was an incoherent shout and it quickly echoed through the entire wing. An electrical system activated and a cell doors locking mechanism buzzed and a cell door opened.

The noise shattered the eerie silence and echoed all through the prison wing. Some not affected by the door opening gave a big sigh of relief.

There were a couple of inmates however that waited with firmly clenched fists.

Cell number 3 was the only padded one on the wing. The padding was in place to prevent one highly volatile inmate from self-damaging or killing himself. The occupant in cell

3 was about to have more sedation drugs administered and he would be left to sleep again.

The inmate would be silent for another few hours, until the next bout of silence was again interrupted.

Another shout and the cell door buzzed closed and locked and the system de-activated. The footsteps returned to their point of origin and there was a stillness and silence in the corridor again.

That's them away.

I know that I do have ears. But they'll be returning later that's for sure. That poor bastard along there has probably been beaten up and they'll have drugged him up to the eyeballs.

How do you know that?

Because I do. That's what these bastards do to you. Beat you senseless and keep you quiet.

They haven't done that to you.

Not for a while.

But you test them

I know. I'm clever.

So go on then. Tell me about your little redhead.

You want me to tell you all about my friend the red-head? Fuck me don't you ever wonder about what's just happened along that corridor?

No.

So it doesn't concern you as to who, or what is along there.

No! Why should it. You know who ever it is has been a bad boy and that's why he's in here. We're all bad boys, so who gives a fuck? 'Cause I don't. They don't. You and I are the

24

ones that are treated like shit, so who cares what they do to that mad fuck along there?

Well I do and I hate those guards.

Listen to him. Oh get the soap box out. You blame them for everything, that's what you really mean to say.

Whatever, that's those fuckers been handing out that Largactyl again. Make sure he swallows it .Sedate the prick and keep the lunatic quiet. He'll be sound asleep for hours.

How do you know they've given him Largactyl and not some new modern drug? You're away behind the times. Largactyl was the 70's, medicine has moved on.

Well maybe it is some new drug they're giving him. Does it really fucking matter what the drug is? I mean does it? They keep him quiet by drugging him day in day out. Are you listening? Same shit every day my friend and that's got to be illegal.

Hark at you, illegal. So what? Just remember where you are.

You don't give a monkey's do you?

No and neither should you, so why are you going on and on about it?

That's why I'm going on and on about it. It's what it's all about. Don't you get it? It's all about routines!

What the hell are you now on about routines for? One minute you're on about the mistreatment of that maniacal bastard along the corridor and now you're on about routines. Hold the press for fuck's sake, we have a new headline coming, this should be good.

I'll tell you what I'm on about my friend; you have to discipline yourself into a routine. That's how you get through this daily shit, this life and through this stinking sentence. That's how I get through every poxy day. You discipline yourself and you—

25

You're telling me how to follow a routine?

All I'm saying—

How do you know he's a lunatic?

What?

I said how do you know he's a lunatic?

'Cause I hear him scream out when he doesn't get his daily fix.

But you said that he gets his meds at the same time every day. It's a routine you said. So how did he miss his daily fix, as you so call it, because if everyone follows a routine, he shouldn't miss out?

I don't know maybe the guard was sick or went for a crap or something. Fuck me, I heard him scream out and it sounded like a lunatic's scream to me.

A scream's a scream in my book.

Are you fucking with me, because if you are, this conversation is over!

Don't be so touchy with me; I'm only saying all screams sound the same to me, so calm down and I'll promise not to annoy you any more, what about the redhead?

You've annoyed me.

You don't say. Now tell the story about the little redhead?

Fuck telling you stories. You've pissed me off.

I know I have, but you like telling stories. It's all part of our daily routine. You said so yourself. Follow the routine. Now please the Red head.

Oh her.

Yes her. Are you calm enough to get on with your story? Tell me all about her and remember what happened. You know its good therapy for you.

Well it was a couple of months after I did the bully.

26

Oh yeah? Can I just correct you on that one pal? A couple of months, it was more like a couple of years.

Was it really?

Aye it was. In fact it was two. If the truth be known.

Was it really two years? Well there you go now. I remember it was after the entire place had been buzzing with police. I remember they had set up an incident room in the Police station, when they discovered that the bully was missing and I remember they brought in sniffer dogs to find him.

Aye I remember the dogs.

So do I. There was a lot of them.

There were a lot of them.

What?

You and your grammar.

Grammar? What you on about?

It's not really proper English. You started the sentence with "there was" when it should be "there were", I'm only trying to help keep you right. But ignore me. You were saying the dogs ...

I can still hear them barking. I nearly got to clap one of them, but the man pulled it away from me.

I know you tried to pet one of them, I was there. Focus on the story, the redhead, are you sure you can remember the whole story?

I remember it fine. It's installed in my memory, but if you don't believe me then I'm not going to tell you.

I'm sorry. I do believe you. I just had to correct you sometimes, that's all. Tell me.

Well she was in a couple of classes above me at school. She was in the third year and she was called Beth and she had lovely long hair and it was the colour of autumn leaves.

Are you getting all romantic with your reminiscing?

I'm only trying to paint you a picture as to the colour of her hair.

I can imagine it. I really can. I know what red hair looks like for fuck's sake. But what age were you when you met her.

Oh I didn't meet her.

Didn't you?

No. I just used to follow her and her pal home from the school bus. They were always laughing and giggling.

So you used to follow them from the primary school.

No the senior school in Kilsyth, don't you listen? I just told you she was in third year.

So you were in the first year.

Give that man a coconut.

Don't be sarky.

We had to get the bus there and back every day. There wasn't a protestant senior school in Lennoxtown. Kilsyth was the closest one in Stirlingshire. So we travelled there and back.

I get the picture. So you followed them home every day?

Well not really. I lived in Netherton Oval and they lived in Whitefield. It was just sometimes I got off the bus one stop early and walked behind them. But I only did that when the weather was nice and sunny

Didn't they become suspicious of you getting off the bus early?

I don't think so.

So they didn't take a blind bit of notice of you did they?

I don't know if they did or not.

Were they laughing at you that day?

Why should they?

Just a thought I had. So you followed at a distance?

Yes.

So she was about 15 years old then?

Aye she must have been

So how did you pick her up if all you did was follow at a distance?

I did pick her up!

Now, now, don't get angry with me. I'm only asking a simple question.

I remember that it was a Saturday and they were playing in the swing park next to where she lived.

So you weren't at school.

No it was a Saturday.

She lived in Whitefield right?

Yes that's where she fucking lived.

You're starting to swear.

Listen to me; there were hundreds of kids there that day. Some of them were—

Hundreds of kids are you sure?

Don't interrupt me.

It's just that I know how you exaggerate.

I'm not exaggerating. There were hundreds.

If you say so.

Well it seemed to me to be hundreds. The play park was really busy.

So it wasn't hundreds then.

Oh for Pete's sake. All right then, there were a lot of kids playing in the sunshine. I think it must have been the school holidays.

What school holidays? The ones in the summer or was it Easter time?

It was the summer holidays.

Are you sure?

Of course I'm sure. I was there wasn't I?

I suppose you must have been. It's your story.

Well I was there. It was the first summer holidays after I went to the High school in Kilsyth.

So how come you were in Whitefield if you lived in Netherton oval? What took you down there? Were you looking for her?

I was down looking for my pal.

This is new. You had a pal, a friend, a playmate?

He was my friend from school.

Oh him; that little odd fucker with the horn-rimmed glasses?

Yes him.

What ever happened to him? Did you kill him, too? Is there something you have forgotten to mention?

I didn't kill him. His family moved away when his dad got a new job.

But you might have killed him?

No he was my friend.

Do you think that was the trigger that sent you on a killing spree your only friend in the world moving away?

What the fuck are you on about?

I'm only asking a question.

Well don't.

So what happened next?

Well if you didn't keep interrupting me then I'd be able to tell you.

I'm sorry. I'll be quiet for a minute.

That'll be a first you – being quiet.

I told you I'll be hushed, I'll be so quiet you'll not know I'm here, go on.

Well I was sitting on a swing and she was on the see-saw with her pal and they were laughing. I saw that they had duffle bags with them and I heard them say they were going for a picnic and a swim

What was she wearing?

A white tee shirt and light blue denim shorts.

Ooo, light blue shorts, the colour of the sky?

Are you trying to piss me off again? Because if you are, let me tell you, you're succeeding. Anyway I thought you were going to shut up for a while.

I'm listening and not saying a dickie bird see?

Well shut the fuck up and let me tell you what happened next. I watched her from my swing and she was beautiful with the outline of her breasts sticking out from under that white tee shirt. The light breeze was blowing her hair and she was laughing. I started to get hard.

So you liked looking at her titties under her shirt.

Don't be so disgusting. That's what the matter with you is. You're disgusting sometimes and so crude.

You said you were getting a hard on looking at her tits under her top. So what was I to think?

I never mentioned hard ons or tits, what's wrong with you?

Come on I know you. You were getting excited. Your imagination was running riot.

No it wasn't.

So why were you getting a hard on then?

I told you not to be crude.

Ok I won't be. But you were excited. Imagining what was underneath the tee shirt and shorts. You can't tell me you weren't. Close your eyes and remember what she looked like.

She was gorgeous.

Can you remember what she smelled like?

I think it was like flowers

Open your eyes she's not there.

I wish she was.

So do I and then we all could have sex?

Don't be disgusting.

So come on then tell the story.

Well she and her friend got up from the see-saw and lifted their duffle bags and went skipping off. So I waited for a while and then followed them.

Followed them again? Christ you liked to follow people didn't you?

Shut up! I could see which direction they went and I got off my swing and casually followed.

Like a bloodhound on a trail.

I had a rough idea where they were headed.

Well done, Sherlock. They did mention they were going swimming.

Piss off.

Are you sure they were skipping? I mean it's not something a pair of 15 year old girls would do now was it?

It doesn't matter if they were skipping or not.

For a story to be true you have to get the facts straight.

They might have been just walking quickly.

So I can cancel the picture I have of them skipping along naked.

You are one weirdo.

Why thank you.

I was walking behind them

At a distance

Yes at a distance. I couldn't just sidle up to them and walk with them now could I? I didn't want them to know I was following them.

So you traipsed after them like a lost puppy.

I wanted to see where they were going.

You liar! You knew damn well where they were going. Do you forget? You overheard them say they were going swimming. How many times do I have to correct your memory?

I knew that they were off to have their picnic somewhere nice.

That nice place on the pebbles, next to the swimming hole.

I guessed that's where they were off to.

Where else could they go eh?

I realized then that I was getting hungry as well. So it must have been about lunchtime.

Lunchtimes out in the open air. I remember them well.

Are you being sarcastic?

Me being sarcastic? Never.

Sarcasm is the lowest form of wit. Someone said that once.

We're not being witty. Get on with your story.

They walked down the road and were heading for the woods and the river.

The woods, oh no! Not the woods in the hospital grounds?

I told you about sarcasm.

I was only trying to build your story up to the scary bit. That's all.

Well don't. I'm telling it, not you, so shut up and listen. Anyway yes those very same woods. So to get into them they would have to climb the wall and follow the path down to the river.

You knew the woods well didn't you? That's where they found the boy you killed. Wasn't it?

Be quiet!

Truth hurts sometimes eh, Nelson? That's the waterfall where you washed all the boy's blood from your tee shirt isn't it?

The place where you stood in the cold running river and smiled.

You knew that spot very well.

Were the girls not afraid to go to a place where a wee boy had been beaten to a pulp, killed and half buried? The rest of the kids seemed to avoid the place.

What can I tell you? I don't know why all the kids stopped playing in the woods. Was I the cause? Maybe I was but I sure as hell played there.

You stopped going to the rope swing.

The rope swing was old hat. I had done that. Games change you know. I liked playing different things.

Yes we had some imagination then. Didn't we? I miss being kids. I wish we could turn back time. Don't you, Nelson?

That's not a fucking option is it?

Ooh, hark at the big hard man. I was only saying that it would be nice to go back and play as kids again. Hell you could even kill that wee boy again.

I saw them climb over the wall and go down the path through the trees down to the river.

Don't get angry now.

You make me angry sometimes.

Your story. Please continue. We're getting to the juicy bit.

I climbed over the wall and ran quietly through the trees so I could look at them. I hid behind a big tree and watched. There was no one else at the swimming hole that day and it was a lovely sunny day. I'd have thought that there would have been hundreds of kids there that day.

But there wasn't.

I told you why it was only them. The rest of the kids were scared.

Yes scared alright. In fact some of them were terrified of playing in the woods after the police found his battered body.

Can I go on?

This is getting exciting. The girls were back in your old stamping ground. They were very close to where you actually killed young Smith.

I said can I go on?

Of course you can! Be my guest.

I remember they put their duffle bags down on the shingles and took their towels out. Her swimming costume fell out and landed on the stones. It was bright fluorescent green.

This was the wee redhead's costume?

That's who I'm talking about.

They looked to see if anyone was watching them ...

You were.

Aye but they couldn't see me. I was peeking out from behind the tree.

So clever the way you hid, so they couldn't see you.

Are you mocking me?

No way would I be mocking the teller of the story.

Just as well, so don't.

Were you not scared in case they did see you?

Not really.

So what did they do next?

They sat down on the dry rocks.

And?

She took her trainers off and her socks

You said she. This is the girl you were infatuated with. The one with the red hair?

I don't know if I was infatuated with her.

"Believe me; you were so infatuated with her. But please go on ..."

She stood up and had one last look around her and then unfastened the top button on her shorts and then unzipped them and ...

Were you getting excited?

No.

I bet you were.

Well maybe a wee bit.

So you did get a bit excited. And you got an erection as she slipped her shorts off over her milky white legs and you saw her pants didn't you?

Stop it.

Well didn't you?

Yes.

So go on what happened?

She took her pants off and I saw

What did you see? Can you remember?

I saw her pubescent shape.

Her pubescent shape? That's a posh word for it. Pubescent shape you mean her ...

I saw her ...

Yes I gathered that.

Then she slipped on her swimming costume and as she pulled it up to her waist, she put her hands round her back and removed

What did she remove?

She took off her white bra and her tee shirt, I think in one go. I could see her breasts. The two girls were giggling as they undressed.

Were they nice? Her breasts were they nice to look at?

Oh Yes. I got an eyeful and then she pulled her costume fully on and...

Did you also see her friend strip naked for you?

I can't remember looking at her.

But you do remember.

All right I do remember seeing her as well.

No wonder you had an erection seeing 2 naked 15 year old girls.

Can I go on?

And then the two girls walked gingerly over the stones and into the cold water. They were laughing all the way in. You could hear them say it was cold. They dipped their toes into the water first and then the two girls laughed out loud as they waded into about hip height and then splash. They were swimming.

No that's not what happened. They dipped their toes in and I could hear them say it was cold yes, but then there was a big splash as they both ran and dived into the water at the same time. That's what happened, not your sordid recollection.

So how was my guess sordid? What were you doing while they were splashing about and having fun? Were you playing with your cock? Were you masturbating?

No I was not. I just watched them play about for a while and when they got out of the water they got dried and then they sat and ate their sandwiches. I was so hungry I could almost smell those sandwiches.

Then what did they do?

They spread their towels down on the grassy bit and they both lay in the sun getting warm I suppose. They were talk, talk talking all the time and laughing. They were talking about boys.

Are you sure they weren't laughing about you with your knob in your hand?

They never saw that.

So you admit you were masturbating?

I never said …

Nelson, lying to me is not part of your therapy now is it? You were masturbating.

Yes I was. I was behind the tree but I was quiet.

Oh that makes it alright then because you were quiet. Do you realize what you just said? You were tossing yourself off hiding behind a tree.

So what?

So what? You lied about not having your …

I had to jack off; I had seen the girl of my dreams. I had seen everything. I had seen all of her, even the wisps of pubic hair. I could have almost touched her.

You wanted to, didn't you?

Oh yes. So much so it was hurting me.

So what did you do then?

After I stopped masturbating?

Yes after.

I watched them go swimming again and playing about in the water and

And?

And they got out and grabbed their towels and started to dry each other and they were still laughing". They didn't know I was there believe me.

Ok then so what happened after they got dried for a second time?

They sat down in the warm sunshine and finished off their picnic.

Bet you could smell those sandwiches eh?

Just about.

So you continued to watch them for how long?

I guess for another half hour or so and then her pal sat up, said something I couldn't hear. It was as if she had just remembered something and she stood up and started putting her clothes back on. She was in a real hurry. I mean, she stood there with not a care in the world and took her swimming costume off and she was naked. Man I saw every small detail of her as well. I couldn't believe my luck. She was dark down there and she had bigger breasts than Beth. Much bigger and her nipples stuck out. I watched her put all her clothes on and Beth still lay on her towel in the sunshine. I strained to hear Rachel say to Beth,

You never told me her name was Rachel

I have so

*No you have not! That's the first time you have **ever** mentioned that the friends name was Rachel. This is good.*

I thought I had.

No you haven't

It doesn't matter, anyway Rachel said that she'd see her later and packed up all her stuff into her duffel bag and left Beth just lying there.

"That was strange leaving her all alone. Why didn't Beth go with her? Did she say she was coming back?"

Rachel left her duffel bag on the stones; I assumed that she must have been coming straight back.

So she just left Beth there. Left her to your mercy. Left her there next to the woods where you killed that boy!

That's not what I said.

I bet you were hard again. Having just seen her pal eh?

I can't remember that, but I do remember wanting to go down and say hello. And then her pal was running along the path. I had to hide by moving round the tree. She very nearly caught sight of me.

So did you go down and say hello?

Yes. I waited till her pal hopped over the wall and onto the road and I went down to where Beth was lying on her tummy sunbathing.

You just walked casually down to see her.

Well no. I tiptoed down because I wanted to surprise her.

Surprise her? That's a bit of an understatement isn't it?

No.

So what did you say to surprise her?

I never got a chance to say anything she must have got a fright because she heard me on the stones,

Heard you on the stones? She heard you crossing the waterfall at the ledge because the water was low. That's how she heard you. You had splashed the water when you tried to cross quietly.

And she must have got a fright because she turned round and screamed.

So what did you say to her to stop her screaming? I mean did you not ask her to be quiet?

I never said anything. I jumped onto her as she was getting up. I had to put my hand over her mouth to quiet her, to stop her from screaming.

And struggling. Isn't that what you mean? I mean she was screaming and struggling and you had your big hand over her mouth stopping her. Is that when she fainted? Because you had your hand on her mouth stopping her screams? She was so terrified that she fainted.

Must have been.

Is that when you ripped off her swimming costume?

I wanted …

So you ripped off her swimming costume and forced yourself into her.

She was …

She was unconscious and you grabbed her tits and felt her mound and you had a hard on. Didn't you?

I can't …

You can't what? Admit that you did all those things to that girl. As she lay on her towel sunbathing by the river, you enjoyed it. You tied her tee shirt round her face and you stuck her socks in her mouth to keep her quiet. Didn't you?

I can't.

Didn't you? And then you had your way with her. Didn't you? You forced your throbbing knob into her, tearing her hymen and you exploded. You had got so excited you shot your load into her and she choked while you were doing it. Didn't you? She was so terrified that she died on you.

Yes. Yes Yes. I had to shag her, she wanted me to.

She wanted you to. That's a fucking laugh. For fuck's sake the girl was unconscious. How could she want you to do anything?

She would have. I know that.

No you don't know that!

I had to have her.

And then what did you do when you realized she was dead? I mean after you had literally shagged her to death?

I shagged her again.

Ha ha ha. You shagged her again. That's so funny. That's called necrophilia you disgusting moron. You were taking a chance weren't you? All that sex out in the open, you could have been seen.

I couldn't think straight.

You couldn't think straight so you just shagged her again? She was dead by that time. And you had to shag her warm body again. You are one sick puppy. Aren't you? You disgust me.

She was beautiful I had to

You had to my arse. You sick fuck. Why don't you just admit it? I am a sick bastard. Say it! I am a sick bastard. Go on its part of your therapy. Say it!

I'm not saying that.

Don't then, but we all know what you are. But come on you sicko; you may as well carry on and tell me the rest of the story.

I packed up all her clothes and carried her away from the waterfall.

You had to be quick in case her friend came back didn't you?

I carried her through the farmer's field's right along the tree line up into the woods. I stopped a couple of times to hide and rest.

She must have weighed a ton.

I can't remember how heavy she was.

You can't remember that. But you can remember the number of times you shagged her.

I saw through the woods and there was some people walking down the ash path down towards the bus stop. I had to be real careful that no-one from the houses saw me and that I didn't bump into any of the kids playing in the woods.

Yeah that could have been a tricky one to explain. Why you were carrying a dead girl.

But I was lucky. The kids must have been playing somewhere else that day.

Did you carry her in your arms or did you put her over your shoulder?

I put her over my shoulder it was easier. She was actually quite a light weight.

Oh so you do remember how heavy she was then?

Okay I remember, anyway I got her through the farmer's fence and started making my way up the wee stream and followed it up towards the pine woods by the South lodge.

And still nobody saw you?

Nobody from the houses could see me paddling up the little stream with all the foliage between the houses and the stream.

Christ, you really were one lucky bastard that no one in Netherton Oval saw you.

I was always lucky.

You left her in that storm drain didn't you. The one deep in the pine forest?

I did and I thought that idea was brilliant. And again I was sure that I left no trace of her at the swimming hole.

Oh you were good at hiding bodies by now. Did they ever find her?

You know they did.

Can you remember how long it took them?

About 3 months.

You were getting to be quite a killer then.

I was not.

Oh yes you were you know. Was it the fame you were looking for that drove you on to kill?

I didn't set out to kill anybody. I didn't want to become famous.

You mean infamous and that's not quite what I meant.

What did you mean?

I meant that you had got a taste for killing. I mean you killed that bully when you were ten or eleven years old? You killed the girl when you were twelve going on thirteen. So you can see what I mean there's a wee bit of a pattern starting.

The girl was an accident.

Accident my arse. You watched her and you planned out the whole thing. You wanted to kill her. Why don't you just admit to your crime? You were a big boy remember, fatter and heavier than the rest of the boys in your class. Remember that's the reason they bullied you.

Why should I want to kill her and then admit it all to you?

Because if you opened up and did admit to it all, you might clear your conscience and you might just get a goodnight's sleep.

What do you think I lose sleep over her, the tease?

Tease? So she's a tease now? How did she tease you?

She knew I fancied her.

She knew did she? Did she ever tell you that?

No. She didn't have to. I knew.

So how do you know she fancied you then?

She was always throwing her beautiful hair back and she was always smiling and laughing when I was near. It was obvious she was doing all that for me.

So you think that she was doing that to tease you?

Well wasn't she?

I don't think so. Girls do that all the time. Throw their long hair back from their face or let it blow in the wind. They're teenagers; they do that stuff all the time. They don't do it just to tease you. Anyway girls that age always fancy someone older. She probably had a crush on someone two classes above her at school, not someone who has just started the Academy.

Anyway you're wrong I didn't want to kill her.

Oh so you're back to that. I didn't want to kill her. But you did. You choked the life out of her as you raped her. She took her last gasp for air as your semen was flying out the end of your cock.

Stop it. I don't want to remember that.

But you do remember.

Yes I do, every day.

Every day is good for you, Nelson.

Only because you make me.

Are you going to go quiet on me again?

Yes. I have a headache.

Chapter 4

Nelson lay down on the mattress trying to shut off the relentless inevitable barrage. He was emotionally drained and had to have quiet. He closed his eyes and attempted to doze off. When he awakened, again the questions and conversation would bombard him again and again. There was no hiding place.

It was Nelson's daily grilling.

It was Nelson's daily punishment.

It was Nelson's daily therapy.

He had to endure the daily shame of listening to the truth. The four stark walls were his only judge and jury.

He held his eyes tightly closed not daring to open them. Knowing when he chose to open them question one, or accusation one, or conversation one, would not take long in coming. Nelson knew that for a hard fact. He would try to sleep and to dream of happier times with his Mum and Dad, but couldn't. He wanted to say sorry to the two people who brought him into the world and who had cared for him and who made him very happy. He wanted to hold his mum and whisper gently into her ear that he was still her little boy. He longed to see his Dad again and hear him laughing and to joke with him one more time. Nelson wanted more than ever to be that child again and to be back home, sitting round the kitchen table with the pair of them all eating their dinner, with the coal fire burning brightly in the living room hearth. Happier times.

It would never happen again.

It was 1988 when they abandoned him, just days before he was convicted of multiple counts of murder in the High Court in Glasgow. They had shown pained revulsion in their eyes during the first days of the trial in courtroom number 2. Every time Nelson looked towards them trying to catch their eye, for some look of hope or some compassion, they quickly averted their eyes in shame. When he stood all alone in the dock there was no one in the world for him. His parents couldn't bear to look at him standing there handcuffed or listen to his prosecution spelling out in detail what he had done. It was his damnation to be alone.

After the initial heartbreak of trying to sit through each day's traumatic testimony, it proved to be too hard, too much for his parents. They had had enough of the questioning stares from the jury and the looks of hatred burning from the eyes from the audience in the gallery.

Patsy couldn't cope and she ended up in tears and it was tears of disbelief. They were both sick to their stomachs and just couldn't believe as to what a monster they had raised.

Nor could the Smiths, but they were different. They sat through the whole trial with utter hatred in their hearts. Nelson could feel the loathing from the pair of them.

He showed no remorse to the Smiths, no saying sorry Mr and Mrs Smith for what I did to your Graham. He couldn't tell them that he was glad he killed their son. That he was a bully and made Nelson's life hell. But he couldn't tell them that and say sorry, there was never going to be any of that.

They're eyes burned deep into Nelson and when the judge passed the 3 life sentences with no parole the Smiths jumped to their feet and cheered.

When the judge brought his gavel down on his desk with a bang, it sounded like a clap of thunder resounding in Nelson's head. It felt like the judge had driven a stake through Nelson's heart. Nelson looked towards the space where his mummy and daddy had been sitting during the beginning of the trial and now there were only two vacant seats. No one had dared sit there and the seats had remained empty.

He remembered his mother had been crying, he had noticed her puffy eyes and the tear-stained cheeks. It broke his heart to think his mummy was suffering. But would she look at him? Nelson had got his answer as no, she was too embarrassed, or was it that she was too afraid to look in his direction. Nelson had witnessed his father putting his arm around his mother to offer her comfort and to console her. Even his dad, the father he loved had been too ashamed; he couldn't bear to see his only son up there in the dock, branded a monster.

That was years ago and here now Nelson felt so isolated and empty. Left to rot in this stinking cell, convicted as a multiple murderer who warranted 3 life sentences.

That vacant space, the empty two seats, the memory would remain with Nelson for the rest of his life. He had wanted to cry out to the pair of them, scream to them, tell them not to worry, that he would be OK. But they weren't there to listen to him if he did try and shout out.

As if they cared. They disowned him. No one cared.

The pain in Nelson's heart told him that they had shut him out of their lives. He no longer existed in their lives.

Cries from the courtroom of, "You bastard I hope you rot in hell", were the last thing Nelson heard over the general melee as the trial judge pronounced sentence. There was uproar as the guards dragged him away from the dock and into the awaiting prison van. Press flashbulbs went off like lightning bolts, hatred shouted at him as the van hit the street. Reporters all pushing to be close to the rear window of the van, pointed cameras hoping for a last picture of the notorious killer.

His parents, whom he desperately needed for their forgiveness and love, had never once tried to contact him in all the time he was banged up in this hole. They had killed him stone dead.

Nelson opened his eyes. He had been crying in his sleep. He wiped the tears away and felt his deep depression begin again. This solitude and this punishment were eating away at his humanity crumb by crumb, piece by piece. It was starting to show its effect on his mind. All he had to think about was his memories and what he would be doing now if he was free. He thought about freedom every day, he held his furrowed brow in his hands and openly wept.

The expected questions began not long after he stopped crying.

Have you finished weeping like a wee girl?

Fuck off!

I'm concerned about you Nelson. I don't like to see you cry.

You're lying.

OK I'm telling fibs. You can cry all you want to. There's only me that can hear you, you big girl.

You're annoying me, I told you to fuck off.

Now, now, language, Nelson. Let's stop the bickering. Tell me what you did between; let me think, between thirteen and the ripe old age of fourteen. Or should I say what or whom did you kill that year. Any more bullies?

Nelson was quiet for a few minutes gathering his thoughts. There was a dull ache festering somewhere in his head. He knew it would soon manifest itself into a real belter of a migraine. The constant headaches were something else that Nelson had to put up with.

Nelson?

No it was just aminals.

You mean animals?

That's what I said aminals.

You can't even pronounce it properly, you moron. The word is animals.

Piss off.

So we're back to telling me to piss off again are we? That's charming. So whose aminals did you kill then?

I won't tell you.

Come on please. You know you want to.

You're an asshole. You know that?

Come on now, Nelson, I know that you don't mean that. I'm your friend.

Friends don't tease.

Oh what a shame you're still upset. Let's see what I can do to help. I know, get on with it!

Remember Old Mrs. Groarty that lived next door.

Oh yes her. I remember she had that wicked black tom cat that used to hiss at us.

Yes well I caught it sleeping one day on top of our coal bunker. It was lying all cosied up there in the sunshine.

And what did you do to it?

Well you know how my mum and dad used to keep that dustpan and the brass poker set next to the fire in the living room?

I'm not sure.

Remember the brass poker, next to the coal scuttle?

Oh that. The one he used to prod the burning coal embers with.

Yep that's the one. I had come round the side of our house and was going into the back garden for my ball when I saw the cat just lying there in the sunshine. It didn't even stir, it was sound asleep.

You already told me that it was sleeping in the sunshine.

I thought that this was too good an opportunity to miss. I knew exactly what I had to do. I hated that cat so much.

I know; we both did.

I went back into my house and grabbed the brass poker from the fireside hearth and went back downstairs and as quietly as I could, sneaked up to the coal bunker and walloped the cat.

Ha ha ha. That's hilarious.

I hit its head as hard as I could. It didn't even make a sound as its brains spread out over the grass when it fell off the bunker. It just lay there twitching. I stood there and watched it die and I said to it as it died that it wouldn't scare me any more. When it finally stopped twitching I took the poker back up the stairs and stuck it into the embers of the fire. The ashes burned off all the evidence of the cat's hairs and the gunge from its brains. The living room smelled a bit with burning hair, but I just opened all the living room windows and the smell was gone after a couple of minutes. I thought that was clever.

That was clever.

So nobody thought that it was me. They all thought it was one of the bigger lads in the street, that had killed her puss, or it had fallen off the roof and used up all its nine lives.

So nobody saw you do it?

Nope

Did she not die shortly after?

Some say she died of a broken heart because she loved that cat so much. I didn't like her or her bloody cat. I always thought that with all that straggly hair she looked like a witch.

She did lack a hair style

Anyway the wicked witch and her evil black cat were out of my life.

So you could say you were responsible for that old lady's death as well.

No not really. I don't want to take the credit for that one.

I don't think you should think of it as taking credit.

That's what I said; she died not because of anything I did to her.

You killed her beloved pussy cat.

Fuck off.

I'm only kidding. So you killed a few animals in the year after the girl with the hair the colour of autumn leaves, and then what.

Would you stop taking the piss? You asked me to tell you something and then you won't listen. Do you want me to go on or what?

You know me. I like a good story and it's not as if we have anywhere to go, now is it? You have my undivided attention.

Nelson stood up and walked around the cell twice before continuing. He leaned against the cell wall facing the doorway. Well as I recall it wasn't long after the girl that I did another one.

Did?

Yeah you know ... did.

You certainly don't mince your words. Very descriptive is the word did.

But it was when we went on our summer holidays. Remember Mum taking me down to Millport?

I remember going down and staying at a boarding house. But I can't remember a girl there.

"No she wasn't in the guesthouse." He sat down. "I came across her the day we hired the bikes to cycle round the island. Everybody cycled away in front of me and I was so far behind,

You were so far behind because you were still a fat bastard.

It was puppy fat.

Yeah right. Puppy fat ha ha.

It was so.

You came across this girl?

Yeah well I'm trying to tell you, I was pedalling my bike trying to catch up to my family, but I had to stop to catch my breath. I stopped my bike at the side of the road next to a lay-by. There was a car parked there it was one of those old Morris Minors. I think it was a grey one. Not that it matters.

Oh it matters. Every detail you remember is good to hear. You stopped your bike to catch your breath and then what?

I caught a glimpse of her behind some gorse bushes. I could see her dark hair blowing about in the wind. She was squatting down and was having a piss. She was totally oblivious of me and everything else all around her. She didn't seem to have a care in the world. You'd have thought that she would have been nervous peeing out in the countryside. Wouldn't you? I mean it's not really ladylike now is it?

She must have been a very confident young lady

That's what I thought later when I remembered all that happened.

So you actually thought about all your actions and what you did?

Listen I'm telling you I got off my bike quickly, looked around to see if anybody else was watching. My wee heart was racing. I laid my bike on the grass and sneaked up on her to give her a fright.

Well she wasn't a girl then if the car was hers and she was old enough to drive.

I don't know if the car was hers or not. It doesn't matter. I laid my bike down on the grass and sneaked round the bush to look. I startled her but all she did was smile at me, which I thought a bit strange.

She saw you and just smiled? I find that very hard to believe. She didn't scream the place down?

Nope. She didn't seem at all scared. She just kept on peeing. After all I was just a big teenager.

I've got to laugh when you said you startled her. You just sneaked up on her having a piss behind a gorse bush. Which in your words is very unladylike and she kept on peeing.

I know but she, oh I don't know, she must have thought it was funny to have got caught. She wasn't a bit embarrassed.

So what happened next?

She finished pissing and then stood up and pulled her knickers up.

Did you see anything?

Oh aye. She lifted up her skirt and pulled up her knickers real slow over her big black bush. My tongue must have been hanging out.

I bet it was.

She said that if I wanted to see her bush again I had to take my cock out and show her it.

Did you show her it?

Too right. I couldn't get it out fast enough.

What did she do then?

Well she gasped at the size of it and then she moved slowly closer to me and put her hand over my cock and playfully gave it a quick couple of tugs. She then took my hand and thrust it down her knickers and I could feel her hair and she was wet.

Well she did just have a piss. That's why she was wet.

Well she took me by the hand and led me further into the bushes and in a grassy spot we stood looking at each other. She kicked her shoes off and then took off her skirt. She stood there in her knickers. She was smiling at me. I dropped my shorts and stepped out of them. She let out a wee laugh when she felt how hard I was.

And did you feel her?

Are you crazy? Of course I did. As soon as she held my knob in her hand I tried to feel her inside her pants. She sat down on the grass and told me to do the same. I mean she lay there on the grass and took her pants off and opened her legs and pulled me on top of her and we had intercourse.

I don't believe you.

I'm telling you. I couldn't believe it either but that's how it happened. In five minutes of sneaking up on her I was on top of her shagging her and exploding into her.

That just doesn't happen.

It did.

Was she drunk?

What do you mean?

There is a complete stranger having a piss behind a gorse bush and you a fourteen-year-old laddie on his bike, somehow stumbles across her and has a shag with her, after showing her your dick? It doesn't happen. So did she smell of alcohol?

I don't remember, maybe.

Now it's beginning to make a wee bit of sense. You never mentioned she had been drinking before.

But I'm telling you it didn't really matter if she was drunk because she went mental as we were having sex. She was moaning and moaning and then she was swearing at me.

Oh oh! You don't like girls swearing at you.

She was cursing and asking me to hurt her.

Hurt her?

Yep that was her words, she said hurt me, baby. Oh yes hurt me, baby, just there, there.

She said that?

Yep she said to bang it into her hard.

She actually said that?

Over and over again.

And did you bang it into her hard?

Well I was enjoying the experience and when she said to hurt her it kinda drove me on

Did you hurt her?

I put my hands on her face to try and kiss her but must have put them round her throat.

So they just slipped and gently found their way to her throat? Did you give a wee gentle squeeze?

I think so.

So you did hurt her then?

She was enjoying it.

So you were still having sex with her as you choked her?

I couldn't stop myself.

So you choked her to death?

I said I couldn't stop myself.

So you came as she died. Same old scenario; Déjà vu eh? You coming as she was dying? Ring any bells?

I think so.

You think so?

All right I remember.

The thing that puzzles me is did she not put up a struggle when you had your hands on her neck?

She did a bit. But it was more exciting then because I was still inside her.

So you shot your load and she died.

Yeah, I suppose so.

So what did you do then?

I stopped shagging her and I wiped my dick clean on her dress. I stood up got dressed in a hurry because I could hear a car coming along the road. I ducked down behind the gorse. But it was all a panic for nothing, the car didn't stop.

So after the car passed by, you just jumped on your bike and continued on your merry way? You didn't go back and shag her again?

No I didn't go back. I wanted to catch up to my mum and dad. I remember I was very careful as I got on my bike. I looked both ways to make sure there were no witnesses.

The amazing thing is that no one ever sees you.

That's because on this occasion there was no one around to see me. It was a small island and all the Glasgow holidaymakers must have been doing other things that day.

I remember the whole island was talking about her murder right enough. 1968 wasn't it?

The Glasgow fair fortnight to be exact. Aye 1968 was a good year.

What do you mean a good year? Was it a good year for murdering people?

No I mean the weather was brilliant for my holidays.

Do you remember the police? Remember the number of police that came onto the island?

Aye. They questioned everybody asked them if they had seen anything.

Did they ask you?

Of course they did.

And you lied to them.

I told them I hadn't noticed the car because I was trying to catch up to my mum and my dad on my bike. I didn't remember seeing it.

And they believed you?

Must have because I was just a kid and we never heard any more about it.

So that was another one you got away with.

Yep.

So who was next? I mean you were getting good at killing and not getting caught. So did you plan for your next victim?

Not plan exactly. Well I suppose I did.

Did you or did you not plan it? That's all I'm asking.

I got a kicking one night coming home from the park at my gran's in Glasgow. There were three of them and all older than me and they jumped me and gave me a thumping. I know I was big for my age but there were three of them. All I could do was try and shield my face with my arms as they knocked me down onto the pavement and kicked me.

So they had you on the deck then?

Yes and I remember recognizing their boots as Doc Martens boots; you remember they were the kind all the boys wore.

What made you remember the type of boots those boys wore? I mean they were kicking the shit out of you and you remember that they had Doc Martens on.

I remember because I felt each and every kick they took and I remember they were laughing with each kick, calling me a fat bastard.

So there was no one passing by that could have helped you or stopped them?

No. It was late.

But you did see who it was?

Aye I glanced up when they stopped. I could see that they were skinheads. Their denim jeans with turn up's, big boots and bald heads. I saw them when they passed under the street lamp. I recognized one of them. I had seen him in the shop just the other day so I remembered him.

So when was that?

It was my fifteenth birthday.

Some birthday present eh?

Yep, I got a sore face and a sore back and my bum was bound to be bruised. Oh and a blood stained jumper, from my nose bleed. My gran was shocked when she saw me. She took me into her kitchen and got me all cleaned up. She checked to see if they had broken any of my ribs or my fingers, which they hadn't. She was going to get the Police and I asked her not to. That would only cause more trouble.

So you knew then he was going to die?

It was going through my mind.

She was a good old lady your gran was.

She was that.

You miss your gran, don't you?

Every day

So tell me, how did you plan your revenge on the thugs that beat the crap out of you?

That was easy. I knew he was a local. I had seen him about the place. All I had to do was catch the boy on his own one night, when he wasn't with his mates and the shoe would be on the other foot so to speak. I visited my gran nearly once a fortnight, so by the time my bruises healed up.

He was as good as dead.

I'd get him when he was vulnerable; he was on his own and not with his gang.

What the one you recognized?

That's what I said. Are you not listening to me?

I'm listening! My question is did you have to wait long?

It wasn't too long about a month maybe.

So how did you get him?

Well I was in the shop one Friday night and who should walk in for fags.

That was the wee corner shop next to the football park?

Aye that's the one. The shop where you could steal anything and not get caught.

And did you steal anything?

Not that night, the shop was too busy. Anyway I saw him pay for his fags and walk out.

He was probably going to meet his pals. Well I followed him at a wee distance.

There we go again, you following someone.

It was getting dark and he was walking back into the estate. Well you remember the street corner with the broken light and the empty house that had all the windows boarded up?

I remember.

Well I caught up to him there. He never heard me coming. He had stopped to light a fag. I punched him on the back of his neck hard and he fell down. As soon as he was on the ground, I started kicking him; I wanted to see how he liked being attacked.

That's my boy. Getting your own back by kicking the shit out of him.

I remember that I kicked him in the face and I must have knocked him out cold. Must have been a lucky kick I think, but I looked around to see if anyone had seen me or was coming to help and saw nobody.

As usual, nobody is ever around to see you do something bad.

Even if someone had seen me they weren't too bothered about two boys fighting.

You knocked him down and he just lay there on the pavement out cold. Did you keep on kicking him?

No I stopped. I could have walked away you know. After all I had thumped him and got my revenge, but he deserved more.

I bet he did and I bet you gave him a bit more of a beating didn't you?

When I was absolutely sure there was no one around, I dragged him along the path to the boarded up house. I dragged him up the stairs into the close and dropped him at one of the first floor doors. I kicked the door open and dragged him inside.

Was he alive and kicking?

Very funny!

Just trying to add a bit of humour

He was alive but really out of it.

You must have kicked him real hard to knock him out for that length of time.

Oh I did and right on the side of his head. Well to be truthful, I was a wee bit scared that I had indeed killed him.

Why were you worried that you had killed a scumbag?

I was a wee bit concerned shall we say that someone might have heard me kicking the door open. The place was empty and I did make a bit of noise. For the first time I was scared of getting caught. So I went back into the close and listened. I couldn't hear a thing except my heart beating and him breathing.

I feel sorry for the poor boy.

I felt nothing. The only thing that I remember, the building smelled of piss. So the druggies and the drunks used it as a toilet. But I was my usual lucky self that night there was nobody there.

As I've said before you were one lucky bastard when it came to killing someone, but it wasn't so lucky for the skinhead eh?

Nope. I woke him up by pissing on his face.

You did not.

I did so.

That's so funny. Did that do the trick and wake the boy up?

Do you know I actually let him stand up?

Were you not scared in case he beat you up again?

Nope. I knew what I was going to do to him.

And that made you brave?

Not brave exactly. More clinical I think.

Clinical or cynical? Was he shouting at you? Was he threatening you?

Yes he was and he was swearing at me.

Swearing at you, oh that's where he made the big mistake.

He was jumping around getting all agitated 'cause he didn't know where the devil he was and who I was and if it was me that had hit him.

He was probably scared shitless at some big lad standing there in front of him and of being all sore and smelling of piss.

I don't know if he was scared shitless, because he started acting all tough again and shouting that he was going to kick my arse. He was looking all around the room for something to grab and hit me with.

And you stood there and let him rant and rave at you?

I suppose I did let him go on and on and threaten me. When he realized that there was nothing at hand to hit me with he made a grab at me. I saw it coming and reacted quicker than he thought and I dropped him again. This time I punched him square on his chin and he fell over.

Fell over like a boxer being knocked out?

Well he sort of reeled and staggered really and then he fell down.

Wham bam, thank you mam.

Mind you he tried to get to his feet too quick and fell over again.

Just like a boxer that's out of it.

He sat there bleeding from his burst lip and he was still determined to find something to attack me with. He looked to his left and then his right just in case he missed something the first time he looked.

Was he looking for a stick? A big stick? Like someone before him that hit you with a big stick.

Aye I guess so. But I started laughing at him

"You laughed at him?"

Yeah at his feeble attempts at threatening me.

So what did he do, when you started laughing?

He threatened to kill me. Well I laughed even more.

I bet that upset him even more.

It must have. He didn't know what I was going to do next.

I think with you laughing at him, you confused him.

Confused is one word for it. I asked him if he could remember me. He looked at me and I could see him trying to remember. But he didn't have a clue.

Even though he was in a lot of pain, he still had the balls to threaten me.

And it was just about to get more painful, right?

He said he was going to kill me and he scrambled to his feet and came at me again just a bit too quickly for his own good.

You let him get up? Why did you do that?

I don't know. Maybe it was to give him a small chance.

But he could have got lucky and hurt you. You should never let anybody get up. Never give up an advantage.

I wasn't afraid of him. He was brave when he had his mates with him. But he on his own, he was scared. And he knew I could really hurt him. I was a different kettle of fish now.

So did he lunge at you?

Yeah but he telegraphed that. I kicked him just below his right knee. I think I broke his leg because he yelled out in pain as he fell down.

What with just a kick you think you broke his leg?

It was like a side kick, you know a karate one. You hit him with the sole of your boot just below the knee and it snaps like a twig.

Where did you learn that?

Just from watching the boys in the school karate class.

I said you were clever.

I asked him again if he remembered me.

And did he?

I said it a wee bit louder and more threatening this time. He swore at me again and there were tears in his eyes.

Oh what a shame.

I asked him the question again and this time, he stared back at me with the frightened look of a wounded animal that knows it's going to die.

Die bastard!

He hadn't a clue who I was. He spat blood from his mouth and asked me why I was doing this.

Did you explain to him why?

I had to tell him where and when he and his pals gave me the kicking.

Yeah, the kicking.

His eyes nearly bulged out of his head when I leaned on his broken leg.

Ha ha ha that must have been excruciatingly painful.

He very nearly passed out.

I bet you he did. Oh I can't imagine the pain.

I asked him who his pals were that night and where I could find them.

Did he tell you?

He was very tearful and not forthcoming with the answer I wanted.

Silly boy.

I broke his wrist and he squealed like a stuck pig.

Oh the poor boy.

He couldn't tell me who his friends were fast enough.

Did you have to break his wrist?

I was in the mood.

So how did you break it? I mean you may as well tell me.

Well I hit him really hard on the back of his hand.

And that was enough to break his wrist was it?

Must have been because I thought I heard it snap and he screamed out in pain.

Were you not scared that someone in the building might hear you torturing the poor bastard?

Not really I was beyond caring. I was beginning to enjoy myself hurting him, the fact that the building was empty and all boarded up, made it very special.

Special what do you mean?

That's maybe the wrong word, but it felt good to be alone with him and knowing that I was getting my full revenge. My gran saw the state of me after what he and his pals did to me that night. She wiped away my tears and got me sorted out that night. It was her that ran my bath. She even put in her bath salts and told me that the bubbles would help the pain go away.

I know.

She got me cleaned up. Remember I got such a beating that I pissed myself in fear. This was payback and there was nobody going to wipe away those fuckers' tears.

What about passers-by. What if they heard you?

I suppose I didn't care who heard.

With you breaking his body bit by bit. I take it he even told you his pals' names?

I told you that already.

So what did you do then?

I took my sheath knife out.

You carried a knife did you? Since when?

Since getting my arse kicked by that gang, it gave me a sense of ...

Security?

Aye that's the word. Security.

So go on, you took your knife out.

I was...

Come on say it.

I'm trying to express what I was thinking

You enjoyed hurting that boy. Didn't you?

He deserved it.

I know he did. He hurt you and now it was time for payback.

I played with my knife making all sorts of waves over his face with the knife.

Bet he couldn't take his eyes off it?

Nope. Then I reached forward and punched him hard with my fist again and this time …

He would have been unconscious when you did all that shit to him. The pain would have been too much for him to stay awake.

So what if he was out of it. I slashed his arms and his legs there was blood everywhere.

So you went to town on him then?

Yes. Because he did it to me.

Now you're making me sick

He deserved everything I did to him that night.

No he didn't. He only used his boots and kicked you a couple of times.

Yes I know but I cried out. It wasn't only him, there were others and they were all kicking me. They took turns and they laughed each time one of them hurt me. I pleaded with them to stop.

So that's why they were laughing at you. You pissed yourself.

No they were laughing because they were enjoying hurting me. They stopped when I pissed myself.

But you used a knife on him. They never used a knife on you. They only used their feet. You slashed him and cut out his tongue before you killed him.

I know. I whispered my name into his ear and the reason as to why he had to die. I heard his last gargle for breath.

So you actually loved watching him die?

Oh yeah and then I left. One down two to go.

You left him bleeding to death in that room.

I did.

No remorse?

Not one bit.

So did you get the other two?

When the body was found the police set up a murder investigation. The building was cordoned off from the public and they conducted house to house enquiries.

You weren't the least bit worried were you?

Nobody saw me so why should I have been worried?

What about his friends?

I suppose the pair of them would have had to go to the police station and give statements because they probably were, or had been with him earlier that day. They were easy to find after that because there wasn't that many skinheads running about Dennistoun at the time.

So you managed to track them down then?

As I said there weren't that many skinheads …

You told me. My you were becoming man the hunter. Weren't you?

I was becoming good at it. And do you know where I got the second one?

No! Where?

Remember the car showroom on Glasgow road at the Riddrie road traffic lights?

Yes on the corner.

Well I got him there. He was standing looking at motors through the window.

What kind of motors.

I don't know. Ford I think. It doesn't matter. I walked passed him heading up towards the bingo hall. Well there's a wee lane between the showroom and the next building.

That's right.

Well I stopped at the lane and shouted at him.

What did you shout?

I called him a baldy headed wanker.

That was good. I bet you that made him mad.

He didn't like that one bit so he ran after me.

He chased you up the lane?

That was the plan. Lure him in and then ...

I pretended to hurt my ankle and started to limp away from him. He nearly crapped himself when I stopped limping and turned round to face him.

I bet that stopped him in his tracks. Seeing you standing there eh?

He realized that I was bigger than him and his initial bravado was quickly disappearing down the leg of his trousers.

He was frightened then?

I could sense his fear and when I took out my knife I stabbed him in the throat. I think he got quite a shock.

That's a bit of an understatement. I think he got a shock. I bet he did. You stuck a bloody sharp knife into his neck and you said he was quite shocked. You're becoming the King of the understatement, one guy was stunned when you bit off a piece of his cock and this guy was shocked when you stuck a knife in his neck. Don't make me laugh.

It seemed funny to me at the time.

But that's a busy road. There are thousands of cars going up and down that road; did no one see you stabbing the boy?

No-one looks down a wee lane. They all drive by it and nobody gives it a second glance. Nobody would remember a skinhead running into a dark lane. Now be honest would they? The traffic lights must have been green because the traffic was moving quite freely when I did him.

You make it all sound so easy, when I did him. Did you do the whispering thing in his ear, like you did with number one?

Yep. As he fell to his knees he tried to grab onto the knife but I pushed it further into his jugular. I leaned over him away from the blood pouring out of his neck and I whispered to him who I was and why he was dying. I turned his head so I could look into his eyes and I wanted to be the last one he ever saw. I looked deep down into his soul and saw death take him. I pulled my knife out of his neck and dried the blade on his jacket as he fell onto the ground.

Did you not feel anything for him?

What do you mean?

I mean did you not feel a wee bit sorry for him as he was dying?

Not one bit. Why should I feel bad about anything? I didn't feel one pang of guilt. I was elated. He deserved to die. It was two down one to go.

You had turned into a ruthless heartless bastard hadn't you?

How dare you call me heartless? Those two skinheads deserved it.

No one deserves to die.

Oh don't start with your sanctimonious crap. Those two did deserve to die and I was glad.

So when did you get number three?

You've gone and annoyed me again.

You have a story to tell me. Can you answer my question?

I got number three about three hours later.

There that's better you've calmed down again.

Just don't start me off again.

I apologise, Nelson. I'm sooooooo sorrrrrrrry!

So you should be. Well I waited at his house for him in the hope that the son of a bitch would turn up and boy was I lucky.

You were getting to be a right wee lucky boy you know?

I couldn't have asked for better timing. He walked into the close and started up the stairs.

Did you have a plan to kill him quickly? Or were you going to torture him?

I'm not really sure.

So you were playing it by ear.

You could say that. I was prepared. I had removed the stair light bulb using my gloves. So the stairway would be in darkness

You had gloves?

Yes didn't I tell you? I used gloves when I killed the skinheads. Black leather ones my dad had in his bedroom drawer.

You failed to mention that detail. So you borrowed your father's gloves. Why?

I didn't want to leave fingerprints.

This is all good therapy, Nelson. You are remembering more and more facts each time you tell me something. You were really prepared then with the gloves. Nice touch, Continue.

The stairway was nice and dark. I stood there waiting, my eyes were accustomed to the dark and I was in a position to—

This is getting exciting.

 See if anybody entered into the close. And lo and behold the next thing I knew, he was there.

He wasn't with anyone then?

No he wasn't. But killing him was too quick. I wanted to pan him out a bit.

But you did kill him quickly

It was too bloody quick.

But you're forgetting some of the story.

No I am not. He entered the close I could see he had a bottle in his hand. It was a sherry bottle I found out later. He was walking a wee bit unsteady. In fact he was swaying about.

He was drunk.

Don't interrupt I'm telling you what happened. You do want to hear don't you?

Yes. Please tell me.

He staggered up the stairs towards where I was standing. I stepped back further into the shadows if that was possible and silently took my knife out.

Did he hear you?

No he was too pissed to be aware of anything.

So he came up the stairs and then what?

He tripped on one of the stairs and went crashing forwards down onto his hands and knees smashing the bottle he was carrying. That was my cue and I was on him in a flash. My weight put him face first onto the stair landing. I had to be quick in case someone heard the bottle smash and come outside to see what all the commotion was about. My knees were on his shoulders and my mouth was by his ear. My weight was enough to keep him pinned down.

So you did whisper?

I did whisper why he had to die. And then I cut his throat. I pulled his head back and slid my blade over his throat.

But you didn't wait until he died this time.

No. But I knew he wouldn't survive.

So that was three out of three then?

Yep. I was satisfied. The only mistake I managed to make was I left a footprint in the blood as I left. But it didn't bother me there were hundreds of people wearing the same type of trainers all walking about Glasgow. The police would be busy getting two murders on the same night. And by the time they would piece them all together it had been too late to save anyone of them. And there was nothing to tie any of them to me.

So you were elated again.

I guess I was.

So your list was growing.

Yep it was taking shape.

You liked to kill didn't you? It was beginning to give you a buzz.

It was my job to sort out the people who broke the law.

Hold on there. Where did that come from? People breaking the law? What made you judge and jury? I mean you were the chief breaker of the law here, you were killing innocent people.

He wasn't that innocent. I was doing the public a favour by killing him. You know he was no good. It was only a matter of time before he killed somebody.

You don't know that, he could have changed into a nice person, given time.

Behave yourself. You know that I'm right.

So you saw yourself as a protector of law-abiding citizens did you? What a mantle to take on. Is that what it was all about?

Oh shut up.

So tell me then really why did you start on a killing spree? I mean all those people?

Who said I killed more than the ones I told you about?

You did.

I did not.

Yes you did. You told me in a different conversation ages ago.

When?

Can't you remember?

No.

You told me weeks ago.

What?

To be truthful you mentioned it yesterday afternoon just before tea.

That crap they called tea.

What didn't you like about the smoked fish then?

76

You know I don't like fish.

But I do.

I know you do but I don't. I prefer steak and chips.

But you said earlier that you would have picked up a lobster dinner when you were on the beach. What's lobster if it isn't fish?

It's a crustacean.

It's shellfish stupid. Fish. Fish. Fish.

I want steak. Steak. Steak.

Ha ha. This is fun isn't it?

It's about as fun as it gets.

So tell me about another one you did when you got older. Now that you were the high and mighty lord protector. So who was next?

I didn't see myself as a lord protector.

But you were.

I just wanted to help.

Tell me about the tramps and homeless people you started killing in 1988.

That's a painful memory for me. I don't want to.

Yes you do. I want to hear about all those poor people

I prefer to call them the unfortunates.

So you think killing these unfortunates was a help to the society?

It took them off the streets. They were probably glad to die. They would have thanked me for ending their miserable lives. They were filthy, dirty, lice filled and a cancer on our society.

Now calm down or you'll give yourself a coronary.

They were really filthy and their clothes were smelly.

Did you whisper in their ears as you took them?

I'm not sure.

Did you or did you not whisper your name into their ears as you stuck that blade into their necks?

I suppose I did.

You know you did.

OK so I told them why they had to die. It was no big deal.

No big deal. Is that what you said? It was a big deal to them as they uttered a last word or took their last breath. It was a very big deal.

You might be right. You know that just seeing the look on some of their faces when they realized what was happening. It was priceless. It made me smile

So how many did you kill then?

About 9.

My my, our memory has gone.

What do you mean?

Your numbers are incorrect it's not nine. Try eight.

No, you're wrong, it was nine!

Eight.

I know how many I killed, it was nine!

Ok tell me about the nine then.

Why did you say eight when you know it was one more?

Because, my friend, you only killed eight tramps that night; eight of those poor miserable wretches, whom you took on your own judgment to kill and to end their hapless lives. Are you listening to me? You were the judge and the jury and the only crime they ever committed was to fall out of society's rat race. You should have taken pity on them not slaughter them. But you had to take your knife out and slit their throats as they were trying to keep warm. You killed all those tramps. But one of them had heard what you had done and hid and stayed quiet before you left. That's why there were eight dead and not nine. You do remember that night don't you?

Of course I do. I was there.

Eight harmless souls that had never did you a bit of harm. Maybe you are right in assuming that they were better off dead. No one will ever know. You should be ashamed.

Ashamed, what? I'm telling you that they were better off dead. They were just things no one wanted to see or to help.

Oh don't go so fucking moral on me pleas – describing them as things. These were people not things. I can't stand your sanctimonious crap.

I wasn't being sanctimonious.

No just murderous.

So what if I ended their lives. No one cared.

I know one person who cared.

Who was that then?

You know fine well. The copper who was put in charge of the investigation, to stop the killings and to catch you – you the serial killer.

Ha that sad person.

How do you know he was sad?

Because he didn't catch me and it wasn't him that stopped the killings. It was me. I took the decision to stop.

Not if my memory serves me well. I think you'll find that's a bit of a lie you're spinning there my friend.

It was my decision.

No it wasn't. You didn't decide to stop killing. Come on now remember!

It was so.

Your memory sometimes is laughable.

I could so have continued if I wanted to. But it was too easy. It wasn't a challenge. I needed a challenge.

So what kind of challenge was it you needed?

I needed to be stimulated

You mean sexually stimulated?

No! I mean intellectually stimulated. I had an idea to plan out a series of killings that would challenge me with the danger of just managing to escape before being caught. I was going to be extra careful and clinically clean and not leave many clues. We were going to play a game of hide and seek.

Wait a minute. You said that you wanted to be challenged? Challenged by the Police? So why not leave them more than just a few clues, in your sick little game?

Why didn't I leave tons of clues for them? I'm not that fucking stupid. I didn't want to get caught.

So why are we in here?

You know why. Because of something called DNA.

It wasn't just that, you were stupid and left someone who could recognize you.

I left no one alive!

I beg to differ. You need to try and remember that whole day and the night with the tramps. Start with the homosexual who tried to pick you up in that gay bar. Then explain to me what happened a week later when you got hurt by another less fortunate one.

Do I have to?

Yes you do. You got us caught. You shouldn't have jacked off after murdering some of those people. Should you have?

There was a momentary lull in the conversation as Nelson thought about what had just been said.

Did you hear me?

Killing excited me. I had to.

No you didn't. You could have just left. But oh no, not you. You had to take out the mighty penis and masturbate. Every drop of semen you left on some of the victims was a piece of the jigsaw puzzle that those bastards needed to catch you. They must have started profiling you in the early days from your first few kills. They probably had a bloody big dossier on you and your crimes. The semen probably tied all the killings down to you anyway.

You're swearing.

No wonder. Do you really comprehend what I am telling you? You shouldn't have wanked over dead bodies.

I told you that I needed to.

That's a lot of people you wanked over.

I suppose so.

Suppose so? Let us count. It's a total of 12 or is it more, so what is it? You didn't jack off over the skinheads now did you?

Never mind counting, I haven't told you about the best ones yet.

Ha. Now we're getting somewhere. Go on, tell me.

Schhhh. Be quiet now, it's about time for the guards to come and feed us. So be quiet just now.

Doesn't the time fly by when you're enjoying yourself? But, Nelson, you do know that you have to tell me everything; it's your only therapy?

I told you to be quiet.

Somewhere in the distance, there was the usual familiar noise of a door being mechanically opened. There was the sound of a trolley being pushed or dragged into a corridor. There were three individuals heard as their boots made differing noises on the polished floor. Three guards approaching the maximum-security wing and a door magically opened electrically. All sounds known to the eight inmates.

The door slid open along its rails allowing entry. The guards stepped into the wing and the crackle of a walkie-talkie shattered the silence. One guard announced where he was and what sequence of doors to open up. The receiver Okayed that and closed the main door behind them. The door returned along its rails and slammed shut.

How did you know they were coming to feed us?
I told you. Be quiet!

The trolley stopped at each door, the guard would radio in the name of the prisoner and the individual cell door would open. Somewhere another guard was pleased that he wasn't on the trolley detail. Each prison door opened slowly outwards giving the guards full view into the maximum-security cell.

As each door opened the three guards would step back and wait to ensure that the prisoner did not charge forward with fists and feet flailing madly. Their nightstick batons were held at the ready to subdue the adventurous. But as times before there were no takers for the beatings this time.

The trolley held polystyrene plates of tepid soup and others of stewed fish and soft vegetables and mashed potatoes.

Nothing the prisoners could choke on whether they tried to do the deed deliberately or otherwise. As all prisoners were deemed as being dangerous only plastic cutlery was ever handed out to them. The more subdued the prisoner then there was a likelihood that one of the guards would spoon feed the prisoner. The other two guards would watch and smile at the unfortunate third guard who had to do the dirty. But it was force-fed more like, cramming food and soup into a being that had no recollection of where he was, or who he was. Medicine would be the dessert course and a nice wee nap would be the next thing on the agenda for the unfortunates.

If the prisoner was alert and not subdued then he was told to clear the doorway and to stand back. The guards would then position themselves on either side of the doorway as the other guard laid the plates on the floor. The three would then leave, as a torrent of abuse would inevitably sound out behind them. It was the prisoners' only way of retribution, questioning the guards' parentage.

Each cell contained a mattress, a thick woollen cover and one standard pillow. No soft duck down quilt with a tog value of 10. No soft pillow your head would sink into. Just bog standard prison issue as it had been described on numerous occasions. The toilet was a four inch diameter hole in the floor located at the opposite side to the door. The prisoners had to squat over it to defecate. The toilet paper went down the same hole. The wall mounted button flush was the only modern appliance in the cell.

The eight cells were all 16-square metres and 2 and a half metres high. There was no running water. Couldn't afford some prisoner self-afflicting pain by crashing his head against a sink. So there was nothing to clean or wash.

Each prisoner was allocated slippers often the wrong size and a cotton button up bright yellow short sleeved coverall for warmth. The coverall was changed out every day at breakfast time; the prisoners would be made to stand naked as new coveralls were issued and the worn ones changed out. This gave the guards the opportunity to look for any sores or marks of self-abuse. Seven of the prisoners were fortunate enough to have a small plastic tray placed on their cell floor containing a small blue safety razor, a can of shaving soap and a plastic cup of cold water. After shaving, all the items were accounted for and returned cleaned; placed by the prisoner onto the tray and put back down on the floor. The prisoner would then be ordered to stand back and one of the guards would retrieve the tray and the worn, sometime soiled coveralls.

This accounted for one of the highlights of a prisoner's day, the routine of breakfast and fresh clean coveralls.

The breakfast always consisted of oatmeal porridge, sometimes of a thick consistency, but the majority of times, thin and runny. It was edible when it was hot and just about passable when it was lukewarm. To get it to being really good was when it was thick and hot and the milk was fresh. Those were rare occasions. Nelson could count on one hand the number of times he had really enjoyed his porridge.

There were also scrambled eggs and two slices of dried toast as an accompaniment. On the occasion that in the real world there was a public holiday, there would be two rashers of greasy bacon and a fried tomato added as extras. But no matter what day it was, you always got a mug of tepid warm milky tea with sugar, even if you didn't like sugar or milk. You had no option. It was a no brainer you either took it or you left it.

The only drawback was that if you were considered a really dangerous inmate, which Nelson was, the guards would sometimes not give the plastic cutlery and let the prisoner eat breakfast with his fingers or drink the porridge like tea. They wanted to de-humanise the prisoner, let him know who governed and who ruled. It was their only way of payback. There were other guards who would just lay the complete breakfast tray down on the floor, stand back and walk away.

Treating human beings like animals is not something new. We have been doing it to each other since the day our species stood upright and walked. And here we are now in the 21st century and still it continues. I can make no excuses for some of the guards' behaviour, but as I have said before, the guards thought that Nelson was an animal.

The breakfast team attended each cell until they came to their penultimate one. They all felt revulsion at the thought of this mass murderer and to be honest with you, they were never quite sure what to expect or find on opening his door.

The guard called in over his radio requesting the opening of Nelsons cell door and they all stepped back, night sticks drawn. Nelson knew the drill and stood at the back wall ready to stare back at his captors. The hairs on the back of the guards' necks stood.

There was no doubt in their minds that this was a monster that stood before them; there was no other word that they could use to describe what they thought of Nelson. They feared him and that was fact. This was someone who had slaughtered people in Glasgow and it made them sick thinking about it.

The door opened slowly and the guards stood ready to repel Nelson's frontal assault. There would have been instant panic if it had happened and instant relief when it did not materialize. But he was back there and he was looking at them through the dark sunken eyes.

It gave them all a feeling of something intangible, somehow threatening but something that felt real. There was no simple explanation of that feeling that each guard felt during the initial contact. Imagine the first time you encounter a wild dangerous animal.

It came from someone who emanated pure evil through every pore, and having once seen that look, the memory never left you. It gave each individual something to think about and something that could possibly disturb you.

No guard would ever stare directly into Nelson's face.

His eyes watched every move you made.

The guards would sometimes attempt to converse with Nelson.

He wouldn't respond. Nelson would never make a sound of acknowledgement.

It pissed the guards off.

That's the way he liked it.

He was in control of the moment not them.

The tray and plates were put down on the concrete floor and a coverall tossed towards him. The guards all stepped back mighty relieved that there had been no incident, no immediate threat. Nelson stepped forward lifted the coverall and put it on. He deliberately took his time buttoning up each button not dropping his stare from the guards. He then lifted his tray and sat against the wall facing his jailers and ate with gusto. They thought he was an animal so fuck them, he ate like a pig. After completing his breakfast he placed the plates calmly onto the tray and then laid the tray back down onto the concrete floor and stepped away. He didn't want to give the guards control or their satisfaction of ordering him or forcing him to stand back.

Nelson played with their minds.

He knew what was expected of him; today he complied with their rules.

There was going to be a time when he wouldn't comply, but today was not the day.

Who knows what tomorrow would bring.

The guards retrieved all the dishes and one of them was then brave enough to place the shaving tray on the floor in front of Nelson. He never took his eyes from Nelson. His heart was pounding. Nelson was sure he could hear it thumping in the man's chest.

Nelson waited for the guard to retreat and again stepped forward and lifted the tray and took two steps back towards his bed. He sat down and methodically slowly began to shave. He knew that all eyes were on him.

They watched his every move with the razor as he slowly scraped the blade over his stubble and then rinsed it in the cup of cold water. They were transfixed. Nelson knew this and his shaving was pure theatre.

This was the most intense and dangerous time for the guards, Nelson had a razor in his hand. A potential weapon because of the steel blade. Nelson found it laughable that they thought that this was a dangerous time. What harm could he seriously do with a wee blue plastic Bic razor? But during each shave Nelson took notice of how each guard behaved. He looked for silly little things, uneasy movements, shifting poses, rapid eye blinking, quick breathing, which one held onto their batons, who was confident enough to take their hands off it. It all racked up in Nelsons mind and he would know which one of today's guards appeared to be the most nervous.

He had in his recollect a mental list of all the guards and he was definite he knew which ones were the scared ones. He just needed them all to be on the same shift at the same time. He looked forward to that day. That was action day.

He cleaned the razor in the cup of water and washed any missed bits of soap from his chin. He dried his face with his sleeve. He stood up and walked the two paces and like before laid the tray out in front of the guards. He returned and leaned against the cell wall.

Their daily trauma of breakfast was over for this day.

Nelson had been in his usual control zone. There would be nothing for them to report.

As each guard exited the cell they all felt a sense of relief.

Nelson remained motionless; he was a statue, making no move or sound as he watched them leave.

The guard radioed in to the control room that they were finished and to close the cell door and seconds later it was done with a thud. All along the corridor you could hear several bolts sliding into place as each door locked.

The three guards would never admit to each other of being scared from that prisoner. Their bravado would never allow them to, but they were all glad that their sphincter muscles had remained inactive as the bolts locked into place.

The breakfast trolley was pushed back along the corridor and after communicating again with the control room, the main corridor door slid open. The three men stepped back through the invisible barrier. One side danger and one side safe. It didn't take a rocket scientist to work out which side was which.

The testosterone levels returned through each man and the machismo strut of the prison guard returned.

The wing returned to silence.

There were seven breakfasts administered that morning.

The eighth was returned uneaten. The recipient remained unconscious.

It was not noted in the log book.

Routines for lunchtimes and evening meals were slightly different. The prisoners were left to eat in silence with no prying eyes. The guards did not want to witness anybody defecating or watch the animalistic way some of the prisoners consumed their meals. Each prisoner had their little bit of privacy.

It was the only act of decency, if you can call it that; that was ever shown to them.

At the end of the meal each item of plastic cutlery was counted back onto each polystyrene plate.

None were ever reported missing.

After breakfast Nelson rested before he exercised as best he could by doing calisthenics. He would push against the cell wall and hold the pose. He would follow that with squat thrusts, running on the spot and then push ups, sit ups and then finish with star jumps.

He sat down and breathed deep and inwardly counted how long he could hold his breath for. He did that several times before having his mid-morning nap. When he woke he continued with strength exercises for a while and then doing more gentle exercises on the run up to lunch.

The afternoons were a change for Nelson.

Between lunch and dinner there was the obligatory 3 o'clock visit to the exercise yard. Sometimes the guards would change the daily routine and try to fuck with your head. You would exercise in the morning, throwing your morning into disarray. Then they would leave you alone and either your lunch or your evening meal would arrive late. Nelson knew all about their mind games, he didn't play.

All he wanted was his twenty minutes under a steaming hot shower just after breakfast. That was his routine. He could exercise anytime that was their rules.

But showering was something that Nelson really looked forward to. Letting the hot water cascade over him was a pleasure he couldn't really explain.

Although the soap remained un-perfumed he felt clean and that feeling of being cleansed bucked up his spirits. He would stand there stock still under the water with his eyes closed until the guard told him his time was up.

Next there would be a question and answer session to partake in; carried out by the prison Doctor or the Warden and sometimes Nelson played his part in it. He gave them a wee bit more of the story each time. It broke the boredom of his solitude before dinner. It was his turn at mind games.

Today the cell door opened for his evening meal and there was a new trio of guards that he hadn't come across before.

Nelson had pre-decided that he wouldn't be arsed getting up. He was delighted that he had made that decision before he knew the combination. Nelson wanted to play his own game with this new mix. He wanted to see how they would react to his not behaving as per their rules. He sat there with his back to the wall. He didn't move a muscle.

The guards screamed to him to get to his feet and stand up.

Nelson never flinched. He showed no emotion. He sat there and watched each man. He thought they would overreact and come in all batons blazing and he would get a beating. The three guards remained stationary, unsure as to what to do.

Nelson smiled to himself. No Alpha male in this threesome he thought.

He knew that all the guards wanted to do was to make as much noise as they could and sound so threatening that Nelson would comply and the situation would calm down.

He had been roared at before, with more or less the same result. He would receive a rollicking from the lead guard for not getting to his feet and end up on report. It would be no big deal. His reckoned his punishment for noncompliance would be no puddings for a week.

Nelson motioned with his hand for them to leave the tray and pointed to a part of the cell to where they should leave it.

He knew that these boys would put their hackles up as soon as he did that, but he didn't care. Today was Nelson's challenge. They were entering Nelson's game room.

The boys had to step up and hit him with their batons. Other guards would have without a shadow of a doubt. Marbury for example would have laid Nelson out cold given half an excuse. These three didn't and in Nelson's eyes they had just failed their first test. Their faces would be etched into his brain. Their non-reaction would also be logged in Nelson's mind.

There would be a time and place.

Not wanting to push this confrontation up to a new level, the three guards were not up for it. They all put it down to the same conclusion that Nelson was just misbehaving. They had done their bit by screaming abuse at him but as they stepped out of his cell and stood in the corridor they looked back at him.

Their shouting had announced to Nelson that they were in charge.

Nelson knew otherwise.

Each man had silently thanked God that they didn't have to physically discipline Nelson. There would have been too many questions to answer. First of all they would have had to explain the berating to the warden and it wasn't worth losing your job over. They would however mention it in their report regarding his behaviour.

What was it today?

Fish as usual. But be quiet. They may be listening at the door.

They're not; they walked away up to number 8 I think. What kind of soup is it?

It's piss soup.

Don't you mean pea soup?

What's the difference between piss and pea soup?

You can piss but you can't pea soup.

That's an old one.

I know. But there were three new guards today. Did you read their name tags on their shirts Nelson?

I got them. Did you see the look on the one called McNiven? Did you see his face when he put the dinner down?

He's scared of us.

I know that. You see the other two, Toland and Strachan pulling their batons out?

They're twitchy.

I'd seriously carve them up if I had my knife.

But you don't have.

Oh to get him in here alone for five minutes. Just five minutes that's all.

Which one?

The one called McNiven of course.

What about the other two?

I'd shove their batons where the sun doesn't shine.

They've never been together on shift before

I realized that when the door opened.

What did you think of their reaction?

You mean their lack of reaction?

Yeah I clocked that. Not one of them was man enough to come at you.

Maybe that's the group I want.

Maybe. Are you going to eat the soup now?

I have to. I have to keep my strength up you know.

Is it pea soup?

I don't know, but it's cold again.

Watch the fish for bones. You know what that chef is like.

Chef? He's a retired cook from the army they have employed in here. He knows how to spin out the meals, to make it all go further. He had to do it in the army for years.

But you don't like fish.

I know, but they say it's good for you .I'll eat it to keep my strength up.

They treat you like a dog. Not giving you cutlery to eat with.

They're scared I use a spoon to attack those three yellow bellied guards. I've heard them when they beat the others. Their big shiny boots giving a new inmate a kicking. Letting him know just who is boss. They're scum.

The water will be on now for the others

I know the routine.

But you are you going to exercise tonight?

My usual 500 push-ups and 500 sit-ups.

And then rest.

But I'll tell you about the cop.

The cop?

Aye him that thought he'd caught me when I knifed that gay bastard that tried to ...

Go on then tell me.

I'll tell you after my exercises before they turn the lights out tonight.

Christ we've got a lot to talk about. You've got a lot to remember: Tramps, a homosexual and a cop.

We've got plenty of time.

That my friend is so true.

Dinner over and cell doors closed for the night, the guards returned to their control room and each one of them returned to where he was before. McNiven took the daily log book down from the shelf and opened it up at the day and an entry was made for 6 p.m.

Solitary. West wing Cell 8.

Harrop unresponsive to guards. Was found sitting down with his back against the wall. Remained in the same position when challenged. Dinner tray left on floor. During the meal prisoner remained silent and tense. Behaviour rebuked by guards, but prisoner offered no verbal response. No action taken by guards. Signed D.A.McNiven.

The book was closed and put back on the shelf. The three guards continued where they had left off, prior to handing out dinner. Toland went back to reading his book and McNiven and Strachan went back to their game of chess. After some time Toland asked if anyone wanted a cup of coffee as he was going to make one. There was a general consensus that having a coffee at that particular time would go down rather well. The chat was of a quiet nature with little small talk of the prison inmates.

No one mentioned cell 8 west wing.

They were free from revisiting Nelson. Breakfast was for another crew, the night shift crew. Their shift would be over at midnight. Their 12 hour shift. The shifts were hard and boring for the most part. The tedium was for, 5 days nightshift, 3 days off and then 5 days dayshift. It was a continental system and part of the new trial on prison officer's duty. It wasn't what the Union wanted; they wanted 3 times 8 hour shifts 5 days a week with 2 days off. That system would have meant recruitment and more men for Nelson to evaluate.

But let me go back to the beginning and explain something to you. Let me tell you how all this started.

Chapter 5

Oct 1955

Nelson Harrop was born in Glasgow's Royal Maternity Hospital just off St Vincent square in Glasgow. The hospital had a chequered history starting life as the Glasgow lying in Hospital and dispensary in 1834 and was located in Greyfriars wynd. It moved to St Andrews square in 1841 and then to Rottenrow in 1860. It had survived 2 world wars and was in a constant state of repair, but the building won over the Glaswegians and they affectionately called the hospital "The Rottenrow".

Nelson was three weeks premature and after a difficult 12 hour labour was seen as a sickly yellow colour. He weighed a measly 5 pounds 10 ounces. The doctor diagnosed the yellowness as jaundice and told the mother not to become too attached to the child, as he did not hold out much hope for it. Nelson's mother cried when she heard those words. She held the wrapped weakling in her arms and sobbed quietly to herself. She looked down on the wee wrinkled face and prayed to god to spare her son and to help him survive. She glanced up at the Doctor wanting to ask him a question, but he had already moved onto another patient.

She looked around at the other girls in the ward and saw that they were either sleeping or lying in bed groaning with labour pains waiting to give birth. Nurses busied themselves between beds and babies.

Those that had given birth had their babies in Moses baskets adjacent to their beds. It seemed like all the babies born that day were all undernourished and sickly. The nurses carried on with ward duties and added their own wee comforting words to the new mums. They would console some or offer quiet congratulations to others. They had seen it all before. They had witnessed all the human frailty in the miracle of birth. It was life or death each time a toddler was born. Until the child was turned upside down and tapped on the back by the midwife and the child wailed nothing was certain.

The new mums were of all ages from 15years old to 25. Some of the mums in waiting were in for their second or third child. For some it was like shelling peas. Not for them the mandatory 5 days of a first birth. No it was one day later and the newborn was off to meet the family.

The year was 1955 and it was late October. Nelson being the result from a drinking session his mother and his father indulged on in the January of that year. They were celebrating the forthcoming Burns night. Celebrating the Bards birthday all to themselves albeit a few days early. Nelsons father had bought half a dozen cans of beer and a half bottle of gin from the pub. His only spending extravagance allowed from his pay packet, before handing the lot over to his wife.

It was one of those awful wet nights when the rain lashed down outside. It ran down the window in torrents, so any thought of going out down to the pub for a drink was out of the question. The room was cosy and warm and with the dark blue velvet curtains drawn, the streetlight was blocked completely.

So the pair of them sat in front of the big coal fire and drank. They sat warming their toes pointing them at the fore. They shared jokes about the day they had just endured. He worked in the shipyards and she worked in the local bakery. They laughed at the thought of pies being the size of battleships and ships being the size of pies. The pair of them were lucky to enjoy working. Post war Glasgow was a hard but flourishing haven for work. The shipyards flourished as Britain came to terms with peace but still required to arm its navy with replacement battleships and cruisers.

They enjoyed a kiss and a cuddle as the flames licked at the coal. She was drinking Gin and lemonade and was in a good mood. He was on his fourth can of beer.

As more of the drink was consumed the braver Nelsons Mother became. Her inhibitions disappeared as each gin took its toll. Their kisses got longer and steamier and hands started to wander. She opened the flies on her husband's trousers with a wicked smile growing on her face and felt his thickening penis. He didn't need any more of a hint. He stood up and took off his braces and dropped his trousers. She stood up and removed her dress. The pair of them never took their eyes off each other. Other pieces of apparel were removed and dumped on the settee. Within minutes the couple were stark naked and copulating on the fireside rug. Clothes were strewn all over the settee, bras and pants and skirts joined with trousers and socks all in a big jumbled heap. The sound from the busy street below had disappeared as the moans of lust took over. All thoughts of the neighbours hearing the cries of sexual acts coming from the living room just didn't cross their minds. The sex had been getting rougher in the last few months as they experimented trying out all kinds of different positions.

The pair of them could have taken their time and prepared the bed settee and could have actually gone to bed for their wanton lust. But they couldn't wait. She was naked and lying down on the rug beckoning him to enter her again and again. He stood over her and his huge penis was ramrod stiff and ready. She opened her legs and he got down and lay in between them. He opened her vagina with his rough fingers and positioned the tip of his penis at the opening and with a thrust from his hips he entered her. She gasped at the suddenness of the entry and as his slow rhythmical thrusts increased it made her moan. Soon his rhythm and her soft moaning were getting a bit faster and then all of a sudden he exploded inside her. She held onto him wrapping her long legs around his waist as he jerked forward for a few more times. A few minutes later and he was spent. He withdrew and rolled off her and lay besides her gasping for air. She turned onto her side and looked long into his eyes and she kissed him.

There were beads of sweat on her brow and on his. There were carpet burns on his knees and one on each of her buttocks. They lay there in each other's arms for some time breathing softly until she could feel him stir again. She put her hand down to his penis and sure enough the monster was awake again.

She giggled as she touched it and rubbed the tip with her thumb He grasped her breast and held it in his hand and licked and squeezed her nipple. She licked his cheek and then kissed him deeply biting his lip. He gave a little yell as he touched his lip and saw the blood. He smiled at her and she giggled. He grabbed a hold of her and kissed her again and forced his fingers into her. He stopped to pull her over onto her tummy with his hand. This was his new favourite position she thought and laid resting her head on top of her arms. He crawled to be behind her and placed both his hands under her hips and motioned that she lift her bum up.

She did as he asked and was on her hands and knees with him directly behind her. He had a hold of his penis with one hand while with the other he was opening her up. He got right in behind her and probed his penis right into her. She gasped in pain this time but like a dog he kept on thrusting. He grabbed her hair and arched her head back. His thrusts were far more theatrical this time. He was enjoying this new position banging her while she ached. He grunted like an animal with each exaggerated slap while she whimpered in satisfaction.

She loved the painful thrusts. The pain satiated her. He let go her hair and leaned forwards and grabbed her breasts and squeezed them hard. She gasped as this new wave of pain further aroused her. He was lying on her arched back and had stopped the banging. He squeezed the breasts harder this time and the tears began to roll down her face. But she didn't want to disappoint her man, she endured and encouraged him with a wanton urge for him to hurt her and swear at her. She wouldn't let him finish and she turned to his exhausted frame and made a grab for his balls. She was really caught up in this experience. Her knees were rubbed raw and her backside would bruise with the contact his hips made. She teased him by licking his shaft; she was fully aroused and whispered that she did not want him to stop.

Patsy pushed Jack onto his back and he watched her straddle him. The ecstasy as she pushed herself down onto his erection again and again forcing him to climax. Recognizing and feeling him climax an out of breath Patsy leaned forward and kissed his chest.

He had come with one final shudder and thrust and he lay there exhausted. He clung onto her dragging his nails down her back, watching her arch it as he did so. He lay there for a few more seconds until she rolled away. She crawled towards the settee for relief and comfort. They were both breathing heavily. She wiped away the tear from her cheek and turned to sit and face him. This was the most intense sex they had done to each other. Both of them knew they would be sore in the morning but for now, the firelight flickered and danced over their sweating bodies. They were so tired they could hardly muster a smile. They sat there in silence for ages and then they drank some more.

Thirty-seven weeks later out popped a sickly small baby whom they called Nelson.

In the beginning after being released from hospital Nelson's mother Patsy found it difficult to cope. The baby cried a lot and wanted fed every few hours. She wondered if she was producing enough milk for him. The powdered milk substitute was expensive to buy now that they had only the one wage coming in. Sleep was difficult with the wee one taking all the attention and sex was a definite no. Jack, Nelson's dad was a help washing the nappies by hand and putting them on the clothesline to dry. If it rained outside he would put the nappies on the clotheshorse in the airing cupboard to dry. The bathroom also had a pulley clothesline hanging over the bath and was always full of wet clothes dripping. The bathroom window was always cracked open and the room was freezing cold. It was not a room to spend any length of time in.

With all the difficulties in bringing up a sickly child Jack and Patsy were struggling to really cope. Life was really difficult and a lack of sleep and quality time together forced the couple to bicker with each other. Arguments caused tension, but they were both strong individuals and knew that they would get through it all.

The midwife would visit on a Wednesday tea time to check on Mother and son and would watch Patsy feed and bath Nelson. After the infant was dry she would weigh Nelson on the kitchen scales. She kept records of his weight in her wee black notebook and would compare his weight with what it was the previous week. She told Patsy that he was putting on weight and that brought a smile to her worried face.

The midwife also commented that she noticed that Nelson's colour had started to improve and although she encouraged Patsy to remain vigilant and watch over Nelson, she was sure everything was going to be alright. Those words of encouragement were all Patsy had wanted to hear. She looked at the bundle she held in her arms and smiled. She laid him down in his cot to sleep.

He was going to be OK after all; he was now over five pounds in weight.

He would soon be a big boy. He would soon be their big boy.

That night after the midwife had gone she couldn't wait to tell Jack the good news about Nelson. As soon as he walked through the front door she told him and watched for the smile on his face and he was genuinely delighted.

His busy shift at the shipyard, the physical effort, the feeling exhausted, all went out the door at the good news. After he had washed his face and hands at the kitchen sink he hugged his wife and said sorry to her. All the arguments were his fault. He kissed her softly on the lips. She loved him so much but laughed at him standing there with water dripping down his chin. She threw Jack a towel to dry himself and laughed as he did so.

Patsy busied herself about the stove. She had managed to cook mince and vegetables earlier as Nelson napped after his feed. All she had to do now was cook the potatoes and re-heat the mince and vegetables.

They sat down at their kitchen table and for the first time in weeks they relaxed in each other's company. They laughed and joked as they ate. When the dinner plates were all washed up and cleared away, they both stood at their front window and watched the rain falling down onto the street below. Jack put his arm round Patsy and gave her a cuddle. Nelson stirred and cried and Patsy went to the crib and lifted Nelson out and prepared herself to feed him. The midwife had shown Patsy how to breast feed her baby and explained to her all about the goodness the baby got from his mum's milk. Although it had been painful to begin with Patsy had persevered. Nelson was now thriving on it. You could see the difference in him physically.

He was putting on ounce after ounce. He was getting bigger and better at feeding. It was less of a struggle now. He was more than five pounds now.

They didn't make love that night in the bed. They had rampant wanton sex. Weeks without sexual contact had made the pair of them lustful and rough.

It was the night she climaxed as he spanked her. He spanked her as a joke but she had egged him on into doing it harder. She had pushed her backside towards him and asked for it to be slapped. Jack laughed softly as he slapped her cheeks.

Patsy wanted more than just a slap. Jack did as he was told and tentatively hit her a wee bit harder. But she called him to hit her even harder. So he did so. She cried out in pain for more and more and Jack was lost in a spanking oblivion. He battered her rump and she climaxed. Her backside was glowing red with the beating and she had loved every painful minute of it. She lay on her back panting wanting so much more. He was so aroused he entered her and in no time he climaxed as she urged him deeper and deeper while swearing aggressively into his ear.

Nelson slept right through all the noise of the spanking session.

Jack and Patsy slept deeply in each other's arms that night through sheer exhaustion.

It was also the first time Nelson didn't wake up in the middle of the night for his feed.

As the first few years passed, Patsy had been lucky to get her old job back in the bakery while her mother watched Nelson during the day. It had come as relief to Patsy, to get away from the chores and the housework for a wee while. It was great to join in the banter at the bakery and to be among the girls again.

Jack had also progressed with a promotion to the shipyard's welding division. More and more clients wanted ships welded together rather than riveted. Progress was being more modern and use up to date technology. The Clyde side shipyards had moved with the times.

Jack had seen this as an opportunity and had jumped at the chance to better himself and earn a bit of extra money. He had worked hard and in doing so caught the foreman's eye and had earned his promotion.

Looking from the outside it appeared that Jack and Patsy seemed to be the normal hard working couple that doted on their young son. The house was always spick and span and there was never a shortage of food or drink. They were just your ordinary happy couple but who would have known, that their sexual antics had taken sadistic and often very masochistic painful turns.

One Friday afternoon while his gran was babysitting, young Nelson was playing on the hall carpet with his toys. The door to his Mum and Dad's bedroom was ajar and young Nelson managed to push it further open with his toy. His gran was sitting in the living room knitting, happy and contented to hear the "vroom vroom" coming from the youngster's lips. She knew there was nothing in the hall that could get Nelson into mischief. He on the other hand was a happy little boy while he could hear the click click of his gran's needles and her humming a tune while she knitted.

He crawled into the bedroom on his knees and pushed the truck along the carpet making his engine noise and stopped as he came to the bed. The valance was a great place to hide your toy behind and Nelson pushed under it with a giggle. Nelson lay flat on the carpet and looked underneath his Mum's bed. There were all sorts of stuff under there and Nelson crawled under to look. He was far too little to understand what all the objects were, but to him they looked like toys.

He touched a riding crop and a big studded dog collar, not knowing what they were. There was a big hard rubber object. Nelson touched that and giggled. He held it and stared at it, his little mind trying to understand what it was. He laid it back down on the carpet and crawled from under the bed with his truck and looked around the room.

He wasn't allowed to sleep with Mummy and Daddy anymore, because he was a big boy and big boys had their own room and their own bed now.

He got to his feet to leave when he noticed that his Mum's cupboard door was open. This was a new place for him to investigate. A child's curiosity took over. He slowly walked towards the open door and with a big smile, opened it even further. He didn't know what to expect or what he would find. It was a cupboard he wasn't allowed into. His mummy had once told him not to go in there as it was naughty to do so. The excitement of the moment was too much for him and he peeked inside.

He saw his Mum and Dad's shoes on the floor and his Mum and Dad's clothes were all hanging up. There was a small pile of discarded clothes tossed in the corner that caught his attention. It may have been the peculiar odour that came from the pile that attracted him to it. Like a moth to a flame Nelson reached out to touch.

Dropping his truck onto the carpet he picked up one of the items. It was his mother's brassiere. He put it to his nose and sniffed at it. He threw it back down on the floor and picked up something else. He sniffed again and did exactly the same with everything he picked up.

There was something telling him to stop doing what he was doing as it was wrong. He was going to be a bad boy if he got caught. His gran would slap his bottom if she caught him in here. Nelson got bolder and lifted a pair of panties. He stared at them noticing they were different from his. These had little flower designs on them and the fact that they had something streaked red stuff on the inside.

He put the panties to his nose and took a deep sniff and then threw them back down onto the pile of washing. He didn't like that smell at all.

Nelson lifted his toy truck and walked out of the cupboard and subconsciously closed the door behind him. He had to get out of this room before his gran started looking for him.

He skipped out of the room and along the hall into the living room to tell his gran that he needed to pee. She looked over the top of her glasses at the sudden intrusion and smiled at him. She put her knitting down and took his hand and led him back along the hall towards the toilet. She took the wooden box from behind the toilet seat and placed it in front of the bowl allowing Nelson to stand and pee all by himself. It was the first time that Nelson's gran had really noticed that he was going to be a big boy. She had stared at the penis that dangled from Nelson and watched it deliver pee right into the bowl. When he was finished she had pulled his pants back up and buttoned his trousers. She flushed the toilet and replaced the box. She couldn't stop thinking about the youngster's penis. If Nelson was like that, was it father like son she wondered. She shook her head dismissing the thought and returned to the living room to continue her knitting. Nelson was back playing with his truck having climbed up onto the settee and his gran noticed that he was beginning to look sleepy.

That night something had disturbed young Nelson and woke him up from his slumbers and for the first time he left the coziness of his bed to investigate. He grabbed his teddy bear and dragged it off to where the noises were coming from. He opened his bedroom door and stepped out into the hall. The noise was getting louder and was coming from his mummy's bedroom. Somebody or something was hurting his mummy he could hear the slaps and her crying. He stretched up and opened her door turning the handle quickly. He was trembling in fear as he peered round the door to find out what was happening.

His daddy was hurting his mummy.

Nelson's little eyes and mouth were wide open; he wanted to cry out but couldn't.

He wanted to scream to his Daddy to stop hurting his mummy, but nothing came out.

Jack and Patsy were far too involved in their sexual antics to hear a door handle turn and see a little face at the door.

Their son was invisible to them.

Nelson's eyes could see images through the dark, helped by the little light the outside streetlamp gave through the curtains.

His mother and father were totally oblivious to the small frightened onlooker. They were engaged in some sort of game and his mummy had something round her arms and was kneeling down on the bed with her arms stretched out. She had no clothes on and his daddy was smacking her bottom with his belt. He stood at the side of the bed and had no pyjamas on either.

Nelson couldn't shout out the words he wanted to. "Daddy please stop because my mummy is crying". He couldn't. Nothing came from his lips. Tears started to fall down his cheeks.

His mummy was crying, but she wasn't crying the way Nelson imagined. She was crying for more and asking Nelson's daddy to hit her harder. For a little boy it was too much for him to understand.

She wanted a lot more of what daddy was doing.

His father lifted the belt once more and sent it down on her backside with an almighty smack. Nelson closed his eyes and more tears welled up and flowed down his cheeks. He couldn't move and watched aghast as his father climbed onto the bed and then he pushed his big penis into her bottom and his Mummy squealed. The words uttered were completely new to Nelson and he had never heard his mummy say them before.

"Fuck me hard, Jack, Oh yes fuck me. Come on give it to me harder you bastard. Come on." Nelson couldn't watch anymore and ran back to his bed. He pulled the covers over his head and cried. The tears flowed down his cheeks and he sobbed uncontrollably. He was so afraid and confused he held his teddy bear really close, trying to keep whatever was happening in his mother's bedroom on the outside of his blankets.

Here underneath the covers with his teddy, Nelson eventually stopped crying and began to slowly feel warmer and safer and after minutes he drifted off to sleep.

Over the next year or so Nelson got a bit bolder and would creep into his parent's bedroom, when they started making their ritualistic noises. Still not understanding what was happening and that this brutal act was for their pleasure, Nelson would hide in the shadows and watch quietly, hardly daring to breathe. He was fascinated at what his parents could do to each other. He had witnessed all kinds of sado-masochistic sex and had watched intently. One night in particular scared Nelson as his Father nearly killed his mother, having got totally lost in what he was doing. Jack didn't realize that he really was choking her and that she was very close to losing consciousness. When Jack got hold of his senses and saw what he had done, he was so apologetic. He cradled Patsy in his arms and sobbed for forgiveness. Patsy laughed it off and told Jack not to worry. Nelson sneaked away leaving his parents saying sorry to each other.

It was every Friday night the sex sessions would start. Routinely Nelson would hide and watch and when he had seen enough he would go back to his bed and tell his teddy what they had done that night.

The year was 1960. Nelson was now 5 years old.

The one way conversation with his teddy bear took on a new meaning one eventful Friday night, the bear answered back.

Jack and Patsy had, like every other young couple in Glasgow, discussed changing their jobs and making more money. Sure the shipyard was fine and it was busy but it was bloody hard going and a very noisy place to work in. Jack wanted a change and to be away from Glasgow and Patsy agreed. There were opportunities aplenty all over the country and all it would take would be for Jack to land something different. Patsy would go along and there would be a job somewhere for her as well.

Jack's brother Ian had told them that there was something happening in the local Labour club on Saturday afternoon and that he had heard that it was some sort of a recruitment drive for some company. Jack and Patsy decided to go along with Ian and find out what and who was going to be recruiting. They had nothing to lose. Patsy's mum could look after Nelson for a wee while.

Saturday came by and as they walked through the club doors, they could sense it was going to be a busy place. New job opportunities advertised by word of mouth and you could fill the place twice over. Jack found them seats and ushered Ian and Patsy towards them. They could see a big table up on the stage and there were 5 empty seats behind it. The club soon filled and as the guest speakers took to the stage and sat down there was a hush descended over the crowd.

The local labour councillor stood up to a warm round of applause. He waited until it died down before he spoke.

"Ladies and Gentlemen, I would like to thank you for all coming here today. I am sure that you will all be very interested in what will be said in the next few minutes. It's good to see so many of my constituents here, it's amazing what a wee rumour started will do to fill our hall"

Some laughter followed the remark.

"We have today two gentlemen and two ladies from the Greater Glasgow Health board wanting to talk to you all about; he turned to the two men sitting to his left. Well I'll let them tell you. I'd first like to introduce you to Doctor Patrick Clyne. A ripple of applause started from somewhere in the back of the hall.

Patrick Clyne stood up; he was a tall man of slender build with a head of silvery grey hair. He wore a dark blue suit over a white shirt and had a spotted yellow bow tie.

Patrick looked over the audience. He placed his hands on the table. There was silence in the hall and you could have heard a pin drop. "I would like to thank Councillor Hall for allowing us to use the Labour club for this afternoon's talk. I on behalf of my colleagues would like to say a few words as to what this afternoon is all about. You have all come here on hearing that someone was having a recruitment drive and I can see on some of your faces quizzical looks of wonder as to what the Greater Glasgow Health board are doing in this club. We are at present short of staff for two of our hospitals in our area. Some of you may have heard of these hospitals, Woodilee hospital in Kirkintilloch and Lennox Castle hospital in Campsie. We are looking for staff, both male and female, to train as nurses."

Some of the audience laughed.

Patrick continued with a smile on his face, "Yes it is true we have male nurses as well as ordinary ones."

Someone raised a hand. Patrick stopped and acknowledged the question "Yes?"

"Aren't these hospitals for loonies?"

This brought more laughter.

"You might say that, but we use kinder terminology and never refer to our patients as loonies."

The laughter died away.

"Our patients are mentally and physically challenged and they have indeed suffered from a lack of care. Some of them if you can imagine, have actually been with us since the war. They were so badly traumatized that no-one could or was willing to help them."

He looked into the audience. "Think of it. Your own family disowning you. He paused, yes ladies and gentlemen, even their own families couldn't offer to help them and having no other place to go, as a last resort, so to speak, they were committed to our care."

Patrick stopped talking and let the audience reflect on that.

"We are offering you today a chance to build a new career. To radically change your lives. To take you away from all this … this town living." He waved his hand in the air, surveying the whole room. "To help you do something different, something meaningful with your lives. We will supply you with all the skills you will need. If any of you are interested in a career with us we offer you training and …"

Another several hands shot up in the air.

"Yes, madam, you there in the fourth row," Patrick said pointing to her.

"Am I too old?"

Patrick laughed out loud, "Too old for what?"

"Certainly not sex" someone shouted out and more laughter lifted the noise in the room. An embarrassed female wishing she never asked the question looked towards Patrick.

"Madam as they say you're never too old to … learn. Please, my colleagues will circulate and pass out application forms if you want one and they will answer any questions that any of you have. All we ask today is for you to be physically fit and want to apply for a job with us. Come and live in the country. Just fill in an application form and hand it back." Patrick smiled at the audience "you won't regret it," he said to end.

So in the January of 1961 after their applications were accepted, Jack, Patsy and a young Nelson moved lock stock and barrel, to their new home in the grounds of Lennox Castle hospital. The housing scheme for the hospital workers was called Netherton oval. It lay surrounded by forest and fields. This was the countryside that Jack always dreamed about. A place of fresh air not polluted by factories, the relative quiet of the countryside in comparison to the hustle and bustle of big city life. Their house was a two bedroom flat in a block of four. They had one of the upper flats with views over the two hospital football parks and onto the hills in the distance. They were also amazed to see, that the hospital even had its own farm, growing fruit and vegetables to help feed its inmates.

Glasgow city council had purchased the Lennox estate in 1931 for 25 thousand pounds. It had come with 8560 acres of wooded forests on which there were deer, pheasants and rabbits and hares galore. This was a hunting paradise for local poachers.

But the City council had other plans for the estate. They desperately needed an out of town Mental hospital to take Glasgow's deranged misfits.

The hospital was built in 1936 pre-war and the wards were red brick built. The small wards each accommodated some 25 to 30 patients of varying ages, mental states and disabilities.

For the ordinary working staff located in Netherton Oval the staff houses were two bed flats with a big bathroom and kitchen and front and back and gardens. For the supervisory staff they were located in semi-detached three bed town houses. For the single nurses they had the splendour of being accommodated in the magnificent Lennox castle, once the home of the Lords of Lennox.

Jack and Patsy loved the place and the rent was far cheaper than they had paid in Glasgow. The air felt cleaner and the place was surrounded with flora and fauna. This was a far cry from the toil and sweat of the shipyards of Glasgow.

The hospital estate looked onto the ancient range of hills that are the Campsie Fells.

The fells are a range of hills in central Scotland that stretch East to West, from Denny Muir to Dumgoyne in East Dunbartonshire. The highest point in the range is the Earl's seat at 1897 ft. The range overlooks the villages of Strathblane, Blanefield and Lennoxtown to the South, Killearn to the west and Fintry to the North.

The hospital grounds were located amid the Lennox forest and the wards were separated with the female patients being located "up the hill" and all the male patients being "down the hill". The main administration offices were all up the hill and each office had glorious views over the surrounding countryside. The staff either walked to the job or cycled depending on which ward you were assigned to and what the weather was like and how fit you were. The hospital worked three shifts. The early shift took over from the night shift at 6am and the back shift as it was called started at 2 p.m. and finished at 10 p.m.

The job wasn't all that hard as you supervised the everyday lives of the inmates.

There was usually three staff to a ward and the patients were fed three times a day. You had to supervise the mealtimes and ensure that everybody got the correct meal and that nobody choked on anything. There were ward orderlies, which were the saner or the trustworthier of the patients. You relied on the orderlies to distribute the food after it was delivered from the onsite kitchens or to clean up any mess.

Jack loved the job, as did Patsy. They both settled quickly into the routine of shift work and Nelson settled down at the wee primary school in Lennoxtown. Jack and Patsy had calmed their sex sessions down and the belts and ropes were forgotten about. Patsy still liked it rough, but the near to death experiences that Nelson witnessed were a thing of the past. Nelson however still had meaningful nightly conversations with his teddy bear.

Chapter 6

The small primary school where Nelson attended was easily reached by double decker bus and the fare was one and a half pence a return. There was always one of the mothers on hand to take all the school children down to the bus stop on the main road. She would escort all the children through the roads by the male wards and over the railway crossing to the bus stop and wait until they were all on the bus. A pied piper with a throng of kids all wrapped up against the chill wind blowing off the Campsies.

All of the children had big woolly scarves and mittens or gloves and back satchels carrying their schoolbooks.

Nelson always had his big woollen hat pulled down over his ears and always wore his matching gloves.

Nelson was in Primary five when his problems started. There was a new older kid who joined the school and immediately took great delight in bullying Nelson. The new kid was in Primary seven and was a misfit in that class. None of his classmates took to him at all. He didn't want to play football or marbles or hide and seek. He was a loner and a bully and took great delight at fighting his classmates. He had something to prove and he wasn't long establishing himself as the best fighter in the school.

He had to have someone to constantly tease and make fun of and he picked out the quiet Nelson. It was mild at first;

name calling that sometimes would reduce Nelson to tears in the playground. It didn't take long for the rest of the children in Nelson's class to join in. This ensured that the new kid didn't bully them. The teasing changed to stealing Nelsons woolly hat and throwing it out of the school gates. More forms of physical abuse followed, a fly slap when Nelson didn't expect it, or painfully kicking his legs or bottom. The only respite from this torture was at the weekends when Nelson could escape from the school at 4 o'clock on a Friday. He could go running off before ever being caught by the bully. He ran until he was out of breath some several hundred yards from the school at a spot he felt he was safe. He could then stroll up the road past Whitefield and on towards the Hospital grounds and his safe haven. He would never see his tormentor on a Saturday or a Sunday that was for sure.

Nelson climbed over the hospital perimeter wall and walked through the path cut in the woods. He passed the big Beech tree where the older boys had a rope swing. Nelson would sometimes see the boys on the swing and could hear the fun they were having. They would shout and holler as they launched themselves from a big branch and in a big arc, swing out from the tree with a scream of delight. It looked really exciting to Nelson but he was too scared to ask them for a try. He feared the rejection as they would most likely mock him. He would look on with envy and walk silently past. He secretly took note of all their actions, how to climb up the tree, where to hold onto the rope, how to launch yourself from the branch and what to scream. When he got a chance he would be prepared and not look like a complete novice.

The path Nelson walked along led down to a small waterfall and the swimming hole. It was a favourite place for the kids in the long hot summer days. All the bigger boys who could swim had been in the hole and lived, but they warned the smaller kids that they would die if they went in there. But Nelson wasn't a small boy; he was the same size as the older ones.

There was a rock ledge on the waterfall where the water levels changed. There was a difference of some twelve feet to the pool below that the kids used for swimming. The water would cascade over the ledge making the pool seem dark and frothy. When the weather was good and there was a dry spell, the river level dropped substantially and you could carefully cross over the waterfall by stepping onto the dry rocks using them as stepping stones.

Today was such a day and Nelson easily negotiated the waterfall and crossed the river to the other side. Here there was a small area where the torrents had cut into the riverbank, eroding it and leaving a half moon shape where smaller pebbles had washed up into. This was called the beach and some of the kids would strip off there and put their swimming costumes on.

Nelson eyed the pebbles but resisted the temptation to stop and throw some into the water. He continued walking through the trees until he reached the hospital cycle path which ran along the edge of the woods. He would soon be home.

It rained cats and dogs on the Friday night and that was enough to keep the kids all inside their homes. Nobody liked playing outside in the rain.

Saturday morning saw the sun shining and Nelson was up and eager to be out and about early. There was nothing Nelson liked better than walking through the woods after rain. There was something magical about the quiet and the smell of the forest. He kicked up dead leaves and picked up sticks and threw them for some imaginary dog. He walked on listening to the birds singing and before he knew it he found himself staring at the waterfall.

This time there were no dry stepping-stones and the water covered the complete ridge. The rains from the previous night had fallen on the Campsies and the little tributaries had swollen and filled. The river Glazert which itself was a tributary to the river Kelvin which fed the Clyde was high. The swimming hole was an ominous deep black and the water tumbling into it made a loud splashing roar.

Nelson was faced with a decision. He could retrace his steps and walk back along the path some four hundred yards to the road. He could cross the bridge and walk along the opposite bank. He could do that or he could attempt to cross the waterfall here and now.

He decided to cross regardless. He sat on the ground and removed his shoes and socks. He put his socks in his pockets and put his shoes back on. He carefully stepped onto the ridge and gasped as the water ran over his baseball shoes. It was cold. He edged forward and the force of the water pushed at his legs. He bravely moved forward. He could feel his feet slipping on the wet stones some several inches underneath. But still he was careful. He was nearly bent in half trying to maintain his balance with his arms outstretched like some deformed tightrope walker.

When the fear hit him he was more than half way across and the force of the water was so great that he was in real danger of being swept away. One slip and he would be over the edge and into the pool. The tears welled up in his eyes and he pushed his legs out through the river towards the far bank. It seemed as if more and more water was hitting him trying to stop him from going on. It was above his knees now and he was considering turning back when something told him to just reach out for the river's edge. He was shaking with fear but forced his legs to power on through the water. As he got near he threw himself towards the riverbank. His lower half ended up in the river and Nelson grabbed out at the clumps of grass and roots and began to pull himself out of danger. The current from the deeper water was still trying to drag him towards the waterfall. But Nelson finally managed to haul himself clear from the clutches of the river.

He stood on the riverbank trembling and soaking wet but the beginning of a smile formed on his face. He had conquered the torrent; he had managed to cross the river that no one else would dare to do when it was in spate. He had pulled himself out of the deep bits of the river because he was a big strong boy. Who was the big boy now? He stared back along the way he had come. He had hoped someone would have seen that crossing and had admired him for being brave. But it was too early. There was no one to witness Nelson's triumph.

The river never let up, the incessant bubbling flow of the dark water tumbling over the falls. But Nelson had conquered it. He stood there for a minute with no thought about his wet clothes and his sodden baseball boots. Then he remembered that he had put his socks in his pocket. They were soaking wet now as well.

There was a spring in his step as he skipped and squelched along the path to the big beech tree and towards challenge number two.

He got there and again there was no one there. No children playing on the swing and no one climbing the tree either. It was perfect. He could take his time.

Nelson could see the branch the rope was tied onto and his eyes traced the rope back to the split in the trunk and to where the rope was secured.

He stood at the base of the trunk and looked up. He would have to climb up about 15 feet to where the swing was. He looked at the tree trunk and saw the six-inch nails hammered into it all the way up the trunk. It suddenly dawned on Nelson that was how the boys got up to the swing. Nelson sat down and took off his baseball boots and took his socks out of his pocket. He squeezed as much water as he could from them. He held the boots upside down expecting more water to empty from them. He then proceeded to put his socks back on, not caring about the wet cold feel of them. He tied his boots, stood up and reached out and started to climb. It was easy and in no time he was up and had the elation from another achievement.

When he reached the split in the trunk he looked down at the rope and the stick the boys had threaded through the knot they had tied onto the rope as a seat. Nelson always thought that the boys had just sat on a big rope knot. Now he knew. Now it all made sense. Nelson lifted the swing from its resting place and put the stick between his legs and sat onto it. He had a good hold of the rope and knew enough to lean back and jump out from the tree. Just like the big boys. He inched forward carefully splaying both legs against both bits of the split trunk. He reached the point of no return. He had to conquer this as well.

He stood there hesitating and trembling, the queasy feeling in his stomach was almost painful. Nelson tightened his grip on the rope and closed his eyes then just fell forward launching him into space. The freefall sensation was thrilling and as he opened his eyes, the rope tightened and arced and Nelson was swinging. He didn't scream out in joy at the feeling. He didn't want to be found nor seen. He didn't want anyone to know that he had done what the other big boys could do. He gripped the rope so tight and marvelled at the feeling. He listened to the creak from the rope and the swishing of the branch leaves above. But no sooner had he jumped out on his first swing, he was slowing down and spinning to a halt. He maneuvered himself off the piece of stick and dropped to the ground. He was exhilarated. He looked at the palm of his hands to see how red they had become with gripping the rope so tightly.

But he had done it and he felt so proud.

He stood a bit taller and looked up at where he had jumped out from. He wasn't scared anymore. He had conquered challenge number two.

Nelson now had to replace the rope before anybody showed up, but he couldn't manage it on his own. He had seen the boys pass the rope to each other up the trunk to the next boy in line and then they would take their turn on the swing. But Nelson's dilemma was there was no one to pass it onto. So with a brief look about to ensure no one was coming along the path, Nelson skipped off along another path through the trees, leaving the rope swing hanging in mid-air for all to see.

Chapter 7

1964

The school week had gone surprisingly quickly according to his mum. She had been so busy working and she now had a few days off and it was the weekend coming up she told young Nelson. He had one more day at school and then it was Saturday. The 9 year old looked forward to his Saturday mornings. That was the day when he got up early and headed for the rope swing. Nelson was now adept at the swing and could have as many shots as he wanted now. He could return the rope to the start, now that some clever clog had put a bit of string on it so you could climb the tree with a good hold of the string and then just pull the swing up to where you were standing. Nelson was happy swinging away with no one in attendance.

Nelson was one of the kids who had school lunches every day and then played with the other kids around the Nissan huts, which formed part of the classrooms.

The kids who stayed to have lunch would play chases or some of them would play football. There were two playgrounds for the boys and one big one for the girls. Heaven help any of the wee boys found in the big playground. They would be chased back to their own playground. Of course some of the wee ones made that a game, too. The majority of kids all knew the playground rules so it wasn't worth the hassle.

Nelson was playing chases and was the catcher this Friday lunchtime. It was nearly bell time and a return to the classroom when running around from the back of the Nissan hut he literally bumped into Graham Smith – Nelson's worst nightmare and tormentor. Nelson sent him flying with a squeal. When Graham picked himself up from the dust he realised who the culprit was and boy was he mad. He picked himself up and made a go at catching a hold of Nelson. But Nelson wasn't stupid and had taken off in a panic. Graham gave chase as the school bell rang out announcing end of lunchtime. Nelson made the class line as Graham made a last grab for him and Nelson felt the wind from Graham's fist just miss his head. Graham lost his balance and stumbled and fell hands first onto the playground. Nelson turned to see Graham sprawling on the ground in pain. His hands and knees were grazed. The first signs of the graze and blood becoming visible. Nelson actually laughed out loud which infuriated Graham and made him even madder and he cursed at Nelson. Graham tried to stand up and have another go at Nelson, but was pushed into his own class line by his teacher. Graham was angry and even more so when Nelson stuck out his tongue mocking him. Nelson's class line started to walk into the school auditorium. Smith's line was next and Graham burst through the doors and there was Nelson in front of him but so was the headmaster. He was ushering the children in to their individual classrooms. Graham couldn't get to Nelson but had managed to catch the attention of the head when the doors swung close with a bang.

A cursory glance from the head was usually enough to have any child quaking in their shoes. Everyone had heard stories about the big black leather belt he kept over his shoulder, under his ominous black cape. The pupils who failed to follow school rules were punished by having their hands warmed by that belt.

Graham shuffled forwards trying desperately to close the gap on Nelson and was stunned when Nelson turned around and spat at him. No teacher witnessed the incident. The headmaster had his attention on something else.

Nelson knew he was for it now.

He could see the look of astonishment on Graham's face and heard the whispered threat, "After school you're dead."

When the 4 o'clock school bell rang out at the end of the day Nelson took off like a scalded cat. With his satchel on his back he ran through the school gates and did not stop running for the next fifteen minutes. He put distance between him and a hiding. He ran past the Town hall, he ran up the road to Whitefield. He only stopped at the pond to quickly catch his breath. Leaning on the wall he glanced back down the road to see if he was being pursued. There was nobody in sight, he was safe for the time being and anyway Smith lived on the opposite side of Lennoxtown.

Nelson was aware he would have to run the gauntlet on Monday morning.

As he reached the bend in the road where normally the kids jumped over the wall to take a shortcut into the hospital grounds, he paused for a moment. He strained to hear if there was any noise at the swing. He could hear nothing coming from the woods only blackbirds singing. He crossed the road, remembering to look left and then right and scaled up the wall and into his woods. Nelson ran along the trodden path to where the path split three ways. You could turn right and that path would take you to the bridge that crossed the river. Or you could go straight on and cross the waterfall along the stones. Turn left and it took you to the swing. He decided to turn right, he had his school shoes on and his mum would be very angry if he got them wet crossing waterfalls. So today he was being sensible. He walked along the bridge path and marvelled at the quiet. Nelson had forgotten all about Graham Smith. He picked up a pebble and tossed it into the river and watched the ripples spread. Oh what a day! He wanted to get home quickly and get changed out of his school clothes into his playing gear and be back out in the woods. He ran on and at the bridge climbed up the banking and went up and over the fence onto the road. He walked over the bridge stopping half way to look over and down at the water to see if he could see any trout. Walking on he came to the cycle path and turned left. The fields of potatoes on his right had started to flower. A sudden gust of wind got up blowing the tree branches above. Nelson spooked hit the path and began to run as if there was someone chasing him.

Run Nelson run the voice in his head warned.

He was breathless in seconds but still he ran on.

He wanted to be home.

He wanted to be in his bedroom.

He wanted to tell his teddy bear all about his day.

He wanted to hear what his bear would say about that

He was only a couple of hundred yards from Netherton Oval and he was running like an Olympic athlete.

Nelson's house had a garden to the side and to the rear. Both gardens were surrounded with a privet hedge. The side garden had a lawn and a small vegetable patch, which his father lovingly tended. His dad grew some vegetables and one of Nelson's chores, was to catch any caterpillars on his lettuce and get rid of them. Nelson ran up the path and opened his outer front door. He found his key which was hanging up on the nail behind the door. He thought that was funny because his mummy and daddy were both going to be home today. It was their day off from work.

As he climbed the stairs he could hear noises coming from inside his house. The hairs on the back of his neck started to rise; Nelson had heard these noises before. He stood at the top of the stairs in front of a glass-panelled door and he held his key in his right hand. He knew what his mummy and daddy were doing. All Nelson wanted to do was sneak into his bedroom, ditch his school clothes, change into his play clothes and be off without his parents hearing him. They were obviously so busy with what abuse they were giving each other they had lost all inkling of time.

Nelson turned the key quietly and pushed the door open gently. He didn't remove the key because he would need it to close the door again. He tip toed into his bedroom and quietly edged his door open and inched it closed. He tried not to listen to his mother shouting for more and to his dad shouting for his mummy to squeal like the bitch she was.

Nelson quickly stripped off his school clothes and as he stood there in his vest and pants he grabbed a pair of shorts and his tee shirt and jumper and dressed as quickly as he could. He reached down and grabbed his baseball boots; he would carry them down the stairs and put them on when he reached the bottom step. He looked at his bear sitting on his bed and nodded hello.

He opened his door as quietly as he could and the bedroom noises stopped. Nelson hesitated before moving, he dreaded being caught because then his parents would know he had heard them. They would be shame faced knowing that their little son had heard them acting like copulating animals.

His parents' bedroom door was cracked open and something told Nelson to peak in and just say he was off out playing. He was drawn to the opening as a moth is to a flame. He couldn't stop himself from looking and saw his mother with his dads' penis in her mouth sucking it. Nelson had seen this scenario a dozen times before. It aroused him. He found that he was smiling although he did not find it amusing.

Nelson watched transfixed for as long as he dared, eyes wide open and his mouth dry and totally unaware that his penis was thickening. He was only 10 years old and was already experiencing erections.

Nelson backed away from the door and tip toed through the main door closing it quietly behind him. He took his key as gently as he could from the lock and hurried down the stairs. At the foot of the stairs he sat on the last step and put his baseball shoes on and tied the laces. He hung his key behind the door and was off out into the sunshine and freedom. He ran down the path onto the pavement and turning right followed the pavement along to the swing park. There he crossed the main road and down onto the black ash path again and down into the serenity of the woods.

Nelson played for a while until hunger drove him back to the house. Back to where his parents had been … He shuddered at the thought. As he got to the outside bottom door he could smell the faint aroma of something cooking. That could only mean that they had stopped the sex games and had returned to the normal family routine of cooking the evening meal for half past five. Desperate for the toilet he took the stairs two at a time. He stood at the glass front and reached into his pocket for the door key only to realize that it was back down the stairs hanging on the nail behind the door. He needed to pee. Going down the stairs for the key was not an option, he rapped his knuckles on the glass panels. He was writhing when his father opened the door for him. Nelson ran past and went straight into the toilet.

His father closed the door with a laugh and as he passed the open toilet door he looked in to see Nelson peeing into the bowl his shorts down at his ankles.

"Wash your hands Nelson and flush the toilet," he said with a smile.

"Yes, Daddy".

"And come and get your dinner. You must be starving"

"Yes, Daddy"

Jack and Patsy had realized that Nelson had come home earlier and had got changed after school and had hurried out. They talked about the possibility that he may have heard them when he came in, but they reckoned that he couldn't have seen anything because the door had been shut. The only thing with that was that Patsy couldn't remember if she had closed it. But both of them agreed that they would have to be more aware of the time especially around 4 o'clock when it came to school finishing.

Nelson dried his hands and hurried into the kitchen where his mum and dad were already seated at the small kitchen table. There was a plate of steaming hot mince and potatoes in front of him and he ate with gusto. Jack and Patsy sat in silence, aware of the speed Nelson was gulping down his food.

Questions of how and when he got home from school were avoided and Nelson was pleased the subject did not come up. His mum sitting across the table with her clothes on saved his awkwardness.

Dinner passed without much more being said and Nelson asked if he could go back out and play. His father said it was OK to play for a while but not to go far and to watch out for rain.

Nelson needed no more than a yes and kissed his mother's cheek; he was off like a whirlwind. He left the table in such a blur, both parents could only laugh.

When Nelson went to bed that night he lay under the covers as usual.

His eyes were wide open because his teddy bear started telling him things he didn't really want to hear.

The next morning on the other side of Lennoxtown, Graham Smith woke up still angry and smarting. He had missed Nelson after school and that had made him even angrier. How he wanted to hurt Nelson, thump the living daylights out of him. He could taste and smell the beating he would soon administer to that brat. He had a reputation to keep up as a fighter. What kind of grief would he get from the rest of the boys in the gang, if they knew what had happened yesterday? He jumped out of his bed and headed off to pee.

Smith quickly washed and dried his face. He dressed quickly and came down stairs quietly into the kitchen to grab a bowl of rice krispies for his breakfast. As he sat at the table in his kitchen his eyes burned with hatred.

Graham had made his mind up he was going to track Nelson down. If it took all day he would find out where he played and he would catch him and kick the living daylights out of him. He washed his plate in the sink and put it on the drying rack before opening the back door and stepping out into a beautiful Saturday morning. He closed the door behind him and set off on a mission. It was seven thirty in the morning. Smith was usually still tucked up in bed sound asleep, but not this morning. His feet would ache that day with every stride as he walked the length of the town heading up to the hospital grounds. He would find Nelson if it killed him. No one treats Graham Smith that way and gets away with it.

No one took much notice of Smith as he passed them in the street. The few people who did see him were too caught up in their own wee world of going to buy a newspaper or get some milk. They would not recall the look of anger on his face or what he was wearing. He was just a kid with somewhere to go. The rest of the shops opened at 9 a.m. and that would be when the town would wake up.

Smith reached the town hall and could now take one or two roads, which would eventually lead him into the hospital grounds. He could walk on and pass by Whitefield pond and go that way to the grounds or he could take the back road past the nail works and go in that way. He decided to walk on to Whitefield past the pond so he could look at the swans and their nest. When he reached the pond he climbed the wall and sat on the other side watching the majestic birds gliding gracefully in the water. It was a momentary lapse from his anger and as he rose to continue his search he picked up a stone and threw it at the birds. It hit the water with a loud plop and sent the birds scattering .The hate returned to his face as he watched them settle down again. A single decker bus passed as he jumped back over the wall to continue his angry trek.

Nelson was also up bright and early that morning. He was down at the big tree playing on the swing. This was his Saturday morning routine when it was dry. Nothing scared him now. He had been doing this routine of swinging on the rope for ages. He felt that he owned the swing because he was really good at it. For all the times that he had used it not one holler of delight had he uttered. It was Nelson's way. He didn't want anybody to know he was having so much fun.

Smith walked past the Whitefield bus stop and was now a mere hundred yards from the boundary wall between the main road and the Hospital forest.

Nelson jumped from the swing as the momentum was slowing and eagerly grabbed for the string. Having got hold of it he started to climb the beech tree for another go.

Smith climbed the boundary wall and disappeared into the woods past the bramble bushes and strode along the path towards the waterfall. He was a boy with a mission. He kicked out at the plants along the path, as he got closer to the waterfall. Oh the things he was going to do with that piece of shit when he caught him. He felt his fists clenching in rage. He picked up a big stick that some kid must have dropped beside the path. Smith was going to throw the stick into the river and watch it flow over the waterfall. He walked quietly along the path when all of a sudden to his left he heard something creak. Smith turned to see someone on a rope swing. He hadn't known about this swing. The boy was good on it as he only had one hand on the rope and he was lying nearly prone as he swung in a pendulum motion. It looked like real fun and Graham temporarily forgot why he was there. He walked towards the boy and was about to ask if he could get a shot when the hairs on the back of his neck stood up. He recognized it was Nelson that was on the swing. Smith's grip on the stick tightened and the loathing returned.

Nelson was enjoying the feeling of exhilaration from the free fall from the tree heard what he thought was a growl and he grabbed the rope with two hands and sat straight up. While he held the rope with two hands, he attempted to focus trying to catch glimpse of the dog that was growling.

It was shock horror for Nelson when he did see what was causing the noise because there was Graham Smith standing at the edge of the clearing with a big stick in his hand. He was growling and getting closer to Nelson. There was nothing Nelson could do as the natural pendulum motion of the swing was dying. He tried desperately to keep his eyes on the threatening Smith, but as the rope spiralled so did Nelson.

Smith stepped forward and hit Nelson with the stick hard on his back. Nelson cried out in pain as he let go the rope and fell. He tried to get to his feet to take flight but to no avail.

"You little bastard so you think you can spit on me, do you?" Smith brought the stick down on Nelson again, harder and with more venom behind it. Nelson yelped in agony.

"You stupid bastard, no one spits on me."

Nelson cried each time Smith hit him begging him to stop.

"You fucker. You made me cut my knees yesterday."

"I'm sorry," Nelson sobbed scared out of his wits. He was in pain lying on the ground squealing as Smith hit him again and again. Nelson covered his head with his hands to offer some protection against the beating.

And then it stopped. Smith stopped hitting him.

In so much pain and sobbing uncontrollably Nelson lay there momentarily stunned waiting for the next attack to start. There was no more from Smith he had tossed the stick to the ground. Nelson attempted to scramble to his feet and flee. But Smith grabbed him by the scruff of his neck stopping him. With teary eyes Nelson looked up at his tormentor.

Smith was standing with his penis out right in front of Nelson's face.

Nelson was dumbfounded as to why Smith was standing there like that. Nelsons sobs were reducing to sniffs as the tears dried.

"Here I want you to kiss it," Smith threatened.

Nelson shook his head in an emphatic no, as his mind shot to his dad and his mum and their scenario. He had seen his mum do it time after time.

"I said kiss it," Smith growled as he pushed it towards Nelson's mouth. Again Nelson shook his head in defiance.

"Kiss it, you piece of shit."

Nelson started crying again. Smith struck him with his open hand in a slap.

"Kiss it, you arse." Smith held it out in front of Nelson's quivering face – daring Nelson to do it.

Smith's eyes were wide open with the look of a madman waiting for Nelson to react. Nelson motioned forward slowly.

Smith was laughing, "Come on do it and make it better for me."

Nelson moved closer.

Smith moved his penis towards Nelson's mouth.

He glanced quickly over his shoulder back along the path he had just come along looking for an adult that would stop this little game. There was no one. He had total power over the quivering Nelson.

Smith turned back and watched as Nelson closed his eyes as he moved his mouth closer.

A voice in Nelson's head told him what to do. Nelson slipped his mouth quickly over the penis taking Smith completely by surprise. Smith gasped as Nelson closed his lips round his penis. He hadn't reckoned that Nelson would fall for his little game. Smith had thought that it would have been complete humiliation for Nelson having to kiss Smith's penis. Nelson would have been in Smith's pocket from then on in. He would do anything to stop Graham telling anybody about the kiss.

Nelson had seen his mother do it to his father.

He had watched his father's reaction and imagined Smith's.

Smith thought he'd only get his dick kissed. He was about to get the biggest shock of his life. Nelson was in charge now. The voice in his head told him what to do.

Nelson clamped his teeth down on the shaft and jerked his head back so violently and so quickly he managed to tear Smith's penis. Blood spurted from Smith's loins and in a state of absolute shock he fell to his knees with his hands on his groin trying to stem the flow of blood. The pain was so intense he couldn't scream.

Nelson spat the piece of penis out. There was blood all over his cheeks and mouth. He stared hard at Smith who was now the one trembling and whimpering in shock. Blood oozed through his hands as he tried to hold onto his crotch and stop the pain.

Nelson eyed the now quivering tormentor and it was he who was the calm one now.

The shoe was on the other foot.

The voice inside his head told him what to do next.

Hit him with the stick he hit you with, Nelson

He had to stand up and go and pick up the wooden club.

With tears in his eyes Smith looked up at Nelson for help.

There was a glazed look in Nelson's eyes as he crashed the piece of wood down over Smith's head.

Smith fell forward face down into the dirt.

Hit him again, Nelson.

Nelson lost control and the blows rained down on Smith.

Again.

It was retribution, it was payback time.

The club held firm and did not break.

Again

The actual blow that killed young Graham Smith no one would ever know. There was one thing for certain, he was most certainly dead.

An out of breath Nelson gazed down at the bloody mess that only seconds before, had been his assailant. Smith was now unrecognizable.

Nelson let the wooden club fall to the ground.

The voice in his head told him it was over and to act quickly now and hide the body. It told him exactly what to do to cover his tracks.

'Make it as if Smith had never been there in the first place'

Smith could no longer be a threat to Nelson.

The teasing and bullying was finished.

Nelson stood there catching his breath and found that he was shaking. He stopped to think and listen to his mind.

"Take a hold of Smith by the ankles and with all your inner strength drag him from here up to that Rhododendron bush about 50 yards up the path. Go deeper into the forest, next to the chestnut tree." The voice told him.

Nelson found it difficult dragging Smith's corpse along the path. When he got to the bush he thought he would hide Smith under the canopy offered by the foliage. Nelson ran back along his path for the big stick and instinctively roughed up the darkened area where Smith's blood had stained the earth. He attempted to cover his tracks by sweeping the stick in a side-to-side motion along the path roughing up the drag marks and it seemed to work.

A dog barked excitedly in the distance which alarmed Nelson. His heart stopped momentarily and he listened. His heartbeat quickened and he held his breath.

He became a statue not daring to move.

He was about to be caught.

He wanted to run but the voice in his head told him to stay calm and don't panic.

There was no dog in the woods. The barking came from the roadside.

Nelson breathed a sigh of relief and resumed what he was doing.

When he got back to the bush, he pulled the limp body through under the foliage and dropped both feet to the ground. He was scared to look out from under the bush in case he had been seen.

Although Nelson was still breathing hard from the exertion, he once again stopped and listened for any noise.

He heard nothing.

He forced himself to come out from under the bush to look around. He saw nothing. His state of fear was subsiding.

The only sound Nelson could hear was his own heart pounding in his chest.

Bury him, Nelson. Dig a hole.

He pushed Smith onto his side and removed all the dead leaves from where Smith was soon going to be. He had to work quickly as time was at a premium and with one big breath he started frantically to tear at the dry soil with his bare hands.

Use the stick. The voice said. Break the soil and then use your hands to remove the sods of turf and dirt.

Do it quickly and we can go and play.

He reached for the piece of wood and began ramming the tip of the stick into the soil time and time again.

He scraped and scratched the earth like a frenzied animal. He paused every now and then to catch his breath. He knew he was making too much noise when he was digging. He imagined the hole getting a bit deeper and wider each time he stopped for a moment's rest.

Panic drove him on.

The fear of being caught was the tool he needed to dig more.

There was no one in the woods that morning.

The voice inside his head drove him on.

He rammed the stick deeper and deeper into the soil and used both hands tearing at even bigger pieces of earth. He heaped the handfuls of earth up to one side forming a formidable mound.

The shallow grave was forming. Smith's resting place was meeting with Nelson's approval.

The voice told him he needed to be a wee bit deeper to hide Smith.

So Nelson clawed and scraped some more like some mad animal. With sweat running down his forehead he had to finish this quickly.

He thought he heard a twig snap and the shock of that moment stopped him immediately. Nelson expected the branches to be pulled back revealing what he was doing. Fearing the worst his panic brought tears to his eyes.

He was going to be caught this time and he would be severely punished. He waited for the inevitable, it never happened.

It had been his imagination. The branches were not pulled back. There were no questions from startled onlookers. There was no forthcoming punishment.

No more twigs had been snapped.

Listening with baited breath for another few seconds and satisfied that it was nothing, he put one final monumental effort in to shaping Smith's grave.

The tear stains were wiped away from his cheeks and a grin started to spread over Nelsons face.

There were no more voices telling him to hurry up. He had done it. His hands and his arms ached but it had been worth it.

He had managed to claw a big enough hole in the ground that he could now hide Smith in.

Smith the bully!

He was never going to bully anyone ever again. Nelson wanted to laugh out loud.

Smith the bastard!

He was never going to see the sunshine ever again.

Smith the tormentor!

He would never torment Nelson again.

Smith the dead boy!

And now he was going to be, hidden from sight for ever, covered by dirt and tree branches and twigs.

Nelson very nearly let out a shout of joy.

Graham Smith had been the bane of Nelson's life, but would be no more. Nelson rolled Smith into the shallow grave and maneuvered the lifeless body into the hole. He had to bend Smith's legs and remove his shoes to fit him in.

He covered the lifeless body with the mounds of earth he had beside him.

He patted each handful of earth down over the body, as a child would do to a sandcastle. When Nelson had finished he grabbed handfuls of leaves and covered the grave. He went outside and hurriedly picked up anything he could find. He grabbed twigs and small branches and brought them back and placed them over Smith.

He had tried not to leave too much of a heap that would be found easily.

The voice in his head had guided him. It had instructed him to do this and to do that. He had done it and had followed the instructions to the letter.

He emerged from under the bush and went to search for bigger branches to further disguise Smith's final resting place. Finding a few and satisfied with all his work he knelt over the mound and urinated on it. Nelson exited for the last time and calmly walked back along the path looking for something he possibly had in his excitement missed. He searched for anything; a piece of Smith's clothing or something that would say Smith had been in the woods.

There was nothing along the track. Nelson used his feet in a sweeping motion to cover over the drag marks that Bastard Smith had made. He looked over the area and again kicked over the stained earth. He caught sight of the piece of penis on the ground and calmly picked it up and coolly walked off towards the waterfall. He stood on the edge of the river and looked up and down the riverbank for any living being. When he saw that there was not a soul in sight he threw the bit of penis into the pool of water not knowing if it would float or sink. He saw the small splash and turned away before he got his answer. Nelson walked further up the bank and when he was confident that he was the only living thing in the woods that morning he quite calmly jumped into the river. He knew by experience that it wasn't a deep bit. He had played here before so he knew just how deep it was. He dipped his head under the cold water and it caught his breath. He rubbed his hands together trying to remove the ingrained dirt from his hands and nails. He was succeeding. He noticed that he had reddening blisters forming on the palms of his hands.

He washed his face to get rid of the tear stains and dipped his head once again into the river. When he surfaced he stood there waist high in the river and felt genuinely happy.

The sun was shining; the birds were singing on this side of the river and it appeared as if there was not another living soul on this earth. Nelson felt happy that there was no one who knew what had just occurred. He stood there as if it was natural for someone to be standing in the middle of a cold running river and calmly wash away all traces of dirt.

He slapped both hands palms down into the water in excitement.

Nelson emerged from the water on the opposite bank from where he jumped in and walked up the small shingles at the shallow side of the river. He stood there for a moment dripping and shivering. He didn't mind one bit. He managed to remove his tee shirt and squeezed some of the water out of it. He had seen his Mother do that before she hung the house washing out on the line in the garden.

He twisted his tee shirt until he could twist it no more; he then shook it and laid it on the rocks to dry. He did the same with his shorts and underpants, socks and shoes. Nelson sat on the stones bollock naked. After squeezing as much water as he could out of his clothes he decided to put his pants back on.

He shivered as a light breeze whispered through the trees and along the riverbank. He listened to the rustle of the leaves and somewhere from deep in the woods a bird sang. The woods it seemed had forgiven him and were returning to normal. The momentary chill hit him but he didn't care.

He was sitting on the pebble stone beach with only his pants on with not a care in the world. He was with nature. He felt the sun's rays on his back and his body warmed. More birds joined the woodland chorus. As Nelson sat in silence he thought about the beating he had received from Smith. He was unsure if his back was bruised although it sure felt like it. He sat there smiling tossing pebbles into the water as if nothing had happened. If anyone had witnessed what he was doing just now they would have assumed he had fallen into the river and was trying to dry his clothes.

That thought hit Nelson and brought him back to reality. He really couldn't hang about in case someone came along the path and saw him sitting there with his clothes off. Questions would have been asked.

He put his wet clothes back on. He couldn't sit there a moment longer. He had to make a move and get out of there. He could only stretch his luck so far.

He dressed quickly.

He left the river and headed home back through the woods. He would have to stay out in the fresh air for ages while he dried. That he didn't mind.

Smith would never bully him again.

When Graham Smith didn't appear for his tea his Mother Margaret promised to spank his backside for being late and for wasting food. His father was doing his usual Saturday spending all afternoon at the Bookmakers and the pub across the road. He also missed his tea. When young Graham didn't show up by 9 o'clock at night his Mother stormed off down to the pub to inform her drunken husband of what was happening.

She pushed the pub door open and stepped into the smoky beer stenched atmosphere. A few of the regulars turned to look at the intruder, some woman who dared enter their bastion, their manly domain, their bar. She stood there, hands on hips searching for him and he spied her first. He had given a big drunken glance as the door opened and had the glazed stupid look on his face of wonderment. No recollection of time or of what she was doing there, just stupefaction. He could see her lips move but there was no forgiving smile. He was in the pub celebrating after his horses won. What was she doing there?

The pub fell silent as they all knew what was coming next.

He had a shit load of money in his pocket, so there would be no fight tonight. He staggered to his feet bumping the table where his fellow revellers sat. An empty glass shattered on the floor as he stood and looked at the woman standing there in front of him.

She started yakking at him about him missing his tea, but it was a Saturday, sometimes he did that. She had never bothered one bit about that before. The pub went back to conversations. They knew that they could all expect a bit of the same when they went home. There were more black eyes administered out on a Saturday night than any other night of the week, and it wasn't always the women that were on the receiving end.

But what the fuck was she droning on and on about, Graham not being home for his tea?

He was late for his tea sometimes on a Saturday because he was out playing? Young lads did that. A grin appeared on his face and that seemed to infuriate his wife and the rant got louder.

Was that all she was bothered about, but she was repeating herself about Graham and his tea. That bit just didn't make sense. He lurched ungainly forward and she caught his arm and dragged him through the pub door out into the fresh air.

"Graham's no back yet from going out this morning," she managed to say.

"No back yet?"

"That's what I told you and he never came back for his tea either."

"Ah about tea! I wiznae aw that hungry," he stammered.

"Am no bothered about you," she said as she squeezed his arm. "You dinnae matter."

"But, Darling," he slobbered. "My horse's won. I've been with ma pals."

"You and your pals. Graham hasn't come home!"

"Listen, woman," he rocked on his feet trying to focus clearly on her

"He'll be out with some of his pals. He'll be back sometime," he slurred. The focus was gone, "Just leave the laddie alone," he said with a burp.

"Have you any bloody idea what time it is?"

"It's—"

"It's nothing! Get yourself up that bloody road you drunken pig. Graham's not back yet!"

At that the conversation stopped as she pushed and pulled and manhandled him ungainly up the road back towards home.

The next morning was Sunday and if you were a Catholic in Lennoxtown then you had early morning mass at 6.15 a.m. Heaven help you if you had a hangover, as the priest would know. The priest would smell the aroma of stale beer or whisky on your breath as you said good morning to him, as he welcomed you through the doors.

Or the sudden whiff of peppermint. There was no hiding place. The priest knew his flock too well. He knew everything about them all. He knew the drinkers and the fornicators; he had heard all their confessions. There were a few more Hail Mary's to come for this lot.

The Protestants had a choice of two churches, the High Church or the Trinity Church. But their services didn't start until 10.30 and 11 a.m., so the Protestants could afford a long lie in. They had an extra few hours in their beds to sleep off the alcohol.

The Smiths were not churchgoers so they usually had a long lie in on a Sunday. But not this Sunday morning, while Mr Smith snored his head off Mrs Smith was up and about. She had not slept a wink worrying about Graham. The rain that morning came down in sheets and thunder rumbled and lightning crashed all around. It was going to be one of those days. Mrs Smith put the kettle on to have a cup of tea. Her hands were trembling and her insides were all churned up with worry. She felt tired and nauseas and had a blistering headache. She looked in hope through the rain hitting off the kitchen window wanting Graham to come skipping up the path. She would give him the row of his life, but would be glad he was home.

She looked at the torrential rain bouncing of the back path and massive puddles forming outside in her garden.

There was no skipping child to scold.

She walked through into her living room and turned the four bar electric fire on and sat down staring at her cup of tea. All thoughts were of Graham – who he was staying with, where he was sleeping? The tears welled in her eyes. Oh he was for it when he came home making her worry like this. Just wait until she got her hands on him.

By the time his Lordship came moaning down the stairs it was 9 a.m. and there was still no sign of Graham. The rain had relented somewhat and Mrs. Smith had his raincoat looked out. It was laid over the back of one of the chairs in the kitchen.

His hangover could wait; his bacon and eggs could also wait, she wanted him out there to find her Graham and bring him home to face her wrath.

Chapter 8

The lights are about to go out

I know

It's time for sleep

I know

So aren't you going to tell me?

Tell you what?

About all the tramps and what you did with them.

I told you before.

I know you did. But you always remember a wee bit more detail each time.

Do I?

You know you do. I think you do that to tease me.

No I don't.

Anyway come on get on with your therapy. I like it when you tell me things.

It's not therapy.

Yes it is so get on with the story.

Would you be quiet for one second, listen. Can you hear it?

What is it?

The faint noise, there it is listen.

There's nothing there

Oh yes there is, it sounds like a … it sounds like a faint hum that runs through the place, just before they turn the lights out.

No I can't hear it.

Just shut up and you will.

The wardens sat drinking tea discussing nothing in particular, clock watching and praying for their shift to end, so they could all go home. The night shift would be there in about fifteen minutes for the hand over and they had the easy shift. The majority of the mad, crazy bastards should be sleeping. The insomniacs would stare into the darkness, scheming, driving themselves even more insane. What else did they have to do, count sheep?

The other prisoners in A, B and C halls would all eventually settle down and sleep. After all what other activity could you do in a maximum security establishment after lights out?

The digital clock on the wall said it was 9.30 p.m. and at that the cell lighting would be switched off shortly. It was routine, on the dot every night 10 p.m. Some of the prisoners would always moan and shout abuse, when their cells plunged into darkness, but would calm down eventually realizing it was all in vain. No amount of shouting or cursing the wardens would change it, so what was the point. Just get on with it; after all, it was another day removed from your sentence.

Others like Nelson knew to the second when the lights would go out and that was the scary bit.

The wardens always sensed it. None of them ever mentioned it.

You never did your sit ups tonight.

I'll do them in a minute.

How many are you going to do tonight?

500. The same as last night.

And the night before.

And the night before that as well.

Well lie down and get on with it.

All right.

So you don't mind doing them in the dark.

I never minded doing them in the dark.

What the sit-ups or the tramps?

Either it didn't matter.

I asked you to remember so have you had total recall about that night?

Are we going to argue about that again?

You need to remember everything, otherwise you'll shut it out forever and you won't know why we're in this place.

I know why we're in this place.

That's what I'm trying to tell you, you don't, your memory has skipped a vital piece in the jigsaw puzzle and you can't complete the picture until you tell me all about that night. Then and only then will you find out who is correct, about the number you killed that night. There are things I know and you do not accept yet. When you do come to realise that I am right, then you will see just why we're in this place.

I need to exercise and think.

Are you going to tell me "about the night of the tramps?"

Later.

At that Nelson lay on the floor and started his sit-ups.

Chapter 9

Smith's father came back without Graham and having no idea where the lad was. His wife looked at the beaten look on his face and sobbed. He had been everywhere his son was known to play to no avail. He had questioned people in the street asking if they had seen Graham. They all shook their head in an emphatic no. He had rung door bells asking Grahams friends if they had seen him and they too had said no. Not since Friday night. He was lost for places to look. Not wanting to think the worst, his son was lying hurt somewhere and needed help.

He held his open arms out for his wife to come forward so he could comfort and console her. She reached into him and put her head on his shoulder and wept uncontrollably. He walked her back into the house and closed the back door behind them.

Nelson had heard the rain battering off his bedroom window and had got out of bed to look. He looked onto the kids swing park and there was water everywhere. He climbed back into bed, turned over and went back to sleep. His teddy bear firmly tucked up beside him.

His mother edged the bedroom door open and sneaked a peek at her sleeping son. He looked like a cherub all cosy tucked up in his blankets. She left the door slightly ajar and tiptoed back up the hallway so as not to waken her wee angel.

"David what are we going to do?"

"Margaret I don't really know"

"I think we should to go to the police?"

Mr Smith thought for a moment. His eyes transfixed staring into the fireplace.

"I suppose we have to tell them," he turned his head and saw the tears streaming down her cheeks.

"Oh, David," she sobbed, "What's happened to our wee boy?"

David took his wife in his arms and held her tight. He did not want to let her see that he too was weeping.

Constable Thomas O'Brien had been stationed in Lennoxtown for the last two years and had got to know some of the community quite well. Some of them whom he locked up in the cells on a Saturday night he knew really well. He often thought that it would be easier for him to just lift them before they got into the pub and got roaring drunk and abusive. It would make his life a hell of a lot easier. He would smile at that thought of just arresting them as soon as they got paid on a Friday and letting them back out on the Sunday morning. That would make Lennoxtown a real wee sleepy hollow.

He lived with his wife in a three bedroom semi-detached Police house at the back of the small Primary School. His next-door neighbour was also his work colleague.

It wasn't really a bad posting being stationed out in the countryside, considering Springburn and Posill and Glasgow were only about thirty minutes from here. Those areas were known to be a lot rougher and tougher and making a policeman's life a lot busier. Stationed there and you never got a minute to yourself.

So when he thought about it, yeah Lennoxtown would do him for a wee while.

He was stationed with another constable called Billy Wilson and the two of them were the only police in the immediate area. They covered the wee villages and hamlets surrounding Lennoxtown.

Both constables were enjoying a quiet morning and were having another mug of tea when the front door opened and Mr and Mrs Smith stepped on up to the desk counter. The pair of them looked like drowned rats having obviously been caught in the latest downpour.

O'Brien put his mug of tea on the table and stood up brushing the biscuit crumbs from his blue shirt.

"Yes Folks what can I do for you?" he asked politely noticing that the wife looked as if she had been crying. The tell-tale signs of that were the baggy and blotchy eyes.

"It's my son Graham," David managed to say.

"And you are?"

"David and Margaret Smith." There was no instant spark of recognition from O'Brien

"… From Bencloich crescent."

"OK so what's your son been up to?" O'Brien asked.

"He's not come home."

O'Brien could hear the tremble in his voice.

Wilson put his tea down and stood up. This could be interesting.

"So you're saying your son hasn't come home?"

"Yes."

"How long has he been out?" O'Brien tried desperately not to say the word missing.

"Since Saturday morning." Smith's wife nodded agreement.

"It's not like him," David continued "He's always come home for his dinner and well we didn't see him at all yesterday. He was gone before we got up."

"OK slow down. I'm sure there will be nothing to worry about."

They were not reassured and he saw that. "I'll have to take down some details." He looked down at the counter shelf for a piece of note paper. He took out his pen and scribbled on the corner of the paper.

"What's your son's full name?"

"Graham Donald Smith."

"Age?"

"Twelve"

"Height?"

They looked at each other. "Eh about this height," David held his hand level at his son's guessed height. O'Brien looked at Wilson and nodded, "About 5 foot 6 inches." He wrote that down and under lined it several times.

"Does he usually get up early and be out and about?"

"Only on a Saturday. He likes a long lie in on a Sunday. Must be all that playing about on Saturday that tires him out."

O'Brien sneaked another glance at Wilson who was taking his notebook out of his pocket.

"Yesterday was a glorious day so he must have got up early and went out to play somewhere," David said with a small shrug of his shoulders.

"Where does he usually play?" O'Brien asked.

"Anywhere, depends, I suppose it'll depend on who he's playing with," David answered.

"What colour is his hair?" Wilson asked.

"It's Black and short. It's not curly," Mrs. Smith butted in.

"What school does he go to?"

"What's that got to do with it?"

"I mean is it the primary up the road or St Machens?"

"The wee school up the road." David answered, puzzling at the question.

"Does he like football?" O'Brien asked.

"What?"

"I said does he like football?"

"Of course he does, he's like every other laddie in Lennoxtown. He's football daft. But what's that got to do with it?"

"Does he like Rangers or Celtic?"

The Smiths were more than confused at O'Brien's line of questions.

"He likes Rangers," Mrs. Smith said.

"So does he have a favourite blue jumper or football jersey that he likes to wear?" O'Brien watched for any reaction from the couple.

"So are you asking what was he wearing yesterday?"

"Yes I suppose I am."

"So why didn't you just ask us then?" David rapped sharply at O'Brien.

"Yeah I should have I'm sorry." O'Brien felt 6 inches high.

"I'll need to check his drawer," Mrs. Smith said,

"Have you tried his best pal's house? He could have been staying over." Wilson asked.

"We have and he would have phoned us. He knows how to phone us," Margaret said as she started to break down again.

O'Brien wanted to keep the couple focused, "What do you think your son would be wearing yesterday remembering it was sunny? Does he run about in football shorts or jeans?"

The two looked at each other and shrugged their shoulders. "I don't know," they said in unison. "Shorts probably."

"Have you tried all his friends, I mean have you been to where his pals live?" O'Brien said.

"Yes I was there this morning. All the ones I know he plays with regularly. I asked them all if they had played with Graham yesterday and they said that they hadn't seen him," David answered and glanced towards Margaret. She was standing there visibly shaking.

Wilson continued to write.

O'Brien continued, "Mr and Mrs Smith I have to ask you this ..."

They both held their breath

"Has Graham ever done anything like this before?"

"No! Definitely not," Mrs Smith said just milliseconds before her husband did.

"And is there any reason that you can think about why he might ... run away?"

"Run away? What do you mean run away?" The Smiths stood in front of the two policemen hurt at someone suggesting that their wee boy would run away.

"How could you even ask a question like that?"

"Because I have to."

"No he hasn't run away. He's not like that. He's a good boy."

"Has Graham fallen out with any of you?" O'Brien said quickly. "I mean have you scolded him recently?"

"No!" came the loud reply.

O'Brien said, "I tell you what, I'll come with you to your house and you can look at his drawers and cupboards and see if you can tell me what he was wearing and we'll start from there."

"Listen, Constable, my son may be lying somewhere hurt and—"

"Mr Smith. Wherever Graham is we will find him. Don't you worry." He was trying to offer some comfort and assurance to them.

"But in order for us to have a full picture of Graham we have to have a full description of what he was wearing yesterday. Listen, I wouldn't worry, wee boys find a million things to do around here. He's maybe—" O'Brien stopped dead in his tracks. Not wanting to say any more.

The two of them were nodding their heads in agreement.

"Bill you hold the fort here and I'll be back shortly. O'Brien called back to his buddy after ushering the Smiths out of the door. "Call it in to Kirkintilloch let the chief know we have a missing kid here and tell the Milton boys and get the local mountain rescue team alerted. I've got a funny feeling about this one."

The look of dread on Bill Wilson's face said it all.

"And another thing, Bill. Phone Lennox Castle Hospital and speak to Donald McPherson the guy in charge there. Tell him what we've got here."

"And what do you think we've got here? Something more than a wee boy staying out late because he's fell out with his mum and dad?"

"Bill, I don't know what to think, but you heard them say they didn't reprimand him and I believe them, but there's a thousand lunatics in that place, so speak to Donald, tell him there may be a wee boy lying hurt somewhere in the grounds."

O'Brien pulled on his coat and put his policeman's hat on and stepped outside into another torrential downpour.

Wilson got to work and carried out the orders that were given to him by Tom. First of all he alerted the main police station in Kirkintilloch some ten miles away and told them that they may have a missing boy in Lennoxtown. He furnished them with the details that he knew so far and said that Tom was with the parents now getting a good description of the boy.

When any child goes missing it always sets a panic going. When somebody goes missing near a mental hospital, well all sorts of alarm bells go off.

Wilson was told to keep Kirkintilloch informed and if the boy did not show up by lunchtime, then they would send the search and rescue team. The two constables were to interview friends and relatives of the boy and ascertain his whereabouts. The phone was replaced on the cradle and Billy wrote all his instructions down in his notebook.

Bill then phoned the small Station at Milton of Campsie and told them the same.

The telephone receptionist at Lennox Castle hospital put Wilson's call through to Donald Macpherson's office at 10.45 a.m. Donald took the call and as always was extremely polite.

"Donald McPherson here."

"Mr McPherson, its Bill Wilson here from Lennoxtown Police station."

"Ah, yes, Constable Wilson, good morning to you."

"Yes good morning Mr McPherson." Bill took a deep breath as an eager McPherson interrupted him.

"Please, constable, call me Donald."

"Donald." Wilson responded

"Yes, Bill?"

"Sir, I was asked to inform you that we may have a missing child from Lennoxtown and—"

"A missing child eh? And I'm thinking that you think he may be somewhere on the hospital grounds? Donald enquired enthusiastically, sensing a piece of excitement on a rather mundane wet Sunday morning.

Bill could hear the upbeat tone from McPherson. "Mr McPherson, in these circumstances we have to inform you that because of the locality of the hospital and of what it is, we have to inform you of …" He hesitated for a split second, searching for the correct words.

He gave up, "Well we don't know for certain if he's missing yet, but there is a possibility that he might be lying hurt somewhere on your grounds."

"Is it one of our kids from Netherton Oval?" Donald asked.

"No sir, it's a kid from Lennoxtown."

"Thank God for that," Wilson heard Donald McPherson say under his breath.

"Anyway, Donald, I'll be in touch and I'll phone you in another few hours as to what our course of action will be." The Police training kicked in and Wilson felt as if he was back in charge of the conversation again "So we may have to search the grounds."

"Certainly and, Bill, keep in touch," and at that the line went dead.

Wilson was left staring into the receiver. "Yes well good day to you as well Mr McPherson," and at that he cradled the receiver.

Donald McPherson replaced his phone and stood up from behind his desk He went to the window and looked out at the rain away in the distance.

From where his office was he could look on the red tiled rooftops of the hospital wards below. As he lifted his gaze he would normally see the lush green Campsie Fells. But not today to his left they were shrouded in mist as the rain swept along the valley. How strange the weather was. Here it was dry but a mile or so towards the hills and it was pissing down. He stood there pondering his course of action. If he had a missing kid from the nearby town on the grounds somewhere where would he be? Where could he be? Christ he could be anywhere. The hospital grounds were in thousands of acres. Where would a kid find so interesting that he would play there and get lost. He thought about of all the places of interest where he would go if he were a kid. There was the fresh water reservoir of course with all the frogs and all the frogspawn. There was the filtration unit for cleaning the water. But surely this was not the season for frogs as this was close to the summer holidays and his holidays were just around the corner.

It was springtime when the frogs spawned, wasn't it? He thought.

The filtration unit building was locked up unless there was maintenance being done on it.

He thought about all the Horse chestnut trees at the hospital farm and up at the back forest. But again McPherson dismissed that as a place to go as they, too, were out of season. It was late September early October when all the kids went searching for chestnuts. McPherson looked up at the dark clouds as if for divine inspiration and turned back towards his desk and sat down behind it. He could hear his secretary tap out letters on her typewriter from the office room next door.

"Bella," he hollered.

No response.

"Bella! Come in here for a minute."

Isobel Davidson stopped her typing at the second call from her master's voice, shrugged her shoulders and wondered what now. She stood up straightened her skirt and walked towards Big Donald's office door and rapped it with her knuckles.

"Come in Bella."

Bella entered, five foot two and twelve stones in weight made her look like a wee mini powerhouse. Her auburn hair was held tight to her head by clasps and hairgrips and she was not the prettiest of secretaries, but that was what Donald required. The last thing he wanted was to be distracted by a young beautiful secretary. His missus would have killed him if he had hired a goddess. No his hire list had a secretary that had to be, fat, grumpy and probably menopausal. Further down the list was she had to be good at her job, all of which was Bella.

She stood there dressed in her grey skirt and brown tights with black flat shoes. She wore a white blouse with a blue woollen cardigan over it. She stood in the doorway and waited for Donald to gather his thoughts. She had gone through this scene dozens of times before.

"Bella, who have we got doing the forestry detail just now?"

Bella stared at Donald inquisitively, "I think the boys have been taken from the wards."

"I know that! I mean what staff have we got doing the detail just now?"

"Oh staff" She exclaimed as if the penny had just dropped.

"Staff, let me see, I'm not sure but I think it was Jack Harrop this week or was that last week, but I can find out for definite for you. Just give me a couple of minutes"

"Good! Do that for me please and, Bella, can you do that quickly?"

"Well I've got those letters to the Greater Glasgow Health board you asked me to type."

"Bella!"

"Yes Mr McPherson."

"The letters after you find out the staff rota please," McPherson stated raising his voice just a little.

"Yes, Mr McPherson," and at that Bella turned on her heels and exited, leaving the door open behind her.

Donald McPherson had the idea about asking the lads from the forestry detail to start a preliminary search for the missing kid around the reservoir and around the chestnut trees just in case. You never know we might get lucky. Maybe the kid was daft enough to look for frogs or chestnuts out of season. Donald picked up his pen and started writing things to do.

He scribbled on a blank piece of paper 'Point number 1 Phone ward N.'

He paused for point number 2, before writing, "See forestry staff."

Point 3 was a doodle and finishing that, he laid the pen down on the desk.

Bella shouted back to Donald that it was Jack Harrop who was the lead staff in charge of the forestry detail.

Donald's first course of action would have to be, phone the hospital ward where the dangerous patients were kept under lock and key and that was ward N. He would ask the staff on shift if any of the patients had been reported as missing or re-caught in the last 48hours. Mind you if any of the patients had escaped he would have seen some sort of report on his desk. He rummaged through his in-tray and saw no reports of missing patients. He dismissed the idea of any patients being the cause for any missing kid.

However regardless of what he thought, he lifted the telephone and called the hospital operator.

Tom O'Brien walked up the street behind the Smiths. He was leaning into the blustery wind and rain and thought what a hell of a day it was. He arrived at the back door of the house and Mr. Smith opened the door and the two men followed Mrs Smith inside. They walked through the small back hall and into the kitchen area. O'Brien noticed the cooker with pans still on the rings and a small refrigerator next to it. The sink area was remarkably clean with only one cup on the draining board. There was a small breakfast table with three seats to the wall side away from the window, which looked onto the back garden. It was a compact kitchen all right.

Mrs Smith shouted for Graham and was met by silence. The two men looked at each other and then towards Mrs Smith.

O'Brien was the first to speak. "Right then, have you a recent photograph of Graham, Mrs Smith?"

"Please, I'm Margaret and this is David," she said pointing at her husband who was now taking his coat off. O'Brien followed suit. He left his coat hanging on the back of the kitchen chair making a nice wee puddle of water on the linoleum floor. Mrs. Smith took off her coat and squeezed past the two men and made her way to the cupboard in the back hall. She opened the cupboard door and hung her coat up on a nail in the inside of the door letting the coat drip-dry.

"David will you take the constable into the living room and I'll go upstairs and see if I can find Graham's school photo." She just managed to say without breaking down.

David duly obliged while Margaret went upstairs to the main bedroom. She went through one of her drawers looking for photographs she had of Graham.

"Please sit down," David said pointing towards one of the armchairs. O'Brien duly obliged. Both men sat in an awkward silence listening to Margaret rummaging about upstairs. O'Brien was extremely conscious of his big black shiny police shoes and tried to focus on something to say.

"Terrible day eh?" he said.

"Aye it's no many days your kid goes missing," David replied

"No I was meaning ..."

"I know."

"... about the weather." Tom bowed his head trying not to look into David's eyes. "It's been terrible. One day sunshine and the next it's pouring down."

"Aye well that's Scotland for you," David said rather uneasily.

"I'll just go and see what's keeping her," and at that he rose up from his chair only to hear Margaret coming down the stairs. So he sat back down.

Margaret entered the living room proudly holding several photographs of Graham in her right hand. She handed them over to O'Brien who looked over each one. He decided on one of them and asked if he could keep it for a while until Graham came home.

"Now Margaret any idea on what Graham was wearing yesterday?"

"Oh I forgot to look when I was up there," she said turning to face her husband. David had already thought about that, what his son would have been wearing and told O'Brien that he thought that Graham would have been in tee shirt and shorts as it had been warm yesterday and he had maybe taken his favourite blue pullover. Margaret turned and walked down the hall and took the stairs in her search for her clues.

The rain relented and the clearing skies could be seen further out to the west. The heavy rain clouds were rushed along the Clyde valley by the prevailing westerly wind and the much awaited blue skies could be seen away in the distance. Loch Lomond and the Trossachs further to the west would now be bathed in beautiful sunshine. So there was a chance that if there was a search for Graham Smith it would start in fine weather.

Donald McPherson sat waiting for Bella to come back through the door with the answers he wanted. She rapped the door as before and before he could call out "Enter" she opened the door and walked in. Donald watched her intently. Bella confirmed it was indeed Jack Harrop and David Thompson who were the staff in charge of the detail. Donald asked where the boys were working and Bella put a sheet of paper down in front of him. It was the week's duties for the forestry boys Sunday through to Saturday. Today they were still clearing on the south side of the Lennox forest. McPherson would have to drive to where they were and have a wee chat with Jack and Davie.

Donald grabbed his Wellington boots and put them on the back seat of his Hillman minx. He told Bella where he was going and to take down any messages. He waved her goodbye and jumped into the car and started the engine. It roared into life and Donald drove down the back road of the hospital to the south side of the forest. He would have to change footwear after he parked the car and walk into the woods to look for Jack and Dave but he knew that anyway. He passed the South Lodge house and slowed to pull in and halt. He parked the car and set about changing his footwear. Having done this he opened the door and stepped out putting his jacket on. He locked the car door and checked the remaining doors to ensure they were also locked. You couldn't be too careful as there were a few characters about who would steal anything and everything. Donald had joked with his wife about him constantly locking up everything by telling her about all the dodgy people and she would answer by telling him to remember that it was a Lunatic asylum he was working in.

Donald crossed the road jumped over the drainage ditch and took the path leading into the forest. It was half past twelve.

Although the path was well used, he struggled to negotiate the steepness between the trees and the wet slippery sections. He stopped for a breather after climbing up a nearly vertical part. He stood under the overhanging branches of a large beech tree catching his breath and grimacing at how out of shape and unfit he was. He would have to exercise more. He decided that he would walk to the pub in future and take the bus home.

Donald looked up at the path winding its way even higher into the forest, hugging the side of the small gorge the stream had carved out of the hillside. As it trickled down among the rocks it made a calming burbling sound. Donald saw grey squirrels jumping about the forest floor on the other side of the gorge. This was all about nature and the peace and quiet of the country. The only noise that didn't fit into this idyllic picture was his laboured breathing. After some twenty odd minutes of climbing, the forest path levelled off at a plateau and now he could hear the sound of a chain saw being used in the distance.

As he got closer the staff noticed him and Jack Harrop started to walk towards him and waved.

The two men shook hands as Jack asked what Donald was doing up here. Donald looked straight into Jack's eyes.

"Jack I've had the police on the phone and there's a wee boy from Campsie missing. It's a possibility he might be on our grounds somewhere."

"He's not about here; we would have seen him. Christ it's not a toddler is it?"

"No he's not, or we would have half of Campsie in our grounds just now looking for him. No he's about 10 or eleven they said, but you know what boys are like, around here, this place is a magnet.

"So how can we help? You want us to start looking for him?"

"Aye I do."

"Alright we'll stop what we're doing here and head off. Anywhere special in mind Donald? I mean the grounds are big enough that you could lose an army in here never mind a youngster." He paused "Any idea who his father is?"

"Nope. The copper didn't tell me. All he said that he would phone me later with an update on what was happening. Christ, Jack, he may already be found, I don't know but if you and the boys check a few places in the next couple of hours for me, I'd be grateful."

"Aye it'll save time. Don't worry, Donald. The boys and I will go anywhere you want us to go, you know that."

"I know that, Jack, and if they find him I'll come and tell you. Okay?"

"Yeah whatever. So where did you want us to start?"

Donald looked over Jack's shoulder. The rest of the squad had stopped working and had sat down on some of the cut logs. Davie had also stopped and was walking towards them.

"I thought that you could look about the reservoir. You know around about that area and walk down the woods to the back of the castle and down towards the old railway line. You know what boys are like. He's probably out collecting birds' eggs or something daft like that."

"Well it's not really the season for bird's eggs, but you're right Donald, he could be anywhere." Jack said turning away.

"And, Jack, check the wee burn that runs along the side of the railway just in case."

Jack looked Donald straight in the eye, "Just in case he's floating?"

Donald nodded.

"Right then I'll tell the boys what the story is and we'll get started. And, Donald, keep your fingers crossed that we find him eh?"

"And, Jack, if you do find him give him a stern fucking talking to, for getting us all this worried."

"I think his Mum and dad will be doing that for sure, but if we find him…"

With a final nod Donald turned away and started back for his car.

O'Brien listened to Margaret rummage about upstairs while the silence continued with David. He imagined her frantically going through her son's cupboards and drawers for what clothes he might be wearing. He heard her as she came down the stairs and as she came into the living room O'Brien made to stand up from his armchair.

"I cannot find his blue jumper or his black football shorts he uses for gym," she hurriedly announced to the pair of them.

"Aye I thought as much," David added. "I told you. Didn't I? About his blue jumper," he said towards O'Brien.

"Aye you did," Tom answered reaching into his breast pocket for his notebook. "Now then ..." He paused, "*Blue jumper*. Is that a vee neck or polo neck or a crew neck?"

Margaret answered, "It's a vee neck because he wears a tee shirt underneath it."

"Now what shade of Blue is it?" O'Brien asked writing *vee neck* into his notebook.

"Dark blue," Margaret blurted out milliseconds before David had the chance to answer.

"Dark *blue,*" Tom pencilled down.

"And Black shorts you said, football ones" O'Brien continued taking notes.

"That's right," Margaret said. David resigned himself to be quiet while Margaret told the officer all she could.

"Now then what kind of shoes was Graham wearing?"

"Oh that's easy," she quipped. "He never has his baseball boots off his feet at the weekend." She smiled as she said that. David saw a momentary lift of his wife's spirits.

"Right then," O'Brien said as he got to his feet. "And this is the most up to date picture you have of your son?" He held it out for them both to see.

Margaret had been holding the other pictures of Graham in her hand and she looked lovingly at the one Tom O'Brien was holding. The tears welled up and rolled down her cheeks.

O'Brien could see how upset she was getting and put the photograph into his notebook. He put that into his breast pocket.

"I'll show you out then," David said.

O'Brien followed David back into the kitchen, retrieved his coat from the back of the chair and put it on. He looked back towards Margaret "Mrs. Smith don't worry. We'll find Graham wherever he is. So please try not to worry yourself." He did not dare look at David.

"Oh and before I forget, can I get your phone number in case of …?" he stopped dead in his tracks before he completed the sentence.

"322666," Margaret piped in.

As O'Brien left, the door closed behind him. He looked skywards as he put his cap back on; he had a bad feeling about this.

Chapter 10

Tom O'Brien sat behind his desk and sipped his mug of tea that Billy had just made. He had written down a plan of search areas just in case the police teams would be dragged into a missing child hunt. There was a feeling gnawing away at his gut.

Lennoxtown had been quiet all day and it was now nearing 3o'clock. The rain had stopped earlier and the valley was now bathed in sunshine. There were no further reports from the family as to where Graham was and the search was about to take on a completely new slant.

Billy had eyed the station clock as he sipped away at his tea. They were due off shift at six when the town went under the control of the nearby Kirkintilloch police. But today they were about to do overtime and they could do without it.

Tom told Billy to phone the Milton of Campsie police and Kirkintilloch for updates. The boy was now missing for 30 hours. The police search teams were told to come to the station house in Lennoxtown and there someone would be appointed team leader. From there a search plan would be put in place and adhered to. There would be no stone unturned, no hiding place missed. Everyone in Lennoxtown would be questioned. Tom sat wondering if there were enough people to cover the initial search area.

Tom had a sheet of paper in front of him. He had itemized the tasks that would probably lie ahead.

Number one: The mountain rescue boys and their dogs would be asked to search the infamous Campsie Fells starting just above Lennoxtown and all the way down to Campsie Glen.

Number two: The Milton police would be asked to walk along both banks of the Glazert River from their station house 2 miles away to the Nail factory in Lennoxtown. They would also be asked to search the disused railway line.

There were places along the river where wire mesh fences had been stretched across and through the river to act as a debris catch point. These would be scrutinized with a fine tooth comb.

Number three: The police from Kirkintilloch would be asked to form small teams and check the coal Bings at the back of the town and the rubbish tip. A thankless task but it had to be done.

Number four: Billy would stay in the local cop shop coordinating while he, Tom drummed up volunteers to start searching the local woods. He would have to move quickly before the two local hotels opened up their bars at half past six and the people of Lennoxtown started drinking.

Tom took a large mouthful of tea and talked to Billy about the volunteers. Billy suggested going to see the priest along the road before he did the next mass at 6 p.m. The priest could ask for volunteers to go and look for a wee boy and that would involve the Catholics in their droves. They wouldn't dare not come and volunteer to search, risking the priest's wrath and their eternal damnation. Tom agreed and asked Billy to phone Donald McPherson again and ask him to drum up some volunteers as well.

Bella had transferred all calls through to Donald's office before she took off for home. It was a beautiful afternoon now as she set off for the walk home to Netherton Oval.

Donald on the other hand was seated behind his desk doodling on a piece of paper, his mind elsewhere and not on the administration of one of the largest mental hospitals in Scotland. He couldn't concentrate as thoughts of the lads finding the boy floating in the burn or caught in one of the poachers snares which were found all over the estate. Poaching rabbits was another local pastime that the natives took upon. It rankled Donald that some of the staff were poachers as well. He knew fine well who it was, but what the hell; it was only rabbits and hares. He found himself attempting to draw a rabbit on the paper in front of him when the telephone rang and brought him back to stark reality. He dropped his pen on the blotter pad and picked up the receiver.

"Donald McPherson here"

"Mr McPherson, its Billy Wilson from Lennoxtown police here .We spoke earlier. I—"

"That we did. Have you found the wee boy yet?"

Wilson was cut off in mid-sentence again "Eh no. Not as yet we—"

"I've got some of my forestry boys searching part of the grounds."

"That's a ..."

"I thought it best to get a bit of a start because of the size of the estate"

"Yes well, as I was about to say ..." an exasperated Wilson cut in. "I was asked to ask you if you could co-ordinate some of your staff and search some of the grounds. But it seems as if—"

"That's what we're doing; I told you we wanted to get a head start."

Bill nodded his head as he listened to Donald go on and on.

Their conversation lasted a few minutes and Donald had commandeered most of it but he bit his lip as he concentrated on what Wilson was telling him. There was a knot building in his gut, this was not good. Bicarbonate of soda would not make this pain go away. He always got pains in his gut when he was worried. Why was that? He wondered thinking he should maybe drink Guinness instead of heavy and that it might be better for his constitution.

"Of course, constable, I'll get some more of my staff," he paused for a moment, while he gathered his thoughts, "and we'll look for as long as we can or as long as we have daylight, or if we have torches we can look in the woods a bit longer."

"Mr McPherson If I may make a suggestion ..." Silence greeted Wilson, "I'd start looking where you know children play."

"Yes, of course, constable, I'll keep you informed," and at that Donald laid the phone back down on the cradle leaving Wilson looking at his receiver having been cut off again.

Donald checked his watch it was nearly the patient's teatime. The main supply kitchens would have the vans picking up the canisters of soup and the main meals and delivering to all the wards. The afternoon shift was half way through their 2 - 10 p.m. haul. The early shift didn't start until 6 a.m. so he could drum up some of them to start a search. The night shift was on in a few hours so you could forget them. He picked the duty roster book up from his desk top and set about going through ward by ward the shifts for the coming few days. He went down the names of the early shift and noted all their telephone numbers. He picked only the ones who were local to Campsie and could get here reasonably quickly. He wrote down names of staff that were on a few days holiday. He would have to ask Bella to come in and give her the list and let her phone all these people.

He stood up from his desk and walked slowly to the window. He would have Jack and Dave in here in a minute with news of how they got on with their part of the search.

He could feel the knot in his gut tightening as he stood there with his hands spread-eagled on the pane of glass, staring out at the estate stretching out in front of him.

He was lost in his thoughts wondering about the wee boy and he asked himself the question, "Where, oh where in God's name are you?" He did not receive a divine answer.

The police in Milton in Campsie had all been called into their station house and told the news. Their sergeant told them the part they were to play in the search plan. The boys were handed out walkie-talkies and told to put them on channel 9.

The Milton boys were told exactly what to do. Look for any signs of a young boy who was missing now for over a day. The constables hated this part of police work, because more often than not, when it came to kids and a river, they dreaded the outcome. Usually the river won and you would not find him or her alive.

A couple of the constables had been fishing on their day off and still had their waders in the back of their car. They were designated the task of searching from the river looking at all the eroded underside of both banks of the river.

The team of six mountain rescue boys showed up in Land Rovers outside Lennoxtown police station and in no time had maps of the Campsies spread out over the bonnet of one of the vans. They scanned the terrain shown in front of them knowing how steep certain areas were. Decisions would have to be made quick regarding likely places to search first.

The dogs sat eagerly in the rear of the lead Land Rover.

The Campsie Fells were an ancient range of hills just to the North of Glasgow formed during the last ice age. They were left sculpted out as melting glaciers spread out over the valley below. The locals were not interested in how old the hills were or how they were formed; to them the hills were just called the Campsies. The hills were beautiful in the summer sunshine and stunningly beautiful covered in winter snow.

As you looked toward the face of the hills you noticed three distinct features. The main one was an area of rock scree high up just below the summit split into three distinct areas at different heights on the hills. This area was called the three steps. To the right of the three steps as you looked east towards Milton, the hill had a deep cleft running from nearly the hilltop to the bottom valley and by the shape of it, was known locally as the banana. Further right still there was another wider deep excavation known as the shovel.

The rescue team had discussed and accepted the decision of the team leader that they would start looking in the shovel and then move onto the banana. They would have to work their way across the face of the hills. Although the weather for the past few days had been showers, the hills were still very slippy with residual moisture. Time was the essence here because of the light would be fading quickly from 9 p.m. onwards. After a quick radio check ensuring all the radios were in working order they set off. Not one of the team smiled at Tom as they set off. He could see the serious look each one of them had on his face.

The locals that showed up to help and the ones that had been cajoled into helping by their priest were quickly gathered round Tom and he briefed them on what was happening.

He asked them to split up into two groups and look around the old coal pit heaps at the back of the field park. They had to pay real attention to any recent landslides and give them a good once over. They had to check along the old railway line as well, tracking up to Campsie and on up to the west lodge. They all looked a bit confused as to who was going with whom, so Tom split the group up and told them to go quickly. One group ambled off in the direction of the disused railway line and the other group walked back towards the Trinity church and down the path towards the coal Bings (slag heaps) at the back of the football park.

More police volunteers showed up and Tom gave them their task of house to house. They would have to check out garden sheds, coal bunkers and garages. Somewhere a kid could have thought was a good hiding place and had either been injured or had taken some liquid chemical thinking it was pop. Lennoxtown wasn't a big place really and the door to door search would to start in the missing child's street.

Tom sat in the office and prayed to himself. If there was a god up there let them find that wee boy alive. He sat and stared hard at the hand held radio set and listened to the buzz from it. Every now and then it would crackle into life and he could hear the progress of the rescue teams as they talked to each other. There was zero to report as each team checked into base. Tom acknowledged each team with the recognized answer, "Roger".

By ten o'clock most of the teams were back at the station with nothing found etched on their faces. The Milton lads had scoured the riverbanks for the mile or so and the boys in the waders had checked under the riverbanks. They would continue the search tomorrow.

The mountain rescue lads were still on the hills with their dogs and would be there for another hour or so before it became too dangerous for them, clambering about in the dark. By now everybody in Lennoxtown knew of the missing boy. There were prayers said in homes up and down streets. Parents tucked their children up in bed and gave them an extra hug and kiss that night.

Jack and Patsy looked in on Nelson as he slept soundly. They too were concerned about the missing boy from the village. Looking at Nelson they whispered to each other about the boy's parents and how they must be feeling. They closed his bedroom door and headed back along the hall, to the comfort of their settee in the living room and they sat staring into the dancing flames in the fireplace. They held each other tight not wanting to be the first to speak; their thoughts were on another family. A family who must be going through hell, their nightmare was that they didn't have their son tucked up in bed all snug and warm.

Nelson had heard the bedroom door quietly open and pretended to be fully asleep. He heard his father whisper to his mother and the door close. Nelson pulled the sheets over his head and listened to what the teddy bear had to tell him. Nelson giggled and agreed with teddy. He gave his bear a big hug and a kiss on its little black nose. He placed his friend on the pillow next to him and gave it another kiss, this time on its furry cheek. He said sweet dreams to his friend and being safe and happy, Nelson snuggled down and was soon sound asleep.

David and Margaret Smith had had a house full all day. Margaret's sister, Violet, had come to the house as soon as she had heard. She sat with Margaret in her bedroom and comforted her every time the tears flowed. David's friends had all popped in to see what they could do to help.

But now it was 10.30 p.m. and they had all gone. The house was quiet with the only sound being the ticking of the clock on the mantelpiece. The doctor had been asked to come to the house and had prescribed some sedative for Margaret. It would give her at least some respite from her dread and allow her to sleep. It had worked she was sleeping upstairs. David sat in the living room on his own with tears rolling down his cheeks. He stared at the photograph of a young smiling Graham in happier times. He just wished for the boy to come walking through the front door and to end this nightmare. But David, too, had an awful feeling that something really bad had happened to his Graham.

Tom O'Brien and Bill Wilson had manned the fort, as they say, all day coordinating the search. It was nearly midnight when they locked the station door. They both tried to look on the brighter side and hoped for a break in the morning. But both knew deep down in their own hearts this was beginning to feel like a lost one.

The rain started to fall as they walked back up school lane and onto their police houses. They said good night to each other as they opened their front doors.

Tom closed his door quietly behind him and took his coat off and hung it up on the coat peg in the hallway. He put his hat on the table beside the phone. He noticed that drips of water from his coat were making a small puddle beneath it. He was too emotionally tired to do anything about it, so he let it drip. It was days like today when he questioned why he was in the police force.

Tom's wife Hannah had lain in bed anticipating Tom's return. She had heard his boots and Bill's echo along the road and as soon as he had said goodnight to Bill, she was up. She came down the stairs wrapping her dressing gown around her. She wanted to hear Tom's story. She wanted to hold her husband because he would probably need it.

Their eyes met and Hannah could see how tired Tom was. She also saw the beaten look that she had not seen for a long time. It was etched across his whole face.

Chapter 11

It was five in the morning and Jack was beginning to stir. Patsy lay beside him sound asleep but Jack had to be up for a wash and make his lunchtime sandwich for his shift which was due to start at 6am. He swung his legs out of the bed and he yawned. Early shift was a killer, so why didn't he just go back to his warm bed and pull the covers over his head? He stood up and stretched yawning again. He tip toed to the curtains quietly and opened them a little bit, just enough to see what kind of day it was. He peeked out and was not pleasantly surprised, with a glorious sunrise. It was pissing it down. It was another typical dull wet day, so he was going to need his oilskins again.

He yawned going to the toilet; he ran the hot water tap until he got enough warm water to fill the bathroom sink allowing him to wash his face and hands. He dressed throwing on his blue serge trousers (Hospital issue) and a dark blue shirt and walked through to the kitchen. There he put on his socks and his work boots. He would put his jumper and jacket on just before he left the house. His first task for the day, however, was to make the tea. He filled the kettle with water and turned the gas cooker on. He took the whistle off the kettle and placed the kettle on the back ring and waited for it to boil. He didn't need the whistle waking everybody up at this time in the morning. He lifted the teapot up and emptied the remnants into the kitchen sink.

He rinsed the pot out before putting two teaspoons of Brook Bond tea into it. He poured the boiling water slowly into the tea pot. He yawned again, why didn't he go back to bed and call in sick?

While he waited for the tea to infuse he went about making his sandwiches for lunch, which today would have to be cheese. After pouring himself a steaming cup of tea he sat down at the kitchen table and had his breakfast, a bowl of cornflakes and a jam sandwich.

He put his cheese sandwiches into his "Lunch box" an old biscuit tin and added an apple and two bananas and closed the lid. He didn't need to take a flask of tea with him because they had billycans and tea up at the clearing site. Before leaving for work he would have a quick look in at the sleeping Patsy and a peek at his son, Nelson.

Jack opened the kitchen cupboard door and grabbed his old woollen jersey that was hanging on a nail. He would need it to keep warm. He pulled it over his head and pulled his shirt collar over the crew neck. Next he took his rain jacket also from behind the door and put that on. He closed the cupboard door very quietly as it sometime squeaked and he tip toed from the kitchen along the hall. He looked in on Patsy who was giving quiet snores. He was happy that he hadn't been too noisy and that she was still sleeping soundly. He moved away and opened up his son's bedroom door. It looked like Nelson hadn't moved an inch and looked really cosy lying there wrapped up in his blankets, with teddy lying alongside. Jack smiled at his little angel as he closed the bedroom door.

"That's Daddy going to work, Nelson"

"I know. Did he look at us as he closed the door?"

"You know he did."

"He always does."

181

"Night, night, Nelson."
"Night, night, Teddy."

Opening the top stairs door Jack thought he heard Nelson talking but it couldn't have been; Nelson was sound asleep.

Jack quietly closed the door behind him and stepped down the staircase to his front door. He could hear the wind and the rain battering at the outside wooden door. He shivered in anticipation. It was twenty to six in the morning and he was just about to get very wet. He buttoned up his jacket right up to his chin and opening the main door, stepped out into the rain.

Bill Wilson's wife Christine had listened intently to her husband telling his story the night before and sleep had been hard to come by as she had tossed and turned most of the night. Policemen were called upon to deal with some situations that were dangerous or frightening, but that was part and parcel of the job and the wives had to accept that. She knew that, she accepted that, but it still didn't detract from the fact that when it involved children it was a different matter.

She had listened to a very tired Bill drop off rather quickly, off to the land of nod. She had found it impossible and turned onto her side wondering and imagining just how awful that poor family must be feeling with their only son missing. She propped up her pillows again and turned to lie on her opposite side. With really heavy eyes the last thing she remembered was Bill snoring.

The next thing she knew was that through the bedroom wall she could hear next door's alarm clock going off and looked towards her own. Christ it was five to five in the morning. The faint ringing of next door's alarm clock had been enough to rouse her from her faint sleep and it would mean that next-door neighbours, Tom and Hannah, would be getting up. Christine put her hand on her alarm clock and pressed the snooze button to prevent it from ringing and turned to snuggle into Bill's back. She gently nudged him awake.

Next door Tom's wife, Hannah, had somehow managed to drift off to sleep although fitfully. She had clock watched for the best part of the night until god knows what time she dozed off. But now as soon as the alarm clock had gone off Tom was up. It always amazed Hannah how Tom could literally bounce up awake after such a deep sleep and get himself organized so quickly. She could already hear him pottering about downstairs in the kitchen. The clatter of cups and saucers signalled she would be getting a cup of tea in bed again. But this morning Hannah decided that she needed to get up and make Tom's breakfast. She pulled the sheets off her warm body and swung her legs over the side of the bed. She felt underneath for her slippers. She wrapped her dressing gown on and went down the stairs to the kitchen. Hannah ran her fingers through her hair and yawned. She had a feeling that this was going to be a very long and emotional day.

All over central Stirlingshire that morning the same scenarios were being played out in ordinary family homes. The men of the house were getting up to resume a search of the hills or forests, for a boy who would now, on this Monday morning, have been missing for two days.

Wives were making their men breakfasts and preparing sandwiches for later, wrapping bread and cheese or whatever they had, in empty biscuit tins for ease of carrying. There were no shops on the hills or in the woods. Today was going to be a long tedious search. Deep down all the searchers knew what kind of day they were going to face. Another day of few smiles on any of the faces.

Tom and Bill exited their homes almost simultaneously and with a courteous good morning hand shake and pat on the back, set off for the five-minute walk to the station house. The shift would start again at six and by five past, the phone would be ringing with calls from Glasgow and Kirkintilloch. There were Chief constables wanting updates and progress reports, so early calls were guaranteed.

Like a well-rehearsed routine Tom opened the station house door and Bill headed for the small kitchen area to put on the first pot of tea. Soon this place would have teams of searchers all wanting their orders and new areas of search mapped out. Tea would have to be administered to them all.

Tom opened up the counter flap and stood behind it. He took off his dripping coat and hat and hung them on the coat stand in the corner to dry. He took the duty log from underneath the counter and placed it on the counter. He opened it at Monday May 29th 1966 and wrote, Staff on Duty Tom O'Brien, Bill Wilson. Time 6 a.m.

He proceeded to pen where all searches were carried out on Sunday, detailing where all the areas would be searched today and that yesterday's search results proved to be fruitless as the young boy Graham Smith was not found.

Police teams from Milton Campsie, Kirkintilloch and the Mountain rescue were due to be here at the station at 6.30 a.m. The two Policemen from Strathblane were also being called on to walk the old railway line from Strathblane down towards Haughhead. It was not going to be a nice way to start the day, walking along a disused railway line in the pouring rain.

Donald McPherson stepped out of his parked car and turned to look towards the hospital wards that spread out below him. The driving rain hit him in the face, which made him shield his eyes against it. Everything that occurred yesterday hadn't been far from his mind and he shuddered at the thought that one of his patients could be responsible for a young boy going missing somewhere on these grounds.

He knew he would have to telephone the police station as soon as he sat behind his desk. Bella would be inside ready to bring him his mug of steaming hot tea, as soon as he sat down.

He decided that today he would have to make a phone call first, and then try to enjoy his cuppa. The tea was a necessity for Donald; it was a big part of his morning routine. He had to sit behind his desk, Bella would hand him his cup of hot tea, and then he could function. The day could then start. He could be ready for whatever being in charge of running a mental hospital could throw at him.

But this morning he had a strange nauseous feeling inside. There were questions left unanswered from yesterday and he didn't like that. He had to find out if the young boy had been found. He closed his car door and walked quickly up the stairs out of the rain and into the admin building.

Nelson threw off his covers and bounced from his bed and went to look out his bedroom window to see what the weather was like. He would soon have to get up and get dressed for school. He pulled back the curtain and looked towards the puddles in the back garden. It was still raining hard. He closed the curtain and jumped back into bed and pulled the covers on top of him. He lay on his side under the covers and talked to his teddy bear about Smith. They both laughed.

Donald sat behind his desk and sipped at his tea. He picked up the phone. He dialled the Lennoxtown police station and spoke to Bill Wilson. Donald bit his lip at the no news so far and he told Bill that his team was planning to look at another part of the Lennox forest today. He put the phone down as Bella showed Jack into Donald's office.

"Sit down, Jack. Won't be a minute." Donald started rummaging through one of his drawers.

"I've got a map of the place somewhere. Bella?" he asked.

"It'll be in the filing cabinet under E for estate." She answered rather abruptly. Donald had missed the tone of her voice as she had answered him. Jack hadn't.

Donald stood up and opened the filing cabinet to his left and seconds later had the map of the estate laid out on his desk in front of Jack.

"Now here's where you looked for that wee boy yesterday" he traced the area with his finger, "and here's where I want you to look today." He pointed at the blue line on the map. "The Glazert from here past Hut N down past the railway station and along to the bridge and down to the waterfall." Jack nodded.

"And, Jack," Donald said hesitatingly. "Look real hard along the riverbanks and under the bridges. I know it's been pissing down and the river is going to be in spate, but ..."

"Don't worry, Donald, we will." Jack said trying hard to reassure the man in front of him. "I'll just go and meet up with the lads and get started and I'll call you later on if we find or don't find anything OK?" Jack turned to leave. "Oh and, Jack, have a wee look in at the old railway station house and the old waiting area, just in case."

"OK, Donald."

"Good luck, Jack." Donald watched as Jack disappeared out the door. He turned back to stare at the map. He spread his hands at each side of it and looked real hard.

"Now, son, where are you?"

The Police station was full. Tom also had a local map spread on the table in the interview room. The team leaders were all briefed as to what area they were to cover that day.

Within minutes all the teams were assembled outside and they were all off. The station house was quiet again. Lennoxtown was quiet with very little traffic moving along in the rain. Bill was washing up cups in the kitchen sink when Tom brought his mug in.

"Tom what do you think about calling Alexander's, you know, the bus company, and have one of our boys from Kirkintilloch pop down and ask some of the drivers if they had seen the boy on Saturday morning. Their buses run every half hour and the Blanefield bus goes up at five to the hour and comes back at quarter past."

"That's a good idea, Bill," Tom said. And then set about telephoning the Station house in Kirkintilloch to tell them.

Alexander's, the bus company, was phoned and the shift manager was told to expect a police car round sometime that morning. He didn't ask for any explanation into the visit nor did he get one.

Two officers from Kirkintilloch drove down to the garage and walked from the car to the shift manager's office. His name was Thomas Donovan.

In his office they were offered seats and the two police constables both sat down and removed their hats.

Asked if they wanted tea they both declined.

They proceeded to ask a few perfunctory questions and offered an explanation to Mr Donovan as to the real reason for their visit. They explained that they would have to have a list of the drivers and the conductors that were on the Campsie Glen to Glasgow route and the Blanefield run on Saturday morning from six o'clock to about 10 a.m. There was a missing boy and the drivers or the conductresses may have seen or even spoken to the lad if he had gotten on that bus.

The manager left his office and spoke quietly to his secretary. She rose from her desk and went to her filing cabinet and looked at the time sheets for last week. She picked out Saturday's list and handed it to the waiting manager. He thanked her and left her office and quickly walked back along the corridor to his own office where the two policemen sat waiting.

The manager returned to behind his desk and sat down. He laid the time sheets in front of him and took from his inside jacket pocket his spectacle case. He opened it and took out his spectacles placing them over his eyes. He closed the case and returned it to the inside of his jacket. He read in silence as the two officers fidgeted. After some moments he sighed, "Ah here we are." The two officers sat forward. "Jimmy Marshall was on the Glasgow, Campsie Glen run in the morning and so was Tony Marshall and before you ask they're not brothers," he said with a smile. "If you're not in a hurry I can find out who their conductresses were on Saturday." He continued looking through the time sheets "Oh and Graham Donaldson was on the Blanefield bus in the morning

"No that's fine, sir. When we talk to the boys I'm sure they'll remember who they were working with … Where can we find them just now, sir?"

"My secretary has a duty list up on her wall. So if you follow me we'll see in a couple of minutes.

They followed the manager along the corridor and walked into the secretary's office. They stood in front of a large wall chart and looked along the names until Jimmy and Tony Marshall was found.

"Jimmy has the Glasgow, Lenzie run this afternoon and Tony has the day off. Graham on the other hand is along in the staff room having a cup of tea just now."

"Can you give me their addresses, sir? We have to talk to these men and can we see Graham Donaldson now?"

"Right this way, officer." Donovan led the two policemen along the hall and down the stairs across the garage forecourt towards the staff room at the back of the garage. When Donovan opened the door he entered a smoke filled room where all the occupants were smoking and drinking tea.

Donovan scanned the room and when he saw Donaldson, called over to him to come here. Graham thought he was in trouble because the bus he should be driving should have left five minutes ago.

He nervously looked down at his watch. Surely five minutes wasn't bad. He wasn't that late. He got up, put his tea down on the table and followed Donovan from the room.

"All right, Thomas?" Graham asked seeing the boys in blue standing there.

"Graham these gentlemen have a few questions for you. They think you may be of a help to them."

One of the constables stepped forward. "You Graham Donaldson?"

Graham had the hair start to rise on the back of his neck "Yes."

"Mister Donovan has informed us that you were driving The Chryston to Blanefield bus Saturday morning. Is that correct?"

Graham's brow furrowed. "Yes."

"What time did you start work Saturday?"

"6 a.m." Graham thought about what actual time he clocked on. "But you should get that from my clock card. What's this all about eh?"

"Did you have a conductress with you?"

"Aye I did."

"What's her name, sir?" the policeman said after a slight pause.

"Debbie," Graham answered.

"Can you give me her full name, sir?"

"Oh aye. She's no in any trouble is she?"

An exasperated policeman said "No She's not in any trouble, sir. Name?"

"Debbie Wren. She's from Milton."

"What time was your first run Saturday?" the policeman continued.

"I left the garage about twenty five to seven to go up to Chryston. That's where I start and …"

"So what time did you arrive and leave Blanefield Saturday morning on your first run?"

"I got to Blanefield about ten to eight and left about ten minutes later. It was quiet on Saturday." Graham replied still puzzled. "So what's this all about eh?"

"When you say it was quiet, what do you mean by quiet?"

"The drive is usually quiet because it's the first bus. I mean there are hardly any passengers and Blanefield is a sleepy wee place and then on the way back, Haughhead is usually still asleep."

"What about Campsie that time in the morning?"

"It's usually dead as well. I mean you'll get a few of the early ones walking about, going for the rolls or the newspapers or to pick up the bacon, but it's usually quite quiet."

Can you remember when you picked up your first passenger on Saturday?"

"Eh` we had a couple of them at Blanefield going to Kirkintilloch, shopping I think."

"Any other stops before Lennoxtown?"

"Aye there was a young boy at Haughhead."

The two policemen stepped forward, "A young boy?"

"Aye he gets on at Haughhead and gets off at Eastside. He plays football through in Kilsyth and he has to get the Kilsyth bus there. But that's every weekend."

Both policemen had thought that they were onto something for a moment, but had that fleeting thought dashed.

"Any other children get on your bus through Campsie?"

"A couple of girls with duffle bags, but they go to the swimming baths every Saturday. They never miss it."

"OK, sir. Can you think for a minute? Did you see a young lad Saturday dressed in a blue jumper walking up the street or ...?"

"Officer. Do you know how many folk in Campsie have Blue jumpers? Jesus, you either wear a blue jumper or a green one." Graham smiled, "Know what I mean?"

"So you can't recall seeing a young boy Saturday morning walking up the street at about 8.15 a.m.?"

"As I said officer ..." Graham shrugged his shoulders.

"Thank you for your time. If you do remember anything else. Give us a call."

"Eh ... What was that all about eh?" Graham enquired. "Can you tell me?"

The policemen didn't even have to think about it. The more people who knew about it the quicker the response they would get from the public.

"We've a young boy missing from Campsie. He went out Saturday morning and has not come home yet. So we're looking for him."

"Oh I get it. You thought he might have jumped on a bus."
The penny dropped.

The policeman watching Graham nodded.

"Debbie's on the Kilsyth run this morning. *She might* have seen something. In fact she ..." Graham looked at his watch "... started her shift at seven."

Chapter 12

As soon as he had completed his exercises in the dark, Nelson had gone to bed. When he slept he was not bombarded with questions that he had to give answers to. He tried to close his eyes and dream. He tried to dream about Lennoxtown and about the swimming hole by the waterfall. He remembered visiting the place when he was in his twenties and had tried to go swimming there. He had been disappointed as the swimming place was a lot smaller than he remembered. That thought did not work at sending him off to sleep, he was still awake. He tossed and turned until eventual exhaustion washed over him and he fell asleep.

Nelson lay there on the bedding on the floor of his cell and with the blanket wrapped tightly around him, he slept fitfully. He never had the nice warm dreams of his childhood to put him to sleep. The dreams he had in the past had been of the cold nights he as a child experienced. He had been too young and frightened, desperately wanting to climb into bed with his mum and dad to keep warm and safe but couldn't. They were engaged in sexual acts that Nelson now knew were depraved and perverse.

He had been the lonely one left standing at the bedroom door shivering.

It felt like he had been spying on them as he stood transfixed like a rabbit in the car's headlights, not being able to move; having to be ultra-quiet to make sure he wasn't caught. Watching the sexual abuse his father gave his mother and her loving every masochistic minute of it and craving more.

But still Nelson dreamt on. Gone were the times when the nightmares would wake him in a sweat. Now he just slept through all that was going through his troubled mind. In the morning he would wake and not have any recollections of any dream.

The night shift warden, Tom Atkinson, was on his rounds. He didn't even bother walking down Nelson's corridor to check on the prisoners. Why should he? They were all sickos down there in their own little private hell holes.

Why should he waste his time on them?

He loathed every last one of them.

It would have only taken seconds to look through the eight peepholes, but why should he have to look at all that waste of human flesh? In his mind they were the scum of the earth. He gritted his teeth in anger and his hand automatically reached down to the nightstick. He felt better and safer that it was there.

He stopped at the big door separating the two corridors. He counted the cells in his mind and thought about each one of the eight prisoners. Starting at cell one and working his way down the corridor he was appalled at the crimes that each one of them had committed. Hideous crimes that were more outrageous as you moved down the cell numbers. Their individual crimes were well known among the warders, but still it brought out his thoughts of loathing against each one of them.

The hairs on the back of his neck rose as his thoughts came round to Nelson. What this guy had done to all those people for so long and got away with made him shudder. And the sad thing was that the charges they could pin on that bastard, were for the victims they knew he killed. They all suspected that there were more dead bodies out there somewhere, but Nelson had never owned up to that fact.

Atkinson paused briefly remembering why Nelson was put in cell number 8. He was the worst offender and deserved cell 8.

As he turned away from the door his mind quickly turned to those politicians on the outside, the ones that shouted for prisoner liberties and fair treatment for the poor prisoners. Now that we were in Europe the European court for Human rights were on about giving prisoners more liberties and less harsh sentences for crimes. He cringed at that thought; these bastards didn't deserve any rights at all, not in his book. These killers weren't human. This type of animal and that's what they were animals, the EU politicians wanted to give them a fair and better treatment while banged up, forget it. Let them come and stand face to face with these animals. Let them be told what they did to other human beings. Then see what they say. If he had his way, he shook his head at the thought, because it angered him so much. What these people would say and do if they knew all about those eight bastards. Prisoner compassion, forget it. Revulsion was all he felt for the evil that lived back there on the other side of that door; he turned on his heels and strolled quietly but quickly, back up the corridor he had just walked down.

The eight were all quiet and settled down. That's what he would put down in his report.

Chapter 13

Nelson sat cross legged with his back against the wall; the time was somewhere around 5 o'clock he guessed. Faint distant noises could be heard from somewhere around the wing. Someone had stirred from their own personal nightmare from a cell along the corridor and the rest of the place would be quickly awake, as soon as he started his ritual screaming and shouting.

This was the quiet time of the day he had to himself. Between waking up and showering and being incarcerated back in his cell. Nelsons own little sanctuary from the pestering voice demanding he respond to, was the only piece of sanity he had. That's if you could term it as sanity. Moments of quiet before the verbal onslaught began, were moments to cherish.

The voice would start pestering him later but not just now. The morning routine would commence shortly with the first disappointment of the day, breakfast. It would trundle along the corridor at 6.30 a.m. pushed by a pissed off guard and escorted by another two with truncheons at the ready.

Nelson always thought the whole scenario of breakfast was pathetic. The small peek hole on the cell door opening up and the guard barking at Nelson to stand away from the door as it was opened. The guard making certain of where

Nelson was in the cell before allowing the other guard to lay his breakfast on the floor in front of him. Like they were putting a dog's dinner down to their pet. 'Here rover, good boy, here's your Pedigree Chum, come and get it.

Instead it was, 'Here Nelson, here's your fucking slop, come and get it.'

The guard who laid the breakfast down on the floor, never took his eyes off Nelson, while the other two arseholes stood in the doorway trying to look threatening, gently slapping truncheons into their free hands. Nelson always stood stock still and very alert, just in case he got lucky and today was the day the guards' combination was the right one. But up to now it never was. He needed a rookie and two of the real soft beggars.

Half hour for breakfast and then the opposite take away scenario would be played out, equally pathetic.

The prisoners were never allowed to meet or talk to each other. Nelson never knew who his fellow inmates were. He didn't really care. To be in there meant that they were just as bad as or worse than he was. En-route to the showers no one called out; if they tried they would be beaten senseless.

Nelson stood and stretched, walked over to the hole in the floor and urinated. The smell of his own piss hit his nostrils and he watched the stream of fluid disappear down the dark hole. The smell from his 'French' urinal, as Nelson called it, didn't bother him. Nelson knew it was all about daily routines, the road to keeping him from going completely bonkers. The daily routine of pissing at half past five, shitting just before breakfast the back of six, the guards marching him off to the showers around 7 a.m., then the lunch routine, then the dinner routine and then lights out. Routines and more routines he had to follow, he hated every goddamn one of them.

Today he decided he would ask for a book to read. He already knew what the answer would be and it would be a big fat no. But his request would have to be vetted by the governor as to what type of book and why now? Certain types of books were banned from Nelson that was sure. 99 percent of the time they always were. Nelson asking for books always aroused suspicion and the authorities looked at such a request as somehow a challenge to their security. The governing body were scared shitless that he would take any little bit of knowledge that could help him escape from their security hell hole.

So there were no DIY books, no books on mechanics, also books on electrics were off the list. So Nelson asking for a book, would wind up the governor and the staff; get them all pissed off, leaving them wondering as to the reason behind the request. They would analyse why he ask for a special type of book. A faint smile was building on Nelson's face knowing that they'd all be puzzled as to why he wanted a book. It was his way of fucking with their minds. His little way of getting one back at the establishment. What else could he do? He only wanted to read the fucking thing.

It was definite he could now hear noises for certain. Breakfast trolleys being pushed along far away corridors, by uninterested fat warders. Thinking about trolleys made Nelson smile. No hotel room service trolley here, no, it was more like a large rectangular bin with wheels transporting food in plastic containers. It was a bonus if it was warm.

There would definitely be no waiter service here, where the waiter would gently knock on your room door, you would open it with a sleepy smile and he would push it past you into your room. He might set up your breakfast and even take the time to open your napkin for you. There would be no piping hot coffee, poached eggs bacon and pork sausages, with brown bread toast and orange juice. There would be none of the hotel pleasantries here.

A bang on the cell door after the flap on the peep hole was lifted, a growl telling you to back away from the door and a plastic tray of slop placed down on the floor in front of you.

No there was no point dwelling on the crap they served up to you here. Meals if you could call them that, served to you by guards, if you could call them that. Delivering the plastic plates to your cell, whether you were ready to eat or not. Keeping it until later when you might get hungry was not an option. As soon as you had finished the meal the guards wanted to see the empty plate and the plastic spoon. Heaven help you if you hid the spoon. The bastards would be in, batons drawn until they found it. You would feel their wrath and the batons would rain down on you until they found it. Once they had it in their possession then the beating would stop. Their lesson for insubordination and for threatening them would be over. Some of the warders enjoyed the physical violence and hit you hard; others were far more subdued and lenient.

Over the last year or so Nelson had hidden the spoon or dropped it on the floor, taking the beatings from the warders on more than one occasion. He had gauged who hit him the hardest and which ones didn't really put their all into it. In his mind he knew who the bad bastards were and who the softer ones were. When he finally got the right combination of warders on shift and in his cell and when the time was right, he would kill them without any hesitation.

Chapter 14

1964

Tom and Bill sat drinking yet another cup of tea. The morning had flown in and with numerous calls made to the station house regarding offers to help in the search and visits from clergy and parish priests it felt as they were doing something positive. In fact they were getting no further forward. As each search team reported back that they had found zero the hopelessness returned to the pair of them.

Tom knew he would have to go and talk to the Smith's again with an update and to sound positive, but he was dreading looking into their faces. They would know he was lying.

The two policemen had stopped the Kilsyth bus at a bus stop near Kirkintilloch and asked Debbie if they could talk to her. The passengers were all watching with interest as she stepped down from the bus and stood arms crossed in front of the two men. She listened intently to what one of the men had to say and after some moments shook her head. Whatever it was she had been asked, the answer was no, most of the passengers surmised.

Debbie got back on the bus and rang the bell twice to tell her driver to drive on. Even he was wondering all sorts of things.

The two policemen got back in their Ford panda car and closed the doors. One of them would have to phone the station with the news that the bus conductress Deborah Wren had not recalled seeing a young boy answering the description given on Saturday morning.

Jack and his team were out early searching the woods to the south of the castle down towards Netherton Oval. The rain had stopped but everything was wet. There was something beautiful about the forest area first thing in the morning. Whether it was the crisp sharp smell of the pine trees or the sounds of the birds chirping their way through the trees Jack didn't know, but it made him feel happy to be alive.

Their orders were to look especially at the storm drains. These drains were 36 inch concrete pipes buried underground and put into parts of the forest to drain excess water away to the river, to alleviate possible floods. Jack had lifted the iron cover off the drain and asked the smallest one of his lads Eamon to enter the drain and to go through it to the next point some 100 yards away. As soon as Jack had removed the iron cover any rats that were there had scarpered so the lad would be safe. All he had to do was crouch down and attempt to walk the length of the drain. Jack knew that the little boy wouldn't be strong enough to have lifted the drain cover off and put it back in place by himself. The kids didn't do that. The bigger ones would have left the cover off when they were playing their games. Jack ordered the boys to take the next cover off to give Eamon a distant light to walk towards. They found nothing in the drains.

The fir trees in this section of the woods had been planted in the late 40s and the forest base was remarkably clear from any major wooded debris. No fallen trees or upended ones caused by recent storm damage, for which the area was prone to. The boys spread out again and searched the part of the pine forest that ran adjacent to the South lodge road and again found nothing.

Patsy had the day off, but got out of her bed in order to get Nelson up for school. She threw on her dressing gown and placed her feet in her slippers. She was humming a tune to herself as she opened Nelson's bedroom door. She saw the lump under the covers and heard the giggles coming from her son. She smiled "Who wants a boiled egg and toast soldiers for breakfast?" She said grabbing at the lump in the covers.

Nelson laughed as his mum started tickling him. "Come on you, time to get up," she said as she left the room. "And remember to wash your hands and face before you get dressed Nelson," she called back along the hall.

Minutes later Nelson sat fully dressed at the kitchen table as his Mum put down an egg cup with his soft-boiled egg and his toast soldiers in front of him. Patsy sat down and with her mug of tea watched Nelson dip his toast into the yolk and hungrily devour the lot.

Jack and his boys had reached the old railway station. There they pushed the broken down disused door open and entered the old waiting room. Graffiti decked the walls with gang slogans, broken glass littered the floor. The smell of urine in the corner was extremely pungent. They looked behind the vandalized ticket counter but there was no sign of the boy. The group exited and started again searching the hospital grounds. They searched under the railway bridge and the woods running parallel to the main road. They set off down towards the main road bridge over the river and down towards the waterfall. They checked every bush on the way and around all the tree trunks in case the wee boy was behind one of them. They passed under and over the main bridge edging along the riverbank towards the waterfall. One of Jack's lads was skirting the boundary wall between the railway line and the woods. All the time they were getting closer to a place where a Rhododendron bush and a big beech tree stood.

No one was aware that as they searched this section of the woods it was very quiet. It was as if the woods wanted to hide a secret and not tell. There were no birds singing in the trees and no little rabbits hopping about. All was very still and quiet. Even the breeze blowing through the trees didn't appear to make a sound. No one noticed.

Jack's team searched in silence. There was no banter between them. No coaxing or moaning about their task of finding the little boy. They all thought inwardly that this search was futile and the hope that the wee boy was still alive was gone. But they didn't want to say it was a waste of time, in case they were the one who jinxed the search.

Bobby was the first to reach the Rhododendron bush and pulled at the foliage to allow him to look under the branches. He made out the pile of leaves and twigs under the canopy. There was also a funny smell here. It didn't dawn on him at first what he was looking at or what the smell was. That's what set the bells ringing. He called out to Jack.

"Jack, I think I've found something."

Jack came running along the path towards the bush. All the other searchers stopped what they were doing to watch Jack run towards the spot where Bobby had called from.

Reaching there in seconds an out of breath Jack looked into Bobby's face, which was now chalk white. Jack could see the fear in his eyes. It made Jack rather edgy.

Bobby pointed "It's under there, look."

Jack moved some of the branches with his left arm allowing him to see under the leafy canopy. He was looking down at a mound of earth, crudely made to disguise and bury something. It had been crudely covered by broken branches and gathered leaves. The hairs on the back of his neck rose, the fear that his dread was coming true made him draw breath. He reluctantly pushed his way under the branches towards the mound and fell to his knees in front of it.

He hoped it was someone's dead pet under this ready-made grave. He wanted desperately to find that it was someone's favourite cat or dog. He silently prayed to God to please let him uncover an animal. He wanted to be able to announce to the rest of the boys that they had found nothing.

There was a growing knot in the pit of his stomach. Jack could smell the faint odour emanating from the mound. He tentatively reached out his shaking hand towards the nearest side of the mound and removed some of the branches. He then brushed away the leaves and clawed some of the dirt away from the base.

Please let it be a pet, please let it be a pet, he repeated to himself.

He touched a lifeless arm.

His heart sank; he knew then that this wasn't someone's favourite moggie.

They had found the wee boy. Here was someone's dead son.

Here was someone's pride and joy.

He felt sick.

He turned to look at Bobby; there were tears in his eyes. "It's him," was all that Jack could say.

Jack stood up as best he could and moved away from the mound. He gently scratched his eyebrow as he looked down at the ground. He gathered himself and turned to tell Bobby to run and get help. Go to the nearest ward. Get whoever is in charge to phone Donald McPherson and the police. Bobby did so and set off running along the path back towards the hospital.

Jack came out from under the bush and saw that the rest of the lads were watching him. He told all the boys to walk away from the bush. Their search was over. It had all been in vain. He could see the sadness etched in their faces.

He realized that this part of the woods was now a crime scene. He walked slowly back to where the group were standing. They were all quiet with their own thoughts.

Who could have done this? What kind of monster kills and buries a young boy?

The call to Donald's office was made at 11-22 a.m. Donald bit his lip at the news. He briefly cradled the phone before dialling 999 and asking for the Police station at Lennoxtown.

Tom and Bill had been discussing about what they were going to tell the parents if ever they got a phone call. Both men deep down feared the worst. Both men could feel it in their water.

The telephone rang and both of them jumped. They looked at each other, neither man wanting to lift the receiver and answer.

Had it been a premonition on their behalf at that point? They both had the strangest feeling when it started to ring. Bill felt the goose bumps rise on his neck and he was sure he could see Tom shaking when he lifted the receiver.

Tom answered on the fifth ring. He never had a chance to speak because on the other end of the line, was an over excited, rambling, Donald Macpherson, telling him that they had discovered the whereabouts of the missing boy and that he was indeed dead. The words hung in Tom's head for ages, "indeed dead". His face took on a frown as he listened to Donald describe the exact location. Bill muttered something incoherent and sat down with his head in his hands. He knew what was being said by the look on his partner's face. The only question now that had to be answered was it an accident? Or was it murder?

Bill looked up at Tom as soon as he laid the receiver back down. The look on his beaten face said volumes. Tom's voice was shaky when he told Bill what had just been said.

"They've found him partially buried."

The question had been answered, it was a murder.

The two men sat silent momentarily, each going over what had just been said.

They had a job to do now and they would have to do it and do it by the book regardless of how they felt. Both men would go and do their thing; each knew they had tasks to do.

Bill went on the radio and started calling the search teams, telling them to return to base.

Tom used the phone and called Kirkintilloch. He was put through and spoke with his immediate superior officer and told him the grim news.

Questions were launched at him; his answers were parried back as quickly as he could get them off his tongue. No he hadn't seen the site yet and no he hadn't informed the parents yet.

The poor parents would have to make a formal identification of their child after the coroner had completed his grizzly task of pronouncing death.

Tom knew that, but that identification would have to wait a bit, he had to move and secure the site as a crime scene. Valuable information could be lost if too many people were allowed to trample all over it. Tom was well aware of that so he nodded agreement at everything his superior was barking down the phone.

Tom's boss would now set the investigative wheels in motion. He had to call in the forensic team from Glasgow and the Detectives who would be assigned to form the integral part of the investigative team. It was their case now by the sounds of it. The full team would be there in less than two hours.

The last order was finally barked at Tom. "Move it and keep me informed," and then the line went dead.

Tom cradled the phone and shrugged his shoulders at Bill, "This is what you get with a looney bin on your doorstep. One of those daft bastards is responsible for this"

Bill just nodded in agreement.

At twelve fifteen the school bell rang and the children all flooded through the school doors into the playground. Nelson was one of them. A cacophony of shouting and laughing and children playing chases ensued. Nelson was happy. He had nothing to fear. His teddy bear had told him that.

Chapter 15

I sat at my desk and quietly shuffled the papers in front of me. I was 24 years old and had been lucky to have come through the Police ranks at an alarming rate, some said too quick.

I had been in the police force since leaving School at 18 years old, joining as a young cadet and then progressing to constable. I had seen a huge change in attitude towards Kenny and me after we started passing exams. We rose quickly through the ranks until here I was now a young detective. This was my first year as a rookie detective and was only let out with the more experienced ones on cases. It was a blooding I reckoned, like the fox hunters and the young followers. You had to blood them before they were allowed to take a full part in a fox hunt. It was the same with Kenny Jackson and I; we were the young fox hunters.

The in tray on my desk had charge sheets for the same old names and the same old faces that I came across every month. Springburn could be a right busy hellhole. I reached for my packet of Kensitas club and opened it and took one out. I lit it and took a drag. This was a first, there were no other coppers scrounging a tab from me. I sat there with my feet on the desk, behind a closed office door, enjoying my little piece of sanctuary. It wasn't very often you got a few moments to yourself, so when you did manage five minutes you made bloody sure they were good ones. Peace and quiet to enjoy my cigarette. The wife had us both smoking the Club because she was saving the coupons for some bath towels she could get from the Kensitas catalogue.

The door got rapped three times and I was rudely brought back to reality. I shouted reluctantly "Come in" knowing fine well that the door was going to be opened anyway and that this was something that was going to annoy me. Our desk sergeant Willie Wood stood there in the open doorway smiling that bloody smile, the one he gave you, which told you he knew you were either in for a bollocking or an arse kicking. It was never good news when Sergeant Wood grinned at you, that was for sure.

"You, my boy, are wanted in the Old man's office pronto."

Willie was an ageing old cop with blue wizened eyes and close-cropped grey silvery hair. He had been a bit of a lad in his heyday and for that he had never made it past sergeant. Misdemeanours or lack of respect for those in authority were bandied about as to the reasons for his zero progression through the ranks. Whatever the truth was it didn't seem to faze him. He didn't seem to hold any grudges when we youngsters passed all the exams the force could throw at us and we moved on up the ladder. He must have at one time stepped onto a snake and slipped all the way back down, although I never knew or asked what the real reason was he stayed a sergeant.

"What's up, Willie?" I asked.

"Pronto, laddie," came his reply and he left the door open for me.

I stubbed the cigarette out in the ashtray and straightened my tie. I thought about throwing my jacket on for appearances but didn't and I ran my fingers through my hair instead. I was as presentable as I was going to be for "The Old man".

Superintendent Daniel McCluskey was 62 years old and built like the proverbial brick shit house. He had come up through the ranks in the Glasgow Police force when lawlessness had reigned and the gangs were real bastards and feared. That's not to say that our current crop were pussycats, because they were far from that. But he had taken on the best of them in his day and won more than he lost. The hoods he managed to get locked up were in places like Barlinnie, Greenock or Peterhead and his name was cursed every day.

Mind you, we also cursed the big so and so when he came down like a ton of bricks on us; make the tiniest of mistakes and his wrath would be felt. Errors were not allowed in his wonderful world. Miss out one piece of detail in a report or fail to record a witness statement and holy fuck look out.

But walking along the corridor to his office, I had not a care in the world. My holidays were about to start and the wife and me were off to Cornwall for a fortnight.

She had seen the holiday advert in the newspaper and decided we needed a wee change. So she telephoned and booked us bed and breakfast in a wee hotel in a place called St Ives. I was about to have some sunshine and sit my arse down on a Cornish beach. There would be Fish and chips, scones and clotted cream. I could hardly wait to get on my Holidays and get the hell away from here. I could sit on an English beach and enjoy the sunshine.

I tapped on his door not quite knowing what to expect, only hoping it was a goodbye handshake and have a nice wee holiday speech. The big gruff voice called me in.

I was about to say "Yes sir what can I do for you", but never got the chance; the not a care in the world smile was quickly wiped off my face.

"Niven I'm giving you your first case."

I think my jaw dropped a mile, but he carried on talking to me

"The department's inundated with case after case at this minute so ..." he held out a brown file. "Here you can type your reports and keep them in this." I reluctantly took it from him.

"What is it?" I pathetically asked.

He looked at me as if I had just grown horns.

"Niven, don't ask me stupid fucking questions. That's an empty file for your case notes; I've got no one else free just now. So get your arse along to Lennoxtown. They've found a missing kid buried under a bush."

The words hit me like a sledgehammer. "But, super, my holiday's start tomorrow; me and the wife are—"

"Well the sooner you get along to Lennoxtown and catch the bastard who has fucked your holidays, the quicker you get going on your jollies," he growled." Lennoxtown now!"

"Can't Jackson take ...?"

"Jackson's going with you!"

"But, super, there's surely someone else," I asked forlornly.

"Niven, we're all fucking busy. I've got gang warfare on just now and stabbings every fucking night and day."

"But, super".

The stare and the growl were enough, I knew it was pointless arguing. My sunshine holiday just clouded over with big dark rain clouds. I was well and truly fucked. I could feel the weight of the world drop onto my shoulders. My very first case and it was going to be a buried kid. I wasn't ready for this.

I turned and stepped out his office only to be hastily called back.

"Niven, the two locals are ..." He paused and glanced down at a piece of paper in front of him, "O'Brien and Wilson. See them at the station house in Lennoxtown and try to beat the newspaper crews. Once they get wind of this it'll be a fucking circus." and with one more bark, "Shut that fucking door!" he was finished with me.

I closed the door and stood for a minute looking at the painted panels and the name plate on the door. My mind was numb, what had just happened?

Missing kid, buried? Lennoxtown?

Me catch the, what on God's green earth just happened? What was I going to tell Deirdre? She would be packing our suitcase and setting out our travel clothes. I was fucked. The rosy picture I had in my mind of a little B&B in St Ives, of beautiful sunny days, ice cream cones walking along the beach hand in hand, just disappeared in one big puff of smoke.

The only thing I had to do today was go to the bank and draw some money and fill the car up with petrol. Buy two train tickets and enjoy the countryside flying past you on the train journey.

My holiday was tomorrow. Two weeks away from all this hassle. Now my day was well and truly shagged. I wanted to rap the door and ask if he was kidding me on, but I thought better of it.

I walked along to my office with the empty brown file in my hand. I had to phone Deirdre and somehow explain to her I would be a wee bit late.

She would understand.

It comes with the job. She'll forgive me I told myself, but who was I kidding. She'll be as mad as hell if we don't get away. Yep I was well and truly fucked. I decided it would be better to phone her later. Once I knew how deep I was in the shit.

The case! How could McCluskey give me a case the day before my holidays? The old bastard had it in for me. I slammed the empty file onto my desk, as out and out panic set in. My wife was about to kill me.

Kenny Jackson popped his head round the door, "You and me eh? Our first case on our own. Exciting eh?"

"Kenny it's not exciting, I'm well and truly fucked. Deirdre is going to kill me. How could that old bastard give me a – I mean us – a murder case the day before my holidays?" Kenny just shook his head and smiled. I didn't know if he agreed with me or he was disagreeing at what I was saying. My mind was racing.

The road from Springburn to Lennoxtown winds its way through Bishopbriggs and Torrance. It takes about 40 minutes from the station and as I drove along my anger abated slightly down to raging. I moaned the face off every driver and found fault with every pedestrian and anybody else I could see. I was having what the wife would call an "Annie Rooney" which in her eyes was a wee mad turn all about me. And the sad thing about my rant was, there was only Jackson to listen to it and he never said a bloody thing. I think he thought I'd get it out my system quicker if he kept quiet, or I would start on him. This bloody road didn't help either it was bend after bend from Torrance to Lennoxtown. I came up to the Tee junction on the Campsie road and with no traffic coming, turned left. A couple of hundred yards further on I could see the slag heaps from the old pits and the Field Park to my left where I had played football there in my younger days. It was the only football park in central Scotland where a river flowed around the touchline. I remember if you shot at goal and the ball flew wide it often ended up in the river. Then the boys from the local team would run and jump into the river to retrieve it. What a place.

I drove on along Main Street passed the Trinity church on the left hand side and the Chapel on the right and the station house was located on the left side of the road another hundred yards on.

I came to a halt outside the station house and I left the engine ticking over, I was wondering what was in store for us and then it started to rain. The BBC radio forecaster had predicted showers for the Glasgow area and I had promised myself bright blue skies for Cornwall. Why didn't I go on holiday last Friday? I swore at McCluskey for assigning me this. I turned the engine off and as I got out of the car I looked up and down the main street of Lennoxtown. I had a pub in front of me, a paper shop and grocers next to that. There were houses all the way up the road to the High Church entrance and a school lane about 30 yards from where I stood. I looked at the grocer's shop and thought the Bobbies here didn't have to go far for their morning rolls and their *Daily Record*. The pub just across the road was pub number four if my mind was right. A couple of big rain drops hit the back of my neck forcing me to slam the car door and hurry inside the station house, before it came bucketing down. Jackson was a whisker behind me.

I opened the station front door and was met with stares from the two cops standing behind the counter in front of me. Their hang dog expressions said it all.

"O'Brien and Wilson I presume," I said reaching out my hand.

"He's O'Brien and I'm Wilson and are you boys lost?"

"If that's an attempt at humour it didn't work. DC Paul Niven and this here is DC Kenny Jackson from Springburn. Don't let the youthful looks fool you. We've been assigned this murder case or should I say, we've been handed this case." The two local cops shot us both a questioning look that saved them from asking us the usual. "You boys not a bit young to be DC's?"

I shrugged off the feeling of inadequacy and noticed that the word "murder" hit deep as the two officers had glanced at each other.

The resignation that this was a murder case and of a local and especially a young local lad, would have had an adverse effect on the pair of them. Christ it would hit me hard if it was one of the kids from around where I lived. Kid's murders were the worst you could work on. There were never any winners, only losers. Everybody felt it.

Immediate family and friends devastated and the devastation always turned to hatred towards the perpetrator.

The media would then whip the general public into the horror and hate mode. The newspapers always made money on a case that they reported on for days and days. The longer they could write headlines, the more money went into the coffers.

"You want a cup of tea or something before we start?" Wilson asked.

The words hung there, I couldn't immediately answer and I must have looked a right prat with my mouth open like a big fish waiting to take the bait.

"Might as well have a cuppa, don't know when I'll get another one. Milk and two sugars for me and DC Jackson will have only milk."

Kenny shot me a look. I ignored it.

"Has anybody showed up from the Procurator Fiscals office yet?"

"No, not yet but we expect he'll be on his way."

I had to start thinking quicker and to be seen to be taking charge, or the two cops could end up questioning our competency.

Wilson lifted the hinged section of the counter. "Come in and sit down in the office here and we'll get you up to speed with what we know."

I followed O'Brien into their office and sat down on one of the chairs on the customer's side of the desk.

O'Brien was the first to speak. He appeared a bit nervous to me but he got down to the nitty gritty and opened a brown folder in front of him. He started to read from his notes.

All I could do at first as he started to speak was to think it looked like the empty brown file I had.

"The body was found by one of the hospital search teams in the woods just up from Whitefield. In the woods next to the waterfall to be exact. The location is on Lennox Castle Hospital grounds. We'll take you there in a couple of minutes. The body was found under a Rhododendron bush in a real shallow grave. Lennox castle hospital has approximately 1000 inmates of various mental disorders and a few hundred staff.

"Has anyone made a formal identification of the boy?" I asked.

"His clothes match the description of what the missing boy was wearing. We told the search team not to dig any more or disturb the crime scene until someone in authority got there."

"So you haven't seen the body?"

O'Brien looked slightly embarrassed and answered that he hadn't.

"So who is watching over the crime scene then?" I asked.

"The lads that found him."

"So long as they don't touch anything that might be evidence," Jackson piped in.

"We told them not to touch anything."

Wilson arrived with the mugs of tea and gave us what we had asked for.

O'Brien went on, "We've also recalled all the other search teams and sent them home.

Again I answered, "Good, but time was marching on. Has anybody spoken to the parents yet?"

"Not yet, but I do know that the local priest and their minister is with them. We were waiting for you to arrive and take over really."

I hated this part but had to tell one of them that they would have to go and tell the parents that a boy answering to the description given was found and that one of the parents would be asked to come down here and formally make an identification, making certain it was their son.

Wilson must have known what was coming next and before I spoke he volunteered to do the necessary.

O'Brien swallowed hard. "Right then come on and I'll take you up to the spot where the boy was found." He turned to his partner, "Bill try not to be too long with the Smiths because the bloke from the Procurator's office will be—" He was stopped mid-sentence

"Okay," was the saddened, subdued answer.

We left the office and walked down the back stairs to the carpark which was at the rear of the Station house. Climbing into the Black Maria as it was fondly known, or the Paddy wagon, the heavens opened and it pissed it down.

Fucking brilliant, here we go again, working in the bloody rain I thought quietly to myself as we drove out of the car park and turned left up the main street. We passed the High Church gates on the right and a Town hall on the left. O'Brien stayed silent as the windscreen wipers struggled to cope with the deluge that was Scotland's weather. Further along the road we passed a small pond on the right hand side with swans gracefully swimming about in the rain, before going down a bit of a hill. There were council houses on the right with a road going off to the right signposted Glen road.

"Whitefield," O'Brien muttered.

The entrance to Lennox castle Hospital was on the left hand side of the road and O'Brien drove through the stone pillars opening next to a small house, which I found out later was the North Lodge house. On either side of the pillars stood large green steel gates, which I also found out, were permanently open. He drove on for about another 200 yards and stopped the van beside several other cars next to a stone built bridge. We got out the van and I pulled my collar up against the rain. We climbed over a green railing fence and gingerly slipped down the side of the bridge and then followed O'Brien along the path by the river's edge. You could hear the rain hitting the tree leaves above and the river gurgling over the rocks on its merry way to the River Kelvin. As I walked along the riverbank, I looked at the diversity of the trees and I couldn't help but notice one thing, there was no birdsong in the woods. Maybe they didn't like singing in the rain. I smiled at that one.

The search team was standing to my left under the canopy of a big chestnut tree for shelter. I could feel everyone's eyes on me as I trudged through the mud towards them.

As we neared, one of the lads from the search team walked forward and O'Brien shook his hand.

"Jack Harrop this is DC Paul Niven and DC Ken Jackson from Springburn."

He offered his hand and I shook it. "So did you find the body?" I asked.

"No, Bobby did," he said, pointing to another one of their group.

"OK I'll speak to him in a minute. Show us where you found him."

"The rest of you stay here," I said curtly.

We came across the bush and Harrop pointed at it. "He's in there."

I have to admit my first thought was that it was a magnificent specimen of a Rhododendron bush. What made that thought jump into my head, I'll never know, but it did. I wanted to look at the scene for myself, so I shot a glance at Jackson and he nodded. He went off to my left and walked carefully back along the bank of the river looking for footprints or anything remotely suspicious.

The search team remained huddled and quiet under the relative shelter of a big old chestnut tree. I knew that we would have to interview them all and take statements as to what they had done during the search. That was going to take time and time was a luxury I didn't have. I wanted to be the hell away from here and have the case wrapped up sharpish. But that wasn't going to happen. The killer was not there to own up to this.

As if by magic the rain stopped and our small attentive audience were all silently watching as a couple of rookie Detectives from Springburn went through their paces.

I slowly approached the bush looking down at the ground looking for signs of a struggle. I touched the leaves on the bush as I walked all around it. There was no blood or broken branches. Mind you my immediate thoughts were that the rain might have washed any signs of blood away anyway. I lifted back a wet branch at the entrance to the bush canopy and I bent down and entered the grave site.

First of all I was amazed at how much room there was under the bush, the branches had formed a canopy. There were no other plants on the ground and I reckoned the reason being that there was no sunlight getting through the dense foliage, so nothing would grow and the ground was bone dry. With all the showers this area had, I was amazed that the ground under the bush was as dry as a stick. Seriously, the things that go through your mind. I had to concentrate.

Looking down at the grave I could see the small hand and a blue sleeve of a child wearing what looked to be a blue jumper. I could make out a set of Footprints in the dirt and what appeared to be depression marks around the grave but there was definitely nothing else to note. So I dismissed the footprints to be the lad that found him.

I checked the ground around my feet and noticed what appeared to be drag marks. It looked like heel marks and that they had been crudely brushed over. It had to be drag marks because this was not where the boy was killed. There was no evidence of any struggle here. There was no blood, then again that was me thinking that the wee boy would have struggled, but what if he had been unconscious and killed here?

I knelt at the makeshift mound but at the opposite side to the footprints. My knees on my trousers were going to get dirty. As gently as I could I removed the remaining twigs and the small branches from the rough grave and carefully brushed the dirt by hand from where I thought the wee boy's face was. I made gentle sweeping actions with the back of my hand and as I got closer to the face, the dirt was giving up evidence of blood.

Giving up evidence of blood what was I saying? You could smell the blood mixed in with earth. As I cleared it away from the corpse, I tried to compose myself, as to what I was about to uncover. There was a wee boy's face under this shit and it did not matter as to how many times you stared down at death, it was horrific when you found yourself looking down at a child.

I don't want to paint such a gruesome picture of what I found, but from what I saw it was obvious to me that this attack had been so brutal that a weapon must have had been used.

I was looking for one very deranged angry individual capable of doing this to a child and he had definitely used some sort of a weapon.

I got up from my knees and brushed the dirt and leaves from my trousers I was going to leave well alone for the coroner and stepped back out from the bush. I looked back along the line from the bush and attempted to follow the directions of the drag marks.

I followed my instinct and walked slowly back a few more yards from the bush. Jackson joined me and we both scoured the terrain for clues.

"What we got in there Paul?"

"A Fucking mess."

"What you reckon, it's him for definite?"

"By the description we have it's him and what appears to me is that he's been savagely beaten to death in a frenzied attack. Hopefully when the Fiscal gets here he will confirm that and tell us what he was beaten with. Go on have a look if you want."

Kenny turned and did the same as I did; he approached the bush ever so gingerly. I kept on looking for a broken plant here and there and I kept tracking back until I reached a big Beech tree, not far from the bush. There was something here, I could sense it. My gut feeling told me so. The area around looked as if it had been roughed up, but that could have been the wind and the weather. Or could it have been a struggle. Could this have been the place where the boy was beaten to death?

I scoured all around the trees and paths and still found no concrete evidence of an assault as far as I could make out. But I would have the rest of the team start looking here for clues. The rain hadn't helped that was for sure. But how long had the wee boy been dead and half buried? How many hours? And in that time how often had it rained since he was posted missing. As I looked around I noticed that there was a rope swing on the beech tree and that it was kept high up in a fork in the branches. Only used by the bigger lads I thought. So kids played here now and then and of course they did. Kids and woods went together, after all this was just a big adventure playground to them.

But that had all changed now; it was no longer a playground.

It was no longer a place where children's laughter rang out as they enjoyed their rope swing.

It was the scene of a horrific murder.

We would have to have the local boys find out which kids played here and if anybody saw anything.

My St Ives Holiday was disappearing fast.

What was I saying; My St Ives holiday was a thing of the past. There was no way this was going to be solved quickly. Even Sherlock Holmes would struggle with this one.

We had a murder in the grounds of a mental hospital.

Any one of a thousand lunatics could have done this.

And how the fuck was I going to find out which one?

I cursed McLuskey.

I cursed Lennox Castle Hospital and all its fucking lunatics.

I cursed the bush that had hidden the wee boy.

I cursed my luck over and over.

I had landed in the biggest pile of shit ever and as I cursed, the heavens opened up again and it pissed it down.

Chapter 16

It was August 1967, McCluskey's last year before he retired. The gruff old bastard would be finally out of our station and Jackson and I could hopefully relax. Ever since we came up with plums, (the case of the murdered boy in the mental hospital grounds what seemed like years ago) he had been on our backs ever since calling us useless fucks. He didn't acknowledge the successes we had, but harked back to our one glorious failure.

That case had us or should I say me and Jackson spending days, weeks, chasing our tails interviewing staff, talking to all the locals getting us nowhere. Nobody had seen a thing. The young lad had managed to walk all the way from his house, all the way through Lennoxtown, past shops, past bus stops, up to Whitefield, jump a wall into the hospital grounds around eight in the morning, as if he was the invisible man. In our defence even Sherlock bloody Holmes would have failed as well.

We had talked to bus drivers, until we were blue in the face, locals who walked their dogs in the morning, paper boys who delivered the *Daily Record*, to folk in houses on the Campsie Glen road and even put an appeal in the *Kirkintilloch Herald*, asking for any information and got fuck all. We had interviewed every staff member of the lunatic asylum and came up with plums.

Even the minutest of evidence we found at the scene, gave us little to go on. We had a few broken branches a few broken plants to establish where the murder had happened and then nothing. In fact failing to have even one definite suspect didn't please the old one at all. Every time one of us got passed his office we hoped the door would be closed because if it was open, you'd hear "useless fuck" uttered. To say it was disconcerting would be an actual understatement. After a while and I mean it was nearly fifteen months I think, people would actually start to believe what the old bastard was saying was right.

The morning of August the 24th was the beginning of another nightmare as I was summoned back into his office.

I dreaded knocking the door and hearing that old grump barking "come in" but I had to do it. I hesitated and then courage or stupidity took over and I rapped his door hard. To hell with him I thought.

"Come in."

I opened the door and stepped back into hell.

The look of distaste wasn't there on his face but it was replaced with more of what I can only describe as a worried look; he was definitely frowning.

"Niven," he began. "I'm going to hand you another belter of a case. I don't know if it's definitely related to the last one but there's a chance." He was hesitant.

I could feel it coming, there was a bombshell and he was about to lay it on me.

"Because it's another missing kid." He looked me straight in the face. It went into my very soul. "It's a girl this time and she's from Lennoxtown. She went missing yesterday afternoon."

My heart genuinely sank and the very expression on my face said "Oh my god".

It was something that I did not want to hear ever again; "another missing kid". That look I must have had on my face at that moment somehow made him feel sorry for me I guess.

"You know the scenario and the locals." He sighed, "So it's down to you and Jackson again, to go over your old stomping ground."

I couldn't say anything, I was dumbstruck.

"Listen, Son, I know that's the last place you wanted to go to and the last thing you probably wanted to hear from me, but this might be the same guy. It really might be the same sad fuck who murdered that wee boy that ..." he hesitated looking for the correct phrase.

"You couldn't catch" was what he meant, but I had caught the resigned look on his face.

"Anyway, you and Jackson have another crack at this bastard. He has to leave some clues this time. He's been away and quiet, but this tells me the bastard's back."

"But, sir, are we to assume that this girl is dead and that we're dealing with the same killer?" The words tumbled out of my mouth before I could think straight.

"Niven, it's another missing child from Lennoxtown and that big fucking mental hospital is still there, right next to the fucking place she has vanished from. Be honest what the fuck do you think? Me – I've got a real bad feeling about this and I haven't had that feeling since the last time that bloody place was mentioned."

I watched him sit forward and spread his hands on the desk as the swearing continued.

"We couldn't catch the bastard the last time because he was real clever in picking his site, remember? He never left us any clues. He vanished into thin air and we never caught him. Now me I'm an old sceptic and I'm going to think the worse here. If I'm wrong and I hope to Christ I am, it'll be a fucking miracle and a bloody nice ending to some family's worst fears. But, Niven, I don't need to tell you to be your usual calm self when you meet everyone again, but I have a feeling that this is some sick bastard just getting started and I don't like it. I can feel it in my gut and it's sickening me. We have to catch this guy before we have to count higher than a definite two."

My breathing must have become shallower as he spoke, because I was aware of taking deep breaths when he finished talking. I noticed that he looked tired and beaten and it was as if someone had just given him some terrible news about his own family. That was the very first time I had seen him as a person getting old. It's something you didn't associate with McCluskey. He was a hard man, a man made of granite with features chiselled in stone, but I saw him that morning in a different light. The only thing I could think of saying was, "Yes, sir."

It was like Déjà vu going back to Lennoxtown and meeting O'Brien and Wilson under similar circumstances. They hadn't moved on and were still in the same old station house, with the same old cream paint on the walls. They even had the same old posters on the notice board if my memory served me right. The only thing I could see that had changed from our last visit was that they had new coffee mugs to offer us. I declined anything to drink as did Kenny.

They personally hadn't changed one bit as far as I could tell. They appeared and looked the same and we shook hands like old friends do, when you come to pay your respects at a funeral.

We immediately got down to questions and answers about the missing girl and I realised just how quick we were to all point the finger again at one of the asylum inmates. We had followed that train of thought with the young boy and that got us travelling down a cul-de sac. I was thinking I could have said a dead end, but I think that would have been inappropriate.

Was this going to be the same?

Were we going to follow the same footsteps as the last enquiry?

Were we going to make the same mistakes?

Kenny and I took the back seats of Wilson's car and I had instant recall, as we drove past the Town hall and the small pond up at Whitefield. Recollections came flooding back and my heart sank even lower when we drove into Lennox Castle Hospital grounds again. It was history repeating itself. We got out of the car and proceeded to walk along the riverbank. I had walked on the opposite riverbank two years before. I tried not to look across the river at the spot where we found Graham Smith. I couldn't help myself and I paused briefly to look over and see the bush. I was actually amazed it was still there. They hadn't cut it down for some reason. I would have done most definitely. The woods were different this time. I got that feeling and I wondered why? Then it dawned on me that this time there was birdsong resounding through the woods.

"She's not here," I said out loud.

"How do you know?" Wilson asked.

"Listen to the birds. They're chirping. The last time we found that wee boy there was nothing only silence. I'm telling you she's not here."

As we walked quietly down to the waterfall, Tom told us when we got there that this was the last known place she had been seen. She had simply vanished from the pebble area on this side of the river.

I could hear Kenny muttering to himself and could make out the odd "Fuck sake".

Tom and Bill were keen to get the whole shebang going again and suggested search teams, dogs and volunteers; I could see that self-same look of inevitability in their faces. I just couldn't believe that I was here again and we would be going over the same old ground. But we had to inspect the pebbled area first in case we could find anything at all.

"Has anybody been over the ground?"

"No. We were told to wait for you guys."

I had questions and they had to be answered at that very moment. We or should I say I forgot the young girl's name and I asked, "What's the girl's name again?"

I know that I as a Detective should have remembered, but sometimes things slip, but what can I tell you, I'm only human.

Tom told me her name was Elizabeth Wilson. My heart dropped a few beats and I felt sick to my stomach as I glanced over at Bill expecting a glare of horror from him. But he shook his head confirming it wasn't his daughter and he said that they were not related. Least that was a bit of a relief, but not much. I know that sounds a bit hard saying I was relieved. But I was glad that it wasn't his daughter.

O'Brien told Kenny and me what they had been told by the last person to see Elizabeth alive.

Rachel McKenzie was a 15 year old teenager full of life and she was in tears telling her story to Tom and Bill. This was her best friend she was trying to tell them about. Through heart-wrenching sobs she eventually managed to relate that they had been swimming and picnicking with Elizabeth and they were having a really good time. Rachel had said that she remembered that her mother had asked her to put the laundry out on the washing line to dry. Rachel had forgotten to do that and she knew she would be chastised for forgetting, so she had asked Elizabeth if she wanted to come and help. Elizabeth had laughed at that and had said she would wait there for Rachel. Rachel had called her lazy bones and they both laughed at that. Rachel had left Elizabeth in a rush with the words that she'd be back in a wee while. When she returned Elizabeth was nowhere to be found and Rachel thought that she must have gone home. But the strange thing that had puzzled Rachel was that her own duffel bag was left there on the stones in the exact same place she had laid it down. She couldn't imagine Elizabeth leaving it there if she had gone home, she would have taken Rachel's bag as well as her own. Rachel had gone round to Elizabeth's house looking for her. She had rung the door bell and had knocked on the door and got no response. She had decided that she would go round later and see Elizabeth. Rachel had returned back around tea time when she knew the whole family would be in, she had been told that Elizabeth hadn't come back and that immediately had set the alarm bells ringing.

The phone lines were red hot.

Everyone in Lennoxtown remembered what had happened to the Smith boy, so panic stations set in. O'Brien and Wilson didn't wait the customary 24 hours this time; they, too, hit the send for help button.

There were certain similarities between the two cases and that was there for all to see, the only major difference this time was the gender of the missing child and the fact that we had all grown older.

We all felt in our hearts that we were about to arrive at the same outcome as the last time. We just couldn't admit it out loud but I guessed that was exactly how we were all feeling.

History was about to repeat itself again I was sure of it.

I told Kenny and O'Brien to start looking on this side of the river and that Wilson and me would cross the waterfall and start looking on the other side. There was a trickle of water going over the falls so crossing was going to be easy. If I was unlucky I was only going to get my shoes wet.

We retraced our steps going over the same old ground and I thought that the weeds had grown a bit and that there were more nettle clumps obvious. It proved that the kids didn't play here anymore.

As we got closer I had to look under the Rhododendron bush where we had found young Smith, just in case. Copy cat killer syndrome sprung to mind. I knew that was one search I'd rather someone else would make, but I felt obligated to do it myself. The hairs on the back of my neck stood up and my skin felt clammy just thinking about what I uncovered the last time. But you never know, if and I say a big if, the killer was one of the asylum in-mates, maybe he was just stupid enough to repeat his last kill. I pulled back the branches and looked under the canopy and felt relieved that there was no mound of earth waiting for me.

We set up to interview the hospital staff and we hoped that they would their usual helpful selves again. We hoped to have a team of them, like the last time, volunteering to help search for Elizabeth. I could imagine and almost see the look of dread on their faces. I had visions of them resigning themselves that it was going to be a thankless task.

Why would I be wrong in that thought?

It had been the last time.

We had all been here before.

My gut feeling was that we were never going to find her alive, but I prayed to god to let this outcome be different from the last one.

But in all truth the odds were stacked against us; we were in a killer's playground, on his field of operandi, treading on the same paths we followed the last time. We were well aware of the secret places kids would hide. We tirelessly checked them again and again. We would have to trample over the six and a half thousand acre woodlands with a fine toothcomb again.

We met the parents in the station house and how can you seriously look a parent in the eye and tell him or her not to worry, to try to stay positive, that we will find her?

There is one theory that you can try to soften their shock by talking to them calmly and softly and this somehow allows them to focus, because they hang on to your every word.

Your soft dulcet tones act as a medicinal tool that they want and crave.

To be honest with you, most of the time it doesn't work. Most can't take in what you're saying to them because they are far too upset to completely listen to your droll. They only want to blame someone for what's happened and they demand action and answers from you. As I said it was only a theory.

I mean how can you stand there while a married couple, experience their worst nightmare right in front of you and you are not allowed to show emotion? It's programmed into us that we can offer sympathy to them, but not to show emotion.

And do you know what the worst thing is? You have to lie to them, knowing what you know from experience. I stood there in front of two human beings who were breaking their hearts and I had to tell them a lie. "Don't worry we'll find her," I said lying through my back teeth. I already had resigned myself to this girl being found with her throat cut.

It is a well-known fact that you have to find abductees within the first 36 hours or you can forget finding them alive.

This time it was three and a half months before we found the body. This time the body was hidden in a culvert where a 36" diameter concrete pipe passed under the main forest track. The track allowed heavy vehicles access to sections of the forest where the lumber was being cut. This track was the main artery for access. It was located in a section of fir woods, to the west of Netherton oval. When our search teams had looked over that section of the woods they had walked over the top of it; somebody hadn't noticed the concrete slab covered in fir cones and dead branches. Someone hadn't looked at the geography of the drainage ditch. Someone hadn't seen the very small amount of water disappearing into the end of a concrete 36" diameter half-buried pipe. Maybe it hadn't rained for days; maybe there was no water in sight. Who knows? The 36" diameter pipe had a rusty mesh grating over it and there was debris clogging up the entrance, so somebody had dismissed looking any further.

We would never have found her, but for some small kid being dared to crawl his way some 30 yards along a buried 36" diameter concrete storm drain by his older brother. What in God's name made them do this?

Why did the older brother remove the mesh from over the front of the pipe?

The youngster must have been terrified as he stumbled along in the dark, in the damp, until the moment he fell over something smelly.

Now you may ask why he did it. Why in God's name was he there crawling along a dark wet cold forest storm drain in November?

It was a dare. The elder brother dared his younger sibling to do it. He goaded him into not being chicken. Not to being a scaredy cat or it was words of that ilk.

The elder brother had said that he would open up the concrete hatch cover to allow light into the tunnel so the younger one knew how far along he had to go.

The elder brother wanted to play a trick on his younger brother by delaying opening up the hatch cover, but it was after hearing his brother's terrifying scream, the hatch cover came off very quickly.

The discovery of the young girl was too much for the brothers. They raced home to tell their parents what they had found. The younger brother cried all the way home.

That wee boy was traumatized for months and I'll bet you he still has nightmares to this day.

The girl's face was unrecognizable.

Three and a half months' of decay and being eaten by vermin could not have been a pretty sight.

She must have looked like a real zombie to that young boy.

CHAPTER 17

1996

I closed the file and closed my eyes. To this day I can still imagine hearing that young lad screaming. I remember both the brothers having to stand in front of us and tell their story. As they sobbed we listened and I was particularly drawn to the younger brother reliving his nightmare. The young lads' father was almost in tears as he held his son close. He, too, was in a state as he listened to the story being told again. I felt for the family and I really cannot explain the way something like that hits you. I felt completely useless.

The older brother tried to explain to us, as to what they were doing in the woods that day and how they came across her.

To this day I will never forget the look on the wee one's face. It will haunt me forever. I had never seen someone look so scared in my life.

I was reading an article in one of the tabloids last Sunday about human rights. I was sitting in my conservatory having a cup of tea, enjoying peace and quiet when the article caught my attention. It was one of those stories you would skip by, or turn the page not wanting to read about it. But this story caught my eye and it made interesting reading. Some female journalist was off on a 'let's put the world to rights' story with a get at one of our establishments, the prison service. The story went on and on about how inhumane it was to incarcerate prisoners in cramped cells and to deny them any form of exercise or recreation for hours on end. That there was no justification for lengthy spells of seclusion and that the British penal system was archaic. It was one of those stories that makes us cops boil. These people haven't a clue as to why those bastards are locked up. Human rights for prisoners, you're having a laugh? What did the writer know about the rights of the people who were killed? For God's sake we just had the Dunblane massacre of all those children by that fucking maniac Thomas Hamilton in March and here she wanted prisoners' rights to be looked at. It really got me incensed.

Dunblane was the reason why we locked up those mad bastards for life and if it was up to me I'd throw away the key. I was so angry that I very nearly wrote into the paper with my side of the argument. But I never did. Spouting off to your own conservatory walls and ranting and raving to the wife was as far as it got. Anyway that got me thinking about our most notorious serial killer and where he was and what he'd be doing at that present time. In fact the next day when I went back to work I pulled some old case files from our archives deep down in the building and set them down on my desk. Why oh why, you ask, did I want to go through all the crap again? Was it a deep down morbid interest, or was it self-gratification that we actually managed to eventually track down and catch the son of a bitch. In fact to be truthful that's not really what I call him. He had to have been the son of the devil; of Old Nick himself.

I placed the two old brown files in front of me and looked at the writing on the front of them. Thirty odd years have passed since he first started killing and it still gives me the shivers to think what he did to his victims.

I opened the first file in front of me and laid it down on my desk. Ask me why we had kept a closed case file in a dusty old cabinet and I couldn't give you a truthful answer. After all, the files had been catalogued onto a hard drive on our main frame computer years ago. Everything relevant to one of our real naughty boys, who were all still locked up, was recorded in a megabyte or gigabyte or something like that. I could log in and trace any case through our data base and have it in front of me on my screen in seconds. I could print it off if I wanted. But there was still something about opening up a file and seeing the actual case notes, we had written all those years ago. It gave me a buzz and there was a distinct aroma from the file, sort of a musty smell and reading the first page was always chilling, as the memory of it kicks in and I remembered both cases, as if it was yesterday.

Both files told of what we thought were Nelson's first and second kills and both cases had remained unsolved for years. What we now know is that the second file, the one we had on the young girl was not his second kill. It was more like number three or four and it was scary to think that Nelson had been an adolescent when he had started killing.

I laid my hands on top of the brown folder and looked at the cover. Did I honestly want to open it up? I can't tell you why I opened it up, but I did. You know it's the age old thing "Should I or shouldn't I".

The front page was a faded A4 grey sheet of paper with the only words typed in capital letters.

File 1. Nelson Harrop.

I hesitantly turned to the next page and a précis of the case was there for me to read.

He had killed a young boy in the grounds of a mental hospital on the outskirts of Glasgow. He was a young boy himself and we officers had followed the wrong line of enquiry and put it down to a frenzied attack by one of the mental asylum's inmates. Trying to get a true statement and a conviction from one of those lunatics was impossible. We had a couple of hundred inmates who owned up to Smith's murder each saying that they did it. Morally the case would have been tossed out of the court. The press would have had a field day if we had tried to pin a murder on someone who didn't know what day it was and couldn't even spell sane.

I closed the file and put it to the side. The second brown folder was in the same format.

I was torturing myself. I looked sadly down at the brown document and I again laid my hands on it. Was I following a ritual? Part of me said "open it up and read it" and the other part of me said "don't be so bloody stupid, you know what it says". I closed the case file and put it down on top of the first one. I didn't need to open it up as the memories of my second visit to Lennoxtown came flooding back. Elizabeth or Beth as she was called would have been married by now and her kids would have been out and about playing somewhere. What a waste of a young life. I sat there feeling defeated as the memories washed over me. There were regrets and thoughts about why we didn't do this or why we didn't do that. Why did we not look there or ... but as I said I was torturing myself needlessly.

It was late in the 70s when three scientists came up with DNA testing and I remember having to go back to Lennoxtown years after to ask the family if we could exhume their daughter's coffin to allow us to re-examine their daughter's clothes. Man I hated that and the hairs still stand up on my neck when I remember the look of sheer horror on the wife's face. But the husband listened to what I had to say and after much deliberation and arguing with his missus, they reluctantly agreed and the coroner and the forensics team got their coffin dug up and miraculously the forensics got a sample of DNA from what was left inside.

Standing in Lennoxtown's High Church graveyard and standing stock still over that young girl's grave, the diggers working under the gaze of the reverend's glare of hatred, I felt so ashamed.

The resigned and embarrassed look on my face that day must have told some story.

The feeling I had in the pit of my stomach then was indescribable. But I knew that we had to do it and by doing that unholy thing, we could possibly get a pointer in the killer's direction. The job sucked when we had to disregard the family's heartache and the wrath of the local vicar. I never went to look when they took the coffin away to their lab in Glasgow to open it up because that bit scares. The typed up forensic report is a much better way of finding out if there is evidence there, rather than looking at a decomposed child being examined. I have seen bodies in different states and it is horrifying what one human being can do to another one and it takes on a real sickening feeling when it's kids involved. Unfortunately that's all part of my job and when I have a choice of looking at the newly murdered or the decomposed remains, give me the new all the time. When you get a result and catch the bastard it makes the entire *Nightmare on Elm Street* worthwhile.

Those two files had been just two of the many murder cases, which had been pushed onto my desk at the time and it was our inability, to find the one piece of conclusive evidence to convict the killer that sucked. Of course he wasn't the only murderer we had on our files. Christ we had dozens of cases on at the time and killers that we were trying miserably to catch. Don't get me wrong there had been plenty successes along the way that we could boast about but this one here being left open, meant that the file got put in a cabinet in archives and marked as unsolved. The cabinet wasn't full, far from it, there were not as many files in the unsolved part, as you would think, but those two files I had in front of me had been.

Sometimes back then, we got lucky and got a wee break or a definite clue and our doggedness got us a result and we managed to trap one of our many felons.

Do you know Glasgow has always had the reputation of being a really dangerous city and in a way I think it was? Right up until it got nominated sometime in the 80s as the City of Culture, 1988 if I can remember right. Somehow it was as if overnight Glasgow changed and all the murdering scum were either in the nick or on a mortuary slab. The advancement of DNA had helped us in our hunt for these animals and to put concrete scientific, irrefutable evidence in front of juries. It helped us convince juries that the guilty were really guilty. It thankfully helped us catch a lot of the bad boys and our job turned more to depending on the Forensics team, to help us nail these people. Yep the Science of Forensics had given us another arrow to our bow and helped us get one up on the baddies.

Glasgow's streets had noticeably become that wee bit safer, or so it seemed way back then. Or was it that the criminals were getting that wee bit cleverer in evasion?

November of 1988 had Kenny Jackson and yours truly doing somersaults. That was the month when all our luck changed and we caught our serial killer.

Chapter 18

Here we go again, Nelson.

Be quiet.

I can hear something coming.

Be quiet they'll hear you.

Routine eh, Nelson, we're expecting this eh?

Don't start on me this early.

The trolley trundled up to Nelson's cell door. The peep hole opened up and a guard's eye sought out the whereabouts of Nelson. There was silence in the cell.

Nelson knew to shut up.

He knew damn fine what the drill was.

What was expected of him? Their rules.

Stand naked facing the guards, with your coverall on the floor.

Do not move when the breakfast tray is laid down on the floor.

But lately Nelson had altered this routine. It was time to start challenging their system. Test the guards, throw them off their game.

Instead of adhering to the warden's prison rules and face the guards and strip for inspection; he would turn his back on them as the door opened and he remove his canary-coloured coverall, tossing it backwards towards the door. He stood naked, arms out in the crucifix position showing his finely honed body – albeit only his rear – to his detainees. He was in excellent shape for being in seclusion; the exercise program he followed was proving dividends. Nelson was one strong individual. He was physically fit and dangerous. He knew the guards looked on with envy. He could feel their eyes burning daggers into his back. There was not one ounce of fat on Nelson's physique. He heard someone shuffle behind him and his replacement coverall, all neatly folded, was thrown down on the floor beside him. The guards didn't want confrontation; they did not want to make Nelson conform to the rules. If they could get these simple breakfast routines over and done with, without Nelson reacting violently then so be it. Let him do what the fuck he wanted. The warden would never know. This fucker was as bad as it got. He was a real monster and only the Americans knew worse. The Ted Bundy's of American notoriety were on a par with Nelson. So the guards played along with his game. No one spoke and no further orders were barked out at the prisoner. Nelson's new game of avoiding direct eye contact when he did turn around freaked some of them out. They expected him to stare, or growl something at them. But he did neither. He stood and let them give him the once over inspecting him for self-abuse on his stomach and groin areas. Nelson reached down, opened up the folded garment and stepped into it and buttoned it up. Nelson knew they were watching him like a hawk. He could feel their hatred, their wanting him to react so they could draw their truncheons and vent all their fury out on him. He felt their nervousness; he could hear the increased levels in their breathing patterns. He could smell their fear.

He felt their uneasiness as his tray of slop was lifted from the trolley and laid down on the floor. It was the same uncertainty as yesterday and the day before that.

Today there was only one medium-sized tray. He saw the plastic spoon put down on the tray. Nelson closed his eyes and concentrated deeply, listening to each one of the guards' movements. He memorised any small sound they inadvertently made. He knew how tall each guard was and their approximate weight, how they walked and how they moved. He knew who sniffed and who had a nervous habit of swallowing. It was all stored in Nelson's memory. All that information would be used in the attack when it came. Nelson knew that and so did the voice. All visits were discussed in detail. Of course any uttered word made Nelson's game ridiculously easy.

After putting the coverall on he stood like a statue. He played along and only at the last moment just as the door was closing sometimes he would thank two guards by name. It scared the shit out of them and Nelson knew that. He was good at mind games. He never mentioned the third member of the breakfast detail on purpose. It made the third guard feel safer and partly invisible. Nelson didn't mention him by name, but he knew who it was.

The cell door slammed shut and the bolts slid into place. It was time for Nelson to turn around and away from any last stare from the peep hole. He knew one of them would cast one last look. The other two would be outside glad that it was all over with nothing to report. They would be standing there trembling all trying to act casual.

He lowered his eyes and grinned. One day it would be him looking in at the three unconscious guards or would he kill them? Should they be unconscious or dead? That was a point still being debated in Nelson's mind. But it was getting close to decision and action time and that much

Nelson was sure of. The grin on his face grew wider, the peep hole closed.

He walked forward to lift the tray of food because this morning he was actually hungry. Bending down to lift the tray, the voice broke in.

So what is the culinary delight the chef has prepared for you today?

Let's see. Eggs Benedict with 2 lightly buttered pieces of wholemeal toast, a lightly buttered kipper and piping hot Kenyan blend coffee,

You jest Nelson. So it's cold Scrambled eggs and slices of dry toast again. Have they graced your breakfast tray with any cereal?

Yeah the usual runny porridge and a thimble of milk.

No stainless steel cutlery from Fortnam and Masons? You should complain, Nelson. This establishment should lose a few of its stars ratings.

Complain? That's a laugh. Not one of those bastards cares a jot about the food, whether it's warm or cold. They probably spat in the eggs when they were making them. Don't you realize I'm not liked?

Nonsense I like you.

Nelson laughed and sat down on the concrete floor to eat his breakfast with his plastic spoon.

Soon, real soon and I'm out of here

This time the voice laughed out loud.

So you've a plan then?

Between mouthfuls of cold scrambled eggs Nelson replied maybe.

You're formulating a way to get us out of here? Oh good!

I said maybe. Are you deaf?

It's just that you haven't mentioned any plan to me.

I know I haven't, but the idea is in its infancy right now. It's at the seed stage growing from a thought to an idea and then it will propagate into a master class of escapology.

Oh a master class of escapology. You're going to become Harry Houdini now?

Oh I am going to get out of here. I have been so patient.

But are we going to kill the guards?

I'm still thinking about that one.

What is there to think about?

I said I'm still at the pondering stage.

I think we should, as a punishment to the bastards that's locked us up here for all this time – the voice hissed *– kill the bastards, let's kill them all.*

Nelson resumed eating

Are you listening to me? I'm saying kill them and anyone else who gets in our way. Kill them with your bare hands. Rip out their fucking hearts and bleed them ...

Shut up! I'm eating here.

I'm only saying.

I know what you're saying and I'll decide where and when and if they die or live.

Well I'm for killing them.

I know what you want to do. You've made that so perfectly clear.

Why did you say if they die or live? It should be if they live or let die. Does that mean you have a preference and that's why you said die first?

I meant live or die.

So you do have a preference?

Shut up and leave me the fuck alone to finish this crap. You go on and on and on, you're giving me a headache, just leave me alone.

But Nelson that was a Bond movie.

What was?

Live or let Die. It starred Roger Moore

Shut up.

Nelson sat in silence the only noise his spoon scraping on the plastic plate. His mind in turmoil with what was said and what was wanted. But he knew it was down to a decision whether the guards would be lucky that day and he let them live.

He finished his breakfast and laid the tray at the door for collection. The guards would return in a few more minutes and take it away. Then a conversation would follow with his Jiminy Cricket until the arrival of the next meal.

The door opened and the tray was removed. There was no shaving routine this morning and that perplexed Nelson for a few minutes. He dismissed it as them playing silly buggers mind games.

No shaving this morning Nelson.

No I'm thinking about growing a beard.

You are a jester Nelson.

You think I couldn't grow one?

They wouldn't let you. Prison policy is no beards.

I know all about prison ...

He could hear something different. Nelson strained his hearing. There was nothing scheduled for this morning, unless they remembered about him not shaving.

He thought that he could make out four sets of footsteps. The fourth set was a lot softer than the noise the guards made, but it was there. Nelson's senses tingled.

There were definitely four sets of shoes. Someone was getting a visit that was for sure.

Was someone about to receive a beating? Guards don't come visiting in fours. The steps got louder where would they stop, which cell?

He clenched and relaxed his fists alternately. The demeanour had changed in an instant; he was now the alpha male again. He stood facing the door waiting in anticipation for the door to fly open and the four of them to come charging into his room with batons flailing beating the shit out of him. But there was no hurriedness, no change in the stride patterns as you would expect as the guards got nervous. Their adrenalin would be at a high and they would be pumped up if they were going to administer a thrashing and especially if they were going to have a crack at Nelson. He knew that they all wanted to, that wasn't rocket science.

They were outside his cell door.

There was a shout.

The door opened.

Nelson clenched both his fists hard.

There was no rush from the guards.

There was nothing barked at him.

No profanities shouted at him.

No batons raised for an attack.

Nelson saw the two big guards Woodall and Marbury, standing around six four and built like proverbial brick shit houses, in the corridor in front of the door and knew that the other guard would be close, but he was out of his line of sight. However there was another smaller grey haired gentleman standing in front of the two main guards. Nelson looked quizzingly at this strange looking apparition. He was wearing a tweed jacket, brown corduroy trousers and pink socks and brown shoes His tortoiseshell glasses balanced delicately on his nose and his ruddy complexion added to his aura and he was smiling at Nelson.

"Nelson, I'm Doctor Scotland. May I come in?"

Now that was new. May I come in? As If I have a fucking option thought Nelson.

There was something about this man's presence that Nelson could tangibly sense. He stepped back without saying anything. Nelson had never seen or heard anything about this man.

Was this a new tactic by the prison service?

But why would they do that? What could they possibly gain out of this?

Nelson's mind started thinking up questions and no sooner answering them in the same instant.

Was this little man there to put him off guard? Was this a ploy to encourage conversation with Nelson? To get him to say something? Is this going to be an interrogation?

"I'll take that as a yes then," the small man continued.

Nelson's eyes burned on the two guards. His mind desperately seeking answers. What was the real purpose behind this non-routine visit? What was their devious plan?

The prison service had to have an ulterior motive. Didn't it?

So what was it?

Provocation?

Intimidation?

Did they want to push Nelson for a violent reaction?

Did the Doctor want Nelson to show aggression? Is that what it was?

Did this new Doctor want clarification that Nelson was a violent criminal?

Did he have to see it for himself?

Dr Scotland stepped into the cell and stood not five feet from Nelson. The guards didn't move. They were poised, watching and waiting for a knee jerk reaction from Nelson.

Nelson transferred his gaze down to the character who stood before him. This was somebody that Nelson knew absolutely nothing about. Should he fear him or ridicule him? The thought of ridicule flashed through Nelson's brain.

The Doctor wasn't trembling or sweating with fear. He was calm and unaffected by Nelson's tense demeanour.

"Nelson, the boys have told me that for some time now you've stopped communicating and that your attitude towards them has changed somewhat. They feel that you're more hostile towards them. Is there anything the matter? Are you feeling OK? Is there anything you—?

"And you are?" Nelson asked quietly breaking all his rules.

Woodall and Marbury glanced at each other. This was new. Nelson actually spoke.

"I'm the new Prison Doctor, Doctor Scotland, and I was wondering if you wanted to tell me if there was something bothering you; or if there is anything physically wrong with you." He hesitated slightly looking at Nelson's face before continuing, "Are you feeling OK?"

Nelson opened his mouth as if to say something, but didn't.

"Regardless of what you did in the past," the Doctor eased himself to Nelson's left." the prison service has moved on and I would like to think that we have progressed …"

Nelson turned his body and followed the Doctor's movements and inwardly smiled. The good Doctor was about to offer Nelson new information he could digest and that at their first encounter. Nelson was inwardly rejoicing. He had detected a slight wobble in the Doctor's response. It was there a small pause between the words. "Doctor … and I was wondering" and another wee pause between, "you" and "regardless".

The guards wouldn't have cottoned on because they were too thick to notice a change in the Doctor's speech. But it was there. Nelson had heard it in the man's voice.

The guards had probably told the good Doctor not to expect any response from Nelson and that the Doctor wouldn't get one word out of him. Nelson wouldn't show any signs of answering.

The complete file the prison had on Nelson could have been read by the new Doctor in the confines of his office. In fact he would have most surely, so he wasn't flying blind. He wasn't stupid. Common sense tells you that you don't go into a lion's den without knowing something about the lion.

"… Progressed to the point where prisoners can honestly trust their Doctor again. I know that in the past few years you have probably become very sceptical of the standards of prison management. But this is 1996 and the new governor and I would like to think that this has all changed and you can tell me anything or ask for any medical help you need. There's a new broom in this prison and we hope to sweep some things clean. What has gone on in the past will stay in the past. This is the future and the way forward."

On the end of that statement he turned ever so slightly and glanced back at Woodall and Marbury. They never flinched. They had heard all the trumped up speeches before.

But this was good for Nelson because he had new information to take in and digest. New Governor, new Doctor, changes in the management system. This was all going to be good news for Nelson's escape plan when he formed one. That he was sure of.

Dr Scotland had stood in the cell for about five minutes now and Nelson was feeling more optimistic every minute he was there.

The seeds of a plan were about to be sown and in time a definite answer as to whether they all lived or died would be harvested.

Nelson broke the temporary silence, "Headaches. I sometimes get sore headaches behind my eyes." Nelson said quietly.

The Doctor pondered for a moment. "Headaches. Is that what's been bothering you? Why didn't you tell the boys? Have you never reported these before?" He turned and looked at Marbury who shook his head to signal no.

The Doctor stepped forward to look into Nelson's face. He reached forward to hold Nelson's face.

Nelson instinctively stepped back.

"Don't worry, Nelson, I have to look into your eyes." The Doctor stepped forward and touched Nelson's cheeks pulling his face slightly down. "Ever had your eyes tested, Nelson? You may need glasses."

This was the first time anybody had physically touched Nelson, (apart from the last beating) and it was the first time Nelson had let anyone get that close.

The Doctor attempted to peer deep into Nelson's eyes.

Nelson looked straight into the good Doctor's.

"That may very well be... what's causing you... to have pain behind your eyes. Something that can be simply treated with a set of ..."

Lead on Doctor, Nelson thought, you're leading me down a path of possibilities.

"... eyesight tests. I'll get that arranged for you".

Chapter 19

Sitting at my desk with the hair on the back of my neck on the rise I had to go and get myself a mug of strong black tea. The memories of those two senseless killings which we eventually tied to Nelson were enough reason for something a lot stronger than black tea. But tea would have to suffice for now. The kitchen was along the corridor to the left of my office and it had a microwave oven and two fridges and a big steaming water urn. All the "tecs kept their favourite cups or mugs in the kitchen and our cleaner was meant to wash them. Sometimes she did and sometimes she didn't. It depended on her mood I think, or was it her menstrual cycle, who knew, but today my mug was washed clean. There was no one else getting a tea when I walked into the kitchen and I was glad. I didn't want conversation just then, I wasn't in the mood. I filled my mug and jiggled my tea bag and when the tea was as dark as I could get it, I dropped the bag into the waste bin. I carried the steaming hot mug back into my office hoping not to meet another living soul. I wanted to be left alone for at least 10 minutes. I just wanted to comfort myself I suppose. Between sips I couldn't get the thoughts of Harrop out of my head. I was real glad that being one of the most dangerous bastards that I have ever come across, he would never get out of maximum security.

He was in Barlinnie for life. The only way he was coming out of there was in a pine box. I only hoped I would still be around to see that day.

I sipped at the tea and I attempted to read my paper. The only sound in my office was that rustle of the newspaper when I turned the pages. I've told you before being this quiet was a rarity and one that should be enjoyed and by Christ I was going to try.

The Prime Minister John Major was on the front page and I passed that story by. It was just the same old usual bullshit from our politicians. Princess Diana had a new boyfriend it was rumoured and I genuinely felt sorry for the girl. She was hounded by the paparazzi from the moment she stepped out of her house in the morning, until she stepped back into it at night. Mind you when you marry into the firm, as the royals are called, you have to accept all the cameras pointing at you. Wishing you to fuck up or pull a face or fall down on your arse. That picture would make someone a lot of money, that's for sure.

The story shared the headlines with John Major. I glanced at it not taking it in. The page 3 girl was an 18 year old from Essex and was indeed a lovely looking girl. Where were they when I was 18 years old I thought? They must have all been locked away or was I just too stupid to notice the really good looking ones?

There were still stories being followed about the new outbreaks of BSE, but that story wasn't for me either. I think my mind was refusing to let me read about the horrors of slaughtering thousands of herds of cattle to protect us, further up the food chain, from catching mad cows disease. There were a few paragraphs on the murderer Thomas Hamilton who killed all those kids in Dunblane primary school. The story said that he was going to Barlinnie for the rest of his life. I could feel my rage starting at that thought. The tax payers would be feeding and keeping him locked up for the rest of his natural. Me I would have shot him there and then. Save us all a packet in the long run. Yep I would have had no qualms at killing that bastard. Sentence him there and then and make him go on his knees in front of you and execute the fuck. By Christ that was the way our laws should be with serial killers and mass murderers. We should be a wee bit like the Chinese, shoot the culprit and then send the bill for the bullet to the killer's family.

I skipped through the rest of the crap until I got to the TV page and checked what the wife and I would be watching that night. I saw that the BBC had *The Vicar of Dibley* on with Dawn French and that brought a smile to my face. That was a funny series and it made me laugh. Her facials and her quick wit appealed to me and it really did make me chuckle. That would do me. My night could get planned around a bottle of Merlot and the vicar. I flicked the pages onto the sport pages at the back to see what or who was getting transferred.

The phone rang which jolted me from my thoughts. I closed the paper and folded it putting it in my in-tray. I hoped I'd get to read it later on. I lifted the phone and a voice at the other end told me my old super McCluskey had just died.

I sat with the phone at my ear stunned at the news. I managed to ask what age he was and how did he die. I got the sharp answer that he was 90 or thereabouts and his heart gave out and that he died in his sleep. I put the phone down. Christ this was turning out to be a funny old day. Someone knocked on my door shattering the silence. Whoever it was opened it before I shouted come in. Jackson popped his head round the door and asked if I had heard about McCluskey. I looked towards my phone and nodded yes and told him that I heard only seconds ago. Before I knew it I was telling Kenny what I had been doing that morning. In a way I was remembering the two kids and McCluskey at the same time.

I swear that Jackson had a smile on his face when he asked if I was going to the funeral.

I lifted my desk diary and wrote down on today's page 'McCluskey died today. Have black suit cleaned for funeral'. I looked back towards Jackson's beaming face and he nodded a very definite yes.

The following day a sympathy card came round the offices and we were all to sign it for McCluskey's family. The desk sergeant would make sure it would be delivered to the family before the funeral. There were no obtuse remarks on the card. No 'Good riddance you old bastard or Rot in Hell' only 'Sorry to hear, deepest sympathy' etc. So maybe he was better remembered by the lads more than I imagined. I added my own signature to the bottom of the card after writing 'You will be long remembered'.

In a way I actually meant it, I'd never forget the abuse he gave me and Jackson over our unsolved cases.

The Funeral would be a welcome day off, a one day distraction from our crime fighting skills, which were constantly tested by Glasgow's criminal fraternity. Ha that was a laugh. Kenny had come up with that sentence once when we were in the pub pissed. He mocked us as superheroes It had given us all a laugh...

So I had a funeral to look forward to and a piss up to celebrate the fact that the old bastard was really gone. I was sure that both Jackson and I would toast the old rascal's demise, by downing several large ones. The only problem I could foresee about that day was how to keep the smile off Kenny's face.

CHAPTER 20

Back in the empty cell Nelson knew that things were moving along now and that he could start formulating a plan. The eyesight tests would have to be conducted at the infirmary.

He was sure all the necessary equipment had to be there. He hoped that there was a visiting optometrist on the books and that the tests were not carried out by the staff doctor. Nelson thought that visitors would be more nervous dealing with prisoners and make his job of surprising him a whole lot easier.

The headache started to wash over him as the voice said –

That's a bit of luck eh?

Nelson closed his eyes as he tried to smile through the ever increasing pain ... Oh yeah.

So we can start to plan eh?

We can start to plan.

Let's kill the lot of them.

I told you before I'm thinking about that.

What's there to think about? We kill them and escape.

I have to …

You have to, what, Nelson, eh? What do you have to fucking do eh? Kill them as we escape and kill any other bastard that gets in our way. That's all you have to do, Nelson. Fuck thinking about it. Make up your mind and that's what we do. These bastards are keeping us locked up in here denying us fresh air. Fresh clean air and blue sky Nelson, blue sky. These are the same bastards that probably spit into your dinner and watch you eat it. So what's to think about?

Nelson covered his face with his hands. He breathed deeply as he gently massaged his temples wanting time to think. A time of real quiet and one where there were no voices to argue with. He needed that. He needed the time to reflect on what his friend was saying. Was he right? Was it that simple? Kill them all: Really? Did each one of them deserve to die?

The pain wasn't getting any better, I need to lie down he said quietly.

Sure you go ahead and lie down. Lie down to all these bastards that are making our lives a misery. You go ahead and do that. I'll think about how we get out of here without you killing anyone. If that's what you want.

Shut up I need time to think. Before Nelson could lie down, the pain washed over him in a rush, there was a blinding flash in his head and he fell forwards into a gaping black dark pit.

When the guards brought lunch, the peep hole opened up and the prone still figure of Nelson was visible. Woodhall watched for a few seconds and he could see no movement at all. Caution took over and as the cell door was opened ever so gingerly, the three guards entered clutching their riot sticks, Woodhall and Marbury were the first into the cell followed by Jack.

Nelson didn't move; he was out of it. Woodhall barked an order to Nelson telling him to get up. Nelson just lay there.

Woodhall prodded Nelson with the end of the stick. He expected Nelson to pounce but there was still no response.

Marbury warned Woodhall to be careful as it could be a trick. Woodhall prodded Nelson again and again stood ready for Nelson to react, but there was nothing. Woodhall put the riot stick down on the floor and turned Nelson over onto his back. Blood had seeped out of his nose and out of his mouth and saliva and spit formed a small pool on the concrete floor.

Marbury looked down at Woodhall and raised his walkie talkie to his mouth and radioed it in.

"Control this is Marbury."

"Control here. Go ahead."

We have a code blue, cell 8. West. Prisoner down. I repeat code blue cell 8 west. Officers Marbury and Woodhall and Jack in attendance. Medical team required immediately"

Woodhall looked up at Marbury, "He's alive, and he's breathing."

Marbury took the radio away from his mouth and let his finger slip off the speak button, "We could do this prison a real favour and smother the fuck."

Woodhall nodded in agreement. "I know don't tempt me. But the post mortem would show asphyxiation. We'd get caught."

"I thought we were in for a wee bit of action there a minute ago. My heart skipped a beat when I saw him on the floor." Jack said nervously.

"Me, too." said Woodhall

This was the very first time Woodall felt relaxed in the knowledge that there was absolutely no threat from Nelson. The fact that an unconscious body lay bleeding before him and could not offer one bit of harm, to any of them, brought a huge sigh of relief.

There was a real temptation presenting itself to the guards at this time, that this serial killer was lying flat out on the floor and all one of them had to do was kneel down beside him, cover his mouth with one hand and pinch his nostrils shut with two fingers on the other and Nelson would suffocate in seconds.

Woodhall was really tempted; he looked up at Marbury and then at Jack, both their eyes goaded him to do it. They were all thinking the very same, let's get rid of this bastard once and for all. Let's do it now.

There would be no more Nelson.

No more being scared shitless.

No more nightmares, waking up in the middle of the night in a cold sweat.

That one Jack knew. His was a recurring one, walking into the cell and Nelson catching him unawares and ... he shook his head trying to dismiss that thought.

Just two minutes of slight pressure and that would be that. End of story.

"Don't tempt me," Woodall repeated shaking his head and smiling back at Marbury.

The radio cracked into life. "Marbury, control, code blue team, on their way. Put prisoner in recovery position". Woodhall had already done that, training had kicked in regardless of his thoughts of how easy it would be to kill Nelson.

Woodhall stood up and sneered at Marbury, "Bastard's alive and that's a pisser."

Jack the smaller of the guards wiped the perspiration off his sweating palms onto his trouser legs. He nervously smiled at the comatose figure on the floor. Nelson was the one guy who scared the shit out of Brian Jack.

"I hope he dies," Jack uttered.

Marbury and Woodhall agreed in unison, "So do we."

The three guards didn't have to wait long until the noise of a stretcher trolley being pushed hurriedly through the corridor was heard. Paramedics and Doctor Scotland ran at its side.

Reaching the cell door and seeing the prone Nelson and the blood pool, Doctor Scotland drew both Marbury and Woodhall an accusing look.

"We never touched him, Doc. Honest," Woodhall said. "We found him like this lying face down on the floor. I checked his pulse and I put him in the recovery position. There was a pool of blood under his cheek."

Scotland reached down and placed 2 fingers on Nelson's neck, he looked at his watch for a half minute. Pulse about 150. He opened Nelson's eyelids and found the pupils dilated.

Scotland said, "First guess, Seizure or stroke. He told me about the headaches. So let's get him lifted onto the trolley."

The guards did as they were asked. "Right let's get him strapped in and off to the med centre."

CHAPTER 21

The Funeral was a well-attended affair with a few hundred of, I wanted to say well-wishers, but that's not the most apt, or indeed the correct description. Apart from his immediate family I thought that the majority of the congregation would be there to make sure that the old bastard was really dead and there was no coming back from this one.

I think I caught a few of the mourners smiling as they took long draws on a last cigarette before the service. Standing outside the crematorium, huddled together deep in conversation it was clique-ish, or so it seemed to me.

Jackson was with our crew from the station and I waved as I walked towards them. The sky was darkening and the forecast said rain showers and some were to be heavy. So as you can imagine everyone's face was like fizz. Real happy campers all being told to attend a funeral they didn't really want to go to. I said hello to the boys and had just time to accept a fag from Jackson. Looking around the waiting throng I noticed a young blonde. She was or should I say, very noticeable. She was extremely attractive and she knew it. The long blonde hair was well cut and shaped and she, I have to admit it, was a looker. She obviously wanted to be noticed and for guys to look at her that was for sure. She had a real nice pair of pins and the short coat highlighted them. My mind was wandering off track again.

The family started to move into the crematorium so I took a last drag and threw the cigarette down on the road. I put my foot on it grinding it out onto the sole of my shoe. Why do people do that thing with the foot, like you're starting to twist or something? And why was it always raining when you went to a funeral, where the hell was the sun?

I suppose I was letting my mind think about anything really, to escape from the moment and not try to think about the word death. I looked up at the heavens and there were some seriously black clouds gathering. You know sunshine certainly brightens everybody's mood. I don't care if any one disagrees with that, I know I'm right. The weather we get her in Scotland can be a right mood swinger, I can tell you.

We all shuffled into the small chapel and Jackson and the squad took seats to the back.

The family had decided on a cremation and I know Jackson agreed with that one. He wanted to be there when the old bastard was toasted. His loathing went a lot deeper than mine. The old man had come down harder on Jackson for some unknown reason and there had been no love lost between the pair of them that was for sure. I was actually surprised that Jackson had stayed on the force. After all the crap he took from the old man after we failed miserably in getting a result with the murder of the kid in Campsie. It was like real blame and as if we were incompetent. The old man went mental as if it had been a child of his that had been murdered and Jackson got it more than me. Maybe that was what the old bastard had wanted all along, he wanted to force Jackson and I to quit. Do you know, I never really thought about it that way before, so maybe it was the reason for the way he had behaved towards us? Mind you he never put the brakes on me becoming a chief inspector, but rumour had it, he stopped Kenny dead in his tracks.

Sitting inside the crematorium having listened to the glowing life story as told by the parish vicar and listening to the old sod's favourite song 'Nessun Dorma' I glanced around me at the rest of the congregation. Some were doing the inevitable staring at their shoes, not trying to catch anyone's attention. Fiddling with the crematorium bible or just playing with the creases on their trousers. Desperately not wanting to catch anyone looking at them, it's a grief thing, it must be and those were the ones who really hated going to funerals. Mind you I'm not that fond of them either. But at least I had my head held up attentively. As the coffin slid along the conveyor belt to oblivion; it had me thinking about my own demise. What would I want when it was time?

The coffin slid through the curtains and you could hear the doors opening up and at that noise a few of the family wept openly. As I watched the coffin slowly disappear from my view, I decided there and then not to think any more about my finality for a very long while.

I looked at Jackson and he was grinning like a Cheshire cat.

Another minute of Pavarotti and more weeping could be heard and then the music stopped. That was it, the old bastard was gone and off to meet his maker. I tapped the grinning Jackson on the leg and we stood up to go. The family moved slowly out first and waited for us all in the vestibule.

You know the reception area before you go into the service. Was it really a vestibule or a chapel of rest? Was that what it was called?

Christ the things that go through your mind at a time like this. Absolute nonsense.

We joined the line of friends giving the family their condolences once more and shook hands with everyone and muttered how sorry we were. As we all made our way to our cars, down came the rain.

In Scotland it seems to be obligatory that after a funeral or a cremation, everyone toddles off to the remembrance meal, for a few cups of tea and whatever. Historically it used to be provided by the co-operative, who not only buried your loved one, but also supplied the egg cress sandwiches and tea, in their very own tea rooms. But in this day and age it was all back to the pub for sandwiches and a few beers.

This family was no exception and they were putting on a finger food buffet and offering a few drinks at the Partick bowling club in downtown Partick for those of us who could manage along. Apparently the old man had been a lifelong member of the club and had been once some sort of club champion. But I wasn't going all the way across town for a few cheese and ham sandwiches and a pint of lager. Nope it was the Crow tavern in Bishopbriggs for me. It was on my way home anyway. Yeah I live in Bishopbriggs, didn't I mention it?

Bishopbriggs is on the edge of Glasgow, between Springburn and Kirkintilloch in the Clyde valley. It's really just another Glasgow district but a wee bit up market from the rest of Glasgow, or so my wife thinks. We live on a rather new estate that had sprung up on the outskirts of Bishopbriggs centre. The estate was a result of Thatcher's time in Government and her dream of everyone owning their own home. That idea had attracted blokes like me to move and mortgage ourselves up to the hilt. Places like Bishopbriggs were builder's paradises and the Briggs was now a place I called home. The strange thing was, from my back garden I could see the Campsie Fells away in the distance and the nightmares of two murdered kids would always come flooding back. But my neighbours were nice and no one in the street ever bothered that I was a cop. Or should I say, that no-one bothered me because I was a cop.

No-one was faintly aware of my past detective failings, so my three bed villa in Avonlea drive, Bishopbriggs was my little sanctuary.

I spoke to Jackson as I pulled the collar of my coat up against the rain.

"You're going to the bowling club in Partick aren't you?" Not so much of a question more of a statement really. I was expecting a yes fucking right I am.

I didn't get that response but I did get that he was.

I explained why I wasn't and that I'd remember the old fuck in the Crow. I told him I'd have a double Grouse with ice and I'd savour it and toast his passing.

I knew why Jackson was heading to the bowling club; his answer was of no real surprise, he would suffer the plastic ham sandwiches and the embarrassing inevitable drivel some folk talk. She was a pretty young blonde, thirty-something, nice legs and possibly newly divorced. So either she was on heat or he was. Anyway I'd seen the tell-tale signs before on many occasions and I'd get the full story of the hunt and the inevitable conquest tomorrow that was for sure. Mind you, every gory detail of the shagging session over a coffee and a digestive biscuit would certainly brighten up the day. I gave one more glance at Jackson heading off in pursuit, I couldn't help thinking about the cat and his mouse and I smiled.

As I turned to go I was almost sure she had looked over and smiled in my direction as well.

I walked back to my car through the puddles and opened the door and jumped in. I was glad to be out of the rain and as I started the engine the rain came down even heavier, it was battering against my windscreen. It was going to be one of those miserable Scottish wet days. I could feel my mood darken because of this depressing weather.

I pulled my seat belt round and fastened it, just habit I suppose or just my routine. Something that I had been taught and something I'd never forget, putting your seat belt on. There have been a few accidents I've seen where the occupants hadn't been wearing their belts and the sight of death by stupidity stays with you for a very long time, I can tell you. But there I go again ranting ...

I pulled out of the car park and turned the car radio on. I needed some music to lift my mood en-route to the Crow tavern. I turned on Radio Clyde and the DJ had a new single from a group called the Spice Girls which he was about to play. A few minutes later and all thoughts of funerals were gone and I was certain a couple of whiskies would definitely make me feel better.

Parking up in the Crow's car park as close to the door as I possibly could, I turned off the engine and got out. I locked the car door and hurriedly walked inside to the bar. Being the cop I looked round the place to see if I recognized anybody. Again that was just habit, me casing the joint, but I always found it useful to know just what was around you. You never know, it drove my wife daft when we were out for a drink and she said I was paranoid and had watched too many American detective shows. Nevertheless there were a couple of the obvious regulars playing dominos to my right and another four guys playing cards at a table to my left. I walked up to the bar and ordered a double grouse with ice. Jimmy the barman made small talk as he poured my drink and I told him the double was for a lost work mate. Jimmy said sorry or something like that and I didn't bother responding. A work mate, who was I kidding? He had been a gruff old bastard that had made my time in the force a misery, right up until the day he retired. I took my drink swirled the whisky round the glass once or twice and downed it in one go. I smiled and remembered that I even put a tenner into the retiring kitty, for the old sod. But mind you, so did Jackson.

I ordered another double and paid the barman. I stood there staring into the bar mirror and at all the bottles on the gantry and I could see everything going on behind me. There was no lull in activity or conversation, or any new comers to the bar, so I was fine. I couldn't be bothered with any trivial conversation, so I stood there quiet. Deep in my own thoughts with the glass in my hand, I sipped at my second whisky and this time let the ice do its work and cool my damn drink.

CHAPTER 22

Dr Scotland ran at the side of the trolley as Woodhall, Marbury and Jack all followed behind. On reaching the Medical centre the medics transferred Nelson onto a bed and immediately started work on him. An intravenous needle went into the back of Nelson's right hand and a saline drip was started. An oxygen mask went over his mouth and heart monitors stuck onto the bare areas of his chest. In a few minutes the two medics had Nelson all wired up and monitors were beeping all around him. The blood had been cleaned from his face and his condition was sufficient to concern the attending doctor.

Dr Scotland had a decision to make now. He had to find out what hospital was set up for taking extremely dangerous prisoners. The Royal Infirmary on the High Street was the closest for any emergency and they had used it before when an inmate's appendix burst. But this was different, Nelson was a serial killer.

Nelson was the most dangerous man in Scotland.

Dr Scotland would have to find out whether he could use the Royal or as an alternative; transport Nelson all the way across Glasgow to the Gartnavel hospital in Pollock.

Doctor Scotland would have to phone Patrick Stewart the governor now and get an answer and action it real quick or

Nelson could die. Nelson's vital signs were erratic which gave the good doctor a real problem.

Scotland was well aware the rule for a stroke, treatment as soon as possible, lessoning the damage to the brain. But he couldn't rule out a blood clot forming and pressure building on the brain and Nelson could die, unless the pressure was released.

He picked up the phone and dialled the governor. After several rings a female voice on the other end answered. The governor would come to the phone in a minute. Scotland could make out a muffled conversation with someone calling for Patrick and telling him to hurry up. When Patrick Stewart answered, Scotland explained just what had happened.

"Patrick, it's John, yes I'm fine. Nelson Harrop has had I think what looks like a stroke. I don't know if it's Ischemic or a Haemorrhagic one. Only tests will answer that. As you know we aren't equipped to deal with that kind of emergency. I have had him moved up to our med centre for observation. But I need to know where we can send him."

Patrick listened and told Scotland to Ambulance Nelson to the Royal Infirmary under two guards. He would telephone the hospital director and then the Chief Constable and inform them of the situation.

Scotland explained the measures he had taken to try and stabilize Nelson, but was told by Patrick to let the Royal do all work, let them do all the X-rays and MRI shit. We didn't have to so let them deal with him.

Scotland was looking towards the watching medics and nodded his agreement. "Ambulance now," Scotland said out loud, "Royal Infirmary."

"Yes, sir, understood. Marbury and Woodall get your gear; you're on guard duty as of now. The Police will take over when you get there.

The ambulance arrived at the accident and emergency entrance of the Royal Infirmary and a trolley was brought out to meet it. Nelson was lifted onto the cart and rushed inside to triage. Marbury and Woodall followed the trolley into the A&E. Two policemen were already inside waiting for their prisoner. Marbury asked one of the officers to sign a temporary release into custody form, which he did and both guards were relieved that Nelson became someone else's problem for a while.

Those two cops were a bundle of laughs eh? Marbury said.

"Would you be? Fuck me, imagine them 30 minutes ago, sitting in the station, feet up with a nice hot cup of tea, not a care in the world and then wham! Getting told they were on guard duty for Scotland's most notorious serial killer. I bet you they've got man-size pampers on." Woodall looked at Marbury's grinning face and laughed out loud, "Fuck 'em."

Nelson was in examination room 3 behind a fully closed curtain and the paramedics briefed the attending Doctor on duty, what had happened and what actions had been taken. Doctor Lee listened as he examined Nelson. A duty nurse wrapped a blood pressure gauge around Nelson's right arm and took his pulse. She worked around Dr Lee trying real hard not to get in his way.

"So this guy is a prisoner then," Lee asked one of the officers. "Anyone infamous?"

"Doctor he's 143 over 95," the nurse said removing the wrap around.

"Thank you nurse."

Officer 1 looked at Officer 2 and shook his head, "Nobody you'd know."

"Should we be shit scared in case he wakes up?" The Doctor asked, not taking his eyes from Nelson.

"No Doctor. As I said he's just another low life criminal."

"Low life eh? So why does he warrant you two boys then?"

Neither officer offered to comment.

Dr Lee continued his preliminary examination and was describing everything he was doing and his findings to a young intern called Foster, who was hastily writing everything down.

"You see his eyes?" The Doctor asked, opening up alternate eye lids. The intern nodded.

"Pupils dilated?"

"Yes, sir."

"And?"

"And, sir?"

"Look at them laddie, are they bloodshot?"

"Only one of them."

"How would we know he hasn't had a full blown heart attack?" Lee asked.

The young intern thought for a few seconds and then blurted out, "The colour of his lips would be blue and his skin very pale. His breathing would be shallow and you could check his pulse to find out."

"Check his pulse to find out what exactly?" The Doctor bellowed. "Explain yourself Foster."

The intern swallowed hard, he hated being on this shift, but knew he was learning from one of the best. "I mean to see if his pulse was racing, or if it was erratic."

"But this happened about an hour ago and the medics said he was given oxygen. His lips would not be blue and his pulse could have settled down. What else are you missing?"

"I don't follow you, sir." Panic in his voice was obvious.

"What about the fact that he's not dead and he's still alive?"

"Yes, sir"

"Myocardial infarction kills in about 30 minutes if not treated. The paras told us what treatment this guy got and they never mentioned any injections, use of defibrillators, etc. The only thing he got was oxygen. You have to learn to listen and to make quick judgments on the information you get from the paras. Their information and you taking the correct decisions could very well save this man's life. Am I making myself clear?"

"Yes, sir."

"Good! It's penetrating your thick skull. So long as your brain keeps taking in all the correct shit I throw your way, you might just learn something."

"Yes, sir."

Lee took an otoscope from his pocket, "Know why we're going to use this?"

Before the intern could answer Lee pressed the otoscope into Nelson's left ear and pressed the switch illuminating the inner ear canal. He looked and then followed the same procedure with his right ear.

"Right, your turn." he handed the tool to the intern. "Know what you're looking for?"

The intern laid his clipboard and pen down, took the otoscope gingerly from the doctor and tested the beam of light from the scope on the palm of his left hand

The intern looked into both ears and shook his head.

"Is there any blood in his elementary canals? And don't shake your bloody head laddie. Talk to me because I have to know. I could be doing other examinations and not have time to look up or hear you rattling your empty head."

"No, sir, there is no sign of any blood in the ears."

"Very good! Now I want X-ray stat on this man's nut and I want you to page Dr Elizabeth Francis from Neurology and tell her that this guy has had a probable Transient ischemic attack and by the looks of the lump on his forehead has had a disagreement with a concrete floor."

The young intern left the triage booth and crossed the emergency floor and picked up the house phone.

"And Foster ..."

"Yes, sir?"

"Tell whoever answers ..." He never got a chance to complete the instruction.

"Yes, sir," Foster answered.

He dialled zero one and told the receptionist to page Dr Francis from neurology.

The tannoy system, Bing bonged into life and Dr Francis was asked to contact triage.

Minutes later Dr Elizabeth Francis knew all the facts so far and was following the trolley into the lift. The two officers joined her and the orderly and they went on their way to X-ray.

Nelson, wake up.

No answer.

Nelson, wake the fuck up.

Still no answer

"Dr Francis the patient is making noises," Officer 1 said.

Elizabeth stopped watching the digital floor numbers and turned towards the officer. "Excuse me?"

It sounded if he mumbled something

Elizabeth leaned towards the bed and lifted Nelson's hand. She checked his pulse and peered into his face for any reaction.

Nelson you have to wake up. I don't know where are we?

I want to sleep he thought.

"Hello can you hear me? Mr. Harrop can you hear me? Elizabeth leaned forward and put her ear close to Nelson's mouth for any response. There was nothing so much as a whisper.

"Mr. Harrop can you hear me? My name is Dr Francis and you're in hospital. Hello?"

Nelson, did you hear that. Her name is Francis. Come on now just open your eyes and see if she's pretty. See if she is shaggable. Come on open your eyes, Nelson, and let's see what kind of mess we're in now.

CHAPTER 23

After having had a nice relaxing quiet night in watching the television with my wife, I woke to the telephone ringing beside my bed. I turned my bed light on and looked at the alarm clock. It was just after 2.30 in the morning. It sounded like I had an excited Jackson on the other end of the line.

"Thought you'd like to know, chief, our old friend Harrop is in the Royal Infirmary. He had some kind of emergency yesterday afternoon and is in there getting treatment.'

My sleepy aura vanished in a flash and I came to a full alert status while Jackson talked, registering as to what he was saying. I think I said, "What the fuck" before my darling wife, who just loves early morning phone calls, piped in with, "Who is that on the phone at this time in the night?" she grumped. (By the way that's the cleaned up version of what she said.)

"It's Jackson."

"Tell him to fuck off. And turn you're bloody light off." (So you get her mood?)

"I will in a minute" and at that she rolled onto her side in an attempt to get back to sleep. It would not take long I can tell you. The woman could fall asleep on a bed of nails.

"Where are you?" I asked.

"I'm in the office."

"I'll call you back in a minute" I put the phone down and turned my bed side light off. I opened and silently closed the bedroom door and hurried down the stairs and into my living room. I turned one of the lights on and picked up the phone and dialled Jackson back. I sat down waiting to hear the worst.

"Right tell me what's going on?"

"The Super got a call earlier from the High and Mighty one in Glasgow telling him the situation regarding Harrop."

"So how's it taken so long for them to tell us?" I asked.

I could tell by Jackson's voice and attitude that he was not amused at this turn of events. "Listen all I know is that the super wanted us to have a heads up about Harrop out of the Bar L. He phoned me about an hour ago on my mobile. He said that he had tried ringing you but you weren't picking yours up."

"I switched mine off at the crematorium. Must have forgotten to put the bloody thing back on."

"Well you'll have a few missed calls when you do turn it back on. So don't be surprised when you check it. Don't go phoning him back."

"So what's happened to Harrop? Hope it's nothing trivial. Is he dying or has the bastard something incurable or what?" I said hoping.

"They reckon he had a Transient ischemic attack and ..."

"What the fuck is that," I butted in.

"That's what I said when they told me. It's apparently a wee mini stroke, but he hit his head on the cell floor when he fell, so they don't know if the fall or the stroke put our boy's lights out. They have to do tests or so they said. Anyway they transferred him from the Prison to the Royal on orders"

"So is he conscious?"

"No idea."

"So how many guys do they have guarding that crazy bastard?" I tried to ask the question in a way that I didn't really sound flustered.

"Two plain clothes from Denniston outside his room and two armed, apparently from the flying squad somewhere else in the building."

"Did they strap the bastard into his bed or Velcro him to the bed sheet? Because they don't have enough guys if he wakes up. And I take it he's going to wake up, if he's not already, from this wee stroke?"

"Yeah he'll wake up alright, because it's only a warning he's had. No lasting damage they hope. Started ringing any alarm bells in your head yet?" Jackson said. "Cause I got a bad feeling about this already."

"Yeah, likewise! But what did the super say? Does he want us to get involved?"

"Nope, he says Harrop's someone else's problem. Not ours. He just wanted us to have an exclusive on this. So go figure"

"It ain't the best news I've ever woke up too, that's for damn sure."

"Me either, but what the Fuck."

"So why are you in the office?" I asked.

"I'm in here checking the armed response stand by list."

I knew that list well. It was a list of policemen from all over Glasgow who were licensed to carry weapons and it was circulated round the stations on the first Sunday of the month. The same guy's names were there week in week out. We were only ever on the bloody thing if there was a fire arm training course we had to attend.

"You staying in the office or are you going back home?"

"There's no point going home now. I'll stay here and dig. I want to throw a few fucks into some of the AR boys we know. They'll want to hear all about our friend that's for sure."

"Alright I'll see you on Monday. I'm going to forget all about our friend. I am going to have a relaxing day and watch some telly later on. After my breakfast the missus and I are going for a long walk. And Kenny, I'll find out on Monday, all about your wee jaunt to the Bowling club yesterday"

"Aye well …"

"Cause I'd thought you'd be ball deep in a wee blond bit and dying to get back there instead of hanging out at the office," I joked.

"Not funny," he said rather too quickly.

"Oh what's the matter, Kenny? Did she knock back the Jackson charm offensive?"

He rapped back, "It was that time of the month."

I laughed at him, "And that stopped you?"

"Still not funny, Paul," and he hung up.

I was still chuckling to myself as I walked into the kitchen to put the kettle on for a cup of tea. There was no point in me trying to go back to bed. She wolf would be snoring her dainty wee head off and I'd never get back to sleep anyway. I'd only toss and turn and wake up her ladyship. It was the mere mention of that bastard's name. I shivered at the thought. As the kettle boiled and I poured the bubbling water over my tea bag I smiled at my image of Kenny.

Poor Kenny he must have tried like a wee bear all afternoon to get into the girls knickers only to get knocked back. I visioned him suffering all through the egg mayonnaise or cheese and ham sandwiches and all the rest of the crap, just to get her to bed and then Sweet Fuck All, I laughed out loud.

As I poured more boiling water over my tea bag I thought back on how lucky we were to catch Harrop in the first place.

CHAPTER 24

OCTOBER 1988

Darkness fell early for Glaswegians in late October and the cold westerly wind blowing in from the Atlantic whistled up the Clyde with an early winter's harsh chill that could find its way deep down into your very bones. Sleet was in the air and there was a suggestion that some areas might even wake up to a sprinkling of snow. Further North the Cockbridge to Tomintoul road was preparing for the snow ploughs to be out and about this early in the season. The road is famous for being the first one blocked by snow in winter. The TV news reports it and 99% of the country haven't the foggiest idea of where the road is. All they know is that it's always the first road in the United Kingdom to be blocked. That's when the rest of Scotland knows for definite that winter is hurrying towards us.

The Scots wrapped themselves up in warm winter coats, as autumn left Scotland in a rush.

Every day cars crossed the Kingston Bridge on the M8 highway, the main route over the River Clyde slowly, they were always nose to tail in rush hour traffic, jammed up in both directions, each driver longing for, hoping for a break in the traffic and for his lane to speed up, oblivious as to what was underneath.

Every driver on the Kingston Bridge had a view of the river Clyde depending on the direction you were heading. If you were heading west towards Glasgow Airport, you could look to your right and see the Broomielaw and the lights of Govan and Ibrox. If you were travelling east you could see the Clyde snake its way towards the centre of the city.

Underneath the bridge, there were many small industrial areas reachable by the many smaller road bridges that spanned the Clyde. The area directly under the Kingston Bridge was a poorer area and was known as a place where the homeless gathered at night. Disused factory units were often broken into and vandalized by young hoodlums who left their spray painted gang slogans on damp walls. These places became shelters for the tramps and homeless street people, Glasgow's city beggars and Glasgow's shame.

Inside the disused building flammable material would be gathered and small fires would be lit for warmth and the homeless would huddle around the flames. Sometimes the make shift shelters would be raided by the police and the fires put out and the tramps moved on. Other times the police just couldn't be bothered moving them on, because it was more of a nuisance to go out and ensure the tramps didn't move right back into the place you had just got them to move from. Those nights when the police didn't come, were the safe nights when the fires seemed to offer hope of a warm night's sleep. They had to find a dry spot in the building away from any drafts and with cardboard boxes laid out for a dry mattress, their layers of clothes all worn at the same time kept them reasonably warm. It was when they had been caught out in the rain and their clothes were wet, you would see steam rise from those closest to the flames. There were very few conversations and fewer friendships, most lost themselves into their own small world. Every one of them would have had a story to tell, but there was no one to listen to them. Food kitchens set up from the Churches in the area were the sole meal providers for them. Their only hot food might be a bowl of vegetable broth but somehow it was sufficient. The Salvation Army workers scoured the South side of Glasgow's streets urging the homeless to seek shelter in God. God would be their saviour.

However God wouldn't be supplying them with a nice warm bed or a three course dinner.

But believe in the Lord and be saved. Yeah right!

They didn't know it then, but late in October, God must have been busy the Friday night a killer came to call.

Nelson was restless and everything seemed to irritate him. Losing his job last week as a kitchen cleaner in the hotel irked. He didn't like it when he fell foul of authority. But this time he had no grievance or a leg to stand on. He had no option than to accept that they were right to sack him: after all he had been caught stealing drink from the store room. He was lucky that the head chef hadn't called the police. Police were the last thing Nelson needed right now.

As he lay in his bedroom growling at the world, downstairs his mother sensed that Nelson was upset. She was concerned, but knew he would tell her what had happened, when he was good and ready. He had gone to his room after tea and hadn't even come downstairs to watch television. With the TV on she couldn't hear Nelson rant.

Stupid for getting caught Teddy chastised.

Don't you start?

Nelson, Nelson, Nelson.

I'm not in the mood, so stop it.

That was a good wee job you had.

I know that. He said angrily.

So why did you steal that can of beer?

I don't know.

You have to stay away from the hotel.

I know.

I mean it Nelson. You have to keep away or else you'll do something stupid.

Like?

Like killing the guy that caught you and got you sacked.

Nelson growled.

No killing that boy, Nelson.

Yes, Teddy.

I mean it, Nelson.

Of course you do, Teddy.

The next morning Nelson was up bright and early and having his breakfast when his Mum came down the stairs into the kitchen. Nelson was like the Nelson of old, chatting and laughing. He got up from the table and asked her if she wanted a cup of tea. He put water into the electric kettle and turned it on. He emptied the tea pot remains into the sink and rinsed out the pot with hot water. He got two mugs from the cupboard and when the kettle boiled he made the tea. They sat and talked and had another cup and talked some more. Nelson could see she was happy with him.

So what if he got fired for being late, he'd get a better job, he was wasted up at that hotel anyway, she assured him with a smile.

Nelson said he was going to the toilet and went upstairs in a blur, taking the stairs two at a time. He closed the bathroom door. He ran the tap water and soaped his hands with the nice soap his mother bought for him. It had to be a brand of soap that was perfumed. It was something that kept Nelson happy.

He turned the tap off and dried his hands using the hand towel from behind the door. He smiled into the bathroom mirror. His reflection did not appear to smile back. Entering into his bedroom he closed his door and looked towards the chair he had in the corner of his room at the side of the bedroom window. His old friend and mentor was just sitting there. He was still in pristine condition; but he didn't appear to be smiling either.

Nelson was just about to ask what the matter was when the bear spoke to him, "*Kill her, Nelson.*"

Nelson stood there open mouthed aghast at what his friend had said. "She's my mum. I can't do that."

"*Kill her. You know she doesn't approve of you drinking and getting sacked, she thinks you're a waste of space. She hates you when you come in here drunk.*"

"No she doesn't."

"*Kill her for fuck's sake.*"

Nelson lifted his wallet from his bedside cabinet and put it into his back pocket. He walked round his bed towards the chair and knelt down on his knees in front of his friend. He reached under the chair and took out his knife that he kept wedged into the fabric. He pressed open the switchblade and it glinted in the light. This blade was as sharp as any surgeon's scalpel. He closed the blade and put it into his jean's pocket. He stood up walked back over to his wardrobe and took his blue parka jacket out and put it on. He stopped at the door and before he opened it he turned and looked at his friend. There was anger in his face, "Don't say anything and no she's my mum," he hissed.

He took the stairs two at a time and hollered to anyone within earshot, that he was off out.

"Bye, see you later," and not waiting to hear his mother's response, he slammed the door behind him and was off down the path and along the road. He decided to take the ash path alongside the woods on his way to the bus stop and whistled all the way there. At the end of the path he turned right onto the asphalt road. He crossed the bridge not looking to his right to see the area where he killed Smith. He wasn't thinking about that, he was thinking about something else. He couldn't hear the river gurgling happily over the riverbed or to the chorus of birds singing in the trees, he was in a different world at that particular moment in time.

Standing waiting for the bus to Glasgow, there was a chill in the air and Nelson put his hood up and zipped up his parka jacket. He buried his hands deep into his coat pockets. When the bus arrived Nelson sat upstairs at the back and paid the bus conductor for a return ticket to Glasgow. Someone had left a *Daily Record* newspaper on the seat in front of him. Nelson lifted it up and started reading it. Published and printed at Anderston Quay. He thought about that for a moment suddenly remembering that he had heard that there was a pub called 'Off the Record' located somewhere close the Newspapers premises. Nelson had set off with no real plan in his head, apart from going into Glasgow and buying a cd from the music shop in Sauchiehall Street. Going for a couple of beers somewhere was an add on. He thought about the pub and decided that was where he was going today. He'd have a pie and a pint in 'Off the Record'.

Maybe if he was lucky he would meet some of the journalists that drank there. He continued to read and take note of the columnists and by the time the bus pulled into the terminal at Dundas Street, Nelson was indeed a happy man.

Nelson got off the bus and walked out of the terminus and down into Buchanan Street. He then cut along bath Street and down Renfield Street. He tried to walk as quickly as he could against the flow of Shoppers and workers out for their lunch break. He headed along and walked into Central Train Station where he cut through, passing all the trains standing at their platforms. He was heading for the far exit. He was a man with a mission and this lunchtime he was focused. All thoughts of his music cd gone.

Walking into the bar he looked around for a seat and saw a table in the corner that was empty. Nelson got a pint of lager and ordered pie beans and chips for lunch. He sat down at the table and took off his parka. It was quite warm in the bar and Nelson delighted in taking in all the conversations all around him. He listened to the couple of guys to his left arguing about football. The girl and her boyfriend to his right were on about music. There were several individual guys at the bar chatting to the waitresses and bar staff. Nelson thought that they must have been regulars to be that friendly.

One of the bar staff brought Nelson his cutlery and put vinegar, ketchup and brown sauce bottles down beside him. "Two minutes, hunny," he said leaving him.

About five minutes later Nelson was enjoying his lunch. The bar had got noticeably busier and noisier with an influx of workers. Nelson finished eating and rose to get another lager. He pushed past some of the guys standing and got to the bar and waited his turn for an order. Got and paid for his lager and returned to his table to find someone sitting at one of the seats. Youngish lad with jet black hair and it looked like he was wearing eye liner. He stood up when Nelson got to the table. "Is it okay if I sit here?" he asked in a quiet voice. "It's just that it's got busy and there's no seats left."

"No problem," Nelson replied. He was annoyed but tried not to show it. The young lad stood up and removed his three quarter length jacket and placed it on his seat. Nelson watched as the lad revealed he was wearing a bright pink vee neck sweater over a white tee shirt. The lad had rolled his sleeves up and Nelson noted a butterfly tattoo on his forearm. He had tight denim jeans showing he had a young girl's thin waistline and figure. Around his neck he wore a gold cross on a chain and had a gold bracelet on his right wrist. He had a gold watch on his left wrist and several rings on his fingers. The black pointed shoes completed the picture. Nelson watched the accentuated walk to the bar and the return with a drink in his hand.

It wasn't long before the young man spoke to Nelson and Nelson in return complimented the young man's watch. "That's a nice watch you have there. Do you mind me asking where you got it?"

"It's not real you know. It's a fake. I bought it in the Barrows a couple of weeks ago for a tenner." He held it in front of Nelson's face so he could have a look. Nelson caught the perfumed scent from the young man's hand.

"It's still very nice to look at. You would never know it was a fake."

"Oh thank you. I do like nice things."

"Yep I think you got yourself a bargain there," Nelson said.

"My name's Terry by the way," and he offered his hand.

"Mine's Nelson" and they shook hands. Nelson noticed that Terry's hand shake was light and that his hands were smooth to touch.

"I haven't seen you in here before, Nelson. Is this your first time in the pub?"

"Yeah I wanted to try something different, I mean somewhere different."

"Know what you mean, Nelson, don't we all want to try something different?" Terry laughed.

Terry looked deep into Nelson's gaze watching for a response to his subtle joke.

Nelson on the other hand was beginning to feel slightly uncomfortable in his new found friend's company. Terry finished his drink and stood up, "Can I get you one Nelson? Lager is it?"

Nelson without thought nodded his head.

Terry stood at the bar and put his empty glass on the bar counter.

"Another Tom Collins, Terry?" Wilson the bar tender asked.

"Yes please and a lager for my friend."

"Got yourself a new friend then, Terry?"

"Mmmm. Never been in here before, never seen him around but, there's an aura about him. Don't you think?"

Wilson looked over at Nelson as he poured the lager. "Bit rough round the edges but OK I guess."

"You think he's rough? Oh good. I like a bit of rough."

"I know you do, love. But be careful," Wilson warned with a smile.

"You know me, Wilson, softly, softly. Soft as gossamer."

Wilson put the pint down in front of Terry and turned to make the Tom Collins.

"How much is that Wilson?"

"For you, Darling, zilch it's on the house."

Terry giggled and took the drinks back to the table. He placed the pint down in front of Nelson and sat back down.

"What's that you're drinking?"

"It's a Tom Collins."

"What's in it?"

Terry looked at Nelson, "You never had one of these before?"

Nelson shook his head.

"It's a shot of gin, a squeeze of lemon juice and my friend Wilson over there puts a half tea spoon of brown sugar and tops it up with soda and ice. Don't you just love brown sugar?"

Nelson sipped at his pint, "Not particularly."

"Well this is delicious. Want to try a sip?" Terry asked.

"Why not?"

Terry handed Nelson his glass and Nelson put the glass to his lips and took a sip.

"Tastes quite zingy," and he handed the glass back to Terry.

"Zingy. Mmmm I like that word. I've never heard someone call it zingy before. But from now on I'll call it zingy as well." Terry put the glass to his lips and sipped from the exact same spot as Nelson had just done moments before.

After several rounds of each other buying drinks Nelson was also on Tom Collins cocktails. He was warming to Terry's company and enjoying the banter. Although some of the stuff he talked about with Wilson was a bit effeminate, it was comical in the way he said it. Nelson was relaxed and getting tipsy.

Terry was drinking Tom Collins without the gin. Wilson warned him to be careful and to have some protection with him. Aids being rife among the careless. Terry just smiled and told Wilson he was jealous because he pulled Nelson before Wilson had.

Another couple of round of cocktails later and Terry had sidled up to Nelson. He laughed at everything Nelson uttered.

"You're really funny, Nelson. You really are," Terry laughed finishing off his drink in a gulp.

Nelson had never been called funny before and looked at his new found friend and playfully punched Terry in the arm, "And so are you my friend."

It was that part of the pull, it was now or never for Terry.

"Nelson let's get out of here. My flats just down the road. What you say we save ourselves money and have real cocktails at mine. I'll make you a Pina Colada."

"Ohh I like the sound of that," Nelson slurred.

"Come on then, stick your jacket on and let's go. We'll say bye to Wilson."

Nelson staggered to his feet bumping the table and scattered his empty pint tumbler. Terry managed to catch it before it shattered on the floor.

"Oh well caught," Nelson slurred with a grin.

He burst out laughing as he struggled to get his arm into his sleeve. Terry helped lovingly. Nelson didn't take any notice of Terry's hand brushing his shoulder or the closeness of Terry's breath on his neck.

"Bye, Wilson." Terry waved and blew a kiss to the bar tender, as the two new best friends left the bar to go out into the bitter cold.

The cold air hit Nelson hard and the alcohol took over. He shivered and put his hands in his pockets, he staggered and giggled. Terry took him by the arm. "This way, Nelson, watch where you're going," and they both laughed.

"Penny Colorado's here we come," Nelson sang quite happily as he waltzed his way down the pavement oblivious of what was to come.

After what seemed like ages to Nelson, Terry announced that they had arrived. Nelson had no clue where they were and Terry opened the front door and ushered Nelson inside. Nelson recognized that he was in a close. Doors to the left and stairway in front of him. The smell of urine was there emanating from the back of the stairs. He felt for the knife in his pocket. Memories came flooding back.

Terry put his hand on the small of Nelson's back and nudged him forward. "My place to the left. Cock and tails to come," he said laughing. Nelson did not join in the laughter.

Terry put the key in the lock and opened the door.

"Be careful, Nelson," the voice inside his head warned.

Nelson stopped at the threshold.

Terry stepped back and smiled. "Nelson, Love come on."

He stepped forward into Nelson's space.

He kissed Nelson on the lips.

The sudden shock hit Nelson. Terry never saw the flash of steel or felt the sharpness of the blade slide over his throat.

He couldn't gasp. His right hand automatically reached up for his throat.

Blood poured through the cut. Terry held his hand firmly over the wound.

He slid down the door frame. The life draining from him.

Nelson bent down and calmly wiped the knife blade on Terry's coat.

There was no remorse. No words to say, "Sorry, Terry. You shouldn't have done that."

He just stood up and looked at his own hands for blood.

Move, Nelson, let's get out of here before someone comes. The voice echoed.

Nelson turned away from the dying Terry and opened the Front door to the flats. He stepped out into the street put his head down into the wind and walked as quickly as he could away from the door. He walked past shop windows all in darkness, premises all closed up for the night. He passed people heading home or heading out to the pub or to restaurants. Nelson didn't care all he wanted was to get away. He wanted to recognize some familiar place, to see some landmark he knew and not hear a shout from behind him "Stop that man".

Nelson turned a corner and walked into Carrick Street breathless. He stood for a moment and had to lean on a car bonnet as a wave of nausea hit him and he puked on the pavement. He retched again and emptied the contents of his stomach. He looked up and down the street to see if anyone had seen him.

He was lucky there was no one to witness his disgusting behaviour. He wiped his mouth with the back of his hand and spat on the ground. He shivered as another retch doubled him over, but there was nothing there to come up.

He walked down onto the Broomilaw and saw a Bridge in front of him. It was George the Fifth Bridge and Nelson walked over it. He dared to steal a look behind him and saw that there were some people following his direction. He quickened his pace. He heard the siren from an Ambulance in the distance. It didn't deter him. He walked on avoiding the traffic on Paisley Road West. He crossed onto Centre Street and turned right into Nelson Street. There was another siren and this one was from a Police car rushing along Paisley Road heading back over the bridge. He paused and looked behind again. This time there was no one walking in his direction. He came to a junction and he looked up at the Street sign it said Patterson Street. There were some derelict buildings in front of him and like a moth to a flame something drew Nelson towards them. He caught the whiff of smoke. He stopped and glanced one more time along the street he had just walked along. It was dark and the streetlights showed him that there was no one behind him. He wished for a mint or a drink of water. He wanted to remove the disgusting taste from his mouth.

He was drawn closer to the building. Senses went to 'tingle' as he stepped past the partially boarded up entrance. He could smell urine and that reminded him that he had to pee. He sidled up to the corner brick wall and unzipped his jeans. He felt relieved. His eyes were becoming accustomed to the darkness very quickly. The smell of smoke was getting a bit stronger.

The moth to the flame.

He moved silently through the big empty space towards a door at the back. He stepped on some glass with a crunch and stopped dead in his tracks. Feeling in his pocket for his knife Nelson wrapped his fingers around the hilt.

He took the knife out and transferred it to his right hand.

Metamorphosis: The moth was changing to something far more dangerous.

He reached for the door handle and turned the knob slowly and quietly. Easing the door open he quietly stepped through. The smell of smoke was much stronger here and he could hear the crackling of wood burning. He had stepped into a corridor with what appeared to be three old office spaces on either side. Nelson's eyes could see that there was only one with a door. The last office on the right. He peered into the first office on his left and there was something lying on cardboard in the corner.

He could make out the outline of a body. The body moved slightly trying to get some comfort from the hard floor. Nelson's hackles rose as he recognized the shape was a tramp. Nelson hated the homeless with a vengeance. His blade flicked open with a click and Nelson moved forward at speed and before the tramp could move, Nelson knelt down and grasped the Tramp's collar baring his neck. The tramp attempted to turn away but Nelson was too quick and covered his mouth with his hand and the blade brought blood. The tramp was too weak to scream and Nelson continued stabbing until the tramp was still.

There was no mercy given and Nelson had killed without as much as a grunt. Adrenalin pulsed through Nelson's system as it does for a wolf on the hunt. He sought to find more and indeed found more. The next office revealed another shape on the floor. Nelson killed again with no thought.

The third office revealed a trickier situation with three shapes in different spots on the floor, but in the blink of an eye, Nelson had stabbed the three sleeping shapes before they knew what was happening.

Old Tommy had been restless and was hungry. The hunger pangs had pained him and he couldn't sleep. He had heard the faint commotion in the first office but wasn't really sure what it was. The second and third rooms were taken, he knew that, but again as to who was in them, he hadn't a clue. He was located in the last office on the right, the one with the only remaining door as was Bill. The office on the other side had a wee fire going, but Tommy had stayed away from that. Fires only brought squabbling as the boys jostled for position closer to the flames.

Tommy was well aware of which offices to keep out of as all the offices had been trashed but his at least this one hadn't been shit in. There was more broken furniture sure, but it was somehow warmer than the other rooms. Bill was huddled up leaning against the wall just behind the door way sound asleep. It was just the usual way that Bill slept. There were definitely no hunger pains for Bill, he had been luckier and had found a half-eaten pie in a trash bin.

Tommy heard the smallest of grunts from somewhere along the corridor. Something nasty was happening he was sure of that and could now make out someone's laboured breathing. His gut warned Tommy to move for safety and he crawled as quietly as he could to hide under the broken desk on the back wall and sat crouched between the desk drawers, hardly daring to breath. He couldn't try to wake Bill, he didn't have time.

He could make out soft footfalls and froze on hearing them stop outside the office. Tommy held his breath. Why hadn't they closed the door? Why had Bill left it ajar?

Nelson had killed in every office. There were two offices left. He looked into the last one and quietly pounced on the sleeping shape. Nelson was surprised to find two bodies under all those clothes. The two tramps were sleeping together and had been having sex. Nelson could smell the semen and took an even greater delight in killing them.

Tommy's heart beat sounded like a drum in his head. It was thumping in his temples.

He daren't breath. He knew deep down what was happening. There was a killer among them and he was in the opposite room.

The door was pushed ever so softly open.

Tommy closed his eyes and waited.

Nelson saw the Tramps feet behind the door. He pushed the door further open and stepped into the room. He stood before his next victim. Bill was lightly snoring.

Tears began to roll down Tommy's cheeks.

Nelson knelt down and pushed the blade straight into Bill's thorax.

Tommy could hear the gurgling and gasping. He could hear his friend's last breath.

He daren't breathe.

Nelson was elated after his killing spree. He was on a high. Tommy heard Nelson masturbate over his dead friend.

CHAPTER 25

Molly and her trolley as she was fondly known as, was one of the street people. Born in Belfast in the early forties she lost everything she had in a house fire. She lost three children and a sleeping husband and a pet dog called Buster. All because of a cigarette butt falling off an ashtray into her sofa and smouldering until it flamed. The acrid smoke killed the youngsters in their beds and her husband who had fallen asleep comforting her youngest. The wee one had had a nightmare and her husband had left their bed and gone through to the kiddies' room to reassure the crying youngster. The dog barking woke Molly and as she opened the bedroom door she was hit with a wall of acrid black smoke and flames. She screamed for her husband to get the kids out but was forced back into her bedroom by the intense heat. She slammed the bedroom door shut and in a blind panic opened the bedroom window and called for help. Terrified she stood with her back against the window listening to the flames crackling and letting the cold air rush inside. There was no more barking and no yelling from her husband. Buster the dog died at his master's feet, but she had somehow managed to escape. She had turned and climbed through the window screaming their names to follow her. But there was never to be an answer. Their voices were lost to the roar of the flames. She managed to jump onto her coal bunker just below and rolled off it onto the grass. Her nightdress had flamed and she had slapped her hand at the burning bit, extinguishing it. She stood in the garden screaming for her family. Lights went on in neighbour's houses, someone called the emergency services. She had screamed herself hoarse as neighbours tried to fight their way into her place but the smoke and the flames were too much for them. Even the bravest of them couldn't fight his way past the heat.

She knelt on her lawn and wept uncontrollably, not believing what was happening.

Molly never fully recovered from the trauma of burying her whole family. She never forgave god for not allowing her to die with them either.

She never looked at another dog. She was consumed with grief every day she was alive and living in Belfast.

One day after sitting in her sisters having her lunch, she made her excuses for leaving early. She put her big woollen winters coat on and waved her sister good bye, with the promise she would see them at the week-end. She took the bus into Belfast city centre and there got on a bus that was going to Larne. She stepped off the bus at the terminus and walked towards the docks. On reaching the Port of Larne, Molly purchased a return ticket for the Larne to Stranraer ferry. With nothing more than 20 pounds left in her handbag. She hitched a lift at Stranraer from a lorry driver going up to Glasgow and got off when he parked up for the night at his destination. That was 16 years ago and she had disappeared from her life. She had sent her sister a letter asking her not to look for her. Molly told her that she would come home when she was ready, but she needed to get away from Belfast.

Molly needed to prove to herself that life was worth living. She had told her sister that she loved her and her family and not to worry about her, that she would be fine.

Molly roamed the streets of Glasgow sleeping where she could and had often resorted to prostitution to allow her to buy food she needed when she was starving. There was an inbuilt will in her to survive. She wasn't aware of it, but it was there. For years she had tramped through the streets finding places where she could beg and receive scraps and sometimes money.

Somehow she had managed to survive.

Her hair had never been professionally cut in all that time and was now a mess. It more or less resembled a bird's nest. She had in the past taken scissors to it, but this last year had given up on that as well.

About five years ago she had stumbled across two young boys playing with an abandoned supermarket trolley on one of the deserted waste grounds, local to where she begged and scavenged.

She watched the boys play for some time, finding herself transfixed by the way they played. She lowered her eyes and bowed her head when she realised that it was not her boys she was watching.

When the two of them had had their fun with the trolley, they set about trying to trash it. She wanted the trolley and appeared as if from nowhere from the shadows, her coat flaying in the wind. She must have looked terrifying to the two boys. Like some sort of spectre appearing from nowhere. They took off in the opposite direction running scared and when they were far enough away and sure she wasn't any harm to them, they started hurling abuse at her and threw stones in her direction. None came near all dropping far short. She gave them one last look as she gathered up the prize. It wasn't badly damaged and it would do very nicely for what she wanted it for. For the first time in years she felt like smiling.

That was five years ago and she had gained a worldly possession, a trolley to carry anything she could find and anything she could scavenge. Anything that she thought could be useful and that she could swap with any of the other street people, if she so desired.

As I said before, there were very few friendships and even fewer conversations between the homeless, as they jealously guarded any possession. Molly had her trolley and the others knew not to touch or try to steal it. She was one mad Irish bitch when it came to her trolley. By day she would be out and about in the streets begging and sometimes got lucky and passers-by would give her a few coppers to get rid of her. She trawled restaurant refuse bins for things to eat. Often she was chased away by staff, other times she was left to it. She had her favourite places where she found food sometimes. And it was coming back from one of those places that she quite literally bumped into Nelson.

A month after he had slaughtered the tramps Nelson was exiting a bar in Argyll Street after having a few celebratory birthday drinks on his own. He stepped out of the bars entrance under Central Station's railway bridge, when he collided with Molly. She was heading for the South side of the river pushing her trolley. He nearly fell into it and was promptly cursed by this apparition. She spat verbal profanities at him which Nelson could not understand. There was not one word of recognizable English except the word "Fucker". He knew that he was being chastised for something that was not his fault. The crash would mean his knee would swell. He gave the bump a vigorous rub to try and alleviate the sharp pain. Nelson growled back at her and offered a few profanities of his own but when he looked up he saw the evil look in her eyes as she drew him a lengthy hateful stare. He was angered by this and he reached down into his pocket for his knife but it wasn't there. He thought about grabbing and cuffing her and giving her a taste of his medicine, but the lank dirty coat and the rank smell emanating from her was enough to stop him from over reacting. She trundled on without so much as a sorry, heading in the direction of St Enoch's square. Nelson's eyes blazed hatred.

"No point in shouting at her pal, that's Irish Molly. She's as daft as a brush."

Nelson turned to see who was talking to him.

"You alright there, sir? The question hit Nelson like a sledgehammer blow. "It looked like that was a nasty bump she gave you with her trolley."

Nelson couldn't answer. There was a policeman standing there on the pavement. He was momentarily stunned into silence.

"Sir, I am saying ..."

"No, I'm fine officer, really," Nelson managed to say, trying to dismiss the incident. "She just surprised me. I should have looked where I was going I suppose ... my fault, should have..." Nelson was fully aware that the policeman was staring at him.

"... when I came out of the pub. It's nothing really it'll heal, it's only a bump," Nelson continued trying to dismiss the whole thing.

The officer's eyes left Nelson and followed Molly going off in the distance "OK, sir. Take it easy the next time," and he walked past.

Nelson mumbled something incoherent and felt relieved watching him go.

The incident had raised a few smiles from the many onlookers and passer byes. Hit by a supermarket trolley and berated by a tramp, how embarrassing.

Nelson swore there and then that she wasn't going to get away with humiliating him in the street like that. He would find her and when he did, she would be the one who would be sorry.

She wouldn't be hard to find, how many female tramps in Glasgow were called Irish Molly.

The constable stopped at the end of the road and looked back at Nelson limping along towards Union Street. Irish Molly had crossed the road and was on the opposite side. He walked on smiling to himself.

Nelson hobbled up Union Street and along Renfield Street heading for the Buchanan St bus station and the bus home to Campsie. The pain in his knee intensified as did his anger. Nelson was not one, who would forgive or forget, this was a birthday he would remember for a long time. He called into the Blue Lagoon chip shop for a fish supper to eat on the bus home.

By the time he got off at his bus stop the pain had subsided mainly through all the self-massage he had administered on the bruised knee. Walking through Lennox Castle hospital grounds towards the home he still shared with his parents, his mood lifted a little. Both his parents would be still up watching the TV, waiting for their birthday boy to come home.

They would poke fun at him asking where he had been and did he have a couple of pints and had he enjoyed himself. He'd tell them the usual lies about being out with his mates and having a whale of a time chatting up girls. He'd tell them about the latest girl he was looking forward to seeing again, a lass called Molly.

But if he wanted to be truthful, he actually had enjoyed his day out to Glasgow.

He had enjoyed having a couple of beers in a bar he had never been in before, talking to complete strangers.

That was how he had wanted to celebrate this birthday, in his own company.

There was no having to lie about where he stayed, because his fellow drinkers didn't care. So what if he did still stay with his mum and dad, no one was the least bit interested.

He was a loner. He would always be one.

He was a killer and killers didn't have many friends.

As he continued through the Hospital grounds, he could see the lights from the houses in the distance. He thought about the best bit about the whole day so far and it was the fish and chips on the way home.

At the same time that Nelson was heading home, Police constable Pat Hendry was completing his shift. He pushed open the front door into Cranstonhill police station. The place was noisy with a couple of drunks giving the arresting officers grief.

Pat was heading to the locker room to change. His shift had been quiet. He had trudged all over the shopper's streets, Argyll Street and Renfield Street. He had answered questions from the many tourists who were in the fair city. But he was now going home.

He passed the desk sergeant and headed to the locker room to change his jacket, when something caught his attention. He always gave a customary glance at the notice board, but never really consciously took much interest in it. He had looked at it hundreds of times without so much of a second thought. This time there was something new on it. Not just the usual 'Crime doesn't pay' shit that had been there for years. Something caught his attention. It was an A4 sheet of paper with artist's sketch and the headlines on the notice read; "If you recognize this man ... call 999 ..." Pat walked on and was just about to open the door to the locker room when he stopped dead in his tracks. He walked back for a second look and as he stared at the wanted poster he brought his right hand up to his chin, feeling the stubble on it. He looked deeply at the sketch in the poster. There was something about the face in the poster that got him thinking: maybe it was the eyes and the nose that grabbed his attention. The face in the poster was wearing a woollen hat. Pat thought that he recognized or had come across this person. He continued to stare into the eyes wondering and the image was staring right back at him. "I've seen you, sunshine. Can't remember where I've seen you, but ..." The nose was maybe a wee bit different; the eyes were maybe a wee bit too close together; maybe you've got dark hair.

"Fuck me," he said out loud, "You look like the fucker that got his leg bumped with a trolley tonight."

CHAPTER 26

Our switchboard was manned 24 hours a day, seven days a week and literally took hundreds of calls a day. Some were kids taking the piss while others were the real thing and our boys and girls had to go and deal with our wonderful public citizens.

David Arthur was working his first nightshift and was sitting at his call centre with his head phones on. He had a mug of coffee in front of him and was enjoying it. The caffeine was a necessity to get David through the next seven hours. It was the only thing that would keep him from falling asleep during the periods of quiet. He had this month's *What Car* magazine on the table and he would read it cover to cover. David Arthur was a proud car nut and petrol head. There was nothing he didn't know about a car and he was proud of that fact.

He lifted up his mug and sipped the hot coffee when his phone rang. His very first call of the night. He grinned to himself wondering what kind of crap he was about to hear.

The British telecom switchboard operator had diverted an emergency call to his unit.

"This is Strathclyde Police, how can I help?"

"This is Constable Patrick Hendry from Cranstonhill station my badge number is 13666. It's about the new Wanted poster you boys on the task force put out."

David sat forward putting his coffee down on the table in front of him.

"It dawned on me that I saw the guy in the poster earlier on tonight."

"Repeat your last message please," David said.

"I saw the guy in the new wanted poster your task force put out"

"Badge number again please?"

Pat reeled off his badge number and David wrote it down he asked him to hold for one second.

David called down to the desk sergeant and within seconds our place was buzzing.

Seconds turned to minutes, the badge number was verified and Pat was told to come up to our station now.

Glasgow's Chief Police commissioner Sir Jonathan Allen had the divisional heads set up a task force to catch our very own serial killer. The commissioner must have had kittens when the initial report landed on his desk.

There was a serial killer in his Glasgow.

He was running free and killing people on the doorstep.

The report must have had the commissioner choke on his morning croissant as he read about one bloke having killed eight of our unfortunate homeless and had attempted to kill a member of the gay community using the same weapon on all of the said on the same night. The homosexual was lucky to be alive having his jugular partially punctured. He was alive by what the doctors described as a miracle really. The knife blade had only nicked the jugular and by rights that usually is enough to cause a fatality. But this time the victim's head had sort of lolled to the side and had somehow partially stemmed the flow of blood. The medics said that it was one in 100 million chances of that happening. It was also luck that the man's neighbour had found him minutes after the attack. It was also lucky that an ambulance was returning from a call and was in the vicinity as well.

As I said the gay chap was a real lucky man. Circumstances had played their part in keeping that guy alive.

The most startling news came from the forensics team on the case. They came up with the fact that whoever our killer was it was the same DNA profile of the killer of Graham Smith and Elizabeth Wilson from all those years ago in Lennoxtown. The DNA found at the scene had kick started our data base back into action. Hence the reason the commissioner set up the task force. Why he picked our station I don't know, history maybe, but our incident room was alive with computers and wall boards. The task force was less than a week old and we had 12 detectives working this case with yours truly as lead.

I got the call around a quarter to 11 and as I sat there in my armchair in front of the TV I couldn't really believe my ears. Thank Christ I was sober was all I could think. I shouted upstairs to my wife who had just gone to bed that I was off out to the station and I'd be back whenever. I never heard her muffled response.

I put my shoes on and sat down on the stairs to tie my laces. I was on a high and shook my head thinking that we were lucky to get such a break. I grabbed my jacket and car keys and I was off out the door. I opened the car door and jumped inside. The new smell was still there and I had no time to drive carefully in our newly purchased Ford Mondeo. I dropped into gear and was off down our road as if there was no tomorrow.

I was lucky enough to get parked in the same street as the station and had to walk about 60 yards to the door. I could see a couple of the boys had beaten me to it and were already in. As I walked through the door you could feel a difference in the place. The boys on the beat were, I was going to say upbeat, but that would be the wrong description. They were all, oh fuck it for the want of a better word, they were upbeat at the news.

I took the stairs two at a time and as I strode slightly breathless into our incident conference room some of the twelve were already there. They too looked different, but as I looked at them, I could recognize their intensity. The place was buzzing.

Kenny was the first to approach me, "OK boss? We didn't get you out your bed did we?"

"No, Kenny, I was up." I took the seat at the head of the table and asked the team to sit down for a heads up briefing. As we sat down more team members joined us. They too were slightly breathless.

"What do we know so far?" I asked.

Colin Brazil spoke up, "A call came into our switchboard at twenty two thirty five from PC Patrick Hendry from the Cranstonhill station. Badge number verified. He told Dave

Arthur on the switchboard, that he had seen our poster and had confirmed seeing someone that resembled the artist's sketch outside Under the Umbrella pub on Argyll Street earlier on tonight. He's on his way here as we speak."

"One of you let the desk know to show PC Hendry straight in here when he comes would you?"

Conversations broke out all around the table as we waited. About ten minutes later there was a knock on the door and in stepped our Patrick Hendry. He looked around the table at all the eager looking faces and I stood up and shook his hand. I took the liberty of all the introductions of my team. It was too much for him to take in all at once, but what the hell I had to do the intros.

He was offered a seat and told to start telling his story. We listened intently and Kenny wrote down the most pertinent points on a flip chart. The rest of the boys used their small notebooks. Questions came thick and fast for Pat Hendry.

How close was the poster to the bloke you saw?

Was it a good identikit likeness?

What colour was the bloke's eyes? Hair? Did he have any visible scars?

What height is he?

Did he have a noticeable accent? You did talk to him?

Which way did he walk away? Did he go along Argyll Street towards Hope Street or along towards Union Street.

I mean the boys fired questions rat a tat tat. Thick and fast and like a good cop, Pat answered them all as best he could.

I stared at Kenny's board and all the points were nearly filled in for us all to digest. After the incident our suspect walked back along Argyll Street towards Union Street. He was limping.

He was around 5 feet 10 inches tall.

He weighed around 180 pounds,

He had dark hair, brown not black.

He had no visible facial scars and he didn't have any noticeable accent.

He was wearing Black trousers and had a black leather jacket that buttoned not zipped up.

After looking at all the answers written down, I started task dividing. I went round the table. Detective Johnny Russell was first.

"Russ, get on the blower and have one of our drive byes keep that pub open. Kenny and Tim will go down there to interview the staff." I was met with a quizzical stare,

"What?" I asked and as I glanced down at my watch and I couldn't believe it was a quarter to midnight.

"Fuck me look at the time. Russ have a squad car try the pub doors anyway, we might get lucky and hopefully they might still be in there cleaning up or having a beer."

Stewart, you and Mike try and rustle up some of our boys and spread the word we need to find out where Irish Molly sleeps. Our guy murdered eight tramps last week so she could be next. Someone on the beat must know where she hangs out.

"Boss you still want me and Tim to head on down to the pub?"

I looked at Kenny and shook my head, "Wait until we hear from the drive by."

"If these boys have been drinking all night they might be in a bit of a state."

"I know, Kenny, but we have to talk to anybody that remembers seeing our guy. You'll have to find out from the bar manager if it was a night for just regulars or what? We need that pub to be breaking the law."

"Les, in case it's shut, try and find out who owns the place. Wake people up if you have to and somebody tell Dave Arthur thanks would you and someone get that sketch artist back in here pronto. We have a better witness folks we need to make the changes."

I could sense something in the room; it might have been a feeling of hope that we were a step closer to catching this guy who had been killing people for a very long time. I hoped that it wasn't something more and that we were getting ahead of ourselves. I knew that every minute we took to get an answer was a minute more he had of putting more distance between him and us.

Around twenty past midnight the police car sent on the drive by radioed in that the doors to the pub were closed and there was no sound of anyone on the premises.

We ordered some coffee and sat round the table waiting for something, anything that could help.

Les came back into the room and announced he had found out who owned the place, but we were fucked there as well as it was a pub chain. We weren't getting anywhere fast, we wouldn't get any answers until the cleaners went in to the place in the morning just before opening. It wasn't a pub any of our boys frequented. I dropped my pen onto the desk and lifted my cup of coffee. I stared again at the points that Kenny had written down on the flip chart. We all sat down and brainstormed. We went over and over again what we now knew.

Detectives chipped in with bits and pieces and in no time I had to have another strong cup of coffee. I was getting tired and so were the rest of the boys.

As I was sipping the hot coffee I piped up, "Now he was walking towards Union Street we know that, so where was he going after that? Was he heading for the underground?" Kenny joined in, "Was he heading for a corporation bus? What buses run along Argyll Street?"

"What's at the top of Union Street?" Another question was shot into the ring.

I continued, "Listen, what if he turned up Union Street, carried on up Renfield Street and then onto Buchanan Street bus station. That's not far. What do you think?"

"It's still Dundas Street bus station," Trevor quipped.

"Is it Fuck, It's now called Buchanan Street ..."

I had to stop the bickering, "Guys please, arguing about trivial things ain't helping. There's a bus station at the top of the road, end of story."

"He could have been heading for George square and Queen Street station. He could have been heading for the big taxi rank or could have got on a train to anywhere. He could have jumped on the Underground and beyond, disappearing into the sticks."

"Yeah thanks for that, Russ, but what if? Just listen for a moment." I paused briefly thinking aloud. "What if this fucker is a local from the Lennoxtown area? The first two murders were from there."

"Clutching at straws, Boss," Kenny said. "Remember the DNA says the 3rd one was in Millport."

"Yeah I know you're right. But humour me for a moment. What if he does come from around there, Lennoxtown, Milton of Campsie or Kirkintilloch? He would have travelled here."

From another one of the team, "He didn't drive here, because he was in a pub drinking. He wouldn't chance getting caught drinking and driving."

Kenny jumped in, "The bus, He came here by bus."

"He had to take the bus because there's no train service from any of those places," Russ chipped in.

"That's fucking right. He had to take the sodding bus. It's a long shot but if we're right …"

The buzz hit the table and resurgence in motivation was apparent. Fatigue was gone and temporarily forgotten about.

"Find out the time of the buses towards," I gestured with my hand, "and someone get a photo fit in front of bus drivers. If he came into the city on a bus maybe someone will recognize our boy. Surely to fuck someone has to remember our man's face; and get the boys on the beat to put a picture in front of taxi drivers, just in case he did take a cab."

I looked round the table at each one of the team and realized that in order to catch our serial killer, we were going to have to rely on our teamwork and get really lucky. I glanced at my watch and couldn't believe the time. Where had the last 6 hours gone?

The morning shift came into the station and the word in the locker room was all about Pat Hendry and his recognition of the photo fit.

The task force was up and out and some of them were heading towards Buchanan St bus Station while others were already waking a lot of tired people up.

Today was going to be a good day I could feel it. I headed off to the toilets to fill a basin full of cold water. I put my face into it and winced at the cold. I grabbed some paper towels and dried my face. The theory was the cold water would refresh me and I'd be feeling less tired. All I felt was cold. I checked my watch and it was a quarter to seven. I'd give the wife another ten minutes and then I'd call her with my news.

By lunchtime I was hoping that we would have more information and dare I say it, a positive identification and we would be a lot closer to our boy. I looked into the mirror and attempted a smile; the wrinkles were more evident every day. Laughter lines the wife called them. I called them stress lines. I had to get myself another coffee.

The phone rang on my desk and I picked it up. Russ gave me the news that none of the bus crews he asked, recognized our photo fit, but he had the names and addresses of the drivers from last night. He'd call later. No sooner had I put the receiver down that it rang again. The cleaners were in the Pub called Under the Umbrella but as expected none of them recognized our guy. The bar manager had been telephoned and she was due in at 9.30

a.m. to check in a delivery. I put the phone down and sighed. So far there was fuck all to get excited about.

Kenny came in and sat down with a cup of something hot. "You get the feeling we missed the bastard?"

I looked at him in earnest and tried to be honest, "Nope, it's early days. Something is going to turn up. We're going to catch this fucker."

"That's if we were right about our assumption that he's a local to the first two killings."

"I know, Kenny. I know. We were both there all those years ago, remember?"

Kenny offered me a cigarette and I refused. I wasn't up to it. I was beyond tired and probably a grump, "We have to be right this time. This fucker is not getting away from you and me this time."

I saw the pained look on Kenny's face and I could see he was fighting back a yawn.

"Kenny, fuck, feeling this tired, be a good lad and shut the door on the way out; I'm going for a lie down. Wake me if something comes up."

Kenny got up stubbed the cigarette out in the ashtray and said sure. The door closed and I hit the settee. I closed my eyes and slept.

I woke with a start later as my office door got rapped hard. I sat up to find several of the team beaming smiles at me. "We got him," Kenny said laughing. "We got him."

"What time is it?"

"Just gone one."

Kenny went on, "We were right; we took a long shot and it paid off, he's a local country boy from Campsie. A bus driver and his conductor have both confirmed that he's a regular on the buses. We know where he's from and what stop he gets off at."

I was gob smacked, the shock of something going right on a guess. "From the beginning someone," I said stretching.

Trevor started by saying, "We put a photo fit in front of most of the drivers that were on last night before they started their afternoon shift or whatever and came up with sod all. But one of the drivers from Kirkintilloch recognized our boy. I asked him what run he was on last night and what time it was that he saw our man and if he was sure and he said he couldn't be one hundred percent sure, but he was ninety percent sure. He was on the Campsie Glen route last night. We then went to another address and asked the bus conductor, who was on shift with him and he also confirmed all of that, when we put the fit in front of him. He said that it looked like the boy that got off at Lennox castle hospital ..."

I shot a glance at Kenny and he was grinning and nodding his head.

"... and that he lives in Netherton Oval."

Memories came flooding back to me of the hospital grounds and of a boy buried under a bush and of a girl left in a storm drain. Of McCluskey sending two young detectives on their first real murder enquiry and us coming up with fuck all. Now here we were years later and we had the bastard nearly in our grasp.

"Task room everybody now and get me the super on the blower, someone should tell him the good news."

CHAPTER 27

Nelson woke up to the sounds of birds chirping outside his bedroom window. His head was sore and his mouth was dry, remnants of too much drink and of him snoring like a pig all night. He wearily threw back the sheets and blankets, got out of his bed and went over to his window. He pulled the curtains back and looked out at the communal swing park. It was bathed in early morning sunshine but quiet with no children at this hour. He looked back at the clock on his bedside cabinet 6.50 a.m. He yawned and stretched and in an instant decided to go back to bed for another hour or so. There was no point in getting up this early he had no job to go to, he had been fired.

The task force had assembled and we went through everything we now knew.

Kenny had started drawing and writing things on a new flip chart and his rough sketch showed that there were three main roads into Lennox Castle hospital and we all were very aware that there was hundreds upon hundreds of acres of open woodland. There was an abandoned railway track that was now used by walkers stretching east to west towards the west lodge and onwards to Blanefield.

We decided that we would gamble on our suspect using the roads. He was either a driver or a walker and used the bus when he went drinking.

We decided on three unmarked cars, Alpha, Bravo and Charlie and a team of three officers per car. The teams were to be stationed one at each road end and that would have to suffice, because if we went heavy handed into Netherton oval as a whole bunch of strangers, our boy could get spooked and be off and running. We didn't want that. We couldn't go in asking folk to look at the photo fit either, because we didn't know just how close the community was. The last thing we needed was to show his image in front of one of his friends, if he had any and he or she, tell him that we were looking for him.

He would vanish like a ghost.

It was also decided that the best thing we could do was to have our plain clothes boys and girls sitting on the Campsie Glen bus in and out of Glasgow, just in case he had slipped past us and he could get on anywhere along the route.

It was moaned at me that sitting on a bus for any length of time was boring and that I would have to change personnel after so many hours.

So we agreed to a quick rota. Occupants of the cars could do longer shifts as they were in comfort. That brought smiles from the picked teams. They would do eight hour shifts before a change. Bus personnel would be changed out every two trips.

Our suspect had the advantage of his local knowledge of the area, but we had an advantage as well. He didn't know we were onto him. Although we didn't have a name for him and we knew very little of his background, we each carried in our head, a mental picture of him. The photo fit was now a very close likeness.

We would have to be patient.

He would have to come to us.

We would have to wait for our recognition of the suspect as a driver, which would be a fleeting glimpse as he drove past, or as a pedestrian on his way to the bus stop. Hopefully it would be the latter and then we could take him down. I didn't fancy a car chase, they always ended badly. I could only hope that he would be on foot.

There was no time to lose. We could only pray that he was still at home and he wasn't out and about already.

We thought that as the first bus of the day was 6 a.m. he wouldn't be on it. It was now nearly two in the afternoon and the last bus was 10.30 p.m. He could have taken any one of them before noon, so we had to station plain clothes at the terminus now. If he was a regular visitor to our city, he could already be here.

With a last look at each one of the boys I told them to be lucky.

I was going to stay at the task room. Kenny was going to take lead car at the main bus stop. All teams drew radios and did a quick check with me. Satisfied they were all working, I nodded to Kenny and he grinned back at me. I really wanted to tell Kenny not to kill the bastard and to leave that for me to do. But I didn't. I reckoned Kenny knew what I was going to say and that's why he just grinned. I could hear the conversations of the boys as they went down the stairs in a hurry.

I could have murdered a scotch at that moment in time only to realize that murder was probably not an appropriate thing to think. I would have to settle for another coffee.

"Nelson, are you getting up?" his mum shouted. "It's gone 12 and I'm off out. Bye, see you later."

Nelson was awake at the front door closing. He had heard her shout something. He threw back the covers and got up from his warm bed. He yawned and stretched and headed through to the toilet. He had a bit of a headache and his knee was sore. He remembered about Irish Molly and as he pissed, the anger returned to his eyes. He looked down at the swelling on his knee, "You're going to pay for that bruise you cow, that's a promise."

He flushed the toilet and moved across to the wash basin. He turned the hot water tap on letting the water run from cold to hot and when he was satisfied that there was sufficient heat he proceeded to wash and shave. After shaving he ran a hot bath and dropped some of his mother's bath salts into the water. As he lay in the warm soothing water he massaged his ego, he was going back into Glasgow and would search for Molly. He knew which part of the city he would start looking. It didn't bother Nelson that he was going back into the same streets where he had killed a month before. It was her time; she was going to pay for the pain she had caused.

She had a date with his knife.

He was going back for retribution.

The pain in his knee would be worth it, if and when he found her.

My radio crackled into life.

"Bravo team in position, South Lodge crossroads."

"Roger that Bravo."

A minute or so later ...

'Charlie team approaching East Lodge gates."

"Roger Charlie."

On the back of that I heard Kenny check in,

"Alpha team in position."

"Keep your fingers crossed Alpha."

"Will do, boss."

I put the hand set back down onto the table and I sat and stared at it. I wanted to pick it up and use it asking any of them for updates but I couldn't. I would have to show patience and lead by example. This was going to be a waiting game and the next few hours were going to be really tense. I closed my eyes and thought about each of the teams in my mind and where they were. I could still visualize the layout of the place from my first encounter with Lennox Castle hospital. The surrounding fields and forests, the Campsie Fells the—

The radio crackled back into life, "Trev here, boss, at the terminus. No one matching our boy came off the Campsie Glen bus."

I grabbed the radio, "Thanks, Trev."

"Two plain clothes going on return journey. Any noise from our boys?"

"All quiet. Over."

I could feel the knot of anxiety pulling at my gut, or was it pangs of hunger?

If my wife had been there she would have told me to go and eat something. Mind you I could have eaten a steak pie and beans and have the whole plate smothered in brown sauce. My mouth was watering at that prospect. The decision was made, I would have to go and search for something soon. I grabbed my radio and headed off to the canteen in the hope there was something left and edible waiting for me.

Nelson dressed quickly and walked through to the kitchen. Opening the fridge he saw that there were bacon rashers and square sausages waiting to be cooked. He decided on a fried breakfast. He got the frying pan out and put some cooking oil in. He turned the gas cooker on and the heat up to mark 3. As he waited he filled the electric kettle with cold water and switched it on. He decided to cook the sausages first as they would take the longest, then the bacon and lastly two eggs.

He was organized and methodical today and as he cooked, he smiled at the thought of finding Molly.

The canteen menu did not have steak pie and beans, which disappointed me, but it did, however, have Lasagne as today's special. I love Lasagne, I could honestly eat it every day and my wife makes it even better than the Italians do. A plate of that with some garlic bread and a glass of red wine and that's me a happy man.

The stuff in the canteen was not Lasagne, I'm not quite sure what it was, but I regretted buying and eating the damn stuff that was for sure. I could feel the indigestion beginning already. But I had eaten something and that after all was the intent and purpose of the canteen visit.

I walked back into the empty task room and stood in front of Kenny's flip chart and stared long and hard at the new sketch that had been drawn up. I could imagine the boys sitting in the cars, windows open and grey cigarette smoke curling from within, as if they had just picked a new pope.

The radio in my right hand remained silent and I had to check it to make sure it was still turned on. I couldn't take the chance and go on it and ask for the teams for updates. Radios crackling into life on a stake out were usually frowned upon. Criminals escaped hearing things like that, like at the beginning of a race when the starter's pistol fired, they were off and running.

Their updates would come in time. I laid the radio down on the table in front of me and I sat down. Should I call my wife and talk to her? Or should I just wait for the news that we had caught our man. If I had a pack of cards I could play solitaire. After all that's what it bloody felt like sitting here on my jack jones. "Talk to me somebody," I said staring at the radio.

Nobody listened to my plea and it remained silent.

Nelson washed up his breakfast dishes and his beloved tea mug and then dried and put them all away. He left the frying pan on the work top adjacent to the gas cooker for further use. He was in an upbeat mood. He took the stairs to his bedroom two at a time; he was in a rush to get his jacket and his knife. After grabbing both he was a bit more careful going back down the stairs. He opened and closed the front door. The sun was shining and it was a beautiful day. It was going to be a beautiful day when I catch Molly thought Nelson. He glanced at his watch and his bus was due in fifteen minutes, if it was on time, he would make it. He started walking quickly along the road, past the football park, past the hospital wards, past the hospital kitchens and the workshops, over the bridge towards the bus stop. Nelson took no notice of the parked car on the other side of the bridge. Took no notice of the occupants, he was too engrossed in his thoughts about Molly, to even register an interest in the stationary vehicle.

"Charlie team checking in with nothing to report, all quiet this end."

I lifted the radio from the table in front of me, "Roger that."

I couldn't help myself and I broke my own rule I pressed the talk button, "Bravo team anything?"

"Bus just passed us heading towards Campsie Glen terminus. Looked empty."

"OK Bravo."

I hesitated conversing with the Alpha team. I don't know why I did at that moment in time. I had the radio at my mouth; I had my fingers poised on the talk button, but something stopped me. My radio crackled into life.

"Alpha team here. Someone approaching, stand by."

I caught my breath for a minute. I was glad I hadn't pressed the talk button. My heart rate must have jumped.

The three detectives were sitting in the car with their backs to the hospital. Andy the driver had parked the car across from the bus stop and had reversed onto hospital property off the main road. They were facing the Campsie Fells. Andy had seen the figure approaching in his rear view mirror. Kenny stubbed the cigarette he was smoking out into the ashtray and stared hard into the passenger side wing mirror. Lyle sitting in the back seat casually turned to get a better look.

"Fuck me it's him," Lyle said. "It's our Man."

"You sure?" Kenny said putting the radio to the side of the seat.

"I'm sure."

"100 percent?"

"Yep."

"How do you want to play this then, guys?" Kenny asked. "Let him go past us and then take him? Or fuck it, open up the door and jump him and you two pile in."

"Yeah."

"Yeah what?"

"You jump him and we'll pile in."

Nelson was approaching the rear of the car and would pass along the passenger side.

Nelson's thoughts were clouding his senses. He was walking into a trap and his gut feeling of danger wasn't there. He had been aware of the car door opening and that a figure was getting out. He tried to step around the person coming out but what happened next was a blur.

Kenny could feel the adrenalin rush as he opened the car door and tried to get out of the car as fast as he could to jump on Nelson. Lyle had simultaneously opened the rear door and got out fast and was the second officer to join the melee. Kenny had swung a haymaker at Nelson catching him totally unawares on his cheekbone and had sent Nelson sprawling. Kenny sprung forward and was lucky enough to hit the falling Nelson again, this time catching him on the side of his head. Nelson lashed out at his assailants hitting one of them but in return was punched again and again.

Andy had run around the front of the car and dived on the falling figure. The three officers had a now fighting mad Nelson face down on the ground as he squirmed for freedom under their combined weight. Kenny was pushing Nelson's face into the tarmac and Lyle grabbed Nelson's right wrist forcing it into the small of his back and slapped the cuffs on him. He repeated the action with Nelson's left hand.

Andy was lying on the wriggling Nelson's legs.

It was over in seconds.

They were all breathing hard. None more so than Kenny. He had taken a punch from Nelson and was now feeling it.

They had won the battle against an incredibly strong Nelson.

The dilemma they now faced was how to get up from being on top of their prisoner.

Kenny told Andy that he could let go the legs and go grab the radio and call Bravo for back up.

My radio burst into life and I almost cheered when I heard Andy calling Bravo team for back up. "Suspect in custody. Bravo team to Alpha position."

Seconds or was it minutes later I radioed, "All teams stand down. Suspect in custody. All teams return to base."

My heart was pounding.

I wanted to see the look on that bastard's face when the boys brought him in.

I wanted to gloat about us catching him.

I wanted to tell him things I can't print here.

I really wanted to hurt the son of a bitch for two main reasons.

One was a small boy.

The other one was a young girl.

CHAPTER 28

The lift doors opened on floor 3 and the orderly pushed Nelson out and along the corridor towards X-ray. The two officers followed on the heels of Dr Francis. On reaching the doors marked 'No Entry X-ray' Elizabeth turned and said to the two officers, "This is as far as you go boys."

"But he's our responsibility ..."

"You'll get him back in a few minutes."

"But, Doctor, you don't understand, we can't leave the prisoner."

"No buts. You see this sign? It means what it says. It says, No entry, unless of course, you boys have been handed a film badge?" Elizabeth caught their surprised looks.

"What no film badge? That's a wee shame. What about you, have you got a personal dosimeter then?" Elizabeth smiled at both their blank expressions. "No? I didn't think so. You boys wait here. We'll be back in a tick." Elizabeth turned on her heels and followed Nelson's trolley into X-ray. The two doors silently closed behind her. The warning light above the door turned from green to red illuminating the No Entry Radiation warning sign.

Both officers shrugged their shoulders with the resignation of having no option but to wait. The prisoner was unconscious and strapped into the gurney. What possible damage could he do?

"What we got, Beth?" Mark Smith the Radiologist asked.

"Possible mini stroke and maybe inter cranial damage, first diagnosis from E.R." Elizabeth handed the new file to Mark. Mark read the notes quickly and put the brown file down on the desk behind the screen.

Mark carefully examined the lump on Nelson's head. "A big old nasty bump there. That'll give him a sore head when he wakes up. Self inflicted or heavy handed screws?" he asked.

Elizabeth shook her head, "Pass."

"OK I'll do the usual angles. Nine straight shots should be finished in about ten minutes. Pop into my office. Beth. Want a coffee? There's one in the percolator."

"No ta, I'm good."

"Well it's there if you want one."

"Thanks anyway, Mark."

Elizabeth walked behind the lead screen along the small corridor and into Mark's small office. The aroma of coffee was appealing and she toyed with the thought of having one. She checked her pager as routine. Saw nothing and decided to sit down and relax for a few moments of well earned rest.

Next door the X-ray controls and the automatic film processing unit hummed, waiting for action. Mark and Tommy the orderly unstrapped Nelson and lifted him onto the unit bed.

Mark then maneuvered the X-ray unit around Nelson's head stopping the target crosshairs on parts of the head that he knew would give the best overall picture of any damage to Nelson.

"Thanks, Tom. Pop back and see if Beth's OK. Sleeping beauty and I are going to be just fine and dandy."

After one final look at the X-ray crosshairs on Nelson, Mark walked silently back into the dark room and checked the X-ray levels from his wall chart; he ran his finger along the scale, knowing the focal distance the KV and Ma values were set in stone. Satisfied he stepped forward to the electronic panel turning each dial he set the Kilovolts first and then Milliamps. Click and a two second buzzing noise and Mark was one X-ray down and ready to re focus the machine again. Minutes later having completed the task, he presented Elizabeth with a full set of nine X-rays illuminated up on the viewer.

"No fractures. No bursts, no bleeding into the skull. Just a sore head when he wakes up, sorry Beth. I know how much you wanted a fractured skull to get your neurological diagnostic teeth into, but zilch this time I'm afraid." Mark grinned.

Elizabeth peered at each image and agreed. "Yep, sore head it is. I have to get him down now and admit him into his very own wee private room downstairs that they're setting up for him. He'll be out of the way down there and back into the watchful and tender care of the police."

Mark asked, "Who is he? Do you know?"

"I don't, but he warrants two plain clothes, Pinky and Perky outside."

"Well if you find out he's someone famous, I'll autograph his head shots for *The News of the World*.

"Yeah right and they both laughed as Tommy and Mark lifted Nelson back onto the trolley and re fixed the straps.

"Velcro is a wonderful thing isn't it?" Mark joked, "Where would we be without it?

Chapter 29

I got into the office around 8 a.m., said good morning to a few of them and went straight to grab myself a coffee. The traffic on this Monday morning wasn't all that bad, compared to some of the days, when I'm gridlocked and the jam doesn't move for ages. That's usually the start of a real bad mood, but today my mood was fine. The blue skies and no road rage that I was witness to would leave everybody, including me feeling upbeat, so there was no bad vibes so far.

I grabbed my cup and put a teaspoonful of Nescafe gold in and topped it up from the steaming urn. Added some milk from the fridge stirred the lot and how easy was that, for a good start to the morning. All I had to do now was ditch the jacket and briefcase and go and wind up Kenny.

I found him sat at his desk reading the *Daily Record* and he was muttering to himself.

"What's up, Kenny?" I asked him.

He glanced up from his paper, "Alright, Paul, how you doing?" he questioned with a smile. He laid the paper down on his desk. I could see that he had black ink stains on his fingertips. He had been reading every news story in the paper.

I answered, "I'm chirpy. The sky is blue; the sun is going to shine all day and my only major case to stress me out, is the car dealership fiasco. So I'm going to have a wonderful day," I told him putting my coffee cup down on his desk.

"Fucking chirpy? Ha ha, you forget who is in Ward 7 in the Royal?"

"Kenny, my boy, he's not our problem. Never mind the ward he's in. Look at the sunshine, think of your holidays, it's the 10th of June." I sipped some of my hot coffee as I sat down. "He's someone else's problem; just think someone from Division, has now just inherited their very own wee nightmare, and therefore he's not ours."

Kenny looked out of his window, "When he wakes up, it's that city that has the problem."

I took another sip of my coffee as I too looked towards the skyline that was Glasgow.

"I phoned some of the boys from armed response and put them in the picture about you know who."

"Well, Kenny, you said you would. So what did they say?"

"They all want to put a bullet into our friend."

I nodded in agreement, "Yeah me too. But you know, fuck him," I said. "Never mind that bastard, tell me what happened on Saturday with the wee blonde bit."

"Never mind her, did you see Steffi Graf and that wee Spanish minx Arantxa Sanchez Vicario on Saturday at the French Open tennis final. Now that was exciting. It was Graf's nineteenth Grand Slam title and the fifth time she's won the French."

"Kenny, you're changing the subject."

"And it's Scotland against Holland tonight in the Euro's."

"Kenny! The wee Blonde bit?"

He looked me straight in the eyes and a smile started to creep all over his face, "Paul, what can I tell you? I wasted my time" I was chasing the wrong bit. It was that time of the month, or so she said. I screwed up, or should I say I didn't."

We both laughed out loud.

Later on having sat and chewed the fat with Kenny earlier, I was sitting at my own desk looking at a file on Davidson's motors. It was a case on what we called the car dealership fiasco. This was a business, a family run company in Shettleston that had a Ford dealership. They had been located in Shettleston since 1963 when they sold Ford Anglias. They hadn't come on our radar screen as being a bit dodgy and had as they say, motored along the straight and narrow. But they had been caught buying and importing the new Ford Focus from Denmark duty free and putting a whacking 3500 pounds on each car. Apparently you could buy the car in Denmark a whole lot cheaper than you could here in Britain.

The story was leaked to the *Daily Record* and was headlines for a few days. The company had then hit a wee bad patch and a few of the pissed off customers had threatened staff. Ford weren't too happy with them either and took back their franchise. Now normally this case wouldn't pass over my desk or anybody else's from our section because we don't deal with fraud cases, but the *Daily Record*'s whistleblower was put in a coma and traction by – it was rumoured on the street – by one of our known Springburn thugs. So the case changed from fraud to attempted murder and hence the reason it was sitting on my desk. To be truthful, I could have put Kenny on it, or one of the other Detectives but it was nice to sometimes get out and about and do what I used to be good at. So I had decided to give it a crack. The case had stalled a wee bit as I couldn't speak to the victim, nor could he identify his attacker, because he was on a machine and that machine was keeping him alive. The other true fact was that there was no sign of him coming out of the coma in the near future. I could only keep my hopes up of a wee mini medical break through and as soon as he woke up, then the case would take on a new dimension and it would make my life a hell of a lot easier. That's if he remembered being attacked and had seen his attacker. I didn't want memory loss from our victim. We hadn't found our thug Sean Mallon either. Sorry I should have said our rumoured thug Sean Mallon. I shouldn't pre judge. But if I was a betting man I would put money on Mallon being our man. He had gone to ground somewhere in the concrete jungle that was Glasgow and I had my boys checking every known associate of Mr. Mallon. It would be difficult to squeeze information out of his friends because they were a tight bunch. We knew that, but we were under an obligation to our whistleblowers family to ascertain and apprehend his alleged attacker. We also suspected that the whistleblower was named by a company man and that one of the families had him done over. We also suspected that he was to be given a kicking for leaking the story and showing disloyalty, but the kicking went over the top and our story teller wasn't meant to end up on a life support machine.

I had to find out which, or should I say if a company director gave the order for the hit and to find out the real reason why. I had left a message with the company secretary at their main showroom in Shettleston that I was coming to see them at 2 p.m. this afternoon. I had some questions for each director, so I had told the secretary, not in a round about way, but firm and direct, to make sure that the three of them were going to be there and not to waste my time. I checked my watch and saw the time was just after 10 a.m. I closed the file and headed back along to the kitchen for another cup of coffee.

Driving to my appointment with the Directors, I was listening to Radio Clyde. I always like background music as I drive, it somehow gets me focused. I stopped on red at the traffic lights on Riddrie road and the DJ played 'Wannabe' by a group called the Spice girls. The Disc jockey gushed about this all girl group. He said this was their first single and he predicted it was destined to be number 1 in the charts. I thought probably, as it was quite catchy. My taste in modern music actually alarmed me. Was it my last cry for help? Was I really, deep down secretly feeling the urge to be young again and was that the real reason I was drumming my fingers on the steering wheel to some young girls singing?

"If you wannabe my lover, you got to get with my friends ..."

Fuck I know where I wanted to be and it wasn't driving along the road to Shettleston. The lights turned amber and then green, I slipped through the gears and accelerated towards the next set of lights.

When I arrived at the Showroom I parked my car in the customer's car park. I got out of my old 88 Mondeo and walked past some forecourt bargains. There were 'For sale' signs on every car. I couldn't help notice the irony that the real bargain specials were on Ford Focus cars Special deals notices on selected other ones, but the Focus's were the ones they really wanted to part with.

I have to admit I could do with a new car. This one was eight years old now and although I've never had a bit of bother with it, you can only be lucky for so long with it not breaking down. Anyway it didn't alter the fact that it was still an eight year old Ford. I should have changed it years ago. I knew that the guys all laughed behind my back about what their Chief Inspector was driving, but fuck them, I liked my old car.

As I passed by a second hand 1995 new shape black Mondeo 2 litre CDI it really caught my eye. I couldn't resist running my hand along the bonnet. I liked the look of this one. It had me written all over it. The alloy wheels, which were all the rage, were shining and as I cast a longing look over it, I could actually imagine myself driving it. I peered inside at the seats which were cream leather. I very nearly opened the door and got in, but I wasn't there on a buying visit. I had a shit load of questions to ask the guys who were waiting for me inside. I let my hand free itself from the door handle and I mused that maybe I should ask how much of a trade in I could get on my old banger. Mind you that question might not be asked if all my other questions were taken the wrong way.

I opened the door into the sales room and the first thing that hit you was the smell of car polish. The cars inside were gleaming and I'm just like everybody else I just wanted to sit inside one of the new ones. Leather and polish and I was sold. The sales room wasn't busy in fact today it was quiet.

I noticed one salesmen busy with another couple at the far end of the showroom looking at an estate car, the other salesman sitting at his desk busy adjusting his tie preparing himself to give me, his next customer the spiel. As he approached me I stopped his smiling face in its tracks when I showed him my badge and told him I had an appointment to see the family. At that moment a blonde vision in a black trouser suit came from the corner office and introduced herself, "Chief Inspector Niven, I'm Penny Livingstone the Company secretary, we've been expecting you. The boys are waiting for you in the manager's office. If you would follow me please."

I thought to myself "I'd follow you anywhere". She was about five foot eight inches tall, slim with long blonde hair, which she had in a ponytail. She had beautiful green eyes with just a hint of eye shadow and a smile to die for. Penny was certainly a picture and had just brightened up my afternoon that was for sure, but she had offered no hand shake and I thought I could hear a wee bit of nervousness in her voice. She had called her bosses the boys. All very family friendly I thought as I followed her the short distance along the corridor. I wondered which one of the boys was banging the arse off "my name's Penny". It was difficult for me to take my eyes from her beautiful rear as she walked in front of me. Rude thoughts were entering my brain, as she stopped at the door to her manager's office.

She knocked on the door and not waiting for any response opened it and introduced me, "Gentlemen, Chief Inspector Niven to see you."

As I stepped into the manager's office, it was obvious that their conversation had stopped as soon as Penny had tapped on the big wooden door. They were silent and all eyes were on me as Penny did the introductions and introduced me. There were four of them seated on two-seater leather sofas to the right hand side of the office, under the big bay window. I had expected to interview only three. I noticed that the sofas were opposite each other, with a coffee table between them. There were neither cups nor drinks on the table. I would have expected that at least. There was a big desk in the centre of the large room with what appeared to be a drinks cabinet behind. First impressions that I had, I suppose was impressive, business must have been good at one time. The manager's desk I noticed was highly polished and devoid of any paperwork. I also noticed that there were no spare seats unless I was meant to sit in the manager's chair.

The four suits stood to greet me as I walked forward to shake each hand offered. It was maybe just a detective thing I guess, but I always look at the quality of what some one is wearing, as to give me a clue to the type of guy I'm about to question. I also quickly look at their shoes, daft eh?

So there I was mentally taking in the bloke in the dark blue suit (Expensive looking), the dark grey suit (Marks and

Sparks), the brown suit (Had seen better days) and the dark blue pin stripe (Italian centre Very Expensive).

Frank Davidson (dark blue) introduced himself as the General Manager and that his brother Nigel (dark grey) was the Company sales manager. His cousin Thomas Franklin (brown) was introduced as fleet manager and as I turned to the youngster of the group, I was introduced to their lawyer Jonathon Brogan. That explained the quality of the suit. I shook his hand firmly and I don't really know why I did that because with the others I only touched them. Maybe it was me subconsciously trying to assert dominance over him by squeezing his hand real hard? Or was it because he was their lawyer, or maybe it was me taking an instant dislike to the rich Italian suit and the false smile.

Frank Davidson asked if I didn't mind if Jonathon sat in on the meeting.

I lied, "Of course not," but I was disappointed that he was there. I was hoping to catch these boys out with my usual flair of verbal trickery. With this son of a bitch present I would have to watch my "P's and Q's".

Penny interrupted the formalities and asked if anyone would like a coffee or a tea. I answered tea and told her how I liked it and there were a couple of coffees preferred. The lawyer declined.

Penny held the door open and as if by magic the salesman I had brushed off seconds ago appeared pushing a leather chair on castors. He offered it to me and I thanked him. I took it from him and moved it closer towards the sofas.

We all sat down and I know it sounds corny but that's what happened; it was like we had all been rehearsing it, to perfect the act of all sitting down in unison.

The two brothers sat on the left hand sofa and Cousin Tom and Jonathon sat to my right.

"Does anyone mind if I tape this conversation?" I said pulling my mini recorder out of my inside jacket pocket. "It helps me remember things we say and saves me loads of paperwork."

The three boys fidgeted nervously in their seats or was that just my imagination?

"It's a handy wee thing right enough and it saves me writing everything down." I laid it down on the coffee table.

They all looked towards their lawyer.

"Do you mind if I have a look?" Brogan asked.

"Be my guest; it's a Panasonic."

He picked it up and pressed the play button and got nothing but a hiss from the machine.

"It's a new tape," I said.

He turned his gaze from me, "Mr. Davidson it will be up to the three of you to decide if you have no objection." He stopped the recorder pressed the rewind button and laid it back down on the table. He could have handed it back to me but didn't, so I picked it up and stupidly put it back into my pocket. Why couldn't I just have left it there? Was this him getting a subtle point across making me bend down in front of him? Putting me in my place as kings do to courtiers?

"But I have to inform you," he continued glancing towards me, "that anything you say here and he records, will be admissible in a court of law. The Scottish courts have indeed recently allowed these recorders to be used as evidence.

Frank Davidson and his brother both shook their heads for no objection and Cousin Tom piped in with, "I don't have any problem with that as we've got nothing to hide," and then shut up. My focus should be on him, I thought, he seemed more nervous than the other two. They were sitting nice and calm, Cousin Tom seemed to me a tad edgy.

Jonathon then turned to me and said rather smugly, "So you won't mind if I tape your questions then, Inspector Niven? To help me, remember things and save me, from writing things down."

Smug young bastard. I was going off this individual rather quickly. "Of course not," I replied smiling through gritted teeth, as I watched him reach down to his hand stitched leather bound briefcase, open it and pullout a Sony Mini recorder. He gave it across to me so I could give it the once over. I handed it back to him unimpressed. I was really getting a bit pissed off with this guy's ways.

There was a knock knock at the door and in walked our Penny with a tray of coffees and one tea and a plate of Kit Kat biscuits.

I thanked her for the tea and took one of the biscuits from the plate. Normally I don't eat chocolate biscuits but it had been a while since I had one of these babies. I removed the wrapper and ran my nail along the silver foil between the two halves. I broke the biscuit in two and bit into the chocolate and at that moment, I could feel all their eyes were on me. The three boys sipped quietly at their coffees and the lawyer just sat silent. I thought that I'd better get the ball rolling. I lifted up my cup and took a sip of tea and placed it back down on the table. I reached back into the inside pocket of my jacket for my recorder. The boys all sat back into their sofas and waited. I showed them the recorder and asked them, "OK?"

Brogan switched his recorder on and placed it down in the middle of the coffee table.

I pressed the play button on mine and also laid it down on the coffee table, thinking ditto.

"It's the 10th of June 1996. D.C I. Niven sitting in the Managers office at Davidson's Motors in Shettleston, with Frank Davidson, General Manager, Nigel Davidson, Company Sales Manager, Thomas Franklin, Fleet Manager and Jonathon Brogan, from Ellis and Carpenter Law firm and," I had to check my watch, "the time is now 14.30 hours."

It was now down to me and the boys and mister smug bastard in the Italian pin stripe. As I asked my questions I wondered just how long it would take Mr Smug to jump in with the "You don't have to answer that" bit. I wanted their answers, if they gave me any, and I also wondered just how long my recorder battery would last.

Chapter 30

Nelson stirred to find himself in strange surroundings; he found that he was all alone in a big room with white walls. His attempt to get up alarmed him somewhat finding he was under some form of restraint. He tried to move against it and realised he was strapped down lying on a bed. He had some sort of cover over him but could feel his bare arse lying on a cold bed sheet. His feet were freezing and he sensed that someone had stripped him of his prison coveralls. He tried lifting his arms again but the strapping had him down tight.

He strained to raise his head to take in as much information as he could before someone came in. His head pained him, it was throbbing and he felt slightly nauseous, there was a strange taste in his mouth. Could he have been sick? Was that why he was here lying prone on this bed.

He struggled to free himself, but it was useless. Whoever did the strapping knew what they were doing. He stared at the ceiling fluorescent light trying hard to remember what events had led him to here, but he couldn't recall. Somewhere in the back of his mind, there was a vague recollection of someone telling him, that he was in hospital, but had he been dreaming that one?

How long had he been out for the count?

What day was it?

He laid his head back onto the flat pillow and closed his eyes and started to memorize his surroundings. He was in a hospital room of some kind that was for sure. To his left hand side there was some kind of machine that beeped. Heart monitor?

There were small cables coming from Nelson to the machine so maybe his guess wasn't too far from the truth. Now that he thought about it he could feel things on his chest and on his right leg. It had to be something to do with his heart.

The room door was towards the bottom of his bed.

Nelson could see some kind of medical thing on the back of his right hand and that there was sticky tape holding it in place. He followed that tube along his right side and up into a small machine on a vertical stand and from there on up to a plastic see through bag with clear fluid dripping into the tube. He assumed that he was being administered some kind of medication or drugs through a drip. It had to be beneficial to whatever he was lying on this bed for, but that didn't really worry Nelson, what did concern him was being strapped into this bed and not being able to move. This was an escape opportunity if there ever was one and somehow he had to be free.

An instant moment of panic spread over Nelson. He was prone, could he walk?

He wiggled his toes and got ten responses, which was good. He could walk. He gave a big sigh of relief.

Apart from the headache he wondered if the rest of him was OK. He drummed the fingers on his left hand onto the bed sheet, so no broken bones there. He couldn't feel any pain from his left arm or from his feet. He pushed and tensed his muscles against the strapping time and time again, not just to test his muscles for pain but it was an attempt to gain any leverage he could against the strapping, but it was useless.

He was well and truly tied down, for now. His chance would have to come later.

He would have to catch someone unawares and action his escape.

He knew he would have to think quickly on his feet for him to make a clean get away.

Nelson would have to somehow manufacture some distance between him and his pursuers. He needed time to do that before the alarm was raised that he was free, because there was nothing more surely; the authorities were going to come after him and with all the men they could muster. Fleeing felons in this day and age would be hunted down. Nelson thought of the Paul Newman film Cool Hand Luke when he was being pursued by bloodhounds. Nelson grinned at the sight of bloodhounds chasing him. But the pain inside his head and behind his eyes came in waves washing over him again. It was enough to stop him smiling, wincing he lay still waiting for the pain to ease.

After several more minutes of relative silence the machine to Nelson's right hand side issued several loud bleeps, warning of an imminent end to his fluid drip.

Nelson made the decision to remain quiet and keep his eyes closed. Learn more about your enemy by observing quietly rather than by confronting them head on.

The room door opened and Nelsons senses caught a perfumed fragrance over a clean soapy smell that this person had just brought in. He heard the door close softly behind who ever had just entered. Nelson thought that it had to be a woman, because this person moved around the room quietly on soft shoes. He was aware of her moving to his left and didn't flinch when she lifted something from the monitor side and lifted his left hand and clipped, what felt like a clothes peg onto his index finger. He was aware of only one person entering the room and as she moved around his bed to attend to changing the bag of solution, he sneaked a quick peek at her, hoping not to get caught looking. He saw her reach up to the hooked stand to his right and take off the empty bag holding it aloft and as she watched the solution empty down the tube to Nelson's hand, Nelson closed his eyes again. It actually hurt his eyes squinting to his right in his attempt to see something. He became aware of her fiddling with something around his wrist and she must have connected him to a new bag of fluid because he opened his eyes when he heard her move to the hooked stand. He was lucky not to get caught as he quickly shut his eyes a millisecond before she looked directly at him. She moved back around the bed and again stood at his left hand side. She removed the digital gauge from his finger and he could hear her return it to the monitor. He then heard her at the foot of his bed and he attempted one last quick look as he heard her lift something metal from the bed rail. He saw that she was standing head down, with a clipboard in one hand and a pen in the other, marking results onto his chart. Pulse rate, time of solution change and his temperature, Nelson guessed.

As she put the chart back onto the bed rail, she had one last look towards her patient and turned and opened the room door. Nelson watched her leaving and could not help but notice there was a man sitting opposite his room door. That man got up from his seat to talk to the nurse as the door closed.

Nelson looked up at the new bag to his right and watched the drips fall into the tube; he looked to his left and saw the Heart rate monitor and the cables. He craned his neck backwards to see if he could see anything behind him, like a window. But there was only a white brick wall.

Nelson thought that he would wait until the nurse's next visit to maybe try something, but he would have to think of a plan and he would have to think quickly. He had to get free of the strapping holding him down; he somehow had to get his hands free. If he could somehow manage to achieve that, he was half way to paradise.

Are you going to kill her, Nelson? Are you?

My head hurts.

She is someone who stands between you and me getting out of here. You do know that, Nelson, don't you?

I know that! Give me a break. My head hurts.

You've said that.

So shut the fuck up.

Thinking about having sex with her before you kill her?

As you can see sex is the last thing on my mind just now. The Velcro straps are my main issue at this present time – Nelson hissed.

Did you see the bloke at the door?

Yeah I saw him.

He has to be Special Branch and that means he's armed.

Maybe.

No maybes about it. Nothing surer. He has a gun for us, Nelson. All you have to do is kill him and we have a gun.

Yes I did see the guy and if you would listen to me for once and think about it. They're not just going to put just one Special branch copper on the door, now are they? Where there's one you can guarantee there will be another one lurking nearby. They always travel in pairs.

Good. We kill him as well and then you'll have two guns.

I have to get out of this bed first before we do anything. The Velcro straps?

That's two to kill Nelson and one to have sex with.

First things first, I have a wee problem of being secured to this bed.

Piss it.

What?

I said piss it.

Piss what?

Piss the bed stupid. They won't let you lie in your own piss. That's got to be in their Hospital rules. Nobody lies in pissy, urine-stained bed sheets. Now do they? The Nurse has to come in and change it and put new clean sheets on it, or she has to get you a new bed. So piss it. They have to take the straps off of you, to move you and get you clean. If they think you're still sleeping then we might just have an opportunity to make a move.

Oh I get it. Maybe the two special branch guys would help move me from the urine-soaked sheets and with their guard down, bang! Surprise the fuck out of them and slaughter everyone in the room quickly.

You like that idea don't you?

I'll admit it has promise but it needs rethinking.

What's to rethink?

Well let me think for a moment. For starters how many Special Branch officers are there outside that door? I don't know for sure, do you? We've seen one guy and we've assumed he's got a mate. What about the ordinary Police? Where do they come into the equation? Where are Marbury and Woodall? Are they going to be sitting on the other side of that door as well? The numbers of personnel on the other side of that door could be mounting up just now. I have to be more certain.

But we have to take a chance if it comes.

I know that. I might only get one chance at flight and I am well aware that I'm going to take it, but we have to find out more information about where we are and with whom?

Oh yes very well put, old chap, with whom. I like that.

Be serious! Nelson hissed. I need to know a whole lot more, before we can plan anything.

Very well put, my man. Yes why don't we find out more and then kill the fucking lot of them.

You're not listening! I need more info, and for example, just where the fuck are we? Are we still in the prison? Is this the prison hospital? I don't know because I've never been in the bloody thing.

Or is this a Glasgow Hospital, or is it Carstairs, you know the secure mental hospital? Have I been transferred? Am I locked securely in a ward, or is it just an ordinary private room, with god knows how many folk outside that door?

Calm down, old chap

Don't you tell me to calm down! Just what the fuck is outside that door? I mean what the fuck happened to me? I need to know!

You're not in a mental hospital!

Are you one hundred percent sure of that?

You're not mental!

Nelson grinned – "Are you one hundred percent sure of that?"

Ok, so go on and do some rethinking. But you haven't asked me the most important question yet.

Which is?

What happened to you and why are you in a hospital?

Do you know?

Of course not, stupid. Why can't you remember? Why have you got a sore head?

Did Marbury and Woodall give me a kicking?

Are you sore anywhere else?

No.

Well you never got a kicking.

Be quiet I need to think about all that stuff.

Nelson lay quiet trying to remember. The only noise was the sound of the machines humming beside him.

His brain waves must have moved off the chart as he started to think about some serious questions. Did Marbury or Woodall cause the sore head? Were they the real cause of this? He couldn't remember having any altercation with them. That did not mean that they were not the cause of this temporary amnesia, he didn't think that it was them, but he couldn't be 100 percent sure. If only he could remember for definite.

He needed to be free. He could do things if he was free. He strained every muscle he could at the straps again, the blood vessels in his neck bulged. Nothing moved.

He had the means to be free. But only in his mind. His anger subsided and he stopped straining his body against the straps. He realized that this effort was tiring, the straps were winning.

His breathing and pulse rate were up at the amount of effort he had expended.

To calm himself he followed deep breathing. It worked when he was in his cell. When he was angry, self meditation and breathing helped change and alter his mood.

He thought again of the idea of urinating the bed. He went over that thought several times until he whispered, "Right the plan is I piss the bed and the nurse discovers it right?"

Go on

Then the next question we have to answer is: who is going to help the nurse change the bed sheets? Will it be other nurses or hospital orderlies? That's assuming that this is a hospital.

Stop assuming. This is a hospital.

OK, this is a hospital and surely their own staff won't be trained to deal with high security risks, now will they?

Not a chance they'll just be ordinary staff. Not used to the likes of us at all.

That's what I wanted to hear. Hospital staff assisting the nurse, then will the cops be looking on armed and waiting? Or will it be the cops helping the nurse?

We need the cops to help.

That would be the bonus.

Yep and as soon as they un-strain you and lift your lifeless carcass up from the mattress and the bastard drops his guard, you grab one of the guns and Surprise, Surprise! Fucking bang, bang, you'll kill the lot of them.

Nelson listened intently and the demeanor changed immediately, the serious look returned to his face, his eyes darkened and his brow furrowed. His fists clenched and his whole body tensed.

He whispered under his breath, "Yeah let's kill the fucking lot of them."

CHAPTER 31

The flight from Washington DC arrived at Glasgow Airport three hours and forty-five minutes late. The young man sat in economy unperturbed. The rest of his fellow passengers were tired and grumpy and some of them had voiced their disproval at the airline staff at the lateness of the landing. Some stewardesses in business class particular got some irate rants. There was nothing they could do, but they apologised anyway. It wasn't their fault that they had to sit on the tarmac at Washington all that time while the ground staff removed someone's luggage. The crew was taught to smile when they apologised, for the smallest of things, they had to grin and bear it, even like on this occasion it had been completely out of their control. It wasn't their fault that Mister whatever his name was, decided to stay in the bar and miss his flight. His luggage had to come off the flight and that was IATA rules.

The young man sat upright, waiting to move. He listened to a passenger bitching further up the aisle; he heard the rough Glasgow accent growling about something. He would have to get used to that accent that was for sure. His ears were still a bit fuzzy and he yawned and swallowed spit to try and de pressurize and clear them. He was also keen to get off the plane. He had stretched his legs going to the toilet just prior to landing. If he was tired he didn't show it. He checked his watch, 3.30 in the afternoon here in Scotland

and 10.30 in the morning back home in Washington. That was right wasn't it five hours of a difference?

This was his first time in Scotland and the first time going to visit his Uncle Thomas, his mother's brother, whom he was named after. His uncle and aunt and his twin cousins would be there to meet him when he cleared customs. That was the deal. He was looking forward to a holiday and seeing the other side of the family. He was actually excited to be visiting Glasgow because for the last few years he had been working tirelessly. Now it was Glasgow and how his mother enthused about the place. Site seeing the Burrell collection, the famous Barrows on a Sunday, the art gallery, the Kelvin Hall, the names of places she remembered whet his appetite. He looked out of the window at the blue sky and the grey terminal building in front of him as the plane taxied to its parking bay. When the plane came to a halt the captain shut down the engines. Welcome to Glasgow. Passengers started to move and lift their hand luggage from the luggage racks above them only to stand in the cabin aisle waiting to exit at the front of the plane.

He hoped the waiting family would not be too disappointed because he was late. He stood up and took his travel bag and his neatly folded jacket down from the luggage rack. He felt his jacket lapel for his new lapel pin. He ran his thumb over the face of the pin.

He felt very proud to have one.

There were only 300 of these wreath pins in the world.

They were very special.

He smiled because he was one of the privileged few to wear it.

He was one of the chosen few from his regiment, specially picked for the service and duty that would allow him to wear it.

He was one of a Band of service Brothers.

He put his jacket on and started for the exit.

Tommy and Millie Woods stood in the arrivals hall waiting for their nephew to appear. They had bored each other while waiting for the Washington plane to arrive. There was only so much coffee you can drink and Thomas was not allowed to go to the bar for a pint. He had read several of the newspapers and listened to Millie for hours. He was told no drinking, because young Thomas didn't drink alcohol, he was not allowed to. Millie also told him no swearing either. Young Thomas didn't swear either. Millie was fussing about like an old mother hen and the laddie wasn't even through customs yet. Tommy felt sorry for young Thomas and for what he was about to go through in the next fortnight. Millie would smother him in kindness that was for sure.

The first passengers appeared and were welcomed by family or friends. There were tears of joy and laughs as friends hugged. Millie and Tommy looked beyond the scene trying to spot Thomas.

Finally a slim, blond six foot plus, good looking young man appeared and Tommy said to Millie "That's him. That's our Thomas."

There was an instant recognition from Thomas and he waved. They looked just like the picture his mum showed him and his uncle was possibly wearing the same jacket.

The smiling couple welcomed Thomas and Millie gave him a big welcome hug. Tommy shook the young man's hand and took his suitcase from him.

"How was your flight Thomas?" Millie asked.

"It was long and so sorry I'm late. You guys must be tired waiting."

"No it was nothing. Planes get delayed all the time. It wasn't your fault so don't you worry, son," Tommy chirped in.

"Some passenger didn't make it onboard and the ground crew had to locate his bags, guess he wanted to stay in Washington I reckon, or maybe just wanted to stay in hospitality."

Tommy licked his lips; he could be doing with a pint just now. Millie saw the subtle lick of the lips and threw Tommy daggers.

"Yeah sounds about right," Tommy said ignoring Millie's glare.

"Come on, Thomas, our car's this way."

"So how you feeling, Thomas? You must be tired with all that flying," Millie said.

"Not tired, Aunt Millie, more excited I reckon. This is my first time out of America."

"Get away with you. First time eh? And you chose to come and visit us. Hear that Millie?"

Millie felt really proud. "Oh I hope you have a nice holiday with us, Thomas."

"Aunt Millie, I'm sure I will. My mom has told me so much about this great place, and all about the history, I'm really looking forward to it."

The arrival terminal doors opened and they stepped out into the open air.

CHAPTER 32

Sitting back in my office with my wee recorder I was bored typing up my interview with the directors and Mr Italian pin stripe. I sat back in my chair and stared at the ceiling as I listened to the tape. I had asked each of them individual questions and I listened to their answers and specifically to the way they answered. After a few minutes I got bored staring at the Artex swirls and shut my eyes to concentrate. The closing my eyes thing was just something I did, as it sometimes helped me picture the interviewees answering. Sometimes subconsciously you miss things that happen during an interview and by shutting my old peepers it did help. Not this time it was all very mechanical. As I listened further I was getting pissed off and eventually I had had enough. I opened my eyes and sat upright and stared at the computer screen. I read the last bit I had typed. I moved the mouse and my wee arrow and clicked on "File" and then "Save as". I was finished for the night; I'd do the rest tomorrow. I glanced down at my watch, it was 8 p.m. Where had the day gone?

Kenny popped his head in, "The lads have had a tip where your Mr Mallon is reportedly in hiding. Coming along for the ride?"

I looked up at him standing there and I could recognize that eager look he had. He desperately wanted to go. I could have and should have let him go on his own. I should have told him no. But it was going to be a long night; I could feel it, "May as well; I'm doing fuck all. She's off to the pictures to see Tom Hanks in *Big*, so I'm on my jack Jones."

"The armed response unit is en-route as we speak. Your boy likes guns apparently."

"Oh he does, does he? Where we going, Kenny?"

He's holed up in a flat in Southbank Avenue next to Glasgow University."

"Who dubbed him up?" I asked putting on my jacket.

"A friend of a friend who doesn't like the bastard it seems."

"With friends like those ..." I didn't feel like I had to complete the phrase.

I closed the office door behind me and followed Kenny along the corridor down the stairs and out to his new shining Ford Granada. I wasn't envious one little bit.

We drove along towards Glasgow and hit the M8 heading west, took the Charing Cross slip road and pushed our way through the traffic lights out onto Woodlands road. We sped along there taking a left down Eldon Street onto Gibson Street. Traffic was backed up and the smell of curry emanating from the restaurants made me think of how hungry I was. We were now minutes away from Mr Sean Mallon. Kenny pulled up and parked behind a black transit van. All windows were blackened which gave it the air of secrecy. Who ever was in the van could see out, but no-one could see in. How good was that? Why I had that thought at that moment I'll never know, but I had a stupid grin on my face thinking it. I could only hope that Kenny hadn't seen it or he would have thought I was mad.

The armed response unit exited the van as we got out. The commander was dressed all in black with the bullet proof

Kevlar vest and held a crash helmet. He quickly introduced himself as Captain David Macasgill. We shook hands and I introduced Kenny to him. As we gathered for a quick tactic meeting he explained what was about to happen.

He told us to follow them in. I nodded agreement; if Mallon was armed let the ARU take the bullets rather than me. We were given the task of relating to the three local bobbies and for them to stay put for now. The commander said that they may be needed to clean up if we found anything. I think they were as glad as me that the ARU were taking over. You could tell that they were as keen as mustard to get involved until they saw the guns.

The six guys in the unit ran up Southbank Avenue keeping close to the line of parked cars and then turned left and ran up a pathway and into the entrance to some flats. The commander was right behind them. We followed them at a distance. There was no point in me getting my arse shot off for being too close.

The biggest lad in the ARU unit carried the ram. The four inch solid metal pipe they were about to use to open the door. Not as subtle as a key but just as effective, or so we found.

The things that go through your mind at a crucial time like this is crazy. All I could think about was one of the guys knocking on the door and Mallon cordially inviting us all into the flat for a beer. We would sit down sup our refreshing lager and then he would admit he was a bad lad and we would arrest him and that was it all over. It would be all very friendly stuff and absolutely no need for violence or guns.

That was not about to happen.

As we entered the flat stairwell there was a deafening noise from above as the ram smashed into the door. Mayhem broke loose above with the ARU shouting abuse at the occupants. When it went sort of quiet, we took the stairs two at a time and when we got there it was all over. I walked into the flat and passed two extremely pumped up ARU exiting to secure the stairs. There was a guy in the first bedroom on the left hand side of the hall, lying prone and his hands cable tied, he was face down bloodied and obviously unconscious. We went further along the hallway into the living room where one of the ARU was picking up a chair he had knocked over. There were another two individuals lying bleeding on the floor, one of them out for the count, while the other one was obviously in a state of shock. Both guys had their hands cable tied. Sean Mallon was not one of our captured occupants. We had missed the bastard. The commander confirmed that fact. I looked around the room surveying the damage.

The one who was conscious was lifted by the ARU and sat on the floor against the wall. He was watching me. I saw his scared look and I asked the commander to give us a couple of minutes. He nodded agreement and walked back out of the living room. Our boy watched him go and then looked up at Kenny and me.

Kenny stood on one side of him and I stood on the other. Blood oozed from his cut lip and his tongue licked it away.

"What the fuck is this, man? We haven't done anything."

"Shut the fuck up and speak when you're spoken to," Kenny said first.

I threw Kenny a look of distaste. I wanted to say that. I never get a chance to say that. Kenny always jumps in first. Kenny knew that and smirked.

"We haven't done nothing is two negatives you stupid fuck, which means you have done something," Kenny rasped at him.

"Where's Mallon?" I said.

"Who?"

"You know who. Your mate, Sean Mallon."

"Aint seen him for months, man."

"Don't fucking lie to me. The bastard was here," Kenny shouted.

"So where is he?" I growled.

"We haven't done anything. I want my lawyer."

"If you haven't done anything, what the fuck do you want a lawyer for?" Kenny shouted.

At that the commander came back into the room, "Inspector you want a look at what we found."

I nodded to Kenny to go and take a look. I wanted this guy in front of me all to myself for a minute.

"I asked you a question. Where's Sean Mallon?"

"You pigs are deaf; I haven't seen him for months."

At that I reached down and punched him hard. I nearly knocked his head off of his neck. He was somewhat surprised I thought...

Man it felt good because it took me back a few years.

"He yelled as blood oozed from his nose. I picked him back up and sat him against the wall.

"Did you hear me? Where's your mate Mallon?"

"What you do that for you fucking pig?"

He was a strong one coming back with that answer, so I had no option than to smack him again. Blood spattered the wall behind him as his head turned from the force of my punch. He hadn't bargained that I would hit him again. I shook my hand as that hurt a bit.

"Where's Mallon?" I screamed into his ear.

He had had enough; He crumbled "He's in the Koh in Noor in Gibson Street. He said he was going for a curry."

"How long ago?" I demanded.

"About an hour I don't know."

Kenny came back into the room holding aloft a heavy duty black plastic bag. "Sawn off and must be about 10 grand in used notes, I reckon at a first look, see?" He opened up the bag for me to look at. I nodded.

"Our friend here just told me where Mallon is," I said.

"Good boy. I had a feeling he would." Kenny looked at the blood dripping out of the boy's nose and the sorry state of his bleeding lip and then back at me. I just shrugged my shoulders.

The local police had been summoned by the on site commander. The three criminals would be bagged, tagged and dragged into Strathclyde Police HQ in West George Street to answer a few more wee questions, re the shotgun and the ten grand for starters.

The ARU assembled at the opening to the Flats and the situation was quickly re-assessed. The boys gathered round their commander and listened to what he had to say. The stakes had just jumped. The target was said to be in a busy restaurant four streets away from where they were standing just now. It was critical to capture the said target with little or no collateral damage to restaurant or diners. There was a strong probability that the subject was armed as there was a concealed weapon found in the flat.

It was decided that Detectives Niven and Jackson would go into the Indian restaurant as diners and assess the situation. We, as it was blissfully made aware to us, were the only ones not in body armour. Made sense really.

The ARU all dived back along the road and jumped into their Transit van. They did a quick U turn in the road, tyres screeching on the tarmac and accelerated back along towards the restaurant. They parked illegally on the pavement just past the bridge over the river Kelvin, on the opposite side of the road across from the restaurant. The darkened windows hid the lads from view. There they would wait for us.

We had agreed to the hasty plan and walked back along Southbank Avenue and into Gibson Street once again. My heartbeat was picking up pace as I walked. I am sure Kenny's was the same.

I wasn't too enamoured with the commander's warning that Mallon most probably would be armed. It hadn't dawned on me that he might be carrying a weapon. It did now and as we passed the Shalimar Indian restaurant, we could see the Koh-in Noor not fifty yards in front of us. The street was busy with pedestrians and a family had exited from Kelvingrove Park and appeared to me to be heading for the restaurant.

Tommy and Millie, Thomas and the twins waited for a lull in the traffic to cross the road. Thomas was being taken to the famous Glasgow curry house. Thomas's mum in Washington had told him that he had to go and try the famous Chicken Tikka Massala from the Koh-in-Noor in Gibson Street. It was a culinary must. Although it was his first day in Glasgow the jet lag hadn't kicked in yet and this was one of the things he could tick off, the "things to do" list.

Sean Mallon sat with his two mates in a booth to the left of the restaurant. They were just about finished and had asked for the bill. Where they were seated Sean could see the front door into the restaurant, look out the large front window and also watch the door into the kitchen. It was a perfect vantage point. He sat there with the remains of his curry in front of him. He reached forward and grabbed the last piece of garlic Nan bread and tore a piece from it. He dipped it into the last of the sauce and wiped his plate with it, while one of his mates paid the bill. The third of the group drained his pint glass and wiped his mouth with the back of his hand.

Sean had seen the dark transit van as it slowly passed the restaurant window and parked on the opposite side of the road. He bit the piece of bread and chewed.

The van had caught his interest; it had blackened out windows: he thought that it had driven past the restaurant too slowly. He looked on as he chewed, it was as if the driver ... was looking for something ... or someone.

He wiped more curry sauce from his plate. His senses were telling him there was something not right about that van. Why had it parked on the opposite side of the road against the flow of traffic?

The waiter approached Sean's table to clean up and gather all the plates and side dishes from the table. He temporarily blocked Sean's view. Sean leaned to his side to keep an eye on the van. He sat forward knowing his .38 calibre was tucked up in his shirt in his jeans in the small of his back. He was packing and so were his mates. This was a dangerous city for Sean and his crew and they were always carrying.

No one exited the van. Sean had seen nobody getting in and moreover had seen nobody coming out.

His eyes were now focused on that van. He couldn't see the driver's side. Had someone exited on the far side?

He whispered to his mates about the van stopping across the road.

This put the other two on yellow alert. Their senses were now heightened. Adrenalin levels were on the way up.

Sean suggested that they all moved the fuck out of there, act casual and not do anything stupid. It was just a feeling but be ready in case this was something. It could very well be nothing and that he was overreacting, but years of experiencing the same, had set the alarm bells ringing. Their situation had moved from yellow to amber.

The commander and the team quickly assessed the situation in the restaurant. They could see Sean Mallon standing up and one of the team had immediately identified the other two as James Kilbryde and Robert Barr as his other standing compatriots. Barr and Kilbryde had outstanding warrants for armed robbery and Mallon was wanted for questioning regarding an attempted murder. The three were identified and confirmed and were observed about to leave the restaurant.

The commander saw the family cross the road and stop at the door.

This was an opportunity to get the team out the van and get in a position for a take down. The family entering the restaurant would give them cover.

They could surprise the three lads and it would be over and done with in seconds. They didn't need to stick to the original plan. Improvise and adapt, but they only had seconds to organize. The commander barked out his orders, Unit team A, B, C left: D, E, F goes right, now. Move!

Sean and his two mates had stood up from the table and were about to leave. Sean couldn't take his eyes from the van, he was fixating on it. His inner senses were tingling with excitement, his gut was knotting up; there was something deep down telling him there was something drastically wrong.

Tommy and Millie stopped in front of the restaurant's front door showing Thomas the advertised menu just to the right under a glass case. The twins already knew what they wanted. One always wanted the beef madras and the other one always had a chicken vindaloo. So they didn't have to look over the à la carte menu.

While Thomas studied the list of meals available he related the story about what his mother had said about the place.

Tommy and Millie laughed, "That's it decided then, Thomas, your mum's recommendation "a Chicken Tikka Massala.""

Kenny and I were ambling towards the restaurant. We saw the family crossing the road and stop at the door. Thinking back, I reckoned that they must have been checking the menu. We must have been about forty yards away, when the back door to the transit opened in a blur and the ARU piled out the back. Crouching they ran quickly over the road. At that point all hell broke loose and shots were fired. My instinct took me down to my knees and I could only watch the scenario unfold. Kenny backed up against a shop front comically trying to become as flat as he could with his hands outstretched beside him. If it had been a scene from *The Sweeney* I would have been impressed at Kenny and probably might have even smiled at the way he did that. But it wasn't a fictitious TV series, this was real, there were guns being fired.

Sean saw the back door open up and the ARU exit. He shouted something to his mates. Barr and Kilbryde had already seen the movement and were in the process of drawing their weapons. They weren't going to get caught like rats in a trap.

The restaurant diners and staff heard all the shouting and had all turned to where Sean was. They saw the three boys raising guns and firing. The surreal scene was one from an American gangster movie. The window exploded through a hail of bullets and shattering glass was thrown in every direction. The Kevlar vests took several rounds and the ARU had no option than to return fire.

The ARU were trained to be more accurate than Mallon, Barr and Kilbryde. All three were targeted and shot dead.

Tommy and Millie had escaped harm in the crossfire but Thomas was dropped when a .38 calibre meant for the ARU somehow got deflected and hit him. He fell backwards onto the edge of the road. There were people running screaming in every direction. It was chaos I can tell you.

As soon as the firing had started, the firing had stopped.

I knew then that there was going to be hell to pay. And believe me that was an understatement. For God's sake this was the west end of Glasgow, things like this do not happen here. This was not downtown Los Angeles or one of the other American cities where gun law ruled. People were out having curries, for fuck's sake, this does not happen here.

I got to my feet and Kenny managed to unglue himself from the shop front window. I assumed that the on scene commander must have had the decision to fire when his team was fired upon taken from him. I found out later that I had been correct in my assumption. This take down was sanctioned strictly shoot if fired upon.

As I looked on I wasn't sure at the time how many shooters had been involved, or if Sean Mallon had been on his own. I was shaking like a leaf as we approached the restaurant. One of the ARU was kneeling over someone lying flat out on the pavement; I could see blood staining onto the road. I wasn't sure if he was dead or alive.

I turned my attention to the restaurant and looked into it through the space where the window used to be. I crunched through glass as I got closer. I looked down on the three bodies on the floor. One of the ARU members had kicked their weapons aside, which he shouldn't have done. Our crime scene forensics team like to photograph everything and I know for a fact they were going to be pissed off at not getting to document the weapons exactly where they had fallen.

The twisted body of Sean Mallon was there on the floor for all to see. He had fallen backwards having taken 3 body shots, one to his right shoulder and two to his upper left chest area. Blood soaked from him and had pooled around his side. The other two lay at odd angles and I noticed that one of them had taken a head shot. There was a rather large bit of his head missing.

There were diners crying hysterically, shaking and holding onto each other for comfort. Staff stood stock still, holding onto each other, their eyes wide in horror, they were scared shitless, and it was not a pretty sight. It never is.

I could just about hear and make out the ARU commander radioing for ambulances.

I felt helpless at that moment in time.

I looked at Kenny and realized that he too was trembling, just like me. "That could have been us," I said.

"Fuck me," was all that he could manage to utter.

In my recollection I can only attempt to describe what I remember of the next set of events.

I think the local boys had stopped the traffic at the top of Gibson Street and started to detour the cars and vans out of the area.

I'm nearly sure that when more local cops arrived on the scene they stopped the cars coming down from Woodlands road.

The diners from the other Indian restaurant in the street had come out onto the road to see what had just happened.

Students had exited their bedsits to find out what all the commotion was. The crowds had gathered. Then again, gunshots in a Glasgow street are certainly going to alert the inquisitive.

An ambulance arrived from the Western Infirmary and took the bloke who was lying injured on the pavement away. I remember thinking at the time I hoped he was still alive. I never checked. I think some of his family jumped into the ambulance and went with him.

A second and a third ambulance arrived and paramedics got out and generally tended to the staff and to the traumatized diners.

As we watched them work, I was thinking that I could have done with a shot of something to calm me down and as I know Kenny, I could guess that he probably wanted the same. But the two of us disappearing and going for a glass of medicinal whisky to calm the nerves was a definite no no.

On hindsight I should have asked the first paramedic that pushed by me, for something like valium to calm me down.

The cigarette Kenny offered me would suffice for now. I noticed that when he held out his lighter, his hands were still shaking. I took a deep drag and exhaled a cloud of smoke. If I remember right, I did it twice. I can still picture that plume of exhaled smoke hanging there and as I looked towards the approaching on scene commander, I could see his steel grey eyes and could sense the bullshit attitude coming towards the very spot where I stood. His explanation as to what the fuck just happened was going to be a beauty.

CHAPTER 33

The next morning I was not a second in the building when our desk sergeant informed me that Kenny and I had to get our butts along into the new super's office. I hadn't even time to grab a cup of coffee. I knew what was coming and that the barrage of incessant questions would demand answers. I met Kenny in the corridor and his look said it all.

"Here we go again," I said.

Kenny rapped his knuckles on the door and we both waited to enter.

Seated behind a large mahogany desk was our new super, a weasel of a man called McTaggart. He was known as a pen pusher and a real stickler for protocol and rules. He looked at us over his horn-rimmed glasses and told us to take a seat. He was younger than me and that fact I did not like one bit. He was polite enough and I wondered how long that would last.

I noticed that there were four seats in a row and I cleverly assumed that we were going to be joined by others. As I said before, the daft things that goes through your mind when you don't need them.

We sat in silence as McTaggart kept on writing something down on a sheet of A4 paper in front of him. I couldn't see what the little bastard was writing but I thought that it wasn't going to be something good.

The door was knocked again and McTaggart without looking up, shouted "Come in". Kenny and I both turned to see the on scene Commander enter the room. I should have guessed it was going to be him. The second person with him I personally did not know.

"Sit down, gentlemen. Won't be long," and McTaggart continued with his writing. He was still being polite and I was sure it was about to change. I felt like a naughty schoolboy sitting there waiting to be chastised for something he didn't do.

It seemed like we sat in silence for ages and when he had finished what ever the hell he was writing, he laid his pen down on the desk and closed the file.

"Gentlemen, before any of you answer, I have a few things to say to you all first. What happened last night was a fuck up. A genuine, monumental fuck up. Three killed and a bystander in a critical condition in the Southern and General's intensive care. A curry house in Gibson Street blown away in a fucking American style cock up." He opened the file on the desk and read out loud.

And this here tells me that another 26 people in the restaurant were treated for cuts from flying glass and most of them suffering from shock."

"This is your preliminary report I have in front of me" Captain Macasgill?"

"Yes, sir."

"I take it that the full report is coming some time today?"

"Yes sir. It will be on your desk by this afternoon."

"It better be. I had the commissioner on the phone at five o'clock this morning asking me questions of which I could only give him partial answers and assurances. Your report will make an interesting read before I have to put it before him. I was told that you preferred to come here with your union lawyer?" He raised his eyes and looked over his glasses at the fourth member of our group. "I take it that you are his union lawyer" It sounded more like an accusation than a question.

"Derek Thompson, pleased to meet you," and he stretched out his hand.

McTaggart did not take it. The look of utter contempt was obvious that union lawyers were not on McTaggart's Christmas card list. Thompson sat back down.

"Niven and Jackson." He paused and I think I stopped breathing for a second.

"You pair saw the whole thing?"

"We were there." I said.

"That's not what I asked."

"We saw 90% of it."

He sat looking at Kenny and me with a disdainful look on his face.

"I want you to remember 100% of last night."

"Yes, sir," we replied in unison.

"I want both your accounts on my desk before lunch."

Again it was a unified "Yes, sir."

"In fact I take that back. Niven, you correlate both accounts and you have the report on my desk before lunch. Any problem?"

"No, sir."

"OK then you two can go."

We were dismissed and as we both moved to stand up and go he added "I want a word with the captain here and … Niven?"

I waited for him to go on, "Find out about the boy in the intensive care. I want to know if he is going to live or die."

He shot such a chilling look at Macasgill I was glad I wasn't on the end of that one.

Kenny and I stood up and relief was the only thing I felt as he opened the door and we stepped out of McTaggart's office. As the door closed and I was sure I couldn't be heard from inside the office, I said to Kenny, "It wasn't that bad now was it?"

"I know. I was expecting a bollocking and I don't know why."

"Me too." I checked my watch and it wasn't even eight o'clock yet. I had four hours to find out about our casualty and to write a report on last night's happenings. But first I needed a coffee and a roll in sausage from the canteen.

The next hour or so flew in and my office door was left open to allow the constant stream of people wandering in and out to hand me pieces of paper with names and addresses. There was going to be a stack of information I would have to sift through.

I had asked Kenny to find out about our casualty in the Southern and General. Delegation was a great thing and having done that to Kenny, I knew that it was one thing less I had to worry about.

I used Microsoft Office and typed out my report trying hard not to leave any bits out. It was going to be more like a story by the time I finished and that's not what McTaggart wanted. He wanted hard facts and expected reports that followed police guidelines on how to complete a report by the book. I knew that but what the hell, I had to give it to him the way I saw it.

CHAPTER 34

Kenny popped his head around my door and asked if I was free.

"From all this bullshit?" I said and offered Kenny to take a look at my desk. There were pieces of paper everywhere.

He took a chair and pulled it towards my desk.

"Here's my recollection," he said and handed over a one page report.

I looked at it and he had started the first paragraph with, Once upon a time.

"Ha fucking Ha, Kenny."

"You're not going to forget anything, Paul. My wee bit will be the same as yours."

He was right. I threw him a smile and laid the sheet down on my desk.

"Right, Guv, First of all, the lad in the Southern General will live."

"Well that's good news."

"Yeah I've been on the blower to the hospital and got some snippy wee receptionist, as you do. She was about to blow me off, so to speak. I told her I needed her to do me a favour and find out what our boy's condition was and it must have been the sweet charming phone voice I gave her, but she said she'd phone me back and she did and gave me the updated news."

"Which is? I have to tell McTaggart shortly."

"The bullet somehow missed his temporal lobe and slid along the side of his skull without doing too much damage".

I looked at Kenny, "I remember seeing him lying in a pool of blood on the pavement. But I didn't go and check to see if he was dead or alive."

"Me neither. All I can remember is that he went into one of the ambulances."

"So the bullet missed. How the ..." I stopped myself saying anymore because I could see Kenny wanting to interrupt me.

"The neurology staff has to ascertain the full extent of the damage but they won't know that for a few days while they run all sorts of tests. He's going to be in intensive care for ages, but the miracle is that he's been awake apparently."

That to me sounded incredulous. "He's been awake after taking a bullet to the old napper: Amazing."

"That bit about no major damage, I don't understand, I mean you take a bullet in your head for Christ's sake. How can that not do damage? I sure as hell wouldn't want that to happen to me."

"Kenny, there's fuck all in your head to damage. You could get shot several times and ..."

"Ha fucking ha."

I chuckled at his answer. "Anyway that's good news for McTaggart. There are only the three dead bodies to answer for."

"Yeah that's what I was thinking, but listen to this. There's a lot more to him." He took out his notebook and before he could read some of the details I asked, "Do we need coffees?"

He nodded his head in agreement, "We need coffees. I'll get them in."

Kenny stood up and left. I went back to rearranging pieces of paper and read Kenny's account. Same as mine. So I hadn't imagined the whole fucking thing. In what seemed no time at all, Kenny returned with our two mugs of steaming hot coffee. He sat down and picked up his notebook and leafed it open.

"Right, Guv, as I was saying, the lad lying in the Southern General with a drip down his nose and another one up his …"

"Kenny! For God's sake no graphic descriptions, please. You'll put me off my lunch." He grinned.

"His name is Thomas Harkins and he's an American."

My first thought was oh shit. My second thought, which happened real quickly after the first one was, do we need to inform the American embassy?

"It gets better. He's in the US infantry."

My heart sank into my mouth, "That's all we need, some GI getting shot in Glasgow. I can see a diplomatic incident or some bull like that happening."

"He's actually a guardsman in the 3rd US Infantry and his aunt told me that for the last two years he's been on guard at the Tomb of the Unknown Soldier."

"What for two years?" I asked sounding incredulous and stupid. I realized that what I said was an opening for Kenny to take the piss. "I know that he wasn't guarding for two years solid."

Kenny had his mouth open waiting for me to put my foot in mine again.

"I know it sounded stupid right?"

"Yep, just a tad. Anyway I googled the 3rd Infantry on the computer and found out the following facts about our casualty."

"Kenny where's the tomb of the Unknown Soldier?" I asked because I genuinely didn't know.

"Arlington National Cemetery."

And that is where exactly?

"Washington."

"Oh there," I commented as if I knew.

"Our lad is a very committed one that's for sure. The 3rd Infantry have been guarding the place since just after the war in 1948. They guard the tomb 24 hours a day and live in barracks under it. They cannot drink any alcohol on or off duty for the rest of their lives."

"Bummer," I said jokingly.

"That stops us becoming a guardsman eh, Guv?"

"Too right, Kenny."

"Anyway he's not allowed to and can't swear in public, and that's for life as well."

"Where's my application form? Show me where to sign?" I reached for my pen.

We both laughed.

"Do you know that for the first six months of his duty he wasn't allowed to talk to anybody or watch TV?"

"He probably never missed a bloody thing. He'll catch what he missed on the repeats. Like us."

Kenny leafed over another page, "Do you know that he has to study all the names of the folk that are buried there? He has to know where each one is. I mean fuck me; I can't remember where I put my car keys sometimes. I'd be piss at his job."

I could only nod my head as I listened in admiration.

"Listen to this one, Joe Lewis the boxer and Audie Murphy the actor ..."

"Not the 24 hour Paddy contractor? Aw day Murphy," I said with a grin.

"... Are buried there. Christ, the old jokes are the best so they say."

"I couldn't help it, Kenny".

"I know you couldn't, Guv. Do you want me to go on or have you heard enough for now?"

"I think I've got enough for McTaggart's report. Thanks Kenny." At that he flipped his notebook shut and stood up. "You finished your coffee?" He asked me.

I looked at the dregs and decided against draining the mug empty, "Yeah you can do me a favour and take it away for me?"

"Sure thing."

As Kenny left my phone rang. I let it ring and ring. I knew it was McTaggart, I could sense it. The snippy wee shit wanted his report and I still had to finish it. I started typing a new paragraph, but this time a little bit quicker.

CHAPTER 35

McTaggart put his phone down with an angry thump after getting no response. Macasgill nearly jumped at the unexpected outburst. He was sitting there also feeling like the proverbial naughty schoolboy awaiting punishment. He had been in these situations before and had expected a question and answer session, but this was going to be more intense, he could feel it. The new superintendant had a temper that was obvious and a grievance with union reps that did not bode well either.

McTaggart looked across his desk at both men and spoke quite calmly. "Captain pray tell me if you would, in your own words, just what the events of last night were."

Macasgill fidgeted and stole a glance at his union rep.

Thompson jumped in, "The captain's report is in front of you, Superintendent."

"I Know that. I can read. I want him to tell me face to face just what actually happened. So you can be quiet for a few minutes. And I'm not asking you politely."

Thompson opened his mouth to answer and Macasgill stopped him dead in his tracks by brushing the rep's leg with his hand.

Macasgill started by adjusting his seating position so that he was sitting more upright. He took a breath and started relating his account.

"Late yesterday afternoon one of the officers from Strathclyde HQ received a phone call from a reliable source of his on the location of one Sean Mallon, a fugitive wanted in connection with a serious assault charge. The tip off also informed us that he was known to carry weapons. My tactical team was brought in and a plan put in place to arrest the suspect."

"Did the plan include shooting up a curry house?" McTaggart exploded.

Macasgill stopped speaking.

"Did it?"

Thompson jumped in, "Superintendent I have to object ..."

"You be quiet!"

"The plan was to arrest the subject at his known location which was a flat in ..."

"So the curry house was an after thought?"

"Sir, when we arrived at the location Mallon was not found, however we recovered weapons and cash and apprehended three suspects, who are at this moment helping the team with their enquiries."

McTaggart resumed the calm demeanor he started the conversation with. The volcano had erupted once and was simmering ready for another outburst.

Macasgill managed to keep his cool and continued to relate the complete incident.

His ass covering exercise continued.

I printed off my incident report and handed it into McTaggart's office just after eleven. There was no sign of the good captain or his union rep. They were long gone. McTaggart took it from me when I offered it to him and he thanked me and said I could go. I left him reading.

As I said before, what a polite wee man.

CHAPTER 36

Muffled conversation surrounded Nelson. He was awake but kept his eyes firmly closed. He felt his cheeks being touched and he showed total restraint in not reacting. It was a difficult thing to do when the headache actually caused you severe pain. He could have cried, but for the first few years of incarceration when self inflicted pain, meant that he was still alive, it had taught him not to show the bastards how much physical abuse hurt you.

He had no memory of the pain getting so severe that it had caused him to fall unconscious again. In this new state of awareness he could distinguish that there were now two female voices in the room and they were talking to two male voices about the state he (Nelson) was in. One of the nurses said, "There satisfied now, he's sound asleep. He would have moved after you nipped his cheek. So can we do our job now?"

"What's actually wrong with our boy?" One male asked.

Nelson's ears pricked up. He was about to find out from the horse's mouth what was wrong with him.

"The Doctor thinks he's had a Transient Ischemic attack."

"Come again?"

"They think he's had a wee stroke. But they won't know how bad he is until they can assess him when he's awake."

You hear that, Nelson? A Transient Ischemic attack. A mini stroke.

"It's a shame they can end up with a whole lot of things wrong after they've had a stroke."

"What kind of things"

"They can be paralysed down one side. Their speech can be affected, oh there's a whole lot of things," she paused. "Yeah it's a shame."

Nelson listened with interest. He knew he wasn't paralysed. His speech was OK. He had heard himself converse.

"So what caused our boy to have a stroke?"

"The million dollar question," she answered. "Can we—"

"Yeah sure. Get on with it."

One of the females uncoupled Nelson from his drip. He almost winced as she withdrew the needle from the back of his hand, but still he didn't make a sound. She pressed something down hard on the back of his hand and seconds later used a medical wipe to clean the residual blood stain off. She then applied a band aid.

The other nurse busied herself; she turned the monitor off, she pulled back the bed sheet and detached all the cables from their pads. She then ripped all the pads from Nelson's body with a quick tug. It was hard for Nelson not to wince in pain ... She gathered all the cables and laid them to one side. She moved the stand and drips to the other side of the bed and placed it in the corner of the room, out of the way. Nelson was thankful that he was no longer attached to the heart monitor. Cables would have just got in his way. Everything that was happening so far was a plus.

One of the Nurses said, "Can you take all the straps off him so we can change the patient and his bedding?"

One of the guys agreed and stepped nearer and pinched Nelsons ear lobe this time. Still Nelson remained as if comatose. Seeing that not even nipping would wake the sleeping beauty, the officer warily undid all the Velcro straps, releasing Nelson to the careful and tender hands of the nurses.

This was an opportunity in the making.

Everything was going in Nelson's favour.

All he had to do was lie still and try to not moving a muscle. Only his shallow breathing announced to the nurses and to how many others in the room, that he was indeed alive. He could feel his legs wet and he knew that the plan had worked.

Piece by piece everything in this jig saw was coming together and it was now crystal clear as to what was happening in this room.

As he had planned, piss the bed and the next time someone checks in on you, they'll smell it and some orderly will come and deal with it. This is what was happening now and it was a pity that Nelson couldn't remember ever pissing it.

Nelson was pleased that this plan had worked. The two nurses were chatting and busying themselves around Nelson, preparing to clean up his mess. The two males were less chatty, but Nelson was aware of where everyone was standing in the room. The bonus part of the plan was that the restraints were gone, albeit temporarily.

Nelson was manhandled and rolled onto his left side by one of the nurses and as she did so, he sneaked a quick glance as to what and who, was in front of him. There was the heart monitor at the corner at the head of the bed, but there was no-one on this left side of the bed, apart from this nurse, who kept a firm hold of him and the other nurse, must have been on the opposite side of the bed. The other nurse quickly pulled the bottom sheet from under him, like the magician's trick of removing the table cloth from under all the glassware in one quick tug.

Nelson could imagine what she was doing.

He knew she was using the same sheet to dry and soak up the remaining urine from the rubber mattress. The nurse holding Nelson rolled him over back onto his back again. Still Nelson didn't flinch. This was not the time to react; there were still too many people in the room.

The two nurses again asked if it was still OK to do what they had to do and one of the men, standing to Nelson's right, said yes that they could. Nelson heard one nurse drop something into water and squeeze the water out. He guessed it as a sponge but listened to her gasp as she lifted Nelsons hospital gown to wash him and dry him down,

"For Christ's sake, Monica," she said with a chuckle," look at the knob on him. God almighty I aint seen one that big. Have you? Christ almighty, I thought my Charlie was a big boy but look at this."

Monica couldn't help but look as did the two cops and as she set about sponging Nelson down she was laughing and teasing the two guys standing at the bedside. "Bet you boys wished you had a tool that size eh?"

Nelson was urging himself not to react, think of something else, anything else just don't thing of her sponging your knob.

He wanted her to stop teasing him.

He wanted her to stop what she was doing right now.

Before it was past the point of no return.

But he knew that deep down he wanted her to carry on washing him; it was so sexy.

The voice was screaming through Nelson's mind, *Not now, Nelson! Not now! Wait for a minute. You have to wait till the time is right.*

The wet sponge was slowly moved over Nelson's lower half. The two nurses giggled and took great delight, as the two embarrassed guys, left the room to … "Fucking get on with it you two and stop playing with his dick and hurry up would you?" Both nurses laughed.

The two girls were flabbergasted at what was in front of them; Monica's eyes sparkled without any embarrassment as she looked at her friend, "Sheila that's got to be the biggest cock I've ever seen."

"Me too."

Sheila was totally lost in the moment and found herself subtly licking her lips and nodding her head in agreement, "I know and what a waste. Shame he's sleeping eh? Can you imagine if that thing was stiff?" Nelson felt his penis being lifted and caressed by two hands. Both nurses were holding it.

The sensation was stirring, he couldn't stop it. He tried to fight it, but it was no use. His erection was beginning and was thickening rapidly. The nurses felt movement and were amazed, as what they were holding in their hands grew. They let go at the same time but they never had a chance to scream out to the police, that their prisoner was stirring.

Nelson sat bolt upright in a flash and in an instant had grabbed each nurse by the throat, his nails biting deep into their soft flesh, crushing the larynx. Startled and unable to scream both girls struggled against the vice like grip on their throats. But it was too late the life was being squeezed from them. Blood oozed through his fingers as Nelson's grip tightened. The intense strain on his arms pained him but he held on. Using his sheer physical strength he pulled the nurses towards him, trying desperately not to make too much of a noise and alert those guards outside.

The gurgling noise as both nurses fought to break free could only be heard by Nelson. Seconds seemed like minutes and as soon as both girls went quiet and limp, he let go and dropped both girls to the floor.

He swung his legs over the edge of the bed and sat for an instant listening for any sound from outside the door. He stood up and faced the door, waiting for the two males to enter, with guns drawn. He was sure they would, the second they didn't hear any more laughter from the girls.

Nelson reached round and pulled at the ties which held the hospital gown on; releasing the knots he pulled at the cloth and shed it from his body. He wiped the blood from his hands and threw the cloth onto the floor. He stood there naked waiting for the inevitable to happen. But nothing did. Outside both officers had opened the fire door and had stepped outside for a smoke. Nelson didn't know that, but he had time.

He became very aware of his massive erection and reached down and turned Sheila onto her back. He lifted her uniform and ripped her panties off and thrust himself into her. If she had been alive who knows what she would have screamed as he ejaculated.

Finished and satisfied he looked around the room for anything he could use as a weapon. There was nothing obvious, basin with water, soap, sponge lying in a puddle on the floor He looked down at the other one of his latest victims and ripped the belt from her uniform. Again he stopped to listen, but still the sound of silence greeted him. It gave him more time to think straight, but think quickly. He lifted the sponge and dipped it into the soapy water and quickly washed his penis.

We have to hurry

And be careful.

You have to hit the first one through that door as hard as you can, Nelson.

I know.

Then pounce on the second guy before he gets a chance to shoot us.

Nelson made hurried preparations to attack the two officers as quickly as he had killed the nurses. He tensed every sinew in his body and he waited in silence. He agreed he would have to act quickly to surprise and take them out. He knew deep down this was his last chance; after all it was they who had the weapons. His only advantage was the speed of his attack. Every one of his senses was operating at 200%. His acuteness and listening heightened. Nelson tried to calm himself down by breathing slowly.

He heard nothing but the faint hum from the fluorescent ceiling light above. The guys had to be coming back in soon. He reached down and lifted the nurse up and laid her on the bed. He quickly put the stained sheet over the top of her and re-attached the Velcro straps and pulled them tight. This might just buy him time when the boys returned, it might just confuse them long enough and to give Nelson the little bit of an edge he needed. They might just think that the nurses had strapped Nelson back down. He thought about strangling the first guy through the door but immediately dismissed that thought. That would take too long and allow the second policeman a chance to get a shot off. He tossed the belt on the bed. Who ever came through the door first had to be hit really hard. That was what was said so stick to it he thought.

The other officer would hopefully be slow to react. It was all down to speed. Nelson clenched both fists and rolled his neck muscles, readying himself for the onslaught.

It didn't dawn on Nelson that there could have been a third man, or a fourth. All he was going on was the two male voices in the room.

Suddenly there was movement and noise coming from along the corridor. A door opened, Nelson could hear voices. The boys were returning, they were laughing.

This was good as the officers were relaxed.

Nelson positioned himself just behind the door and waited for it open. He crouched down and waited to spring forward. The voices were getting louder; Nelson could hear one guy talking and then more laughter. Nelson held his breath.

He was seconds away from mayhem.

Seconds away from freedom.

Seconds away from dying.

The leopard and its prey. Not every Leopard attack results in success. But this one had to.

It was natural to him; he was about to do what he did best. Kill someone.

These two innocent strangers didn't make one bit of difference to Nelson.

They were going to die. They had to so that Nelson could escape.

They would never know what hit them.

The door opened and the first guy never finished his question "Have you pair—"

Nelson pounced like the leopard from a crouching position with a yell and hit the first officer hard with his right hand on his throat. Shocked the guy dropped to his knees clutching both hands to his throat gasping for breath. His partner was also momentarily stunned and he hesitated. He couldn't fathom out what had just happened. The slow reaction was to be his downfall as Nelson hit him right between the eyes and all sorts of coloured lights went off in his head. There was a reactionary curse at Nelson and the officer blindly lashed out at his assailant and luckily managed to get off a punch of his own, hitting Nelson in the shoulder. Nelson launched himself again into the officer with all his weight and knocked him down and began raining punches on his face. The officer's vain attempt to fight back, trying desperately to stop the whirlwind of blows raining down on him was futile.

The stunning attack had been successful. He had been far too quick for any meaningful response. It was over in seconds.

Nelson sat astride the weakening man and summoning all his energy for one last punch hit him hard on his nose sending splintering bone into his brain. The man wouldn't draw another ounce of breath.

Nelson quickly turned his attention to the gasping individual lying on his back on the room floor. Nelson watched the officer with his hands round his throat gasping for air, his bulging eyes watching Nelson's every movement. The officer tried to rise from the floor and confront his naked assailant but couldn't. Human instincts told him he had to react; this was his last chance to stop Nelson. He tried in a vain struggle to get to his feet, draw his gun and shoot the mad man, but it was going to be too late.

There was nothing in the training manual in how to handle a wild uncontrollable animal called Nelson.

Nelson jumped on top of him, knocking him back down to the ground.

Nelson smiled as he dropped his naked frame onto the prone figure and met little resistance. The officer weakly raised his arms against Nelson. Somewhere deep down in his memory bank something was telling him that he should be fighting for his life, but he was too fucked up to do it. He couldn't breathe, his wind pipe was shattered.

He tried to speak to Nelson and beg for his life, but could only rasp a whisper. Nelson wasn't listening; the voice was egging him on, *Kill this one as well, Nelson. Come on do it.*

His hands dropped automatically around the officer's throat, his thumbs pressing down hard and deep onto his fractured windpipe. One last effort from the policeman as his hands tried to pull Nelson desperately from his throat. But there was no strength remaining there. There was just the inevitability. The rasping sound of trying to gain breath, eyes widening at the strangulation. Nelson smiling as the dying man tried one last time to shift his weight. One last ditch attempt to turn his body and throw Nelson off of him. But it was useless Nelson choked the last breath out of him.

Be quick now, Nelson. We've still got a lot of work to do. Grab the guy in the corridor and bring him in here. Hurry because there may be more.

Nelson let go of the policeman's throat and stood up and did as he was told. He put his hands under the dead policeman's armpits and dragged him into the room.

There now that was easier than we thought. Wasn't it, Nelson?

Nelson stood with his fists clenched and his arms up above his head as if taking applause and surveyed his kill. Like the solitary leopard proud of what he had done.

We're free, Nelson. Hurry now. Put some clothes on and be quick about it. Someone will be missing these people. Come on hurry up and don't even think about sodomising Monica or Sheila again. You don't have the time.

Nelson calmly assessed each man and stripped the one closest to his size. He removed jacket, shirt, trousers and socks, but refused to take the boxer shorts off to wear.

He looked round at the dead nurse lying on the floor and a minute later was wearing her lace undies.

He dressed as quickly as he could, but the shoes were too small. He tried the second cop and his were slightly bigger than Nelson would normally have worn. He removed the second cop's socks and put them on also. It would make his feet sweat, but what the hell; it would be worth it when he got out of here.

Gun, Nelson! Wallets Nelson! Think man, think. We also need money and take his watch.

Nelson did as he was ordered. He took the money from both wallets and what each man had in his pockets. He counted it as sixty-five pounds and fifty-two pence. He slipped a watch from a dead man's wrist and saw that it was 8.35. Whether it was a.m. or p.m. it didn't say. Nelson didn't really care. The pain in his head was subsiding due to the adrenalin rush from the attack. His shoulder pained a bit but he could get over that. He was unscathed.

He took both guns and checked the firing mechanisms of both. He held one of the guns out in front of him at arms length and looked along the barrel at an imaginary target in the distance. **Bang bang**, he whispered for the audience of corpses.

Obeying the commands to the letter, Nelson put the side arm into his jacket pocket and the other one he tucked into the waistband at the small of his back. He was ready to move out. Where to, he was unsure, he would have to wing it. There was no ongoing planned escape. He didn't know where he was, the only thing that mattered was that he wasn't going back to Barlinnie.

No one was going to stop him taking in the fresh air, his first for a very long time.

No one was going to stop him and ask him what he was doing outside this building.

He was heading for somewhere that was for sure.

With one last look at his handiwork he opened the door quietly and stepped out into the corridor. He looked to his left and right and decided that he would turn right and head towards the glass door at the end. He smiled as he passed a solid wooden door with a sign that read, Danger Bio hazard. Only authorized personnel allowed. He walked on to the end of the corridor and was pleased to see that he was on the ground floor and that the glass door in front of him was a fire hazard door. He assumed that this was where the boys had come for a smoke. Ignoring the sign that said 'Use in Emergency only', he hit the push bar and shouldered the door open. There were cigarette butts strewn all over the ground. He had been correct; they had their last cigarettes here.

He shut the door behind him. He found the pavement and walked along the front of the hospital buildings, he didn't care to look back once.

He strolled out the main gate and stepped onto Cathedral Street and out towards freedom.

He turned left and strode with an air of confidence down High Street. No one stopped him. He was just another Glaswegian out for an evening stroll. He stopped for a moment at Glasgow Cathedral and looked left towards the graveyard. He could smell the newly cut grass so he stopped to breathe deep, drinking in all the fragrances.

He closed his eyes for a moment and imagined children playing and running around his park. He walked on and grinned as he recognized a rhododendron bush.